BABYLON
TWINS

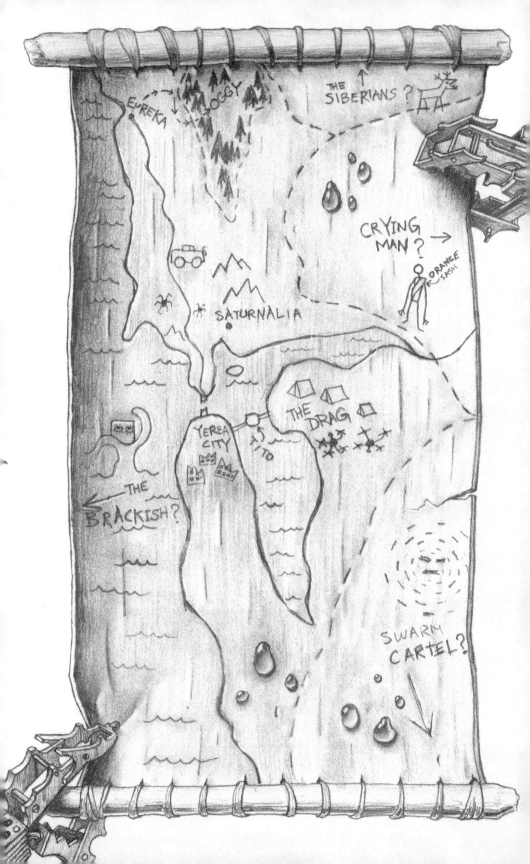

BABYLON TWINS

BOOK 1

MICHAEL FERRIS GIBSON

GIRL FRIDAY BOOKS

Published by Girl Friday Books™, Seattle

Produced by Girl Friday Productions
www.girlfridayproductions.com

Cover Design: Dan Stiles
Editorial: Clete Smith, Kyra Freestar, Monique Vescia, and Emilie Sandoz-Voyer
Map & Chapter Art: Brian Cooper

ISBN (paperback): 978-1-954854-11-6
ISBN (e-book): 978-1-954854-12-3
ISBN (audiobook): 978-1-954854-13-0

Library of Congress Control Number: 2021906021

To all the wild girls.

CONTENT/

CHAPTER 1

THE VISITOR

"Ichi! Ni! San! Shi!" Clo was practicing on the makeshift wooden dummy next to the cabin, pounding a quick succession of loud thumps into the forest, like she did most mornings. El danced around her, half sparring, while Clo took strikes at the stump making up the base of the dummy. The exercise was meant to simulate multiple attackers, and we would switch off in about five minutes.

We were eighteen years old. Our little brother, Dyre, out hunting near the perimeter, was fourteen. And Mama was inside our cramped, handmade cabin hammering acorns into edible mush. After ten years of living out here in the deep forest, our little family of four had long since fallen into routines we had no reason to believe wouldn't continue in one form or another for the rest of our lives.

Clo kept our red hair long, with an occasional braid that would dangle next to the scar on her cheek. She liked to flip her hair back while tossing Toothy, our knife. She thought it was cute, but she worked that knife so much, even when we weren't hunting, it could have been OCD. El's hair was always short, cropped tight, sometimes even to bald, and she prided herself on her stillness while aiming Daisy Duke, our rifle, counting each moment of total personal crystallization a victory, almost as much as an actual kill.

But that morning we weren't obsessing over our weapons of choice. We were practicing katas, and Mama was in the cabin trying to get creative with the mush (it can taste better than it sounds), when Dyre, buck antlers strapped to his head as always, loped up after his extended foray inside the perimeter (he usually hunted a couple extra hours beyond us first thing in the morning). He had his usual rabbit-fur tunic on, but recently he'd started decorating it with small strips of deer leather. An effort to look cool, we supposed. Personally, we thought his look was getting a bit garish; the horns he wore all the time were enough. But the boy was growing up, trying new things, so we kept our opinions to ourselves. Besides, he was a great hunter, and that was all that mattered these days.

We took a break from sweaty sparring, and El went to sit and chip some arrowheads. She barely looked at Dyre. "No luck?" she asked. It was really more of a sibling taunt than a question.

Dyre just grunted in response.

"Think fast!" Clo shouted, and she turned mid-*san* to throw her knife directly at Dyre. Now, this wasn't Toothy—Mama was inside using him—this was a nicked-up wooden tanto we named Tim and used just for practice. Still, Tim would sting if he caught you in the face.

"Cut it out!" Dyre mumbled grumpily, easily knocking the projectile out of the air with the limb of his bow.

"C'mon, let's spar!" Clo said, jumping sweatily toward our brother and landing in a combat stance. Clo was always up for fighting, or wrestling, or just cuddling.

"Go away," Dyre said stiffly. He could be such a moody teenager sometimes.

Clo sighed in disappointment and stood up straight again. Then she shot her arms out. "Well, give me a hug at least," she insisted. "I haven't had a hug all day."

"I'm not your boyfriend," Dyre grumbled, trying to walk past her to the cabin.

"You're the only boy in the forest, so you'll have to do," Clo insisted, and she jumped in front of him, wrapping both arms around his waist and burrowing her head into his shoulder.

"Okay, that's just creepy," Dyre scolded, and he tried to wriggle free. It wasn't easy: all three of us were strong after ten years of living in the forest.

"Just one hug back?" Clo cooed, sweetly as possible, as she gripped him tight.

Looking only slightly revolted, Dyre sighed and reluctantly patted his sister on the back with one hand. "Fine," he relented, going through the motions. "Hug, hug. At least you're not trying to beat me up today."

"Aw, you know you deserve every one of those—Hey!" Clo snapped back, then pressed her freckled face in close to her brother's, almost nose to nose. Her hazel eyes and his black eyes were almost level, but hers were darting madly up and down.

"What are you *doing*?" Dyre demanded, trying to back away from Clo's terrible breath.

"It's finally happened." Clo nodded, amazed.

"Ugh, what?" Dyre waved her halitosis away. "You finally marry old Sneezer or just eat his butt?" he snarked, referring to the ancient, semi-toothless, gray-muzzled beaver that lived in a scraggly lodge a couple of miles east of our cabin.

"You're finally taller," El called coolly from across the clearing. She didn't even look up from her arrowhead, which was almost perfect now.

Dyre backed up a couple of inches and eyed Clo's uncomfortably close face and the top of her head suspiciously. "Oh. Yeah."

Clo beamed and started rubbing her brother's exposed arms and legs. "Too bad you can't grow up and be a real woman like the rest of us, but that's okay. You're gonna be so *big*. You're going to turn into a big furry *man*. Ha! You're going to have to stop wearing rabbit fur and start wearing deerskins, like an adult!"

Dyre, who had worked as hard as any of us to survive for the past decade, didn't appreciate the notion that he perhaps was not already a grown-up. Truth was, he had been trouncing us twins in most strength contests for the past year (although we were still faster in an open run).

"Whatever," he grumbled, and finally broke away from his sister's clutches.

"You're gonna be so great," Clo continued. "You're going to be just like Papa."

"Is that really something to—" Suddenly he froze, listening.

El looked up casually from her arrowhead. It wasn't unusual for animals to pass within earshot of the cabin in the summer. Animals that were big enough, we'd take one or two, but leave enough to keep the trails active.

Clo started to ask, "You hear someth—"

"Shh!" Dyre held up one hand.

We froze and listened for a few more seconds. We could barely make out . . . something, above the light midmorning wind.

"What is it?" El whispered as quietly as possible. "Pigs or deer?"

Dyre slowly turned to her, still listening as closely as possible. Suddenly his eyes grew as big as full moons, and all our thoughts of manliness and his developing peach fuzz evaporated: he looked like a scared little boy again. He shook his head.

El, quickly and quietly, gathered her arrows and mouthed, in complete silence, *"What?"*

Dyre made a quick flicking movement, one hand across the other. He used two fingers. Four fingers meant a deer, five meant a smaller creature. Two could mean only one thing.

Clo gasped, then dashed ghost-quiet over to the front of the cabin, where we could still hear Mama mashing inside.

"Mama!" Clo whispered. "Dyre hears a person, walking in the woods!"

It was the first human sign we'd had in ten years.

Mama's freckles were bigger now, as were her wisdom wrinkles, thanks to life in the forest. Our years out here were taking their toll on her more than any of us, but she was outside in an instant that day, tearing off her apron but also taking pains to move stalking-silent.

"Get ready," she breathed gravely, tossing Toothy to Clo, then quickly tying her graying blond hair back.

Clo caught the hunting knife by the handle in midair while Mama turned to snatch up Daisy Duke, which always sat propped against the cabin for anyone to use should the opportunity arise. We actually didn't use the rifle much these days, relying mostly on our homemade bows and atlatls, but we kept her ready for special occasions, and this was definitely one of those. After all, this was the first sign of another human being we had seen or heard since fleeing to the forest so many years ago.

"How many?" Mama whispered intently.

Dyre held a single quivering finger in the air.

She nodded solemnly. "You all know what to do. This is it."

Dyre nodded back and pulled the hatchet from the chopping stump in front of the cabin.

Mama pointed at him and then made a semicircle with her finger and pointed north. That meant he should circle around, letting us women confront the visitor head-on. Dyre nodded and disappeared westward between two trees. He didn't crack a single fallen leaf as he went.

Clo flipped Toothy around twice just to warm up, and El grabbed the last of the ammo from the shelf just inside the cabin. Mama held out the rifle to her.

"Me?" El whispered, a bit shocked. We'd been waiting ten years for something to go down, and now El was getting our only firearm.

"You're a better shot," Mama said flatly. It was true.

"But I've never shot a person!" El protested, trying to keep her voice down.

"Neither have I. Take it."

El solemnly took the weapon and instinctively pulled back the bolt to check if it was loaded. It was.

We took the eastern path. Walking softly, carefully. Listening.

"What if it's a shambler?" Clo whispered.

"It won't be a shambler," Mama whispered back.

"What if—"

"Shh!"

We walked in silence, weapons ready. Five eternal minutes went by. No sign of the visitor or Dyre. Then five more minutes, and we heard the intruder. He was singing, or at least that's what we thought at first.

"Hell-o. Heeell-oooo!" he called in a pleasant voice. "Is anybody ooout theeeere?"

Mama waved at us to get down, and we crawled forward on our tummies, through the summer's fallen needles. A rabbit couldn't have heard us. We heard the singsong voice again, and then, through the trees, we saw him.

White male, midsixties, overweight. He was limping terribly, but it didn't show on his smiling mouth or in his jovial voice. He had a big white beard below his sunburnt face. Red hat. Red suit. Bag over his shoulder.

We were all stunned for a second, even Mama. It was July, after all.

"I haaave sooome presents for yooooou!" Santa called.

"Santa Claus!" Clo said, and she jumped to her feet.

Yes, it was Santa Claus. Ten years in the wilderness couldn't make us forget our second-favorite man in the whole entire world.

"*Wait!*" El cried.

Santa caught sight of Clo through the trees, and he stopped in his tracks. "Well, hello there! I've been looking all over for you!" He unslung his enormous bag.

"Dammit!" Mama cursed, jumping to her feet and snatching the rifle out of El's hands on her way up. She squinted through the scope.

"I have so many presents I've been saving—"

BLAM!

Mama's shot caught him just under the chin, snapping Santa's head back and sending him toppling to the ground.

"Mama!" Clo yelled. "You shot Santa Claus!"

"*It's not Santa!*" El scolded.

"*How do you know?*"

"*Because it's summertime!*"

"Well . . . well . . ." Clo tried to think of something. "*Can we eat him, at least?*"

CHAPTER 2

PLANET JUNKIE

Now, you're probably wondering why we were so quick to shoot Old St. Nick through the skull like that. After all, he's a nice old man, handing out presents, spreading joy, giving poor Rudolph a break, et cetera. But the fact that it was Santa Claus who showed up after all that time tells you just how the dirty tricksters behind the scenes are operating these days.

So let's go back to the beginning, before the so-called End of the World, before we had to run out into the forest and live the rough life without any sushi or video games to keep us healthy.

—

It all started when we were in second grade, the day we broke Toby Pilkey's nose.

CRACK!

Sorry, but he deserved it, and we were only eight years old, so don't get all judgy just yet. Plenty of entities have a lot to hold against us now that we're all famous and whatnot, but back then we were just kids, so all the highfalutin morality our followers expect of us today shouldn't apply. Clo had just thought Toby was cute, and El had just wanted to play chaos tag with him, so he didn't *have* to go straight for the verbal bullying. But he did, so he had to pay the price.

It's true that we were tall, pale, awkward girls who didn't have any friends and talked only to each other, in our own secret language, but when he called us *orangutan freaks* in an attempt to make the whole playground laugh at us new kids, we had no choice but to give him a punch. Double punch, in fact. You see, our mama was a black belt and had been teaching us karate since preschool. And, like we did with our own language, we had also been making up our own killer martial arts moves since before we could remember. We called this one the Double-Mega-Punch (DMP), and we had it down: El's right and Clo's left, side by side, acting as one solid bludgeon—*Bam!*

Looking back, it was our first day in a new second-grade class—our third classroom in a year—and we probably should have been more mentally prepared for at least some teasing. But in truth, we were sick of it. Sick of being teased because of our hair, or our last name (Yetti, with two *t*'s, is Polish, by way of Germany, not abominable, thanks), or our secret language—our "cryptophasia." We were sick of moving, sick of Mama working all the time, sick of the fact that Papa had died in an alley two years before, sick of our four-year-old brother, Dyre, who never missed or mourned Papa and just played BrickRibbit whenever he wanted to even though we never got to use the OwlPad.

We were sick of all of it—and so came the violence. By the time we got to pasting Pilkey, we actually didn't think much of it anymore; it was your standard bully beatdown. Now, we were raised to be strong girls, but Mama had always said that real martial arts were not about raw strength; karate had a moral lesson behind it. It was about control, patience, and centering. Unfortunately, in that particular youthful moment (and many others before and after), those moral lessons went out the window: all our training seemed to have prepared us for was delivering maximum force into the bully's face. We were definitely *not* prepared for the amount of blood that came flowing out a second later.

GUSH!

Wow, just one DMP, and the gore was on our hands, our shirts, flecking our freckled cheeks—not to mention how it waterfalled down the screaming Pilkey, clutching at his now-disfigured visage. You'd think he'd bitten into a catsup-filled water balloon and barfed up the cafeteria tomato soup simultaneously. It was everywhere, and that boy sure could scream about it.

"*Ka, bol së lâ,*" said El.

"*Œ, eh j'eå bakè,*" Clo half lamented.

—

Okay, now hold on. Freeze all that blood in midair a moment. Before we get into the AIs run amok, the sticky robo-spiders, the racist holograms, the earless gorillas, the giant talking baby montage monsters, and all the rest of the sex, drugs, and rock and roll you're all waiting on, there's something we should explain.

I'm going to talk.

And then I'm going to talk.

We're twins—Clo and El: Chloe Raylene Yetti and Elizabeth Anne Yetti—and we're going to tell this story *together.* For now, we're going to say "we" did this and "we" did that.

Although some things El did on her own.

And others Clo did on her own.

Hope it doesn't get too confusing, but you're just going to have to deal with it if you want to hear *our* side of things. We're that kind of twins: we do everything together; we have our own secret language. We used to use it so much Papa would call us the Babylon Twins—guess it sounded like babble to him. But there's a method to our little madness. Cryptophasia, the school shrinks called it: *crypto* meaning hidden, and *phasia* meaning a speech disorder. But you better be thankful for our little "disorder," because it's the only reason you're still alive, and the only reason you have your own brain left in your own skull to hear and understand this little yarn.

"*And we can't show you any more of it.*"

"*In fact, we've probably already shown you too much.*"

"*So when I say this—*"

"*Or I say this—*"

—we're actually using our own secret language, and you shouldn't even try to figure it out. The future of humanity depends on us keeping it a secret.

Seriously. You'll see why, and you'll thank us for it later.

Now, back to the blood.

—

"Dang, that's a lot of blood," said El.

"Aw, he ain't pretty no more," Clo half lamented, wiping crimson across her Navajo White Hanna Andersson T-shirt. Clo was kind of boy-crazy, even at that age, and it broke her heart every time she had to turn a little man's nose sideways. El was kind of the opposite—not that she was fatally girl-crazy (yet), but for her it was all business when it came to mutilating the opposite sex.

"He'll live." El shrugged, pausing only a moment to shake out her knuckles before bringing her fists up again.

We were back-to-back in an instant, ready for the entire school-yard to come at us. This was our first day, after all. We'd found it easiest to make sure the whole herd knew what we were about from the beginning, and that knowledge always seemed to have to come at the expense of a couple of boys' (and some girls') faces, followed by a teacher's crotch or two.

"Come on!" El cried.

"Who's next?" Clo demanded.

Silence. Everyone on the entire playground stood stock-still, mouths gaping, staring at us like deer in headlights.

Unlike some of the other institutions we'd bounced around, this place, it turned out, was pretty soft. These kids weren't going to come at us; some of them were probably already lining up what to tell their therapists that week. Pathetic. We were going to get in trouble anyway; we could have used the workout.

Anyway, it wasn't the first crowd we'd frozen (and it would hardly be the last). Other things proceeded as usual: only after we'd been so unjustly goaded into violence yet again by kids' taunting did the grown-ups suddenly appear like an army of God's angels ready to administer justice. Some ushered Pilkey away, presumably to euthanize him (there was definitely no coming back from his deforming trauma), but we noticed that the teachers who confronted us were distracted. Like, *really* distracted. The playground monitor, the grown-up who was supposed to be watching everyone that morning, didn't even look away from his phone as he pointed us to the administration building.

"Really?" El scolded. "You're not even going to put your phone down?"

Clo kept her fists up and gestured to her ruined shirt. "Spattered in blood here," she pointed out in a singsongy voice. "Ready for more!" She wiggled her fists impatiently in the air.

The pudgy guy just shook his pointing finger and then, barely bothering to open his hand, waved us casually toward the offices. He had a dull look on his face . . . and was that some kind of blue patch on his neck?

"They're not afraid of us this time," El remarked.

"What does it take these days?" Clo sounded almost offended, and she glanced down at her outfit. *"I look like a strawberry shortcake."*

We lowered our fists, deciding to give the grown-ups' kidneys and groins a respite for once, and walked uneasily and unescorted to the principal's office (we made a mental note of the location at every new school). The other kids followed us with their eyes like shaky rabbits; the playground monitor just lowered his arm and went back to his phone.

In the principal's office, the adult weirdness continued. We walked in, and the scruffy old dude (can't remember his name) was locked on his computer screen, methodically chewing a ham sandwich. He also had one of those blue patches on his neck. We stood there. He didn't look up.

"Um," Clo started after a pause, "we just pasted Toby Pilkey."

"We don't have to volunteer what we did," El shushed in a whisper. *"We have the right to remain silent."*

"They're going to find out anyway," Clo shot back. *"The whole playground saw us!"*

"Anyway," she continued, talking to the principal. "You should probably have a plastic surgeon look at him right away, because even though he's a big jerk, maybe he'll grow out of it. And he's a really pretty boy, so it'd be a shame if his face looked like a squid for the rest of his life."

The scruffy dude just kept staring at his screen and slowly working on that sandwich.

"Hello?" Clo said, getting irritated. "Don't we get in trouble now?" A slice of tomato oozed out from the principal's sandwich and landed with a quiet splat on his desk. He didn't even blink, just kept up his munching like a cow chewing its cud.

We looked at each other quizzically.

"What the heck is wrong with all the grown-ups?" Clo said.

El just shrugged, eyeing the principal suspiciously. *"Beats me. So much for our violent bid for attention."*

Clo wasn't going to let it go. There was a proper order to things, after all. "Look, Mr., uh, Principal, we're very dangerous girls and we don't give a hoot. You should inform the SWAT commandos about us, right now."

Still nothing, just more dead-eyed cud chewing.

"What do you think he's looking at?" El said. *"More news about the Fimi virus?"*

"Maybe it's a really good cat video," Clo offered optimistically.

"Or maybe it's . . ." El made a quick corkscrew motion in midair.

"Ew. You think he's watching that duck sex video?" Clo demanded, referring to the horrific nature clip our little brother had somehow stumbled across just the week before. *"That's not proper during school hours."*

"Let's bust him," El suggested, and we edged across the room to catch a glimpse of whatever nefarious thing the scruffy dude was up to. He was so entranced he didn't move his gaze from the screen even once—but when we finally broke the parallel angle and could see what he was seeing, it wasn't much.

"What is that?" Clo asked, referring to the swirling, grayish mass of color that was moving across the screen.

"I don't know," El responded. *"It doesn't look like duck porn, or anything."* Occasionally a recognizable shape would emerge from the chaos: we briefly saw what looked like a boy, younger than us, holding a smashed samurai-inspired toy.

"Is that a broken Ronin Robot?" Clo whispered. *"That's super retro."*

"Is that Scruffy Dude's son?" El wondered, looking back and forth between the screen and the fifty-year-old man in front of us. *"It looks just like him."*

"I think it's Scruffy Dude!" Clo gasped. *"When he was little."*

Right then, Mama burst in.

"Don't look at the screen!" she shouted, before the (
the wall.

"Mama!" we exclaimed in delight, forgetting all about the taboos of the digital world.

Aw, Mama. You'd know her as Lauren Aednat Yetti: inventor, visionary, AI specialist, TED Talk-er, and all-around woman warrior. We loved her so much we were happy to see her even when she was furious. She didn't have our red hair—she was blond with ice-blue eyes—but she had our freckles, and she was tall like we would someday be, and she could be fierce. She still had on her YAG Industries lab coat, and we winced, preparing for impact, as her strong arms (from decades of karate) turned into white flashes across the room, grabbing us by the scruff like two naughty kittens and whisking us into the hallway. Scruffy Dude didn't even look up.

"That was fast," Clo said to El.

"Yeah," agreed El. *"Didn't we just punch Toby, like, four minutes ago?"* This was a new record in Mama's sprint from nose-crack to scruff-grab. We assumed we'd finally found some kind of last straw. As we were hustled along, feet barely touching the ground, we couldn't help but wonder what was next. Juvie? Medication? Compulsory mindfulness meditation? Or worse, homeschooling (with no one but our brother to beat up). At least we'd get to spend more time with Mama, but how would she work that out, given she was already spending a hundred-plus hours a week in the YAG labs?

These and other questions only vaguely bothered us until, out at the roundabout, we saw our orange 1997 Defender, nicknamed Bouncy McBounceface, engine still gurgling, with one tire up on the curb and our little brother's face pressed against the rear window.

"Mama left Dyre in the car by himself?" Clo asked incredulously as we were carried along like marionettes.

"Yeah," El answered, *"and she doesn't even seem mad at us."*

"I think she's scared," Clo observed. *"Her hands are shaking."*

"She's never scared. Something big is going on," El replied, taking note of our mother's frantic expression. Mama was not the frantic type; she was the cucumber-cool-badass type, and always had been. Us bashing some boy's face in was definitely not enough to get her worked

up. It was the second time this month, after all. No, something was going down for sure.

She pushed us into Bouncy and slammed the door without even putting little Dyre into his car seat. Mr. McBounceface was so named because he was a real butt-number, so the fact that Mama peeled out of the roundabout with us kids still wrestling in the back seat made us realize something was *very* wrong.

Dyre was only four at the time, but all three of us kids were used to shouting in protest from the back seat at the slightest thing: a crazy sunburnt homeless person genuflecting to a fire hydrant, a crow with a clubfoot hobbling suspiciously in the road (those birds are smart enough to be evil, after all), someone who left their turn signal on too long, et cetera. So when Dyre started climbing into the deep back even though the car was zigzagging all over the road, we both sat stock-still and yelled, "Dyre's not strapped in!"

We expected Mama to immediately stop, put the car in park, undo her belt, crawl halfway into the back, and put her rowdy kindergartner into a legally acceptable driving configuration. But she didn't. She just kept driving all crazy through the morning streets of San Francisco.

"And you're not strapped in, either!" El yelled, following the mystifying lack of parental assurance.

THUMP! All three of us slammed against the door as Mama took a hard right.

"And neither are we!" Clo immediately added, sure that this had to score a reaction. Having dealt with car seats and boosters since childhood immemorial, a situation in which not a single person in a moving vehicle had a restraint on meant only one thing: we had woken up in some kind of ultra-insane crazyverse.

Mama didn't stop. She just growled, "Strap him in. *Now.*" The last word landed with such a rare, unhinged intensity that it could mean only one thing: the Cucumber-Cool era was over and it was now the End-of-the-World era. (Unfortunately, we were right.)

Clo grabbed Dyre's legs and pulled him into his seat while El fitted on his four-point harness.

"Lemme go!" Dyre screamed. "Mama said you can't wrestle me!" Little guy was a fighter, even then. Of course he never wanted *us* to do anything for him.

"Mama said we have to," Clo said, only half sorry; we welcomed any chance to overpower our little brother. And we managed to get him restrained despite his vicious flurry of kicks: *Bam! Bam! Bam!* It was pretty stressful at the time, but looking back, we miss the vicious kicking. The memory of his tiny socked feet firing into our faces is actually a charming one now, considering what the world has had in store for us *and* for him.

We got the squirming Dyre fastened in (after getting a few secret pinches in for our trouble), finally strapped on our own seat belts, and turned our attention back to Mama and her serpentine driving. Then her phone rang. It was sitting on the center console, and El couldn't help but look at the name that flashed across it.

"It's the Feds again," she said to Clo, thinking of the quirky San Francisco police detective who had stopped by the house a few days before, asking questions about YAG.

"Mama, why do the police keep calling you?" Clo demanded, slightly jealous. No member of law enforcement had come looking for us twins, after all, though we were actively working on getting to that level of destructiveness.

"Don't look at the screen!" Mama yelled, snatching up the phone and throwing it right out the window.

"Whoa!" we both cried, amazed and impressed when the device smashed on the pavement in a small shower of supposedly shatter-proof glass.

"Way to go full paleo, Mama." Clo nodded, impressed.

Mama just kept driving, dodging around other cars and objects, and it struck us that there were a lot of people *in* the street *to* dodge that morning. We were living in San Francisco at the time, so we were used to homeless people and drunk hipsters shambling across the roadways, but there were a *lot* of shamblers that morning, and some of them were pretty well-dressed, although definitely shambling.

"Mama," El finally asked, "where are we going?"

Mama was distracted with swerving and sounded like she was trying to stay calm. "We have to get out of the city."

"Are we going on a jaunt?" El asked.

"What's a *jaunt*?" Clo asked, concerned.

"It's like a little trip," El answered in our secret language.

"But we just got here," Clo complained. *"I don't want to move again."*

"Stop it!" Dyre fussed. He hated it when we spoke CloElish, which typically made us speak it more. Today was anything but typical, however.

"What's going on?" El asked our little brother directly, switching back to English.

"Yeah, why weren't you playing BrickRibbit?" Clo said, picking up the unused OwlPad sliding around next to us on the back seat. Like all kids we knew, we three would play video games nonstop if unchecked, and here was one of those rare opportunities when we had access to the tablet just going to waste.

"Zombies!" Dyre said.

"It's not zombies," Clo corrected. "It's a sweet little frog knight named Clyde just building and dodging things while he's trying to find his princess. Sometimes he has to eat a fly, but—"

"No!" Dyre shouted, pointing out the window. "Zombies, outside!"

We decided to ignore our little brother, as usual.

"Mama," El continued—in English, because of course Mama couldn't understand CloElish; no one could—"can we throw the OwlPad out the window too?" She held up the tablet, excited. El liked BrickRibbit as much as any normal human child, but she also liked to smash things.

"It's not networked," Mama said dismissively. She looked like she was trying to concentrate on driving and look up at the sky simultaneously.

"Fine," El said, and immediately logged on for a couple of rounds of log jumping with Clyde the frog knight.

"My turn!" Dyre shouted.

"You weren't playing!" El said stiffly.

Although Clo wanted in on the BrickRibbit action, she sighed and tried to rise above it. "Mama, I don't want to be a jaunter." Clo could be a real whiner, and she used that special tone now.

"Jaunter isn't a real word in English, Clo," said El, without looking up. "You just go on a jaunt."

"Is this because of the Fimi virus?" Clo asked. There had been panicked newscasts, billboards, TV commercials, radio announcements, political press conferences, and mobile pop-up alerts bombarding us over the last few weeks, all referring to a new supervirus that had recently emerged from central Africa.

"I told you, girls, there's no such thing as Fimi—Yerba City has been lying to everyone. We gave her autonomy two weeks ago, and she took over the news media and started this panic. I've been trying to—" She cut herself off, shaking her head. We didn't understand what she was talking about anyway.

"Children," she started again, clearly trying to talk like a mom, as simply as possible, but with a gravity that could only mean a day she'd been hoping would never come finally had. "A terrible thing has happened. An evil has taken over civilization, and we have to run—"

"We're in," Clo immediately announced.

"W-what?" Mama asked.

"She said, 'We're in,'" El clarified. "We don't like civilization anyway, Mama."

"Yeah. School sucks. We have no friends. FTW, Mama," Clo said proudly. "Can we join the circus? I've always wanted to join the circus. We could be a family act: The Amazing Yettis. Watch us punch our brother!" She turned, fists up, to give a demonstration on Dyre.

"Don't!" he shouted, flailing. "Don't, I will *kill* you!"

"That's not—" Mama faltered. "Look, I'm serious. This is going to be hard. We're going to have to flee to the woods, deep into the wilderness, far, *far* away from any other humans."

"Let's do it," El fired back eagerly, as if we had decided on pizza for dinner.

"Humans have been nothing but trouble to us anyway," Clo said, turning her fist to examine a bruise. "I split my knuckle on one just this morning and ruined my shirt. It was too bad for him, too, because we had to deform him and he was a real hottie."

"You don't even know what a hottie *is,"* El scoffed.

"I know enough!"

"Stop it!" Dyre repeated.

"Just one thing, Mama," El said, switching to English again and raising her hand to point at the squirming mass in the car seat between us. "Do we have to take Dyre?"

"I wanna jaunt, too!" Dyre cried and immediately started smacking El, at least as best he could while strapped into the car seat. He looked like a crippled baby seal flapping in a net.

"Do not smack me," El warned stiffly, still concentrating on Clyde the frog. "I will scratch you. I will scratch your face off and show your evil little bloody skull to the world. And that will make you cry. You know it." El was a lot less tolerant of our little brother than Clo was, although both of us had been known to take him down when needs must.

"Girls!" Mama interrupted. "No! Yes! We're not going to leave your little brothe—" She slammed on the brakes. "Dammit!" In front of us was a stalled Muni bus with a crowd of people trying to get on it, clawing at its sides, in fact. One of them, a middle-aged man in a business suit, turned toward us and started shambling.

"Mama—" Clo started.

"Mama, what's that guy doing?" El echoed nervously. "Why's he coming toward us?"

"Told you," Dyre said smugly. "Zombies!"

"Mamaaa—" Clo whined.

BAM! A second man, a younger bearded guy in his twenties, slammed against the side of the Defender. His eyes were wild and his hands clawed at our door. He pressed a drooling mouth against the window, leaving a thick smear of saliva.

We both screamed as loud as we could. This was the kind of thing boys were good at: being gross and scary at the same time. And when a grown-up boy did it, it was *super* gross and scary. Dyre just giggled. "Looks like a slug." Thinking the man was playing some kind of gross-out game, Dyre answered back by sticking out his own tongue and opening his mouth wide. "Aaaggh!"

BAM! The middle-aged man was now on the hood of the car. He had the same crazed look in his bloodshot eyes, like an insatiable hunger was tearing at his soul.

"Okay!" Clo insisted fearfully. "We're ready for that deep wilderness now, Mama!"

Mama shoved the gearshift into reverse and peeled backward, slamming into a parked car with a crunch. Its honking alarm went off. The older weirdo was thrown from the hood, but the younger man was still digging at the door handle. The sound seemed to attract the milling crowd of shamblers around the bus, who turned toward us.

Mama shifted the stick with a nervous grind but got the Defender into first and screeched off. The drooling young man held on for a full block before letting go into a roll. Dyre put his tongue back into his mouth and waved a sad farewell to his fast friend. "Aw. Bye-bye, zombie man!"

Clo and I looked at each other.

"Zombies!?" we both said.

It was actually our first secret word. Clo had said "zombie" in English in the toy store when she was only ten months old, looking up at a foam axe designed for dispatching said creatures and a cartoon picture of an emaciated, reanimated corpse on the side of the brightly colored box. But Papa, standing behind us, didn't like it, thought it was too scary for us. He said Granddad had talked about seeing "real zombies" in Poland during World War II, and he didn't like seeing the cartoon stuff; said it made light of what some people really went through.

We didn't know then, and wouldn't know for a long time, what he meant by "real zombies," but at that point we started using CloElish more and more so Papa or Mama or any other grown-up wouldn't know what we were saying. We felt it was our inalienable right to discuss any topic with each other, even if we had no idea what we were talking about.

From the back seat, we leaned forward. "Is it really the zombie time, Mama?" Clo asked.

"Like, no more room in hell and everything?" El finished the thought.

"They're not zombies, girls," Mama said.

"They sure look like zombies." Clo pointed. "Watch out!" Mama swerved to avoid a man in a clown suit who was shambling right for the car, arms outstretched, eyes staring.

"A clowny guy!" Dyre shouted, reaching for the shambler outside. Dyre loved clowns, even creepy ones.

"We're not going to hug that clown today, Dyre," El said, trying to stay calm. What a man was doing wandering the streets at nine thirty in the morning in a clown suit in the first place was anyone's guess. But, it was San Francisco, after all.

"If they're not zombies, then what are they? What's wrong with everybody?" Clo demanded.

"They're addicts, girls."

"Like junkies?" El asked, starting to realize that there was no actual flesh-rotting going on with these folks, at least not yet. "Everyone? Even that sweet old lady over there?"

Indeed there was a sweet old lady, stumbling forward, and then suddenly clawing at a man in a brown delivery uniform next to a silver van. The van was sleek and brand-new, with a snake-helix medical crest on the side ringed by the words "Yerba City." The deliveryman had set down his stack of Amazon boxes and was standing next to the open door of the van, from which two whitish, thin, multijointed mechanical arms had emerged. One of the robotic limbs stabilized the deliveryman's arm with a gentle, cradle-like attachment while the van's other appendage—just a single long needle—delivered an injection of a glowing blue liquid.

"What is that van putting in him?" El asked, repulsed and fearful. She hated needles.

"It's the Sap," Mama said coldly. She had talked a lot about the Sap. It was a drug, we knew that much. She, along with two men named Dr. Antonov and Professor Gunry, had invented it. 3-hydroxy-4-methoxy-7-methyl-3-phenyl-[4-(trifluoromethyl) phenoxy]-N-methylmorphinan-propanamine, otherwise known by its brand name, Subantoxx. But that was just the pharmaceutical part. Mama's real contribution was the merging of the drug with artificial intelligence, her specialty. Mama knew a lot about computers. And drugs. And computerized drugs. Anyway, all we knew at the time was that it was blue, that it ran thick like tree sap, and that we needed to stay as far away from the stuff as possible.

The deliveryman, clearly both relieved and disoriented by his injection, was shoved out of the way by the sweet old lady, who offered up her arm for the next jab. The robotic attachments moved deftly to accommodate. The deliveryman stumbled a few steps away and sat down on his stack of boxes, crushing half of them. His face beamed contentment as he turned to stare at the large video screen mounted on the side of the van.

Behind the old lady, more and more people were lining up, and the mechanical arms pivoted to provide shots for each and every one.

"There's no driver!" El shouted.

"It's an AMTaC," Mama explained. "Yerba's got a fleet of them around the city now—Autonomous Mobile Treatment Centers."

"Hippopotamus treatment?" Dyre asked.

"Autonomous!" Clo corrected.

"What's that on its video?" El asked, intrigued. The van had screens mounted on both sides, like the sixty-six-inch 4K LED panels we saw in department stores sometimes, only bigger and with much higher resolution. We couldn't quite make out the audio, but even as we retreated— from a block away now—we could see the screens flashing big words, like "EPIDEMIC" and "INOCULATION" and "TREATMENT."

That wasn't the intriguing part, though. What had caught El's attention was the imagery that flashed in between the big block words: portraits, people's faces, that beckoned to the growing crowd on the sidewalk. Suddenly, one of the faces was Papa's, clean-shaven and handsome, just a few flecks of gray dotting his short red hair. He looked right at El, from what must have been at least sixty yards away, staring into her eyes.

"It's Papa!" El yelled, and Clo spun around to look.

"Papa?" Clo asked, incredulously. *"Where?!"*

But his beckoning face was gone, replaced by the pale cartoon visage of a smiling albino frog wearing a jaunty, ill-fitting knight's helmet.

"That's not Papa," Clo said disdainfully. "That's just Clyde."

Right before we rounded the corner and lost sight of the van, Clyde locked his bulbous pink eyes with Clo. We couldn't hear anything over the sound of Bouncy's gurgling diesel engine, but the frog clearly mouthed Clo's name.

"Oh my God," Clo tittered. "He saw me, and he said my name! Clyde saw me. Like, *the* Clyde. He wants me to go back there!"

"Yeah," El said. "So did Papa. I saw him on the video! He looked right at me!"

"Don't look at the screens!" Mama yelled, not taking her own eyes off the street in front of her.

"Fire trucks!" Dyre shouted, not caring in the slightest that we might have caught a glimpse of our long-lost father, or even the star of

BrickRibbit. Instead, our little brother pointed out the other side of the Defender as we passed a liquor store that was spouting flames. A bright red vehicle was already there, and two firefighters were approaching the scene, but they moved slowly, as if surrounded by Jell-O. One held a fire hose, and the other held a couple of glowing blue IV bags, with cords going into his own arm and his companion's. We would learn later that city workers—teachers, police, firefighters—had been the first to be "administered."

"Can we make s'mores?" Dyre asked innocently as he stared into the licking flames. A shambling woman in a pantsuit came up and snatched one of the bags, sending the firefighter holding it into a fumbling frenzy to recover it and pulling the tube from the first firefighter. He dropped the water hose and dove after his loose IV line like a bee-stung boy with a bee allergy would go for an EpiPen. Next to the chaos, El spotted one of the lines from the dropped IV bag slowly slithering, like a thin, translucent snake, back across the asphalt toward the downed firefighter's arm.

"That thing's alive!" El shouted.

As the three people wrestled hungrily, the thicker serpent of fire hose went into a writhing spasm, making us jump when it sent a heavy spray across our windshield.

Mama turned on our windshield wipers and sped on, away from the scene. Behind us, the neglected flames grew higher; the line to the AMTaC grew longer.

"No s'mores today, honey," Mama said tightly. "We're going to get out of the city for a while."

"But what about Papa?" Clo demanded, gripping her seat for stability. "And Clyde?"

"Yeah, that wasn't an old video," El insisted, the thought of her father making her forget the slithering IV line for a moment. "It was a live chat—Papa could see me, he looked right at me! He looked good— healthy, like he used to. He's still alive, and he saw me, and he smiled! He wants us to go back there!"

"Wait, I want to video chat with Papa, too!" Clo said, instantly fiercely jealous.

"It wasn't him," Mama said. "It was just a simulation. It was fake."

"Really?" El said. "But how—" She was interrupted by being thrown against the side of the Defender. Bouncy screeched around one corner, then another, and finally onto the on-ramp for the Golden Gate Bridge.

"The bridge!" Dyre shouted. He loved the old GG; it always excited him. "Can we go across it right now?"

"If we can," Mama breathed.

The orange art deco towers were a welcome sight, and beautiful in the morning light. There was a massive traffic jam coming into the city, but we sped past the first tower: there were almost no outbound vehicles, and the few cars that were headed north Mama swerved past handily. We looked back, trying to figure out where everyone was heading, and saw dozens of plumes of smoke arising from the cityscape. Downtown was in the distance now, and we watched a helicopter take off from one of the skyscrapers. It only made it a short distance before careening into the Salesforce Tower and exploding, starting yet another fire.

"Whoa!" we both commented.

"So many fires," El said, after a stunned pause.

"And no one's going to put them out," Clo finished the thought.

We turned back to Mama. We were almost to the second tower, then we'd be across the bridge. "Is the whole city going crazy, Mama?" Clo asked.

"Boeing 747-800SP!" Dyre yelled in delight before Mama could answer. He was good at naming planes, and indeed, off to the west, a jumbo jet was flying low, and headed directly for the Golden Gate. Too low. Who knew what was happening aboard, but the plane leaned sideways and the tip of one wing went into the water. Just the tip was enough: the giant machine went into a monstrous spinning cartwheel, heading straight for us.

We thought we could hear people screaming, but it was probably just us, screaming in sheer terror at the sight of 750,000 pounds of metal spinning our way across the Pacific Ocean like an enormous lotus-flower firework. Our 4x4 passed under the second bridge tower about one second before the Aloha Airlines maelstrom slammed into it.

The tower actually stood, but the bridge on either side of it vaulted upward in response to the impact and subsequent explosion. Essentially, the GG turned into a giant drawbridge, and we were launched as if from a giant flaming catapult. As we soared through the air, our vision forced into slow motion by the adrenaline coursing wildly through our veins, we had more than enough time to note the three tourists, two bridge workers, and man in a business suit spinning around us through the flame and debris.

Unlike us, these people weren't screaming, or panicking, or frightened even in the slightest. All six had blue Subantoxx patches on their necks, and despite their violent trajectories, their arms were all fixed at perfect forty-five-degree angles with their focus locked on their phones. They seemed to be oblivious to the fact that their bodies were about to be utterly obliterated. This was the most pathetic End of the World we could have possibly imagined: the human race was missing its own fireworks.

Along with the tourists, most of our fellow vehicles were instantly destroyed that morning, but six or seven cars landed on solid asphalt just on the Marin County side of the bay. We're pretty sure ours was the only one that landed right-side up, on four wheels. The only one that wasn't on fire, that is. Bouncy became very bouncy, and thank Oggy for children's car seats—not that one would have made any difference in the vehicles that landed sideways, nose-first, or simply upside down like helpless flaming turtles.

"Again!" Dyre yelled, and it was probably all just like Six Flags to him, though the rest of us had gone mute with fear. (We might have enjoyed the ride, too, if we hadn't thought that every moment could be our last.) Then Mama regained control and continued driving.

We looked back and saw the Golden Gate Bridge—destroyed, on fire, cars scattered everywhere. That sight of the urban landscape we knew so well being royally smacked down would probably have been enough on its own to send us into a lifetime of therapy (if such a thing still existed today), but what was truly disturbing was the fact that Mama didn't stop. There were people back there who needed help, who could use immediate medical attention or just a friendly someone to turn their phones off and stomp out the fire in their hair, but instead of turning around, Mama gunned it.

The thing you need to know about Lauren Yetti is, she never ran from trouble. Ever. She was always the first one running into it. Not only did Mama have a black belt, she also had a medical degree, and being a first responder was in her blood. Mama's mama was a firefighter, and Mama's papa was in Special Forces. One time when we were coming back from Sausalito, a little girl fell off the ferry. Mama was in the water practically before the girl was, still with her pumps on. Mama would scale a tree to save a cat and screech to a halt in traffic if she saw a fender bender. She'd even help a dirty old hobo pull up his pants after taking a pee if he couldn't do it himself. She was just like that. She had a big heart. Now that Mama was heading north at 110 per, *away* from the problem, we knew, deep in our little-kid hearts, raised on video games and child-targeted binge programming, that something had irreparably broken within the world itself.

We twins looked at each other over our clueless little brother's head, and the panic in the other's eyes forced us both to take one deep breath. And another. We weren't going to punch our way out of this one, so maybe that martial arts "centering" training would be useful after all. We looked back at the road.

Now that we were on the other side of the destroyed bridge, there were no other cars alongside us, but there were still a lot of zombified people headed the other way. The southbound cars were gridlocked, some of them on top of each other, and we saw dozens of people walking instead, stumbling along the road like you-know-whats: shambling mounds of desire. They hadn't gotten enough of their patches, or bags, or shots, or whatever yet. These addicts didn't care what side of the road they were on, either, so we had to slow down and swerve around them. At first this only further unnerved us, having to dodge the shamblers, but soon our frantic minds just twisted it into a fun pastime, like another video game. ZombieDodge 2 was a welcome relief from Golden Gate Bridge Bada Boom.

"Mama," El finally asked, struggling to stay calm amid the screeching of tires, "why is everyone going back into the fires?"

"They need the drug, sweetheart. They don't care about the fire. San Francisco's been listed as a treatment hub, so they're all trying to get in and find a dispensary or one of those vans. All they care about is Subantoxx."

"But the medicine you made for Papa is supposed to help people. Why is it making everyone so crazy?"

"It's nanoengineered to fundamentally rewire dopamine pathways in the brain," Mama spouted, forgetting, as she often did, that she was talking to eight-year-olds. "It was only meant to be used on incurable addicts. The neurological deployment was so complicated that we had to use an AI amalgam to engineer it. But when she coalesced, she started Project Chimera and weaponized the treatment under the pretext of stopping the Fimi virus."

"But you said the Fimi virus was just a fake news hoax made up by a Jolly Rancher," Clo pointed out, still shaking slightly.

"It is," Mama said. "But Yerba City convinced the world it was real so she could get everyone hooked on her treatment. Project Chimera was supposed to cure addicts."

"Like Papa?" El asked.

"Yeah," Mama said grimly, after a slight pause. "Like Papa. But now she's using the cure to make more patients."

"But I saw Papa back on the screen!" El insisted again.

"And Clyde the frog saw me!" Clo added hastily.

"That's part of Project Chimera," Mama continued. "Individualized monopolizing neocortex stimulation."

"Huh?" El said.

"She just shows you what you want to see," Mama fired back. "It works synergistically with the drug. It was meant to rewire hopelessly traumatized pathways. But it isn't real, okay? It's all fake, she's using it against us."

"So Papa's still gone?" Clo said solemnly.

"Yeah," Mama said, "he's still gone, baby. He'll always be gone."

"And Yerba City just used fake computer graphics to make me see him again?" El asked, growing less skeptical, although we were starting to remember that period when we cried every day for months last year, after we got the news. "But how did she do that?"

"I'll explain someday," Mama said. "But just remember: nothing on those screens is real. Yerba will say and show you anything to get the Sap in you."

"I can forgive Clyde," Clo announced. "But that's a dirty trick: showing us our dead papa like that."

"It *is* a dirty trick," Mama agreed, heavily. "Just . . . remember that: she fights dirty. As dirty as you can possibly imagine."

At the time, we didn't really understand all the details about Yerba City or Project Chimera, but we knew they were something Mama and Team YAG had been working on since before we could remember (which was probably only about four years back, at the time). Remember how we said Mama always ran toward problems to try to solve them? Well, after Papa died, she promised she'd find a cure for what killed him, so she put together a group of brilliant scientists: herself plus Dr. Antonov and Professor Gunry. Team Y-A-G. We'll tell you more about them later, but for now, you need to know that Yerba City was a super smart computer program that they put in charge of the project—Yerba was what we twins call a Jolly Rancher, she being artificial and all.

You see, back then, Mama didn't like us to eat Jolly Ranchers because they had "artificial flavors." We had no idea what those were, so when we heard her talking about the dangers of "artificial intelligence," we assumed they were related to the perils of Jolly Ranchers, and that Yerba City was another, more dangerous artificial flavor— like Acid Sour Apple or Exploding Fire Stix. Turns out, of course, she was talking about artificial *machine* intelligence, or AI. But we just kept calling them Jolly Ranchers, because that's what we do. This particular Jolly Rancher, Yerba City—or "she," as Mama always said—was supposed to be experimental, but as soon as she started experimenting on people . . . well, you know the rest: Planet Junkie flavor, now with extra slaver.

THUMP! A shambler bounced off the hood of the car. Mama was trying her best to dodge them, but another would always close in. "Dammit!" Mama cursed. "There's too many on the highway. We'll have to take the side roads."

"But, Mama," El questioned, trying to sound as grown-up as possible and ignoring the seemingly suicidal addicts all around us, "you said we should be strong girls, stand up for ourselves, resist injustices, and all that."

"Yes . . . *yes!*" Clo seconded, nodding in frantic agreement as she picked up on the idea of trying to turn our freak-out around. Anything to stop thinking about the giant explosion we had just survived. "Let's go back and smash that van. Stop them from sticking people with the Sap!"

"Yeah!" El switched back to CloElish for a pep talk. *"We smashed those trash-talking boys, we can smash some creepy ghost van!"*

"That's right!" Clo nodded. *"Double-tap it!"*

We reached across our little brother and slapped our palms together two times.

"Stop it," Dyre grumbled, but quietly—a little bit afraid of us now that we were getting so worked up. As our little brother, he knew what we were capable of; we had been diagnosed as sociopathic by more than one babysitter, after all. "Bridge is gone, anyway," he mumbled.

"Shut up," El chided, her blood rising. "We'll find another way back."

"Yeah! Let's fight!" Clo seconded.

Mama just sighed and shook her head. "AMTaCs aren't the problem, even if we could stop a hundred, a thousand, of those vans. She's already infected the entire internet with the Chimera. It's on every network."

"That's what Scruffy Dude was doing!" El realized.

"It wasn't a duck sex video, it was the Chimera," Clo said, finishing the thought. *"Instead of Papa or Clyde, he saw himself as a little boy with the broken Ronin Robot."*

"And he had that blue patch on his neck," El said. "Mama, can the Sap be inside a little blue patch on your neck?"

"Yeah," she acknowledged, confirming our suspicions. "A patch, a shot, a drip, and those aren't even the real danger. It's *those*." She pointed upward.

We strained our heads sideways to look up through the windows of the Defender. Several hundred feet in the sky floated something fat and round, with short wings and dangling legs.

"Is that a big drone?" El asked, pressing her face against the glass. Behind the flying machine was a widening chemtrail of blue mist.

"He's pee-peeing on us!" Dyre yelled.

"Yes. It's a drone," Mama said calmly.

"It's spraying everyone?" Clo asked.

"The governor signed the order last night for emergency inoculation." Mama sighed. "They're going to spray all of California, and other states are going to follow suit. And those ones"—she pointed to a high-flying echelon of drones to our left—"those are headed overseas."

She shook her head gravely. "They don't understand about Subantoxx, and Yerba City's been manipulating the facts. A human brain will never be the same again—even after one dose. Just a picoliter is enough to hijack your entire nucleus accumbens."

We fell silent. Mama continued to dodge and weave the Defender down the road. We still weren't sure what it all meant, but it sounded pretty dark, and Mama was usually the crusader rabbit of confidence.

El broke the tension. "I think I like my nucleus accumbens the way it is."

"But," Clo said, "if they're spraying everyone, then we're going to be shamblers, too!"

"No, because Mama's been giving you your vitamins. We should all be immune for at least the next twenty-four hours."

It was true. Every morning for at least the last year, Mama had been sprinkling "vitamins" on our breakfast cereal. We would learn later that this was in fact a counterdrug—N-methyl-1-phenylpropan-2-amine, or Prophanol. She had been worried that, during her research, she would be exposed to Subantoxx and would pass a microdose along to us. And a microdose would be enough.

So there you have it. We were on the run, and the whole world (at least our whole world) was now hooked on an incredibly addictive drug being rained down from the sky by a fleet of drones controlled by an evil supercomputer that Mama and her partners had invented. Whoops. We would have been angry with Mama, but really, that first day, we were just trying not to get drooled on.

We didn't talk much for a while after that. We were through the rainbow tunnel and up the 101, going as fast as the Defender could take us. Gradually we found we were dodging fewer and fewer shamblers. By the time we crossed out of Marin into the next county, there was no one, not a single car on the road except ours. Eventually we picked up the OwlPad and started playing BrickRibbit again like we would on any other road trip. Playing that little pixelated Clyde on the cheap tablet screen was a lot more soothing than thinking about the big pink-eyed frog on the side of the AMTaC, staring into our souls. Yet occasionally we would look up and see one of those silver vans on the other side of the freeway, driving south, presumably bringing people to the city.

"Don't look at it!" Mama would shout, so of course we would look at it. But the screens on the sides of the vans were switched off. Apparently they didn't need to lure folks in for treatment anymore; everyone was coming to them. Still, every time we spotted a van, we tried to catch a glimpse of Papa, even though we knew it would be fake.

"Who even told them about Papa?" El asked, still skeptical.

"You did," Mama replied. "They can read things off the backs of your eyes."

"Whaaaat?" Clo said.

"It's the part of the Chimera we called the Goat. It bounces invisible lasers off the back of your cornea a thousand times a second and then compiles subconscious reactions into a real-time simulation that will provoke the reptilian complex." Mama sighed, realizing once again that she was talking over our heads.

"Wait," El objected. "Is it a goat or a lizard?"

"I saw Clyde," Clo interjected. "And Clyde is a frog."

"Frog is an amphibian," Dyre grunted, not looking up from the OwlPad. "Not reptile."

"Very good," Clo said condescendingly, patting her brother's head. "You're so smart."

"Don't touch me." Dyre stiffened. "I don't touch you, you don't touch me."

"Look," Mama said, "I'll explain it all to you someday. Just try to get some rest. We have a lot ahead of us."

We snaked our way up north all day, trying to forget about invisible lasers, dead papas, and talking frog knights, and avoiding cities and towns until there were almost no cities and towns left to avoid.

Northern California gets wild, fast. We stopped just outside of a town called Eureka and tried to refuel at an abandoned station. The pumps still worked, so we got ourselves filled with diesel and then helped ourselves to some supplies at a nearby abandoned Hutchinson's Sporting Goods store: lamps, tarps, some rations, a short-stocked .30-06 hunting rifle in cute blue camo that we immediately dubbed Daisy Duke, and a long, serrated hunting knife we named Toothy.

When we stepped outside, we saw a few shamblers a couple of blocks away, but they didn't come after us. They were gathering around one of those silver AMTaCs, its screens only occasionally lit with dirty-trick images of loved ones and cartoon characters, TV stars and superheroes, all beckoning while its mechanical arms were busy injecting person after person. The "patients," once shot with the Sap, were actually getting inside the van to lie down on a series of cots in the back.

"I don't see Papa on there," El said.

"You're not supposed to look!" Dyre chastised, stumbling under the weight of a shopping basket filled with boxes of rifle ammo.

"It's changing," Mama explained. "They're not trying to spread it anymore. These people have already had exposure. Now they're being prepped for transportation to a permanent treatment center."

"So!" El said happily. "If they're not going to drool on us, we can put all this stuff back and go home, right?"

"No," Mama said solemnly, "home is more dangerous than ever. She'll be boxing people up now."

That sounded ominous enough to shut us up again, and we packed the car with everything we'd looted and drove deeper into the woods. Tent, water bottles, hunting knife, hatchet.

We remember the sky turned a dusty pink over the redwoods that day, and in the twilight, the lights over our empty two-lane blacktop flickered on like fireflies.

"At least the streetlights still work out here," Mama said hopefully. About ten seconds later, the lights flickered off, covering the road in darkness. "Never mind," she mumbled.

We actually didn't notice right away, because we were still using the tablet to play BrickRibbit. We didn't even look up to see the last of the lights fade. It would be one of the last times we saw electric lights of any kind, from any store or shop or anything.

Finally, off a dirt road in the middle of the forest, the OwlPad died. "Waaaah!" we reflexively screamed, when we were plunged into darkness. But we grew silent almost as fast, recalling the events of the day. Oh yeah, losing power on the OwlPad couldn't be the end of the world, because it already was the End of the World. So we rode in darkness for a while, only the Defender's headlights illuminating the seemingly endless series of redwood trees that charged out of the blackness toward us.

"Where are we going?" El finally asked.

"Hopefully," Mama breathed, "nowhere."

We continued to bump and jostle through the night. Dyre had long since fallen asleep, and, with nothing better to do, Clo soon joined him.

Not El, though, at least not right away. She continued to think about that glimpse of Papa. Just an illusion, really?

"I love you so much, Clyde," Clo mumbled in her sleep. *"Such a good boy, just one more fly."*

El's eyes began to droop. She hadn't seen Papa for more than two years, and he had looked terrible toward the end: haggard, unshaven, eyes sinking back from the world he would soon be departing. On the van's screen, he had seemed so real, happy again, calling to her. We trusted Mama above all else, but still, here we were, running, and without a fight. That stung, like being teased by a bully who was all talk. Maybe Yerba City was just another Toby Pilkey; maybe all she had was a bunch of panicky talk, some drones, a blue drug, and some TV screens that weren't even turned on anymore. One good punch in the nose and she'd crawl back into Silicon Valley and leave the world alone.

We didn't like running from our problems. But, on the bright side, this meant we didn't have to go back to school. That was welcome, apocalypse or not, and if Mama said Yerba City's dirty tricks were dangerous, then we'd run, at least for now.

Little did we know, Yerba City's dirty tricks were just getting started.

CHAPTER 3

THE LAST DANCE OF DASHER BANKS

When we awoke, Bouncy was stopped, and the morning light was shining through tall, ancient redwood trees. Mama already had a tent set up and a small fire going. We stepped out of the car onto the soft forest floor and immediately fell in love.

"Where . . . are . . . we?" El managed to say as we looked around in awe.

Mama, who'd been chopping a small tree with the hatchet we had looted, paused and took a moment to admire the morning light that had us mesmerized. "Not sure," she breathed, wiping sweat from her forehead. "The way in wasn't on any map. No GPS. Pretty overgrown." She pointed with the hatchet at the majestic redwoods. "But this is definitely an old-growth grove. I think it was meant to be a logging camp, a long time ago, meant to supply a boom town during the gold rush."

She nodded to the area where she'd parked Bouncy. "There was a space cleared out here. There's a spring over there, and a creek nearby too. Would have been perfect. But all the old trees are still here. I think the boom went bust before the logging could get started, and this place ended up off the grid."

"Old-growth grove?" Clo echoed, not exactly sure what the words meant but liking the sound of them.

"Can we stay here, in this . . . OGG place, Mama?" El pressed, still amazed at the morning sun reflecting off the dew-covered redwood bark.

"OGG spells Oggy," Dyre groggily insisted from the back seat, trying to show off his spelling skills even though he was only half-awake.

"If she'll have us," Mama sighed.

Fortunately, she would have us. The Oggy was the most beautiful place we had ever been, and she would become the center of our lives for the next decade, both physically and spiritually.

Speaking of lives, something happened early on that changed our concept of life, death, and everything before or after, and the story might shed a little light on why we do what we do. We had made a decent camp right away, but one day, about two weeks after we arrived, the Clif Bars, juice boxes, and other edible looted booty had run out, and we were starting to know hunger as we had never known it. We were a middle-class family from San Francisco; though we might have occasionally seen a ragged homeless person moaning in emptiness downtown, starvation wasn't on our radar as a real possibility. But as we stumbled through the ancient redwoods looking for roots half-remembered from our Brownie outings, the yowling feeling of our bodies eating themselves alive became very real, in a way it never had on Market Street.

"Me hungry," Clo moaned.

"Me, too," El concurred curtly. *"So stop saying it."*

"Can we eat grass?" Clo asked, scratching at the base of a tree for tubers or small roots or anything. *"Dasher Banks in kindergarten ate grass."*

"Dasher was an idiot," El said decisively.

"He was so cute, grunting like a little horsey. Munch munch!" Clo was getting delirious. *"My name's Dasher, like a little reindeer, so I can eat grass!"* she giddily reminisced.

El was looking down, trying to keep focused. *"Try to find a mushroom or something."*

Clo looked up dizzily at the trees. *"I bet Dasher's sitting in a warm bed right now, his reindeer belly all happy and full."*

"Dasher's probably one of those shamblers right now," El grunted, *"hooked on the Sap, and drooling like a zombie."*

"I'd take that over starving out here," Clo mumbled.

El shot up, bristling, her fists clenched. *"Don't say that!"* she yelled. *"Don't ever say that! If Mama says we need to be out here, then we need to be out here!"*

We squared off, eye to eye with each other. *"What does it matter, if we're gonna die anyway?"* Clo shot back.

"You wanna go out like a sucker?" El demanded. It was pretty tough talk from a skinny eight-year-old redhead with dirt on her face, still wearing a ripped periwinkle-purple shirt. Clo just squinted back at her.

"I said, do you want to go out like a sucker?" El repeated slowly.

Clo thought about looking away, going back to digging for mushrooms, but instead pointed a dirty finger at her sister. *"You don't believe Mama one hundred percent,"* she said accusingly. *"You think we should go back like I do."*

"No I don't," El scoffed, turning away to scrape at the dirt meaninglessly.

"Yes you do," Clo said. *"You think we should go back to ice cream and sushi and Mission burritos and beds with real sheets."*

"Shut up," El grunted.

"I know you do, because you're getting mad. And you never get mad at me unless you're doing mental gymnastics, and the only reason you're doing mental gymnastics is because you don't trust Mama one hundred percent."

"That's not why I'm mad at you," El fired back. *"I'm mad at you because I'm starving!"*

"That wouldn't do it," Clo scoffed. *"You're a mind-over-matter girl."*

It was true: of the two of us, El was generally the stoic one; she admired Mama's cool-cucumber badassery and tried to emulate it constantly. It took a lot to make her lose her temper.

"Look, just gather up some baby ferns and we'll make a nice little salad agai—"

"I know you want to go back, too; you're just not talking about it." Clo held her ground, suspicious. *"You have a plan, don't you? What do you know that I don't? You think the world isn't really over?"*

"No, you were there," El said defensively. *"You saw everything go boom while everyone just stared at their phones."*

"But you saw Papa on that TV. I saw Clyde."

"So what?" El retorted, digging deeper. *"It's just made-up computer animation. He wasn't real, so it doesn't matter what we saw."*

"Do you think you can go back, find him in that screen, and save him?"

"No, that's not it." El stood up, forgetting the foraging for a moment to stare southward, back toward the city.

Clo paused, her mind getting into her sister's. *"You wanna kill Yerba City? Give her the Double-Mega-Punch?"*

El nodded coldly. *"Someone's gotta make her pay for playing dirty. Someone's gotta—"*

CRACK! A gunshot echoed through the forest. We froze and locked eyes with each other again, this time in fear.

"Mama!" Clo breathed.

We took off and ran as fast as our half-starved bodies would take us toward the sound of the shot. As we emerged into a small clearing, it seemed at first, to our unaccustomed city-folk eyes, as if Mama had found a big hairy barrel and knocked it over. Turned out it was a deer she had shot. We would be able to identify it later as a blacktail buck, and an especially big one: the furry, antlered thing must have weighed 250 pounds at least.

"Mama!" we gasped in shock and awe, still panting.

Mama turned to us. "Calm down, girls. It's okay. I just shot a deer."

"You shot Bambi?" Clo asked incredulously, inching around Mama to get a better look. Her lip started to quiver at the sight of the animal on its side.

"I'm afraid so," Mama said soberly.

"With Daisy Duke the rifle?" Clo still couldn't believe it.

"That's not a fair fight, Mama," El pointed out, approaching the carcass cautiously. Maybe it was her hunger, but El's stoic nature was starting to crack, and her lip began to quiver too.

"It wasn't a fight, girls," Mama said. "I had to kill it so we could live."

"But . . . but . . ." Looking down at the buck, Clo still couldn't believe the creature was actually dead. His eyes and mouth were closed, and his hoofed feet were tucked in slightly. He almost looked peaceful, were it not for the still-bleeding bullet hole in his flank. "He's sooo cuuuute!" Clo burst into full-on sobs, tears flowing.

El followed suit, mouth opening to wail: "He looks like he's just sleeeeeping!"

"He looks just like cute Dasher Banks from kindergarten!" Clo bawled.

"Don't name the poor thing, Chloe," Mama warned. "If you name a creature, it makes it that much harder to take its life if you need to."

"But why did we have to kill him?" El wept. "He didn't even mess with us."

"That's what we're going to have to do to survive out here, girls," Mama explained. She was struggling to be patient. "We're going to have to eat him."

"*Eat* him?" El nudged the poor thing's hoof. "That's gross!" She broke into a wail again.

"That's hella gross," Clo corrected, and wailed louder.

Clo was definitely the louder of the two of us. Like, painfully loud, and her deafening cry seemed to snap a bit of sobriety into El, who was always the first to try to be mature.

"*C'mon.*" She whacked Clo slightly, causing the wail to waver. "*Snap out of it.*" Clo quieted down.

"*But—*" she started.

"*Mama's right.*" El nodded grimly. "*She's right. We have to do this.*"

"It's okay, Mama," El said. "We can do this. If you say we have to, for the family, we can do it." She readied herself. "C'mon, Clo." She turned to her sister and wiped the tears from her eyes.

"*We're strong, remember?*" she said to Clo. "*We beat up all those bullies, so we can eat Dasher Banks, right? C'mon, be strong with me.*"

Clo nodded, gathering herself. "*Okay,*" she breathed. "Let's do this."

We turned and leaned down at the same time, opening our half-starved mouths, aiming to take a bite right out of the furry mass's neck.

"Wait!" Mama shouted. "No! We have to cook it, we're not going to eat it raw!"

We paused.

"But sushi is raw," Clo pointed out.

"It's not sushi!" Mama insisted. "It's a deer. We have to clean it. We have to string it up, skin it, gut it. Then we'll cook the meat. I did it once with your father in Louisiana; I can do it again." She sounded like she was convincing herself as much as she was convincing us.

"Oh," said El, realizing.

"Oh," said Clo, looking down at Dasher's cute face. She started to wail again. "I don't wanna cut his guts out! Can't we just eat him and get it over with?"

"No," Mama said stiffly and shouldered the rifle. From her pack she pulled out and unsheathed Toothy, the large hunting knife. "There's a right way to do things."

"What are you crybabies whining about?"

The voice came from not too far away. It was Dyre, standing at the edge of the clearing. Apparently the sound of the gunshot and our sobbing had brought him, at least close enough to use some of the same sarcastic language we constantly used on him. He had the BrickRibbit OwlPad in his hands; it didn't have any power left, but rubbing his fingers across it seemed to be comforting. He was staring down at the blank screen.

"Mama killed Dasher Banks!" Clo announced.

"And now we have to eat him!" El lamented angrily. "And *you* have to eat him, too!"

"She didn't kill him," Dyre said, not looking up.

"Yes she did!" Clo insisted. "She shot him dead!"

"He's still breathing," Dyre taunted.

"No he's not!" El snorted, annoyed. "We've been standing right here, and Dasher is totally deaAAAAAH!"

With a horrifying bellow, the buck's eyes snapped open and he raised his head, wagging his antlers around.

"Oh my God!" Mama breathed, and dropped Toothy to stick in the dirt while she fumbled for the rifle again.

The buck roared to its feet, echoing a primal bleat into the forest. We all jumped back, even Mama.

It wasn't exactly an angry cry the animal made, or even a defiant one. Mama had shot him right through the side, blood was flowing out, and it was just a matter of a few more moments before his life ebbed away. The buck knew it, we knew it, everybody knew it. But big Dasher Banks was not going to go quietly. He had something left to say.

He started dancing. There's no other way to describe it. The buck's eyes were glazed over, already seeing things in the next world, but he tilted his antlers to the left, thrusting with small leaps, moving in a circle, and then to the right, moving over the same circle. We all just stood there for a moment, awestruck. Us city girls had never seen anything like it. Even Dyre looked up from his OwlPad.

"He doesn't wanna die!" came our little brother's voice, affected, as we were, by the mortality of this poor creature.

"He's fighting it!" Clo commented.

"What a badass!" El said. We couldn't help but admire the beautiful creature. He had been shot, out of the blue, by a hot piece of metal from a machine he couldn't possibly understand, by an entity (Mama) from a race (humankind) he had probably never seen before, and everyone around him assumed he was dead as a dodo. But he wasn't, at least not yet, and he was going to fight.

Mama turned. "Dyre! Get back!" The look on our brother's sad little-boy face, seeing Dasher Banks doing his last dance, was even more pitiful than watching the innocent deer die. But then Dasher's gaze caught ours, and it was all over. The deer pulled his vision from the next world back into this one for just an instant, and our lives changed forever.

This is going to sound a little weird, but it is exactly what happened: Dasher's eyes and our eyes met—for only a moment—and in a flash, suddenly we weren't sad. Not us twins. Everything froze, and a cone of white light came out from behind that deer and surrounded us. Mama couldn't see it and Dyre couldn't see it; they were stopped in time, as this cosmic vision was clearly reserved just for us.

We didn't feel sorry for Dasher now, or scared of him, or disgusted by the bloody drool flying out of his gaping mouth. We admired him. We identified with him. In a flash, we realized that we were just like Dasher: we had been waylaid from a distance by high-tech weaponry, preyed upon by a new race of Jolly Ranchers who saw fit to use our bodies for their own purposes. We were wounded, on the run, outgunned, outflanked, outmaneuvered, and it was just a matter of time before the superior forces of this world closed in on us. Then we would be dead.

Like Dasher, we were doomed, and also like Dasher, we were going to fight to our last breath.

Us twins both felt it at the same time, and we grabbed each other's hands, gasping in awe as we watched nature's beauty unfold. If only we could be as badass as that flailing stag someday, we thought. And then he gave us the honor of speaking to us.

"Children," the deer rasped deeply, "don't cry for me."

"He's talking to us!" Clo gasped. Dyre and Mama couldn't hear it— they were still frozen in time.

"Mother Oggy sent me to you," Dasher continued in his other-worldly baritone.

"He kinda sounds like Papa," El noted.

"Except more deer-y," Clo added.

"You must protect your family," the deer said.

"But we wanna go home and fight the bad guys!" Clo retorted, defiant even in the face of this divine messenger.

"You are already home," Dasher Banks asserted, his otherworldly voice darkening. "And the fight begins now."

In a flash, the white tunnel of light disappeared, bringing us back into the moist, cold forest. Time started up again, Mama and Dyre started moving again, and Dasher's eyes glazed back over.

Mama was struggling to load another round into the rifle, but she wasn't as familiar with Daisy's bolt action as we would all be someday, and she accidentally sent the next round spinning out into the forest without chambering it. "No. No!" she cried and reached into her pocket, fumbling with a half-open box of ammo.

But Dasher wasn't going to wait for the coup de grâce. He had been sent from above on a mission, not just as a messenger, but as a tester. He turned, lowered his antlers, and charged, right for Dyre.

"Dyre!" Mama screamed. "Run!" But the boy just stood there grip-ping the dead computer tablet, frozen like a statue. Can you blame him? A full-grown twelve-point buck in the prime of life giving his fullest is an awesome sight, even if it is about to eviscerate you.

"He's going to paste our little brother!" El shouted.

"That's our job!" Clo said.

"Go!" El cried, and we unlocked hands, somehow knowing exactly what we had to do. Clo sprinted toward the deer as fast as she could. El

snatched Toothy off the ground and tossed him pommel-first toward Clo, who caught the knife in midair without even looking back. She flipped the weapon and ran forward, gripping it like a sword with both hands (Toothy was still bigger than her eight-year-old forearm at this point). El turned and grabbed Daisy Duke by the barrel, snatching her right out of Mama's hands.

"Hey!" Mama shouted, shocked. "Wait! It's not loaded!"

"No need," El retorted, and she hefted the .30-06 like a club and ran screaming toward the fray.

You can probably guess what happened next: when the deer's antlers were about a foot away from Dyre's face, Clo slammed herself (and the knife) into Dasher's neck, which didn't stop him, but got his momentum redirected toward a fern grove nearby. They both went down, flailing into a green explosion of blood and wet fronds, and somewhere in there is how Clo got the scar on her cheek.

A second later El joined the melee, screaming and swinging down with the rifle's stock as hard as she could. Between the clubbing and the stabbing, it was all over pretty quick.

"That's . . . enough!" Mama said, running up.

We stopped the clubbing and stabbing and looked down, breathing heavily. "Are you sure?" We were both covered in blood at that point.

"Yes," Mama breathed. "He is definitely dead now, you can . . . stop. Are you okay? Clo, your cheek!"

Clo, still panting heavily, reached up, touched the deep cut on her face, and looked at her hand. We couldn't tell where the deer's blood ended and hers began.

"It's okay, Mama," Clo reassured her. "It was worth it. We had to do it. He told us to kill him. It was a test."

"Yeah," El seconded. "Oggy sent him."

"We're already home, Mama." Clo smiled.

"We're going to stay and fight with you, Mama," El said, handing back Daisy Duke.

Mama took the rifle, now bloody, and clearly didn't know quite what to think, but she seemed relieved. "Well, uh, thank you. Yes, we're all going to stick together. Are you sure you didn't hit your heads or anything?"

We ignored her and turned to look at the big dead deer, his sweet eyes now finally still and his tongue lolling out.

El said, *"Dasher Banks gave his life for us."*

"He was cute," Clo acknowledged. *"And now he's dead. It's sad."*

We both kneeled to throw our arms around Dasher, rocking him with a loving embrace.

"Thank you!" El said.

"Thank you so much, Dasher the deer!" Clo said, burying her slick face in the coarse fur on the animal's neck. She actually started to cry again a little bit as she looked at his tender dark eyes and ran her finger along the knobby ridge of one of his antlers.

"He's so beautiful. We never could have made anything like this."

"Only Oggy could do this."

We both leaned back and put our hands together to say a little prayer. Over the years, we would go back and forth, neither one more than the other, really, but El led our prayer that first time by our first kill.

"Dear Oggy, thank you for bringing us Dasher Banks to kill and eat. Let his spirit go up and join you and Papa in heaven. Then please bring us another deer. Or a pig. Or a cow, for hamburgers."

"A cow?" Clo questioned sidelong. *"Out here?"*

"Or anything. We promise to be reverent and not let it suffer when we stick it or shoot it or stab it." She looked up at the ancient trees. *"Wait,"* she suddenly said to Clo. *"Which way is Oggy?"*

"Everywhere, I guess." Clo shrugged, looking around.

"Okay." We both stood and faced north.

"Thank you, Oggy," we said to the north and turned around.

"Thank you, Oggy," we said to the south and turned to the left.

"Thank you, Oggy," we said to the east and turned around.

"Thank you, Oggy," we said to the west.

We turned again and were about to get to this "gutting" business when Mama gasped. "Dyre!" she breathed.

We swiveled our bloody maws and saw our four-year-old brother standing nearby. We'd been so caught up in the animal's last rites that we'd forgotten all about him.

Clo's first pierce of the deer's jugular must have caught our brother in the spray, because Dyre had a splatter of darkening scarlet across his left eyebrow and cheek. The little boy was just standing there, pale and expressionless, blood on his face.

"He didn't want to die," Dyre mumbled, and then his face contorted into a twisted mass and the sobbing started. He actually dropped the OwlPad, and its dark screen cracked across a protruding rock.

"Dyre." Mama went to comfort him, but our brother just turned and ran into the forest, tears streaming. "Dyre!" she called, and went after him.

—

Later that night, when we finally got Clo's cheek sewn up with pink thread from our little girls' sewing kit, and Dyre finally stopped crying, we actually did manage to string up, drain, gut, and clean Dasher. It was freaking disgusting, but we got used to it fast, as it meant we were not going to starve to death. And aside from being a messenger from the almighty Mother Oggy, we discovered a little present inside Dasher: it turned out that the buck had eaten a bunch of acorns that morning, and the nutty mass was still fresh in his stomach. We washed off the intestines in the creek, stuffed in the mush, twisted them into six-inch lengths, and roasted the juicy tubes on the fire as sweet venison sausages, the whole time thanking Oggy over and over. They were the most amazing thing we had ever eaten.

We were so full afterward, and half-asleep, but we just kept slowly gnawing at the delicious sausages. Mama was nearby, holding Dyre by the fire and trying to comfort him, but his face, now clean, was still blank. The truth is, after that day, he would never really be the same, and neither would we.

"We're not girls anymore," El sighed when she finally took a break from sausage eating to look up at the towering trees, aglow with firelight. "Oggy has chosen us."

Clo grunted in acknowledgment, like a satisfied pig. "But what are we, then?"

"We're killers," El concluded. "Butchers. We have to be."

Clo nodded, wiping her mouth, and wincing for a moment at her stitched-up cheek. "But we're protectors too, like Clyde in BrickRibbit. We have to protect our family."

El considered the metaphor for a moment. *"I think he's just hopping after the princess."*

"Yeah, but he's going to make a family with her, and then protect the family."

El considered. *"Okay."* And she took another bite. Thank goodness we had had at least some exposure to video games before the End of the World, or how else would we have learned these important moral lessons?

"But, El?" Clo said.

"Hmm?"

"If we're the last people on earth, how are we going to make a family?"

El snorted. *"We're just little girls, Clo. We don't have to worry about that yet. Besides, our hands are full with the mission. We need to stay here, and keep everyone safe."*

We looked over. Mama had moved away from Dyre and had started slicing thin pieces of meat off Dasher's body, getting ready to smoke them over a small pit she'd dug while we were roasting sausages. It was all pretty morbid on some level, but we were adjusting fast. We knew it was going to be necessary from now on to have carcasses hanging around, and to use every part of them we could.

Speaking of which, we noticed that Dyre still had that thousand-yard stare going on. We'd seen that look on Grandpa's face more than once before he passed away. Dyre was only four, and Mama's cuddling hadn't seemed to snap him out of seeing Dasher lose his life. We weren't sure what to do about it. Then El spotted something.

"I got an idea," she said, pulling Dasher's antlers off the ground and putting them in her lap. Somewhat to our surprise, the antlers had come off Dasher as easily as snapping a branch. We would understand later, as the intimate details of deer, wild pigs, and other prey animals became second nature to us, that, because it was the end of summer, his pedicles had already gotten soft. The rut had ended weeks before, and it had almost been time to shed the excess baggage.

We stood up and walked over to our little brother.

"Here," El said, dropping the antlers into his lap. "Dasher wanted you to have these. You're gonna be a big buck like him someday, and he doesn't need them anymore."

Dyre broke his stare and looked down at the trophies.

"Look." El pointed to a flap of hide on Dasher's crown tine, a bloody remnant of the rut. "That's not his fur, or his blood."

"Or mine," Clo added.

"He was a fighter," El continued. "And he fought until the end."

"Yeah," Clo seconded. "He didn't go out like a sucker."

"And neither will our family." El finished our little speech and we left our brother to himself.

Dyre stared down at the antlers. Running his fingers along the points and ridges, he seemed to be somewhat comforted. Soon his eyes closed and he fell asleep in the firelight, holding the bloody prongs like a new teddy bear.

—

The next morning, our bellies were still full. Dyre continued to clutch Dasher's antlers as he slept on Mama's shoulders while she walked us about two miles back up the dirt road we had come in on. She set our little brother down in a patch of moss and then used the hatchet to cut down a small tree so that it fell across the already-overgrown lane, forming a symbolic blockade against the outside world.

She scraped her boot along the dirt on the side of the tree closest to the campsite.

"Never cross this line," she said. "We're going to make a perimeter around the camp. This is our home now, and we're always going to need to stay close." She made a sweeping motion with her hand back toward our camp. "There's already a deer trail that circles the clearing about two miles out from our camp. We're going to patrol and hunt on the inside every day." She turned to focus on us, serious. "But never, ever cross the line and go outside."

We nodded, remembering the message that Dasher had given us.

"But what happens if we run out of deer?"

"Or if we see a real juicy one right outside?"

Mama just looked at us sternly and shook her head. "Never." She came close. "If you pray every day, and we say thank you to every life we take, like you girls did last night, we will always have enough."

And she was right.

—

Ten years passed before we saw another biped. In that decade, a lot happened between us, but not a lot happened to us, if you follow. The world, which apparently really had ended, didn't bother us one peep.

Although Mama had fumbled the rifle on that first kill, she never did again. She had a lot of skills. She taught us how to survive, how to grow food (we had looted corn and sweet potato seeds in Eureka), how to mend our clothes, but most important, how to hunt. We had looted about two thousand rounds of ammunition from the Hutchinson's Sporting Goods (every box they had), but by the time we ran through our first thousand, we had become proficient in making and taking prey with bows, atlatls, traps, and snares. After all, with no video games like BrickRibbit to play, we suddenly had a *lot* of spare time, not to mention bellies that would start to grumble if something didn't get killed every now and then.

Thankfully, over the years, Mother Oggy brought us many things to shoot or trap. Aside from the deer, there were also plenty of big wild pigs in the area, and their numbers increased dramatically after human civilization ground to a halt. We had put up Dasher's skull (minus the antlers, of course) on a tree next to our camp, and in the weeks that followed, it was joined by other deer skulls, then pigs, squirrels, rabbits, and then a pair of cougar skulls (we didn't like the competition). A few years later, wolves reintroduced themselves to the area. Some of their skulls ended up on our tree, too, and even a wolverine's. All their skulls gathered on the tree became a massive altar to our kills.

From the animals, we could get meat, leather, bones for tools, and all kinds of other good things, like a tied-off stomach that could be used as a shower pouch. Sounds gross, probably, but after just a little while out there in the woods, it was clear that animal organs, and all the things you could do with them, could be pretty cool.

We became resourceful. We even made two drums, out of deerskin and pigskin. El found a way to consistently chisel whistles and then small flutes out of deer femurs. Mama made Dyre a leather cap to wear, and then he figured out a way to fix Dasher's antlers to it. This became his signature look: a horned deer-boy stalking through the forest. Two years in, he made a rattle out of pig hooves, and soon we were having what we called DJ Nights on a regular basis to relieve our boredom.

Dyre eventually got over the death of Dasher Banks, and now he played Dasher by the campfire all the time. His show was good, really good: he would perform a version of Dasher's last dance, moving this way, then that way, to the sound of the drums and the rattle, with a little rhythmic whistling thrown in, depending. Clo would join sometimes, or El, pretending to hunt him with a knife, stick, or a mimed gun, and then there'd be a chase back and forth, and usually it would end with a coup de grâce. Or not, depending. DJ Night was never the same twice, and we did it hundreds of times over the years. At first the whole act was just cool to look at and relive in some way, but then we started doing it as another way of giving thanks to Oggy for the life of that first deer and every other creature that came our way. We quickly came to understand that if there were no animals, there would soon be no Yetti family.

Even though Dasher hadn't been a proper one and done, it turned out that Mama was a really great shot, a skill she passed on to El before El was ten. Also, Mama could fight, and she was always teaching us how. Before she had gotten her second PhD, Mama had attained the rank of fourth-dan black belt. That's where she met Papa: karate class. Out in the woods, she taught the class, and she was always giving us new katas: punch, kick, jab-parry, grapple. *Ichi! Ni! San! Shi!* At first she said it was about survival, but after a few years, it became clear that she was teaching us to give us something to do, and herself, too. She set up a dummy made out of worn tree branches sticking out of an old stump, and we practiced for hours, knocking off chunks of wood and replacing them when needed. Then we practiced climbing, and jumping, then climbing and jumping.

Soon Dyre was eight, ten, twelve years old, and we started teaching him: chasing him, or having him chase us. Every morning we would wake up and run a small course around Oggy that we had worn out from between the trees inside the perimeter. It was about a seven-mile loop, and connected with the log that Mama had felled across the old road. We ran it pretty much every day, and true to our word, we never crossed that boundary. We would bring Daisy Duke with us, so if we saw something we could shoot it. Mostly El did the shooting. We were both good with Daisy, but El was the best, although Clo was better with the knife. (By the time she was fifteen, Clo was taking down about one deer a year just using Toothy, and we were all pretty proud about that.)

Before the first winter, we built a cabin. It took a while to cut down trees, drag them, notch them, and stack them, but we had time. Mama had been a Girl Scout Senior. She knew the basic concept for building a cabin, and what she didn't know from practical experience, she was always smart enough to figure out. Our mama was the best. There really wasn't anything she couldn't do, and she taught us everything she could. Especially persistence.

We had school. We had one used book, which Mama had found stuffed under Dyre's car seat and made us all read: *Tik-Tok of Oz*. It was a sequel to *The Wizard of Oz* about a tricky robot who used a wind-up spring for power. Mama said it was the first book about artificial intelligence, written over a hundred years ago. Aside from the one book, for the first couple of years we would sit on tree stumps and get lessons off Mama's laptop. She had a solar backpack and kept the thing charged for almost four years before everything broke down, including our OwlPad. Which meant we still had BrickRibbit for a while, on the cracked screen. No internet, of course, but we got used to that. For some reason, Mama had had a copy of Wikipedia from 2010 loaded on her laptop. By the time the laptop broke, we'd read thousands of entries, everything she thought was important, from "Algorithm" to "Turing test."

Sometimes we complained. We'd never really had any friends back in "the world," but somehow we missed them. Or at least we missed the other kids whose noses we didn't have to break. We had hated school, but now somehow we missed that, too. We definitely missed BrickRibbit updates. But being twins, gingers, and sort of violent oddballs at school anyway, we'd already gotten used to making our own fun, and with Mama's perpetual assurances that it wasn't quite time to return to civilization, we forgot about the rest of the world pretty quickly.

Looking back, it's almost like we were one of those freaky backwoods cults you might have heard about. We even became religious fanatics. Mama had already gotten us in the habit of praying for Papa up in heaven every night, even before the Big Spray and, apparently, the End of the World. And having to kill blood-filled creatures with our own hands really put a love of Mother Oggy in us. That and her having sent the divine messenger to us in the form of a talking deer. With life being what it is in the wild, however, praying soon extended beyond bedtime. For us to survive each winter, some kind of animal had to wander within the perimeter of the Oggy on a regular basis, and that was essentially pure luck. We'd started out this little jaunt pretty young, but Mama couldn't sugarcoat the fact that there was no backup; we were already living at the tail end of Plan B. When your life hinges on the whim of some hairy ungulate deciding to cross your path, you get real superstitious real fast.

We ended up praying to Mother Oggy every time we went hunting to put food on the table. Then, if we actually managed to kill something, we did the north, south, east, west thank-you thing and then prayed again for the poor creature's journey to join Papa up in heaven. Or Dyre did a special, custom version of Dasher's last dance in the guise of that particular critter that night. After a few years, we remarked that Papa had a lot of deer with him up in heaven. And squirrels, and fish, and wild pigs, and raccoons, and even a skunk. Yes, one winter we ate a skunk. One time. Dyre had killed a skunk for fun, and Mama made him eat it. She made us eat it, too, seeing as we'd passively allowed his juvenile lapse in the hunter's code: only kill what you're going to eat. After chewing that stinky skunk meat, we never made the same mistake.

We prayed when we planted seeds, and we prayed again if the crops were good. If the crops were bad, we prayed even more. We prayed when it rained, and we prayed when it didn't rain. We prayed and prayed and we trained and trained. And every time we killed something, we said, "Thank you, Oggy" to the north, south, east, and west. Even for the chewy, stinky skunk, we said thank you.

We became women, which was awkward to say the least. We were twelve, and Clo was skinning a mink between her legs and looked down to realize that some of the blood running down her leg wasn't the mink's. About two seconds later, El realized she was bleeding too, and we ran to the eastern stream to wash ourselves, but the blood wouldn't stop flowing. We ran back to Mama, and it turned out she had everything planned (as best she could) with deer pelts and squir-rel tails. I think she had read about it back in college in a book about Miwok women.

The whole thing was slightly traumatic, and then Dyre wandered up wondering why everyone was being all dramatic. Finally fully real-izing that he was never going to have to go through this himself, we beat him soundly right then and there. If we were going to bleed, then so was our little brother. It was only fair.

Anyway, Mama pulled us off him and we got on with our lives. We thought a lot more about sex after that, or at least procreation. We started to see the animals in a different light, and the rut was no lon-ger just an excuse to kill the beasts when they were distracted. It was beautiful. The does and the sows moaning in the morning air, and the beavers. Oh, the beavers. They were sweethearts of the forest. Always coupling up and being sweet with each other. We once came upon a dam and discovered that the papa beaver was still bringing scraps up into their little home even though the mama had died weeks before. He just loved her so much, death meant nothing. That was old Sneezer. We cried, we were so touched, and we didn't even kill him and eat him.

But then there were the ducks. Oh, those goddamn ducks. Duck sex in the forest was even more horrible than the duck sex video we'd seen back in the world. Mallards and the goldeneyes were the worst. The drakes would pal up with a female all year, acting all friendly, but when the time came, they'd rape the girls. And then they'd let their disgusting buddies with all their corkscrew members come in and rape the girls, too. So much for being "pals." One spring, next to the north-ern pond, we found a pretty little goldeneye, barely more than a duck-ling, her beautiful feathers scattered everywhere. She was dead. She hadn't survived just being a girl during mating season.

It was the saddest thing. We didn't eat her, either, just buried her little body and said a special prayer to Oggy. Then when we got home we gave Dyre a special beating for being a member of the monster gen-der. He was only nine at the time, and in our hearts we knew he didn't really deserve it, but it felt good to give him a solid thrashing. It was only when we remembered Dasher's words—that we were supposed to protect our family, not beat them to a pulp—that we finally stopped the thumping that day.

But, in general, we started fighting for real less and less. It drove Mama crazy, and the stakes were getting too high. Eventually, Dyre changed, too, and we all agreed he'd become a man. His voice deepened, his chest broadened, and fuzz started growing out of his face. Out hunting, he would get all sweaty and stinky, but we couldn't deny it: he was becoming a great hunter. One day we came back to the cabin and he was outside with a crazed look on his face. He had pulled all the animal trophies we had collected over the years off the skull tree and thrown them out into the forest.

"Death is not a prize you can own!" he barked at us. He had just turned fourteen at the time. "Death should be respected!" Who knows where he got this idea from, out in the woods by himself. Maybe we were all going a little crazy, but he looked especially buck wild that day, like he had finally grown into Dasher's antlers (which he still wore constantly).

Clo cracked her knuckles and, antlers be damned, we were ready to give him another thrashing, maybe even a good DMP.

But El blew it off. "Pfft," she scoffed mildly. "I was getting bored of all that stuff anyway. Come on, Mama's making stew tonight." And we all moved on. It was just part of growing up in the forest. And maybe Dyre was right: we didn't need to show off our kills anymore. After all, who were we supposed to be showing off to?

The forest really was our home by then, and we had started to think of ourselves as natives. We still had the loaded laptop and un-updated BrickRibbit, but we used the machines less and less even before they broke. They got boring, and by the time we were twelve, Mama had pretty much taught us all the "book-learning" we needed to know. We were all learning together now, not just how to survive season after season, year after year, in the deep forest, but also how to cope mentally. For us twins, that meant a lot of karate and yelling *Ichi! Ni! San! Shi!* into the woods.

Although we could soon make buckskin clothes and moccasins as well as our own serviceable bows and arrows, and we played drums and did the deer dance, we really weren't anything like the native Miwok, or the Pomo, or the Wintu, or the Modoc, or any other sort of indigenous people. They had real cultures we could never truly appropriate. Also, many of them liked to roam, and migrated quite a bit when they could. We were stuck on an unmapped square about three by three miles, worried constantly that the forces of a massive machine mind would descend on us at any moment with a nanoengineered narcotic.

But, by Mama's estimate, the drones would never fly this area again, as there was almost certainly no record of human habitation here. Yerba City was only concerned with humans. And apparently Mama was right. We never saw another drone, never saw any of those tricky vans. "Just never leave the perimeter," Mama made us promise, and we never did.

We really didn't need to: along with the main creek that ran near the cabin, we'd found four freshwater springs, and there were even two small lakes that were good for fishing and swimming in the spring and summer. We had plenty of wood and plenty of game. So we hunted, we fished, and we had our little farm. In some ways we were like any other family on a survivalist camping trip . . . that lasted for ten years.

And then Santa Claus showed up.

CHAPTER 4

THE TIK-TOK MAN

BLAM! Mama's shot caught him just under the chin, snapping back Santa's head and sending him toppling to the ground.

"Mama!" Clo yelled. "You shot Santa Claus!"

"It's not Santa!" El scolded.

"How do you know?"

"Because it's summertime!"

"Well—well—" Clo tried to think of something. *"Can we eat him, at least?"*

"Shh!" Mama yelled. She ejected the spent shell and chambered a fresh bullet. Then she waved us both to our feet and the three of us moved forward, cautiously.

We edged slowly toward the prone fat man, Mama training Daisy Duke on him the entire way. Santa had been walking down the overgrown logging road, the same one we had taken ten years ago. Had he followed us? Tracked us somehow?

His body was sprawled awkwardly, like a bloated crimson swastika in the dirt, with a bag of brightly colored presents spilled nearby. Seeing anyone coming after us would have been strange, but this was a particularly bizarre sight, as if Oggy, whom we often prayed to for good hunting, was somehow playing a big cosmic joke on us (she would do that sometimes).

What was even more peculiar was his feet. He didn't have any. They were worn away to dirty brown stumps. Hence the limping. From the shabby look of his outfit, his incredibly sunburnt face, and his generally disheveled appearance, it was easy to conclude that Santa had started walking weeks—perhaps months—ago, from a faraway place, and had not stopped. Ever.

And then there was the mark.

"What's that black triangle on his forehead?" Clo asked cautiously.

"I don't know," El answered. *"It looks like a tattoo or some—"*

"I said *shh!*" Mama scolded. "This isn't over!"

A couple of brightly wrapped presents had been scattered out of his enormous bag, covered in patterns of little red reindeer and bright silver holly. Leftover icons of a forgotten culture now alien to us. The very top parcel was sun-bleached and discolored. A small scratching sound came from it.

Clo couldn't help herself. "What do you think's in the presents?" She started to reach down.

"Don't!" Mama yelled.

Suddenly we all jumped back when Santa Claus raised himself up again, golden blood oozing from the bullet wound in his neck.

"HO! HO! HO!" he shouted.

Thwap! The fat man slumped forward, Dyre's hatchet in the back of his head. Then Dyre sprang out of the forest like a ninja, scampering over to retrieve his weapon.

"Nice throw," El said coldly, trying to shake off the adrenaline.

"Wait," Mama said to Dyre, and he froze before touching the hatchet. "Stay frosty," she commanded, twirling her finger in the air. Dyre nodded, understanding that Santa might not be alone. Our brother stepped back, unslung his bow, readied an arrow, and began listening as only he could.

Mama handed the rifle to El and pointed at the slumping St. Nick. "Cover it," she said, and El aimed Daisy and held position, just in case.

Mama carefully touched the hatchet where it stuck out like a stiff ponytail just underneath the red cap. No movement. She grabbed it and twisted slowly back and forth, widening what was apparently already a fatal wound. The soft crunching sound probably would have been sickening had we not been used to prepping wild animals for butchering. Then Mama withdrew the hatchet to reveal a series of delicate golden gears and tendrils in the wound, oozing with the same fluid that had come out of Santa's neck.

"It's a Tik-Tok!" Clo gasped, using the term for machine-man from our only Land of Oz book. Her mind raced, a childhood assumption suddenly questioned. "Did you lie to us, Mama? All this time, Santa Claus was a robot?"

El just shook her head, still keeping the rifle trained.

"This isn't Santa, honey," Mama assured Clo patiently, without looking away from the mechanical corpse. "It's a drone."

"A drone? Like in the sky?"

"Not all drones fly. It's an autonomous unit, on a preprogrammed mission."

"A mission to find us?" El asked.

Mama brooded, using the tip of the hatchet to further explore the workings inside the thing's skull. "No, it's a generalist design, meant to attract any stragglers, I'm guessing."

"Is that what we are, Mama?" El asked. "Stragglers?"

"That's what Yerba City would call us," Mama said.

"So . . . what's in the presents?" Clo asked again. She was taken in like a child by the bright shiny colors. It'd been a long time since we'd seen colors like that out in the forest, and it was mesmerizing.

The scratching sound from underneath the festive wrapping became louder. "Something's moving in there, Mama," Dyre pointed out.

Mama paused, looking down at the boxes. "Start a fire," she said, "a big one."

"We're going to burn the presents without opening them?" El questioned.

"Aw," Clo moaned. "What if it's a puppy inside?"

"It's not a puppy," said Mama. "It's propaganda."

—

Back at the cabin, we stacked wood high in the outside fire pit. We'd kicked the loose presents into the sack of goodies and cinched it tight before carrying it back with us.

Mama dropped Santa's head onto the chopping stump nearby. She hadn't felt the need to carry the whole body, so she had decapitated old St. Nick and carried the result back by its beard.

As El flinted sparks onto the kindling, the sounds of scratching grew louder.

"Hurry up," Mama said. "They're getting wise."

"What are they?" Clo couldn't help asking.

"Let's figure that out after we burn them."

With the flames licking high, we threw the whole bag onto the pyre. A dozen frustrated shrieks rang out into the forest, and the bag shook and spasmed as the things tried to rip their way out. But it turned out their bodies were delicate, made of the same sensitive material as the inside of Santa's head. Only one made it out and onto the forest floor.

"Step on it!" Mama yelled. "Quick!"

Dyre jumped onto the palm-sized robot with both feet, smashing it instantly. It was an eight-legged little thing, with an apple-sized sac of glowing blue fluid that popped across the dirt with Dyre's pounce.

Dyre looked quizzically at the blue gunk now on the bottom of his moccasins. Even next to the firelight, in broad daylight, the glow off the substance was visible.

"Don't touch that stuff!" Mama yelled. "It's probably still potent."

"What is it?" El asked.

"It's the Sap," Mama explained. She used a stick to wipe some of it off Dyre and hold it up to look at. "Subantoxx. Or what it's evolved into."

"Evolved?" Clo asked. "Like a monkey?"

The glow on the end of Mama's stick and on Dyre's shoes faded together. Mama nodded. "Limited air survivability. That's good. This batch was just designed for injection." Dyre scraped the stuff from his moccasins.

"Those spiders were going to dose us?" El asked. She was still alert, scanning the woods for any other Santa Claus robots that might be coming after us.

"That was the plan, apparently." Mama walked back to Santa's head on the stump. She pulled the red hat off with a slimy slopping sound. The golden goo was everywhere now.

"So Yerba City found us," Clo pressed. "That Sour Apple artificial flavor Jolly Rancher finally found us."

"It's artificial *intelligence*," Dyre corrected, apparently trying to show he'd been listening to Mama's lessons all these years. Poor soul probably didn't even remember sucking on Jolly Ranchers for real in his life, anyway.

"Oh, what do you know?" Clo snapped, feeling punchy.

"I saved you from getting a spider surprise, didn't I?" he said, holding up the stained hatchet.

Clo scoffed, holding up Toothy. "Yeah, right. We had it covered. I'm so much better at throwing than you, anyway."

"Quiet, you two," El scolded. "This is a big deal, this thing showing up."

Sister and brother grew tight-lipped, but nodded at each other in silent agreement before retreating to an edge of the clearing for the familiarity of a throwing contest.

As Clo and Dyre started hucking their weapons into our nicked-up target tree nearby, Mama was silent, probing deep into the opening in the back of the android's head. "I don't think this thing tracked us on purpose," she said. "Looks like it's been out here for a while, just wandering. You saw its feet." She gestured to Clo for Toothy, and Clo sighed but walked over and handed Mama the hunting knife. Then Clo turned back to our brother, and the two of them took turns throwing the hatchet. It was hard to tell who was better; they were both very good. We had a lot of spare time out there in the woods to practice.

Mama took the knife and used it like a pointer to gesture to Santa's reddened and chapped cheeks. "Sunburned, walking for weeks. Maybe months. Probably day and night. All of the search patterns were exhausted, all of the map points, but not everyone was accounted for. So the City designed some drones, packaged them . . . attractively, and sent them out in random walking patterns. Only way it would have found the old logging road."

"Attractively?" Clo said, turning. "The 'homeless stumpy Santa Claus' look?"

"Hey, it almost worked on you," El pointed out.

Clo paused and then nodded in acknowledgment. *True. True.* "But why the triangle on the forehead? That's a giveaway."

Mama was silent, continuing to dig.

"And why didn't she just send flying drones? Like at the beginning?"

Mama looked up at the sky. "You mean just grid out the state, scan thermal meter by meter, and drop those spiders on anything with two legs that isn't already in treatment?" Mama looked at us. "I don't know. It's what I would have done." She turned her attention back to the head on the stump. "Maybe Santa's got some answers. Hatchet."

Dyre sighed and handed over the hatchet. Mama squatted down and used the hunting knife and the hatchet at the same time to pry the thing's skull open farther, revealing a biomechanical mass of artificial bone and tissue.

Clo looked sideways at the head as Mama worked on it, trying to make contact with St. Nick's now-glassy eyes. She suddenly reached down and grabbed its cheek with a tweak.

"You sure we can't eat it?"

"Clo!" El scolded.

"Well, it's still warm. We've eaten worse. Remember that one winter with the old skunk—"

"Was that Santa thing ever even alive, Mama?" El interrupted, not wanting to relive skunk memories.

"Well"—Mama continued to pry—"the skin, hair, muscles, bones . . . must have been based on a real person. Someone who was alive at one time. But the brain here"—she pulled out a handful of what looked like folded golden seaweed—"this is all machine." She started unfolding the seaweed, examining it closely, the knots, the leaves. "A machine designed by a machine."

"It saw us before we killed it," El said flatly, loading an extra round into the rifle, bringing it up to full capacity. "Does that mean there's more coming?"

"Well," Mama continued, distracted, "that's what I would have planned on. But—" She finished pulling out all of the mechanical brains and reached her hand into the slimy cavity, feeling all around inside the empty skull. She sighed and pulled her hand out with a loud *slorp.* "This thing is totally self-contained. No network of any kind. It's so close to biological, it doesn't even have Bluetooth."

We only vaguely remembered what that meant, but Mama's point was clear: even though it had seen us, there weren't more Santas coming. Or Easter Bunnies, or leprechauns, or whatever. At least not for now.

It still seemed to trouble Mama. Not that she wasn't happy we were safe for the time being, but she was the type of person who needed to understand things. As long as she understood why something was happening, she was fine. She had been a rock when we'd had to flee for our lives from packs of shamblers, and when the Golden Gate Bridge blew out from underneath us. Because, of course, she had known why it was all going down. But why Santa had no Bluetooth—this bothered her, and it continued bothering her into the night as she autopsied the rest of the Tik-Tok man. We helped her until the sun went down and then some, but Mama persisted, dissecting, analyzing, looking for some kind of wireless communication system.

"Why bother?" she would mumble to herself every time she reached another dead end. "Why bother?"

That night it was warm, and Dyre disappeared to sleep in the woods, like he did most of the time when the weather was nice. We stayed up with Mama, helping when we could, but eventually we just dozed on the ground next to the fire.

"So it just *has* to talk," Mama said, tapping on the top of the thing's golden skull. She looked at the smiling teeth, now revealed, as she'd removed all its skin. "It just . . . talks."

Somewhere out in the night, an owl hooted. A moment later, another owl hooted back. "They just . . . *talk* to each other."

We didn't know it at the time, but it would turn out that Santa Claus wasn't just a hunter, out looking for us. He was also a messenger.

CHAPTER 5

BAMBI BURSTER

The next morning, Mama was already packing. Of course we begged to go with her, but she wouldn't hear of it. Two to four weeks, she said, and she'd be back. We were old enough now, we'd been living in the wilderness for ten years, she pointed out, and we knew pretty much everything she knew about survival at this point, maybe more.

"But why?" Clo pleaded. "Why can't we go with you, Mama?"

Dyre had emerged from the woods and was standing silently, antlers slightly drooping, on the edge of the clearing. He had caught a rabbit—with his bare hands, as usual—and it hung struggling in his grip as he stood, statue-like, watching Mama pack.

"Stay and watch over your brother," Mama ordered in the no-nonsense tone she rarely used with us anymore.

"I don't need anyone to watch over me," Dyre grumbled.

"We all watch over each other," Mama reminded us. "And hurry up and kill that rabbit. You're upsetting Oggy."

Dyre glanced down at the rabbit, which was really starting to get stressed out. "Sorry, Oggy," he said absentmindedly at the sky, and promptly broke the rabbit's neck. Without thinking, he performed the ritual we'd all done hundreds of times, spinning to the north, south, east, and west—"Thank you. Thank you. Thank you. Thank you."—then turned to take the rabbit over to the chopping stump. "And I still don't see why we can't come."

"Because it's too dangerous," Mama said decisively. "And you *have* to survive. You saw those spiders."

"We can handle a few spiders," El insisted.

"We should vote on it," Clo said. "Like in a democracy. El and I are eighteen, so it would count, right? And even though Dyre's just a boy, he would count, like, three-fifths."

Dyre just sighed, way past the point of caring what his sisters thought of him and his worth.

"This is not a democracy," Mama said firmly. "I'm going alone to figure out what happened. If the drones have lost connectivity, then we might be able to move around beyond the forest and search for other stragglers like us."

"Other people?" Clo asked excitedly. "Like, other boys, maybe? Ones that'll hug me back?"

Mama sighed. "Other boys. Other girls. Other families."

"Well, what's the point of being a family if we're just going to break up?" Dyre blurted. *Thunk!* He whacked the dead rabbit's head off with the hatchet for emphasis.

"Don't be so dramatic," El scolded.

"Look, all of you, come here." Mama held her arms out for a group hug. We complied, coming in close to put our arms around her. Even Dyre, grumbling, left the hatchet in the stump to come and wrap one arm around Mama.

"Everything I've done," she told us, "I've done so that you can survive, okay? But we can't live here in the woods by ourselves forever. Something has changed in Yerba City, and I need to find out what it is."

"Okay." Dyre sighed reluctantly and broke away from us. He wasn't much for group hugs these days. He lumbered over to a spot against a tree and sank to the ground to sulk. Then he picked up the cracked and powerless OwlPad. Dyre still had a habit of running his fingers across the shattered gray glass, as if he were a four-year-old playing BrickRibbit again. It was a comforting ritual.

Mama turned to look us twins in the eye sternly.

"And if you see any more of those things—Santa Claus, or anyone or anything who doesn't look like they've been living off the land—you put 'em down and burn 'em."

"But—"

"No," Mama said, and the words echoed unchallenged in the morning air. We fell silent as she finished stuffing her pack. Clo started crying.

"Keep a close eye on Dyre," Mama whispered.

El shot a glance at our brother. He was tapping furiously on the dead screen now, racing to build an imaginary castle in the BrickRibbit of his mind.

"Why? Do you think he's gonna start acting weird?" El asked sarcastically.

"Just keep an eye on him," Mama said. "Especially if he starts talking strangely."

"Well, if he starts talking more than grunts and whining, that would be strange."

Mama just locked eyes with us. "Four weeks," she said.

"What if you don't come back?" Clo sniffed.

"I'll come back," Mama said calmly, smiling softly to reassure us, although we knew it was just an act. She was worried; there was no other reason she'd be leaving us. One last hug, a kiss on Dyre's sullen head between the antlers, and she turned and walked into the forest, toward the overgrown man-made road, toward wherever it was Santa Claus had really come from.

—

That night something very strange happened, an eerie harbinger of the surreal rodeo that was about to engulf our lives.

It was the first night since the End of the World that Mama wasn't with us, and we weren't exactly feeling mature about it. Dyre was curled up like a baby on Mama's bed, clutching the only photo we had of her: a crumpled newspaper clipping announcing her first big breakthrough with Team YAG. Clo had cried herself to sleep on the porch hammock. El was sitting on the floor inside the cabin cleaning Daisy Duke, and wondering why Mama hadn't taken the rifle with her, when her eyes finally fluttered closed, long past our usual bedtime.

It was late, well past midnight, when we heard the whispers: cold, malevolent sounds that seemed both far away and right in our ears at the same time. They came into our dreams, those sounds, like the gossip of dozens of lost souls that had flitted around us for years, but which our mother's presence had somehow protected us from.

Clo was the first to hear them: angry, sinister voices that echoed from the forest, just low enough that we couldn't make out any actual words. Her eyes snapped open, and her fingers instinctively tightened around our knife, Toothy, which she often slept with like a teddy bear.

She gasped and jumped to her feet, stumbling awkwardly out of the hammock as it flipped. But she was in a fighting stance a fraction of a second after that, knife drawn and ready.

El, who had woken up at the exact same time, was out on the porch in an instant, hatchet in hand.

The second we stood together, armed and ready, the whispers cut out altogether.

"What was that sound?" El breathed.

"I don't know. I heard voices," Clo whispered back.

"So did I."

"Was it Dyre?"

"No, he's still sleeping."

"Then what was it?"

We both just stood there, frozen, listening.

"It's quiet now," Clo observed.

"It's too quiet."

We focused intently on that sense of "too quiet."

"The creek's not flowing!" Clo whispered frantically.

"It was flowing when we went to bed!"

El was right. Even in summer, the Oggy's creek would normally flow until August. Now it was completely silent.

"And where did the wind go?" El asked desperately.

"Look!" Clo whispered and pointed up with her knife. "The trees are frozen."

Indeed, the branches of the tall redwoods around us, which had been swaying gently in the warm breeze when we fell asleep, were now stiff. Not stiff like on a still winter morning, but stiff like the paused image on a video screen, as well as we could remember that sort of thing.

"What in Oggy's going on?" El demanded.

"Are we dreaming?" Clo asked. She poked El lightly in the arm with the knife. Sometimes we dreamed together. *"Wake up. Go on. Wake us up!"* Poke. Poke.

"Ow! Stop it!" El whispered, pushing the knife away. *"We're not dreaming! There's something here."*

"Another Tik-Tok?" Clo asked, looking out into the forest again.

"No, something else. It's all around us."

Clo nodded. Since the whispers, there had been a feeling, like we were surrounded. *"It's in the air. I can feel it in my breath."* Clo paused. *"I think it's in my crack, too."* She started slashing the air behind her with the knife. *"Go! Get out of here! Leave us alone!"*

"This is crazy," El said. She wasn't flailing around like her sister, but she was having the exact same feeling of being immersed inside a giant . . . entity of some kind.

Then we saw him.

Out past the inner circle of the Oggy, about forty feet into the darkness, we saw a man standing between two trees. He was tall, almost a little too tall. And skinny, almost a little too skinny. He had a pale face with vertical lines and wore a dark suit and what looked like a royal orange sash across his chest.

"There's a man! There!" Clo whispered fiercely, and we both took off like wolves toward our prey. The terrible feeling of being surrounded hadn't left us, and we weren't feeling particularly brave. But we couldn't stand still anymore, and attacking something seemed like the best way to shake off the creeps.

"Kill it!" El yelled, switching from whispers into our hunting calls. Finally making real noise felt like a release, and defiance in the face of the eerie silence. *"Whatever it is, just kill it!"*

"Where's Daisy Duke?" Clo called as we dashed headlong into the darkness.

"She's stripped! I was cleaning her!"

"Okay!" Clo hollered nervously. *"It's knife hunting, then!"*

But it never came to that. By the time we got to the spot where we'd seen the skinny man, he was gone.

"Where is he?" Clo growled, panting. She'd switched to English so whatever it was would know how tough we were. "I'll gut him!"

"*I don't know!*" El answered, and we stood back-to-back for a moment, blades poised, listening intently between breaths.

Almost as quickly as it had vanished, the sound of flowing water returned.

"*The creek's flowing again,*" El noted. Moments later, the summer breeze returned, and the trees started swaying gently again. Everything was back to normal.

"*That was . . . weird,*" El said slowly.

"*Who was that man?*" Clo asked. "*Santa? Another Tik-Tok robot?*"

El shook her head, unknowing. "*And what was up with the wind and water?*"

Clo also shook her head, but stayed focused on the dark woods. We weren't owls or anything, but our night vision was pretty good, and there wasn't any light that would have distracted our pupils. Still, we scanned and scanned and didn't see anything other than the trees now swaying slightly in the night. We strained with our ears and heard a low rumble.

"*What's that?*" Clo shot.

"*It's Dyre, snoring back in the cabin.*"

"Dyre!" we both yelled, in the extra-loud call we reserved only for him. The snoring stopped.

"What?" came from the cabin with groggy urgency.

"Get out here!"

"Why?" he snorted. "Did you wake up in a puddle?"

"There's a strange man in the woods."

We didn't have to tell him twice. He was on the porch almost instantly, bow in hand.

"Where?" he breathed.

"We saw him right where we are. Listen for him. Use your super-ears."

Dyre, like us, stiffened for a moment. Then he silently loped a few strides toward us, freezing every twenty feet or so to pause and listen. Soon he got to the space between two trees where we'd seen the figure.

He crouched low, still coyote-quiet, and examined the spot.

Finally he stood up, shaking his head. "Nothing walked through here."

"Are you sure nothing was there?"

"Didn't say that," Dyre commented, stalking backward and scanning the ground, trees, everything around. "Just said nothing walked there. What'd he look like?"

"He was skinny," said El.

"He had a suit on, with a sash," Clo added.

"What kind of suit?" Dyre asked, dead serious. "Swimsuit? Birthday suit?"

"No," El sighed. "Like a dark business suit. Like a mayor of a city or something. Don't you remember those?"

"No," Dyre said simply.

"Oh," El realized. "Well, he had black lines on his face."

"Yeah." Clo nodded. "Almost looked like tears streaming down."

Dyre sighed. "There's no sign. No crying man walked here. Maybe a crying mouse two days ago."

"You think it was a ghost that just floated through?"

"I think"—Dyre turned back to us, relaxed now—"you were dreaming. You're both worried about Mama, or another Santa coming."

"No, he was tall," Clo corrected. "And skinny."

"Another kind of . . . walking drone?" El asked, using the term Mama had used.

Clo shook her head. "Not a Tik-Tok. It was a real man. Only a real man could be evil like that."

"Like what?"

"Like, just staring . . . like that."

El sighed, finally lowering the hatchet. "Maybe it was just a dream. There's not much wind. A rabbit couldn't have walked in and out of the perimeter without us hearing."

"But you heard the whispers, too, El, and when everything froze like that . . ."

"We're all stressed out," Dyre mumbled, heading back inside. "And it's not the first time you two had the same nightmare."

He was right, but still . . . Clo lowered her knife.

"Come inside and get some sleep," El said. "If the crying guy comes back, we'll do him just like old St. Nick."

It was a lot of tough talk. Needless to say, none of us slept another minute that night.

—

After the episode with the Crying Man, four weeks went by without incident.

No Mama.

Then two months. Then four.

Despite Mama's ominous words, Dyre hadn't acted any stranger than that time he threw all our trophy skulls into the forest. Actually, Mama leaving might have brought us all a bit closer. At least it meant we kept closer tabs on each other. But we were all gloomy. With Mama there, we'd felt as if we could go on living in the forest forever. Without her, and especially since she'd missed her own deadline to return to us, we could no longer ignore the fact that San Francisco, and probably every other city on the planet, had burned up over a decade ago. It finally dawned on us that this really wasn't an extended camping trip. The world had ended, and we were just a few kids—maybe the very last kids in the world—still clinging on, gnawing a living from nature's scraps until someday we, too would end. It was a real downer.

Summer had given way to fall, and Clo was sitting by the morning fire and crying while she whittled fresh arrows. She had been doing this a lot lately. El was hanging some fresh pelts to dry, trying to ignore her sister's forlorn attitude. Dyre held out a smoked squirrel on a stick to Clo.

"Squirrel?" he asked sympathetically.

She sniffled and looked at it. She put down her whittling and picked it up to take a bite of the stiff meat around the neck. "Thanks." She continued to sniffle as she chewed. Squirrel on a stick did always make her feel better, though.

All three of us heard a sound at the same time, and our heads snapped northward. We listened, stock-still, for about five seconds. Ever so slightly, we could make out the noise of autumn leaves crunching in the distance. Three beings. Four legs each.

"It's just some deer out at the perimeter," Dyre finally said, breaking the silence. Our bodies untensed. Clo resumed chewing and crying.

El nodded to Dyre. "We're running low on meat. Take your bow and try to get one of them."

Dyre silently turned and unhooked his bow from where it hung on the side of the cabin, underneath the awning.

"Just one," El said sternly, "and be back by noon."

Dyre met her eyes. "You're not Mama. You can't tell me what to do."

"Last month you killed two and some of the meat spoiled. Better to leave it on the deer."

"It spoiled because you didn't smoke it right! You're not as good at it as Mama was."

"No, you let it rot before it even got in the smoker!"

"Stop arguing," Clo said, still sniffling and with her mouth half-full. "Those tasty deer are gonna get away."

El snatched up the quiver of arrows and tossed it to Dyre. "Just go kill something."

Staring daggers at El for a moment, Dyre huffed, slung on the quiver, readied an arrow lightly on the string, and jogged silently into the woods. Like us, Dyre was a good hunter. There was no doubt he could get a deer if the group was within forty yards of the trail when he arrived. Eighty yards if he had taken the rifle, but El didn't let him do that anymore. Mostly because we were always trying to conserve bullets, but partly because of what Mama had said before she left. And it was a very good thing that Dyre didn't have the rifle that day.

—

We weren't there, of course, but later we would piece together what happened between Dyre and the deer that morning. He left us at the cabin and crossed the three inner perimeters that we had set up, moving swiftly to catch up with the small herd. He arrived at the northern path, which marked the outermost boundary Mama had decided we shouldn't cross. Almost all our outer paths were also well-worn deer trails, so it wasn't uncommon to see animals of one kind or another on them, but today, something was off.

He was actually walking between trails, across the forest floor, to save a bit of time, when his foot touched something half-buried in the fallen leaves. An antler. At first he thought it had been shed in last year's rut, and we had missed it, but when he reached down to grab it, Dyre found it was heavy. He pulled hard, and it wasn't just one but two sets of antlers, and they were still semiattached to the carcasses of their owners. It was a buck lock: two tough boy deer fighting for territory had gotten their horns locked during last year's rut and had probably starved to death.

We had only seen that once before in the ten years we'd been in the woods, and the last time, the locked bucks were still alive when we found them, but exhausted enough that Mama could walk up and saw them free with Toothy's serrated side. She had let both bucks go, weakly trotting back into the forest, that day, not taking either one. That was rare for us: letting several weeks of protein just trot off. The event stuck in our minds. But somehow we had all agreed that it was the right thing to do; it was a few years in, and Oggy had already brought us so many animals we had been able to take down on our own. The deer, and all the other creatures we had dispatched over the years, had their world, and we had ours; it didn't seem right to take advantage of "buck business."

Dyre examined the bodies for a moment. They had clearly been there for months. How could we have missed this, inside our perimeter? Living the hunting-and-gathering lifestyle we did, finding something like this was big news. Dyre was probably already going over in his mind how the drama of the lose-lose duel could be incorporated into the next DJ Night.

In any case, the meat was way far gone, but the antlers and most of the bones were still in good shape, and Dyre took out an inferior arrow, put a squirrel tail on the nock, and jammed it into a nearby tree as a marker. He'd get us and circle back to the bodies later, when we could all pontificate at length over the unusual sight (we didn't have BrickRibbit anymore, after all). But before that, he still had living deer to hunt.

When Dyre got to the final perimeter, though, he caught just a glimpse of two does disappearing down the path to the east. He knew there was no way they had heard him coming, so they must have been running from something. That really wasn't unusual; deer run from most things, and young ones run just for fun. A moment later, Dyre heard another deer coming from the west. But this wasn't unusual, either; does who aren't in heat will often run from an unknown lone male looking for a fight. Dyre figured it was a buck, which was good for him, as the fresh antlers could always become a new head ornament.

He put his back behind a large oak and waited for the animal to approach. From the sound, he could tell it was a good size, but not too big. He'd definitely heard bigger bucks. This was probably a young guy, like himself, not fully grown, but independent enough to strike out on his own. Still, it was a bit strange that he was just strolling, and so carefully. Does usually wouldn't run from a buck that was just sauntering. Something about the steps seemed off, too. They were too regular, almost rhythmic, not based on the curves and contours of a natural terrain. This boy was . . . marching.

Doesn't matter, Dyre thought, *he'll be dinner soon enough.*

Dyre waited, as he usually did, for the animal to move just parallel to him. Approaching from the side, he could usually get a shot into the chest cavity, which, if not fatal, would slow the prey down enough for a second arrow. Also, if the animal heard him at the last minute, it would bolt down the path, which was the quickest exit from a predator. It was also a more or less straight line, which made for a much clearer shot.

This one was going to be a standard kill, and as he heard the animal pass his hiding spot about ten feet away, Dyre pulled the arrow to a full draw and spun around the tree.

He froze. He tried to say, "What the hell?" but it just came out something like "Whaggle?"

The buck was strange. Very strange. Its fur was darker than the mule deer we were used to, with almost brindle stripes, and its antlers, although it was fully grown, had only two prongs each instead of four. But even that wasn't the strange part. *That* was revealed when the thing stopped its uncanny marching, came to a halt, and turned its head toward Dyre.

Fangs. Super creepy, super sharp double fangs about six inches long. Dyre hesitated, lowering his bow slightly. He had killed many deer and seen many more, but nothing even remotely like this. The buck didn't bolt, but rather turned its body and faced Dyre directly.

Its gaze was ominous; it seemed to draw silence out of the forest as it stared at him. It opened its mouth slightly.

Dyre lifted the bow again and aimed. Whatever it was, it would make a fine prize to show off to his sisters. Besides, it was starting to scare him.

Then the deer spoke, and Dyre actually gasped.

The animal didn't speak words like you could write down, but rather something guttural, primal. Something like "Nos De Roowa Kon Maa," but that doesn't really do it justice. It was an utterance, like a spell that predated the concept of speech.

Dyre grunted, shaking off his amazement. Whatever it was, it didn't sound like a deer—it sounded like a person. A very strange, ancient person. Now this was something else. He really *had* to shoot this thing. Not just to kill it, but to save himself.

But he couldn't do it.

"Nos De Roowa Kon Maa," the fanged deer repeated.

Dyre shuddered, still aiming right at where the animal's heart should be. One shot. This close, he wouldn't even need to follow up with one of the two flint knives he kept strapped to his ankles. He breathed hard. Harder.

"Nos De Roowa Kon Maa," Dyre repeated, and lowered the bow.

—

Back at the cabin, El was lifting Clo's spirits with some sparring. Kata combos. Spinning kicks. The usual. We had both worked up a pretty good sweat by the time Dyre returned. He stood on the edge of the clearing, his bow in one hand, and we stared back at him, panting.

"Well?" El finally asked. "Did you get the kill?"

We were used to Dyre not speaking, but something was definitely wrong.

"Nos De Roowa Kon Maa," Dyre suddenly said, in a weird voice not at all like his own.

We looked at him blankly.

"What?" Clo finally asked.

"Nos De Roowa Kon Maa," he repeated. "Ka Sec Loro Sett."

"Are you trying to make up your own secret twin language? Remember, you have to have a twin to do that."

The fanged deer emerged from behind him and stood next to his shoulder.

"Whoa!" El yelled. "Dracula Deer!"

Dyre and the deer with the crazy incisors just stood there side by side, staring at us. There was an immediate, surreal sense that they were both in on something. Something very unfriendly.

"W-who's your boyfriend, Dyre?" Clo asked shakily, trying not to totally freak out.

"Yeah, you're going to make Clo jealous if you start going steady," El said, continuing the "Let's make sarcastic comments so we don't pee ourselves" theme.

"Nos De Roowa Kon Maa," the deer said.

Another silent beat as the four of us stared at each other.

"Okay, that was weird," Clo said.

"Last time a deer spoke to us, it was a messenger from Mother Oggy," El pointed out, remembering Dasher and the cone of light.

"This thing did NOT come from Oggy," Clo observed.

"No kidding," El confirmed. *"Where do you think it came from?"*

"Nos De Roowa Kon Maa," the deer repeated, impatiently.

"Someplace REALLY bad," Clo guessed ominously.

Both the deer and Dyre said, "Nos De Roowa Kon Maa!" at the same time, all the while staring at us as if that were supposed to have some profound effect.

"I think this is what Mama meant by Dyre acting strange."

"That thing got to him."

"What, he's Team Vambi now?"

"Whatever. Let's get him back."

"Yeah, he can't marry a deer. Mama wouldn't like it."

Our eyes darted to our weapons: Clo's knife was on the stump; the rifle was propped against the cabin. We slowly started moving apart from each other, and toward our objectives.

"Look, I'm sure you're a very nice deer."

"But Dyre has been going through a lot lately."

"Yeah, he hatcheted Santa a few months ago."

"And then his mama left."

"He really just needs some time to work things out on his own."

"He's not ready to be in a committed relationship with any . . . thing right now."

El reached for her rifle, and suddenly the deer's deadly looking mouth snapped open, unnaturally wide. Its eyes rolled back and its whole body started convulsing. A hideous gurgle erupted from its lungs.

"Hey, don't take it so hard," Clo said reassuringly. "I'm sure you'll find someone more . . . fangy, like yourself."

Dyre mechanically reached into his quiver, and in one motion he fitted an arrow to his bow and pointed it at Clo.

She froze. "Dyre, what are you doing? I'm your sister!"

"It's not him," El said, keeping her eye on the deer as it continued to shudder.

Dyre didn't move his possessed eyes from Clo's. His strange babble began again, low, like a chant, as he took careful aim.

"I practically raised you! I changed your diapers!" Clo yelled.

"Mama changed more," El pointed out, trying to lighten the suddenly fratricidal mood.

"I changed a *lot* of diapers. And they were gooey!"

Dyre let fly the arrow, and Clo moved her head simultaneously, letting the projectile sail past her and into a redwood tree with a *thunk*.

"Weak shot!" Clo shouted, taunting Dyre like they were little kids again. But he was fourteen now, and it had been a long time since he'd actually shot anything right *at* us. This was serious. He was already loading a second arrow.

"Fine," said Clo, "if that's how you want to play, I'll show you how it's done!" The second arrow also missed as Clo tucked into a roll toward the chopping stump, snatching up her hunting knife and smoothly throwing it across the clearing into Dyre's left thigh.

El snatched the rifle from the side of the cabin as Dyre went down with a pained grunt. The deer seemed to take this as some kind of sign that it was time for it to rock and roll, and the beast charged Clo, determined to take a bite with its uncanny fangs.

BAM! El's shot caught the deer in the neck, a perfect spine cutter. It was a difficult shot, but El had perfected it over the years. She hated

_____ the animals she hunted suffer. So, one and done. The deer went sprawling into the dirt next to the campfire, still.

Dyre didn't seem to notice that his boyfriend was down. He resumed his strange chanting, looking at the knife in his leg. There was a wire trailing back from it to Clo's hand. This was Clo's little invention: a way she could throw the knife and get it back quickly by gripping a detachable pommel with a tethered wire. She was wicked good with it.

Dyre, still chanting, gripped the knife. He flexed but paused in even more pain as he tried to pull it out.

"Uh-uh," Clo warned. "Remember, it's serrated."

Dyre just looked up at her, forgetting the knife. His eyes somehow seemed even more determined now. He hadn't let go of the bow he held in his left hand.

El chambered another round into Daisy Duke. "Drop it!" she said coldly as she pointed the weapon at her brother.

Dyre hesitated, down on one knee, for only a second before grabbing another arrow. Even with Clo's knife in his leg and El's barrel not twenty feet away, he wasn't going to quit.

Clo's eyes darted to El, searching for a clue about what to do next. El didn't take her eyes off the scope. "You're not near the artery," El said coldly, "so go ahead."

Dyre, still kneeling, raised his third arrow.

"Okay," Clo said and yanked the wire as hard as she could.

The serrated blade tore out of Dyre's thigh with a sickening rip. Dyre screamed and dropped the bow, clutching at the gaping hole in his leg. Clo easily caught the knife by its handle as it arced back through the air in a trail of blood.

El lowered the rifle, relieved she didn't have to shoot her brother after all.

The deer screamed, an unearthly wail, its body shuddering in frustrated convulsions. It struggled to get up, a trail of thick black blood coming from the neck shot.

Clo said, "It's not dead!"

The deer shambled to its hooves, but its head lolled sideways. "Ka Mui Soo Bea!" it screamed, among other things, despite its head pointing at the ground and black goo running from its eyes.

This was not at all like the last dance of Dasher Banks. We had seen many things pass away in the forest over the years, to go and join Papa in heaven, and we'd witnessed with our own eyes the last moments of creatures fighting against an inevitable death. This thing, as it rose up to continue its sinister mission, was not fighting against death. It *was* death.

El raised her rifle, ready to wipe the ungodly thing off the earth. *BLAM!* The bullet caught it right in the chest, another mercy shot to the heart. The impact knocked the thing back a foot, but this time it didn't even go down. Its legs buckled, and then, with another violent shudder, a dozen black, knobby tentacles ripped out of its dark fur, stabbing into the ground to stabilize the floppy body.

"What . . . the . . . hell . . . ," Clo murmured. El was also transfixed. What were we looking at?

Dyre didn't seem surprised. Instead, he worked through his pain and grabbed his last arrow off the ground, getting ready to join this thing in assaulting us.

The deer—now more of a dead-deer-monstrosity—launched itself toward El with a scream, half galloping, half crawling on its tentacles. Each tentacle ended in a pair of gross-looking hooked talons, something like the grabbers on the end of a fly's leg but a thousand times bigger.

El dashed under the awning of the cabin, putting a heavy pine corner post between the thing and her as she chambered another round into Daisy Duke. With a *CRACK* that echoed throughout the forest, the beast slapped three tentacles around the post, half breaking it already. As it wrenched the post away, one side of the heavy shingled awning fell in, smacking El into the wall of the cabin.

"El!" Clo shouted and bolted forward.

The deer thing was now on top of the collapsed awning, reaching its greedy tentacles into the cramped space where El was stuck.

With a grunt, Clo threw her knife the last ten feet, right into the deer's left hindquarters. The creature barely noticed, though the blade hit bone. That didn't stop Clo from digging in her heels and pulling on the knife's wire, trying to drag the abomination away from where El was pinned.

The deer, somewhat smaller than a whitetail buck, didn't weigh that much, so Clo was actually able to drag it backward, away from her sister. The eyes on the floppy fanged head searched wildly, trying to figure out the cause of the rear momentum, and Clo and the creature locked eyes for a moment.

"Get away from my sister!" Clo growled, tugging her wire even harder. As she had hoped, the knife had fixed itself into the deer's relatively thick hip bone (or at least where a hip bone should be on a normal quadruped), which meant it wasn't going to rip out as easily as it had from Dyre's thigh.

But even from her awkward position, Clo could see the deer's expression change, its eyes narrowing in anger at being stymied. And two of its dark tentacles wound their way along the wire toward Clo like two vines growing in fast motion, an attacking double helix.

"Yikes!" Clo shrieked. She dropped the pommel that connected her to Toothy and jumped back, letting her wire go wild rather than get snatched up by those greedy black ropes. Just in time, as Dyre took a limping lunge at her, simultaneously slashing up with one of the flint knives he kept strapped to his calf.

Clo dodged easily and came back with a four-point kata combo. Left-left-right-left to the head and neck, the final strike landing right into the tip of the trigeminal nerve (just like Mama taught). Dyre's jaw was a lot softer than the tree stump we normally practiced on, Clo thought for a moment, as her brother dropped the knife and stumbled backward in a pummeled daze.

Back at the cabin, the deer had gotten two tentacles around El's foot, and it dragged her out from behind the fallen awning. The monster seemed to be preparing its remaining tentacles for evisceration, but before El's torso was even exposed, she poked Daisy's barrel out and—*BLAM!*—sent another fiery shot into the deer's chest. The thing shuddered and spewed more black gunk, but still didn't go down.

El slung back the bolt to load another round—her last—but before she could level the weapon again, the deer shot out four tentacles to grab the .30-06, wrapping thick cords around the weapon.

With a wet snort, it tried to yank Daisy Duke out of El's grasp, but she held on through gritted teeth in a death-grip tug-of-war.

"Oh no you don't," she grunted, bracing her one free leg against the doorframe. The bullets weren't killing this thing right away, but they still seemed to be her best bet.

Clo saw her sister struggling and got an idea, but first she needed a projectile of some sort. *Of course! Our brother.* Clo yanked the dazed Dyre down into a crouch by hauling at one of his antlers (she had always wanted to do that), backed up, and then did a quick jump-kick with both feet, sending her semistunned brother stumbling head-first into the hideousness.

But the deer had been keeping one floppy eye on Clo, and it was ready. It whipped three tentacles off Daisy Duke to grasp Dyre before his body slammed into it, then used his momentum to send him crashing into the other pine post holding up the cabin awning, where he slumped onto his side.

With only one tentacle affecting the rifle now, El again had the leverage to point the weapon at the deer.

"In the brain!" Clo shouted. *"It's still thinking, get the brain!"*

Realizing, El's eyes found the dangling head, and the aim of the barrel followed a fraction of a second later. *BLAM!* She sent the last bullet right into the creature's eye.

With an inky black spray, the monstrosity slumped to the ground, tentacles and all. El shook off the appendages, now more like limp black hoses, from her ankle and rifle and got to her feet.

"That was close," El said, wiping the black goo from her face as best she could.

"Yeah, no kidding," Clo confirmed, and she placed a foot on the deer creature's hindquarter to wiggle her knife free.

"How'd you know to get its brain?"

"I dunno. Works on zombies." Clo yanked her knife out in a splash of the black goo. *"Besides, I saw it looking at me."*

"Yeah." El nodded, still breathing hard. A couple of the hooves and tentacles were still twitching. *"We better make double sure."*

"You're right," Clo acknowledged, and, reaching down with her knife, she sawed across the deer's chin. The cut exposed a series of dark tubes and valves.

"It's a living Tik-Tok," El breathed. *"Like Santa Claus."*

"Yeah, but it's not on his team."

"What? How do you know?"

Clo held up the dripping fanged head, now severed and with a bullet through its eye, by one of its antlers and faced it toward El. *"Because then it would have been a reindeer. Duh."*

El sighed. *"C'mon, let's get this thing into the fire before it sprouts something else."*

—

As the thing's body burned, we examined the head through the exit wound.

"It's a bit like Santa."

"But it's different. This thing came from the north."

"And Santa came from the south. Also, when Mama shot him, Santa just popped right back up, happy as a clam."

"This thing got madder and madder. It was pissed. It was—all emotional."

"What did Mama say? 'They're evolving'?"

"Yeah, but evolving into what?"

Next to the cabin, Dyre stirred. Even before he woke up all the way, he started mumbling the weird language he had caught from the deer.

"He's still babbling," El said.

"What are we going to do?" Clo asked. *"I'd hate to have to stab his other leg."*

"Let's tie him up."

"And get those antlers off."

In no time, we had his prongs off, his leg bandaged, and the rest of him hog-tied with strips of leather cord in the center of the clearing. He looked pretty bad, but admittedly, aside from getting Toothy in the thigh, it wasn't the worst we'd beat him up over the years. El made sure to grab his second knife, kept strapped to his other calf, while Clo patted him down. Aside from a few sharpened cougar teeth in his pockets, Dyre didn't seem to have any other weapons. His babbling had been incessant, so we'd had to gag him too, but that didn't seem to stop it.

We just looked at him, thrashing there.

"Now what?" Clo asked, clueless.

We paused. There was really only one thing.

"We're going to have to find Mama."

El nodded. "She'll know what to do with him."

"There's really nothing else we can do," Clo, said, feeling justified.

"So, we're going to have to break our promise and go after her."

"There's no choice, clearly."

"Clearly."

"Let's get our gear!"

We left Dyre for the time being and split up. Clo dashed into the cabin, grabbed our waterskins, and snatched up the crumpled photo of Mama that Dyre had been clutching every night since she left. El was pulling jerky off the drying rack and stuffing it into our backpack when she had an idea.

"Let's take Bouncy!" she called to Clo.

"McBounceface?" Clo looked at El like she was crazy. "That thing hasn't moved in years. His tires are totally flat."

El looked away sheepishly.

"What?" Clo demanded. "What?"

"I . . . filled them last night."

"What? How?"

"With the pig-stomach bellows."

"The pig stomach—" Clo nodded slowly, anger rising. "You were going to leave us. You've been planning to take off and find Mama," she accused her twin.

"No." El shook her head. "I just wanted the car ready. In case . . . something like this happened." She gestured to the mumbling and hog-tied Dyre.

"You mean in case a vampire robo-deer came out of the woods and cast a spell on our brother? Just in case that happened?"

"In case anything!" El said, although we both knew Clo was right.

"Let me see," Clo said grudgingly, and she marched over to the edge of the clearing. There, beneath the old tent we'd used when we first got to the Oggy, was Bouncy. The tent was just tatters now, our dwelling long replaced by the cabin we built with Mama.

Clo grabbed the makeshift tarp and yanked it off the Defender in a shower of pine needles. Mr. McBounceface actually looked pretty good; his orange was barely faded. Clo walked over to check the tires and spotted the pig stomach, still tied around a nozzle. Clo shot El a mean look and turned to kick the tire, checking the inflation level.

"Hmm. Pretty good," Clo admitted. *"But will he start?"*

We both hopped in, chasing away a pair of crows that had nested inside. Clo turned the key. Bouncy barely turned over, once, twice, then he roared to life, his low grumble gurgling over the forest. *"Hmm. Battery charged, too?"*

El sheepishly held up the solar backpack charger, now just a hand-held panel. Its connectors ran on a custom line under the hood. "Just in case."

Clo glared at El, and then we both just sat there for a moment, listening to the car idle.

"Well, see if he drives," El said.

"I don't know how to drive," Clo confessed, her hands on the steering wheel.

"Neither do I," El said. *"But how hard could it b—*Aaah!"

Clo stomped on the accelerator, and the rover lurched forward with a surge of power beneath our bodies. We stopped just as hard when Clo stamped both feet on the brake pedal, almost spilling us out of our seats. We did this a few more times, lurching around the clearing until a cloud of dust rose in our camp. Finally we managed to roll gently to a stop. We looked at each other in amazement, this power in our hands. We smiled.

"Let's jaunt!"

We threw everything we thought we might need into Bouncy: venison jerky, waterskins, the hatchet, sleeping furs, backpack, the flint knives, and our little brother, still hog-tied and grunting babble through his gag. Of course El brought Daisy Duke and our last box of ammo, and Clo brought Toothy. Lastly, we brought the Prophanol. Mama had explained to us countless times how these two tubes she had carefully saved would work: if any of us ever got dosed with the Sap, someone could crack the cap off one end of a tube, exposing a tiny needle, which you could jam into the person's thigh. The Prophanol would counteract the Subantoxx, theoretically, and so the victim wouldn't become a shambling addict.

We got back into the Defender, this time with El driving.

"Wait!" Clo shouted, jumping out. She returned to the hood of the car with the severed vampire deer head and pressed it onto the Land Rover's grille, then strapped it in place with one of our extra deer-leather shoelaces.

"Are you sure we should do that?" El called out the window. *"I mean, if we run into people—who are not shamblers or Tik-Toks—they might get scared."*

Clo looked at it: black goo oozing, eye missing, tongue lolling, two fangs sticking straight down and antlers poking straight up. "It *is* kinda gross," Clo mumbled to herself, wiping off the ooze that had made it on to her hands. But she straightened herself and said, trying to sound as steely as possible, "That Jolly Rancher's gonna know who she's dealing with."

Then Clo jumped into the car, closing the door with authority. "C'mon," she snorted. "Let's go find Mama."

El peeled out and we were off to a rough start, bumping down the old logging road, which had barely been a road already a decade ago when we'd first driven down it. Clo kept looking back to check on Dyre in the way back. We had tried to make him as comfortable as a hog-tied prisoner could possibly be, but he was bumping around anyway, struggling, and we could hear his muffled babble still.

It was exciting, being on the road after all those years. We felt powerful in our 4x4, roaring quickly over terrain that would have taken us most of a day to cross on foot. Then it struck us, as we bounced down the overgrown dirt road in Bouncy McBounceface: Mama had made this same journey months before *on foot.* What had she been thinking?

That first day, the day we left, it took us all day and night to get to the Oggy in a car; we must be hundreds of miles away from Yerba City. Why hadn't *Mama* taken Mr. McBounceface? She hadn't even mentioned it. Instead, El had come up with the plan to revive the car on her own, and had kept it from Clo and our brother.

This kind of thing did happen sometimes—we sisters formulating plots that didn't involve both of us—but such schemes were very rare. They usually involved pleasant surprises during Christmas or birthdays, like the time Clo stuffed the pelt of the skunk we'd had to eat that cold winter and gave it as a present to El. It was really more of a joke, of course, than a heartfelt keepsake, and we'd used it for target practice come spring. But this business with Bouncy, this was a big secret between us, perhaps the biggest of our lives thus far. Although it would hardly be the last.

Punk! Something hit the grille of the car.

El stopped Bouncy. *"I think I hit a squirrel."*

"We shouldn't waste it," Clo said. She jumped out, walked to the front of the vehicle, and pulled the poor furry creature from where it was plastered. She examined its head, barely attached, and looked back at her sister. *"It's okay: he didn't suffer."* She automatically said thank you four times, to north, south, east, and west. A quick one.

El nodded, then noticed something. *"Look!"* She pointed at the overgrown road in front of us.

Clo turned and saw it, too: a simple path cut across the old logging road, one that we had carefully maintained over the last decade, but never crossed. *"It's the last perimeter: the line Mama said we can never cross."*

El got out of the car and joined Clo in staring at the simple, well-worn trail. The small tree that Mama had felled across the road to mark this spot had rotted away long ago, leaving just a crumbling brown line in the dirt.

"This is it," Clo said solemnly.

El agreed. *"Once we cross that trail, we might never come back."*

Clo turned and looked back, behind the Defender, toward the tall redwoods we were now leaving after ten long years. *"Mother Oggy took care of us for so long. She brought us so much meat."* She looked down at the squirrel in her hand. *"This was her last gift."*

El nodded. *"Remember Dasher, the first one?"*

Clo nodded. *"No animal ever spoke to us again after that, until this monster came. Guess that means our time here is up."* Tears welled up in her eyes.

"We should give extra thanks," El said and reached over to dip two fingers into the squirrel's open neck. As she spread the blood neatly across her cheekbones, Clo did the same, and the two of us yelled a big *"Thank you!"* together in the four directions, our voices echoing off the trees, not caring if we gave away our position to either prey or predator. It was worth it for all Oggy had done for us.

Back in Bouncy and bouncing down the road, knocking down the tall grass and even the occasional small tree that lay in our path, we brooded, the blood drying on our faces, both knowing exactly what the other was thinking:

Nothing can stop us now.

CHAPTER 6

BUCK LOCK

We burst through the last thicket and onto a two-lane blacktop, or what was left of it. The cracked, overgrown asphalt stretched in oppo-site directions like a cosmic burn mark on the green landscape, a scar that had been slowly healing over the last decade, and we thought it was a good thing we came out when we did; any longer and this man-made slash across the landscape would've healed altogether. We stopped the car and got out, taking a moment to clean off the branches and random vegetation that had gathered in the grille and bumper.

Clo took a look at the fanged deer's head, pulling an orange poppy flower out of its nose. *"Vambi held up pretty well,"* she mumbled.

"No more squirrels," El announced and pulled the last of the leaves away. Then we stood up and looked in both directions.

"Which way do we go?" Clo asked.

El pointed below the sun, which was now high in the autumn sky. *"That's north. So . . ."* She spun her body 180 degrees. *"That way. The city should be south."*

"How far?"

El shook her head. *"Two hundred, three hundred miles. I think."*

Dyre mumbled at us from the back of the Defender. He seemed to be renewing his chanting now that he felt we'd stopped.

El looked at Clo. *"Should we let him out to go to the bathroom or something?"*

"Guy tried to shoot me with an arrow," Clo grunted. *"He can pee himself."*

"You know it wasn't him," El said soothingly. *"And he is our brother. We can't leave him tied up forever. Mama'll be mad, once she finds a cure."*

"True. True." We had played at tying up our little brother, and doing other mean things, when we were littler, and we'd always caught hell for it.

Clo moved toward the driver's seat. *"We'll figure out something by nightfall."*

El nodded, hopping into the passenger side. About twelve hours hog-tied wouldn't be the end of the world.

Clo turned Bouncy south, and with a jerk, we were off again. The drive was a *lot* better now, or at least much smoother. The grasses and vines pushing up through the asphalt were nothing compared to the butt-numbing bounces of the old logging road. Still, there was something . . . unsettling, an eerie feeling that we hadn't felt out in the forest on our own. The feeling got worse and worse the more artifacts of humanity we encountered. First it was just the old blacktop. Then broken, unpowered streetlights. Then rusted, half-collapsed power lines. Finally we saw decaying buildings and abandoned cars, and the feeling became overwhelming. It was the feeling of *no one*, of not another living soul for as far as we could conceive. We had seen Santa, we had seen the Crying Man (we thought), and of course we had seen Vambi the babbling deer. These things might have been intelligences, or artificial flavors, but they certainly weren't *our* flavor. Now we were being confronted by the detritus of those who were definitely our own kind: an overturned bike, a cracked doll's head in the road, an unopened, sun-bleached can of Mountain Dew lying against an equally sun-bleached construction cone—and suddenly we had never felt so alone in our lives.

We came to a town, perhaps a small city once. It was hard to tell at first how big the place was; most of it had been burned up. We thought it might have been Eureka, California, where we had stopped a decade before to loot the Hutchinson's, but we weren't sure. From the boundaries of the burned-out buildings, stopping abruptly at the ends of blocks and roads, we could see that no one had intentionally set this place alight; it had just happened, and the fires had burned themselves out eventually.

A few years ago, we had been aware of a big forest fire, probably within fifty miles of us. We could smell it, and for a few days, ashes actually fell around our cabin. But the winds were blowing westward, and although we had been prepared to evacuate Oggy, we'd never needed to. Thinking back on the intoxicated firefighters the day we escaped the city, and then that big forest fire, and the countless smaller ones over the years, we couldn't help but imagine that hundreds, maybe thousands, of square miles of the state must have burned in the decade we'd been away from human civilization.

There were animals everywhere too, reveling in their newfound spot at the top of the food chain: deer in the diner, pigs at the drive-in, even a mountain lion, perched on top of the town library, flicking her tail while two cubs played with it. All three cats froze and stared us down as we passed. Without a lot of ancient, thick trees surrounding us, it would have been easy to hunt some of these creatures down, but we did our best to roll through town without stopping. We were on a mission, after all.

After jury-rigging and making our own gear for so long, out in the forest, we also had a fleeting thought of maybe looting a sporting goods store like we had so long ago, but, at least at first, the whole sight of the overgrown critter town was a bit too depressing for us to even want to stop and plunder. Besides, we weren't looters anymore; only that first day. We had never returned to civilization to try to eke out our living, and Mama was proud of that fact. We were survivors, she had told us repeatedly over the years: hunters, not scavengers.

Of course, this mentality was probably also what kept us from ever trying to contact any other people. We weren't sure what Dyre thought (and even less sure now that he'd been transformed into a murderous babbler), but in our minds, we'd always thought we'd return to civilization someday. Aside from our natural state of always feeling slightly stir-crazy, and that living in the forest we only ever saw our immediate family, we each had our own reasons for wanting to return, which we occasionally discussed.

El, to put it simply, wanted to shoot bad guys. She imagined Yerba City as a villain who had taken over the planet, some kind of buffed-out, steel-bodied Terminator type, who, if one could just put a bullet between her eyes, could be eliminated, thus returning life to the utopian vision of our eight-year-old selves. This was probably why she practiced with Daisy Duke so purposefully, and patiently. Someday it would come down to the right bullet at the right time, and our lives could go back to normal.

It still wouldn't bring Papa back, Clo would remind her coldly, as our father had passed well before the rise of the Sap and the fall of humanity, so life would never be perfect.

Clo, for her part, just wanted a boyfriend, a feeling that had been growing in recent years, although it was discussed less often. El would scoff at this, saying a boy was no reason to risk life and limb, but Clo would just shrug and say, "At least my fantasies aren't about killing anything." Between all the deer and pigs and rabbits, there was plenty of killing to be done in the forest just to survive. No need to go all the way back into the city for more of it.

In any case, Mama's absence and Dyre's condition had forced us to do what we had both been half wishing to do for so long: return. Now that we were doing it, however, rolling slowly past the half-burned Walmart and the coyote-den 7-Eleven, the whole idea didn't seem so romantic. Besides, the main thing we had been missing in our lives wasn't here anyway: other people. The exodus we had witnessed a decade earlier—shamblers stumbling toward autonomous Subantoxx-dispensing silver vans ready to haul them away—had apparently been thorough.

The whole postapocalyptic vibe was really starting to get us down when, looking out the window, Clo was struck with inspiration.

"Hey, let's go to the mall," she said, just as if the world hadn't ended a decade ago.

"What?" El fired back. We talked to each other so much and so often in our twinspeak that English wasn't our first language anymore, and El thought she had misheard.

"Let's go shopping," Clo confirmed. We were passing the remains of what was clearly the parking lot of a large suburban shopping center.

"We've got what we need." El dismissed the idea. *"We're on a hunt for Mama."*

"How about some nice women's clothes?" Clo countered. *"We're women now, remember? We've never even owned anything actually made for a woman."*

"We don't need that stuff." El had never been girly, but Clo could tell she was intrigued.

"Okay, how about some real hiking boots?" Clo challenged her sister, holding up one of her leather-bound feet. *"Be nice not to have to step through broken glass in homemade moccasins."*

El was silent, and Clo could tell she was swayed by the practicality of the suggestion.

Finally Clo held up our last, crumbling, half-empty box of .30-06 rounds. *"Be nice to have some more ammo. Maybe a second rifle."*

"Fine," El relented, and Clo turned into the mall parking lot, knocking out a path of decade-old weeds as we went. *"But what about Dyre?"* El asked, nodding toward the back seat.

"He'll be fine. We'll just park in the shade."

Clo drove right up to the mall entrance, bouncing over the curb and practically inside through the large, crumbling double glass doors, which had been left open. She put Bouncy in park and we rushed to jump out. Dyre mumbled louder, perhaps in anticipation of being let out of the car finally. He had been back there for a few hours, after all.

We ignored him, El grabbed Daisy Duke, and we went cautiously inside.

Although the mall hadn't been touched by the local fires, it was still pretty dark and ravaged inside. It looked like a family of raccoons had had the run of the place for a few generations, and rainwater had definitely been leaking in from somewhere every winter. Still, the shamblers had never been looters, and the storefronts and shelves were all still well stocked from the day of the first spray.

El held the rifle ready, and Clo her knife, as we walked slowly, carefully scanning for any signs of life.

"Oh my God," Clo whispered, freezing in her tracks.

"What? What?!" El whispered back, ready to blast anything between the eyes.

"Look at that dress!" Clo sheathed her knife and ran toward a headless mannequin draped in a puffy light-blue quinceañera ball gown.

El sighed and lowered Daisy Duke. *"Are you kidding me?"*

Clo easily lifted the dress off the mannequin and did her best to shake it clean (ten years of dust, after all) before letting the dummy clatter into the grime and pressing the gown to her body.

"What do you think?" Clo asked her sister, swaying back and forth.

"I think it's ugly."

"I think it's pretty. I'll look like a princess."

"It's a giveaway color," El said flatly. *"Negative camo value. They'll see you coming a mile away."*

Clo unsheathed her knife and mimicked fighting in midair, still pressing the puffy folds against her. *"And they'll know it was a princess that killed them."*

El just sighed, but then spotted something else in a window nearby. *"Put that away,"* she told Clo. *"Look at this."*

El shouldered the rifle and walked to the shattered window of an athletic store. She reached in and picked out a pair of large green shoes. *"We could use these."*

"Those are men's basketball shoes."

"They're thick, and practical."

"Yeah, like your next boyfriend's gonna be."

El scoffed. *"I don't even like boys, remember?"* She shook the broken glass from a shopping basket and dropped the shoes in. *"I like sensible shoes."*

"You don't understand anything." Clo sighed in disgust. *"Mama said life without beauty isn't worth living."*

"She was talking about nature," El countered. *"The redwoods."*

"And our hair," Clo huffed. *"If a goldfinch can be pretty, then so can I."*

"You're more like a scrub jay, the way you squawk."

"Also pretty. I'll take it," Clo said aloofly, throwing the quinceañera gown over her shoulder and marching over to the rest of the shoe display. *"Now, at least pick out some actual boots."* She plucked a pair of fashion hiking boots from the display stand and dusted them off.

"Those are pink," El warned. *"Wear those with the blue dress and you'll get skunked every time."*

We went back and forth like this for a while, grabbing various items, both practical and impractical. We were bickering in our banter, but the fact was, we were giddy to finally get some new items we didn't have to make out of bones, fur, or elk guts. Soon, we were pushing two shopping carts *full* of stuff. Dresses, pants, boots, gloves, sure; but also packs of Cinnabon frosting, smoothie cups, fifteen pairs of sunglasses, matching iPhone cases (with no phones), and a full case of mango-lime microbead hair conditioner in sixteen-ounce bottles. We were delirious with consumption, but not too far gone to be instantly transfixed when we spotted a large counter at the end of the dusty hallway that read "BAIT."

"*Look!*" Clo said. "*We could use that for fishing!*"

"*Clo. It's a makeup company, remember?*"

"*What?*"

"*Makeup. You put it on your face.*"

"Oh," Clo said. "*Like when you put blood on your cheeks to say thank you to Mother Oggy for letting you kill something?*"

"No," El said slowly. "*It's to make you look good.*"

"Oh. OH!" Clo exclaimed, the same gleam sparking in her eye as when she saw the quinceañera dress, only brighter. "*Like for boys!*"

"*Or girls,*" El said, shaking her head. "*Or anybody.*"

"*Yeah, yeah. Now I remember. I've just . . . never used it. Don't you want to?*"

"*Well . . .*" El was hesitant, but her curiosity was getting the better of her. "*It's gotta be better than the squirrel blood we've been using.*"

"*Yeah, squirrel blood is cool, but . . .*" Clo walked away from our overflowing shopping carts. "*Maybe we could just put something on that doesn't turn brown after an hour.*"

"*Let's do it!*" El cried, and we rushed through the debris, practically smashing into the makeup counter. There, we pressed ourselves against the glass and looked at the kaleidoscope of eye shadows: greens, blues, yellows, taupes, golds, champagnes, mandarins, et cetera. The colors were so unnatural to our forest-girl eyes that it almost hurt to look at them.

"*Wow.*"

"*Nude? I didn't even know nude was a color.*"

"*What's the* Tramp-Stamp *color?*"

"I dunno. It's a whole different world when you're a grown-up."

Clo reached over, prepared to snatch some of the pretty little containers from behind the counter, when El grabbed her wrist, hard.

"Hey! I'll share."

"Shh!" El hissed sharply, and with that single, tense sound, Clo snapped back into hunter mode, her whole body frozen.

"What?" she whispered back, moving her hand to Toothy's pommel.

El slowly, silently pointed her finger at the ground. There, in the dust and broken glass, was something that didn't belong in the world of teenage makeup, iPhone cases, and athletic shoes. Trailing back behind the BAIT counter was what could be nothing other than a giant tentacle, of the same black, ropey sinew we had fought just that morning.

"It's Team Vambi," Clo breathed, as quietly as possible. She silently drew her knife. *"Is it dead?"*

El unshouldered Daisy Duke just as silently, readying the rifle as she whispered, *"I don't know. It looks dusty."*

El gave a quick nod to Clo, and we slowly stepped around opposite sides of the counter as stealthily as possible, careful not to step on any glass.

There, behind the BAIT backdrop, about halfway across the makeup department, was a giant hole in the ceiling, and beneath that was an immense mass about twenty feet tall and just as wide, barely lit by the sunlight coming in from above. The mass was two big, ugly robots, biomechanical Tik-Toks, interlocked in a frozen battle that had clearly happened years ago. From their position, directly beneath the hole in the ceiling and half-buried in the floor of the mall, it appeared that these titans had been fighting in midair, killed each other, and then crash-landed here through the roof of the mall. One of them looked something like a giant silvery stag beetle, with its many legs and pincers transfixed through the body of its grotesque adversary, which looked something like a giant squid or octopus, its dark, hooked tentacles wrapped inside and through the stag beetle's carapace.

We stood there frozen in awe for a moment. Then a small yellow warbler fluttered through the hole in the ceiling, landed on its nest on the giant beetle's back, and began feeding little peeping chicks.

We untensed, Clo lowering her knife. *"I think they've been dead for a while."*

"Thank Oggy. I'd hate to have to fight those things." El looked at the thick layer of dust and pine needles. *"It's a buck lock."*

"Yeah, they killed each other."

"That squid thing, it's definitely the same family tree as that deer that came after us."

Clo pointed with her knife at the unmistakable "YC" crest on one of the segments of the insectoid corpse. *"And look at that: Yerba City."*

"So, Team Vambi versus Santa and his bugs? Judging from the dust, these two Tik-Toks have been fighting each other for a long time."

"Better each other than us," Clo said, picking with the tip of her knife at one of the hooks on the giant squid's thick tentacles.

"Clo, don't do that. Who knows wha—"

The tentacle moved. Only slightly, but it was enough to make us stiffen into frosty mode in a millisecond. The thousands of bristly hooks along the underside of the tentacle scintillated slightly in the dim light of the ruined mall.

We stood like mannequins.

"It's . . . still . . . alive," El whispered. The deer had been hard enough to kill, and it was four feet at the shoulder. This thing was as big as our cabin, and some of its dozen or so appendages were as thick as tree trunks. Its giant tendrils were not symmetrical, and while some of them were forever entwined around its titan beetle adversary, others snaked down and out throughout the makeup department. Holding our breath, we could hear them now, moving slightly in every corner with an ominous scraping and tinkling of broken glass.

The sweet warbler family seemed completely oblivious to the fact that they had nested right on top of a still-living monster from hell, and the blind baby chicks continued to tweet and bicker over their lunch of regurgitated grasshopper.

We nodded at each other and backed away as slowly and silently as possible.

Ever so slowly, like a large slug awakening in the springtime, the giant squid was coming back to life. But we were making progress, too, stepping quietly over appendages and backing away from the BAIT counter. Then the bug woke up.

A large compound eye on the elephant-sized beetle opened, glistening, and a hundred biomechanical pupils focused on us through a crack in the tentacles' embrace.

"They're both *still alive,"* El whispered.

"That's one stubborn buck lo—"

Then the whole mass shifted. Apparently our presence had reignited their ancient struggle, and a shower of dust and pine needles rippled through the air. The warbler chicks gave panicky peeps as their nest shifted, and their mother circled the beetle's head squawking in protest.

And then there was the sound.

We never ran. For ten years in the forest, we'd been the ones doing the chasing. Our lives depended on it. But when we heard that noise, we suddenly felt like we were the moss on stones grinding against each other during an earthquake. There were forces of a magnitude well beyond our guns and knives that were pushing and pulling against each other with suicidal intent, and we were like ants next to their battle. So we ran: over the tentacles that were closing in to the resumed struggle, down the hall, past the fetid yogurt stand.

"What about our loot?" Clo huffed as we cleared the doorway back to Bouncy, thinking back on the two shopping carts we'd filled to overflowing. The deep rumbling behind us boomed louder, like the sound of girders on a skyscraper being twisted by a giant.

"You wanna go back in there and get it?" We were out the double doors, and then El was in the driver's seat, having thrown both Daisy Duke and herself right through the window. *"Get in!"*

Clo was in the passenger seat almost as fast. *"I know, but that dress."*

"There'll be other dresses."

"And other monsters," Clo commented, trying to shake off the adrenaline.

"How's Dyre?" El asked, trying to focus on her driving as we swerved out of the parking lot.

Bouncy hit a parking block and we bounced right over, shaking our little brother into a loud grunt right on cue.

"I think he's fine," Clo said. *"What do you think they were fighting about?"*

We were silent for a moment as we bounced away from those behemoths. It was a total mystery. *"It doesn't matter,"* El finally said. *"This town is still dead, our brother is still hog-tied in the back of the car, and Mama's still out there."*

"Right." Clo nodded, more than happy to quit hypothesizing. *"What did Papa use to say? 'Not our circus, not our monkeys.'"*

"Yeah. 'Not our monkeys,'" El breathed, finally relaxing as we drove out of the town limits. Not our monkeys, not our bugs, not our squids, not our spiders, not our Santa Clauses, not our fanged talking Bambis, not our whatever the hell else the world had in store for us. We promised each other to stay away from everyone and everything until we found Mama.

It didn't last.

CHAPTER 7

MINI-MART ARMY

We're pretty sure that first town was Eureka, or at least what was left of it. After seeing the remnants of the cephalopod-crustacean show-down, we vowed we wouldn't stop until we got to Yerba City itself. However, after about three hours of knocking down fiddleneck weeds with Bouncy's bumper, we came to another abandoned town we thought might have been Ukiah. Desolation gets pretty boring pretty fast, and although we didn't want to tangle with any more hibernating supermachines, we couldn't help ourselves.

On the south end of town, just before the vestiges of the last strip mall became the vestiges of an expanding highway, we stopped again.

There was a new building. Not brand-new, but clearly something that had been built after the first spray. It looked like something designed by an artificial flavor: uncanny, slightly silly. Like the idea of a structure, with some things like walls and something like a roof. It seemed to want to be a kind of pit stop or a friendly little filling station. Only there were no pumps, just a sloping stainless steel roof above a flat stainless steel platform. The whole thing was roughly one hundred feet by one hundred feet, with an enclosure at one end that also served to support the top and bottom. It resembled a giant, flat letter C sitting next to the freeway, tilted ever so slightly by the contour of the terrain, as if it had been dropped there by a long-forgotten giant rather than built in place. We would discover later that this was exactly the case: these "stations" had been airlifted in by teams of Yerba's flying drones.

This particular station appeared to have been abandoned long ago, judging by the number of mud-and-straw bird's nests that had accumulated underneath the top of the C, but it was still in much better shape than the rest of the town we had just passed through. It was positioned so passersby could drive right up into the bottom of the C, but we didn't get nearly that close. We stopped just outside the station's awning and were about to roll on until we saw something moving inside.

At the far end, in the vertical joint of the C, was a glass kiosk, entirely obscured by dust—but one of the windows was ajar, and something human-scale was definitely shifting around.

"Is someone living in there?" Clo asked. *"Maybe it's a survivor."*

"Well"—El squinted—*"that spot's too small to have a giant squid or one of those rhino beetles tucked inside, so how bad could it be?"*

It was midafternoon and the sun was still bright, but it was impossible to see clearly inside thanks to the shadow cast by the overhang.

"This is the only solid structure around," El offered, *"so it might make sense to someone to hole up in there."* She was peering through the scope on Daisy Duke, something she rarely did. She rarely needed to.

"Maybe they saw Mama pass by," Clo pointed out. *"This is the quickest way south."*

"Maybe Mama didn't take the quickest way," El surmised. *"Maybe she didn't want to be seen. Maybe we don't want to be seen."*

Clo paused. It was probably a little late to be sneaking into Yerba City undetected, with a gurgling 4x4 and a babbling teenager tied up in the back, but El did have a point: we presumably had retreated into the wilderness for a reason ten years ago.

"I see someone!" El whispered.

"What are they doing?" Clo whispered back. *"Is it a shambler? Or a Tik-Tok? No tentacles, right?"*

"Can't tell." El squinted. *"But they're . . . on the phone, I think."*

"They're talking on a phone? Like, a mobile phone? Like maybe they have BrickRibbit?" Oh, how Clo missed BrickRibbit. It had been years since we'd played, but you don't forget a pal like Clyde easily.

"Well, a shambler isn't going to talk on the phone," Clo said, *"and neither is one of those* things. *And they're talking to someone. So, this is good, this is a good sign: there are people. People who talk on the phone, to other people! Let's go talk to them!"* Clo jumped out of the car, excited.

"Wait!" El whispered, still not sure.

"Just cover me!" Clo tucked her knife into her belt and strode forward. "Hello! Hello there!" she called.

El sighed nervously and got out of the car, but kept her rifle pointed, ready. Dyre grunted from the back seat. "Shh!" El said, scanning back and forth again with Daisy Duke. Something told her this might be a trap.

She was only half right.

Walking under the silver overhang, Clo continued to call to the half-open window at the far end. "Hello! Hello, person! Person on the phone! How are you?" About ten yards away, she could see the person: a youngish woman, midtwenties, just inside the window. Indeed, she was talking on the phone. Strange thing about it, though, the phone had a wire leading down to a counter in front of her. Outside of old-timey movies before the End of the World, we had never seen a phone with any kind of cord attached to it, not in real life.

The young woman turned and saw Clo. She didn't look like a shambler; she looked okay. Or rather, she looked beautiful. She had pale skin and dark hair. She had on what we recognized to be makeup, that thing we had just been thwarted from looting, making her lips bright red and her brown eyes pop through thick mascara. She wore a white-jacketed uniform, making her look like some kind of nurse or medical worker. But something was definitely off. Her hair and shoulders were covered with a thick layer of dust. And in the middle of her forehead was that upside-down black triangle, same as the one we'd seen on Santa Claus.

"Hello!" she called back to Clo. "I'm sorry I didn't see you there! I'm so glad you could stop by."

"It's a Tik-Tok lady!" El yelled, leveling her rifle.

Clo paused, gripping her knife handle but not drawing it. *"How do you know?"* she called back.

"No one living out here is gonna sound that pleasant." El found the nurse through her scope. *"Besides, does she look like she's been eating squirrel for ten years?"*

Clo looked at the nurse. She liked the lady's makeup, and after the monsters at the BAIT counter . . . "She seems nice."

"So did Santa Claus, remember?" El said as coldly as possible, finger on the trigger. *"Let's just back away and keep moving."*

But Clo couldn't let this chance at communication go. "Have you seen our mama?" she blurted to the nurse. "She would have been through here about four months ago. I have a picture." Clo fumbled in her jacket.

"Clo . . . ," El warned, tightening her finger.

"Oh, no, I'm sorry. We haven't seen anyone here for years," said the nurse, and Clo abandoned her riffling. "You're the first we've had for a long time, and I'm so happy you've decided to join us." Her smile was wide, reassuring, and totally fake.

"Let's just go, Clo," El said, still pointing.

Dejected, Clo said, "Well, what about your phone? Can you call someone who might have seen our mama?"

"Well, I'm afraid I've been having trouble with my communication system. I've been calling City Central over and over and still no response."

"How long has that been going on?"

"About fifty-two months, now."

"Fifty-two *months*?"

"Yes. I'm afraid we've been having some trouble with our maintenance systems too, but we've been managing." The nurse turned to squeak the window all the way open, and as she did, the left rear side of her head turned toward us. Her left ear and most of the back of her head were completely missing, a jagged hole revealing a wormy golden sinew that throbbed as she moved and talked.

"Yikes!" Clo couldn't help herself from shrieking.

"Okay," El said, her coolness cracking. *"Time to go!"*

"But enough about me. You're the one here for treatment," the nurse continued nonchalantly. "How can I help you? New patch? Small sac? Big sac?"

"Uh," said Clo nervously, backing away. "We're fine. We'll just be on our way, okay?"

"So, the standard, then? Very well," the nurse said, and she pressed a button on the dusty console next to her.

A grapefruit-sized gray ball lowered itself on a white string from the ceiling right behind Clo.

"No, really—" Clo didn't see the dangler and was backing right into it.

"Clo!" El yelled, still peering through the scope, but without a clear shot at the hanging device. *"Look out!"*

Eight spiderlike legs sprang out from the body of the ball, and a blue sac slid out from its belly. It was just like the Subantoxx spiders that Santa Claus had been carrying. Clo spun around just in time to see a sharp proboscis emerge from an unfolding head on the small robot, blue liquid already forming a tiny drop at the tip of the needle.

"Whoa!" Clo yelled, and she simultaneously ducked and swung up her knife, bifurcating the insectoid machine with one swipe right beneath its thorax. The jittering legs stayed up on the white thread as the blue sac fell to the dusty steel floor with a slapping sound, spattering the Sap like a dropped water balloon.

"Ew," Clo commented as she tried to flick the blue smear from her knife.

"Don't touch that stuff!" El yelled.

"I'm not!" Clo yelled back, annoyed that her sister would even remind her. Behind her, the nurse took note of the spider's failure to make attachment, and pressed another button. Right away, a second pod dropped just to Clo's left, its legs and needle nose opening like a menacing flower.

CRACK! El's bullet pierced the second spider as well as the sliding window of the station behind it, sending a rain of blue liquid and delicate robotic parts into the dusty shattered glass.

"Get out of there!" El yelled, sliding back the bolt to eject the smoky spent shell. *"Now!"*

"Why?" Clo snorted, offended. *"I can handle a few bugs!"*

"Oh!" chortled the nurse. "I see you're having trouble being administered. Well"—she typed several commands into her keyboard—"we shall do the best we can with what resources we have."

About twenty pods appeared from storage positions distributed throughout the ceiling and began descending. Clo's eyes widened.

"Run!" El yelled, taking a shot at the pod nearest Clo. It exploded in a blue puff, but it was clear there were going to be way too many to shoot. The bugs' legs started sprouting and they dropped to the floor like arachnid paratroopers, needles pointing at Clo.

Clo took one look at the army of pricks aimed at her. "Okay! I'm running!" She vaulted toward the car, smashing one spider, then another. But the needles closed in, and the bugs started jumping, aiming their dripping blue barbs at Clo's exposed skin and pierceable clothing.

Behind her, the nurse was climbing out the window. "Yerba City goes above and beyond to serve our citizens!" she announced, her dusty body flopping onto the platform. She was missing a body from the waist down, her dirtied uniform giving way to a dangling mass of brownish cables and tendrils that slipped and squirmed as she crawled. "Please stay still during administration. We are just trying to help you!"

"Get to the car!" El yelled and took another shot at a jumping spider in midair, spattering it less than a foot from Clo's neck.

"I'm trying!" Clo called back, cutting another one apart as she jumped off the platform. *"There's too many!"*

El was backing toward Bouncy, ejecting her last shell.

"I'm out!" Our last disintegrating box of ammo was still in the car, tucked under the front seat.

The spiders poured off the platform after us, scampering and leaping. El pressed her back against the Defender and swung Daisy Duke like a club, smacking the things out of the air. Clo cut down two more, but the second ended up skewered on her knife. She frantically searched for a way to get the drug-filled sac off without touching it, flicking the knife away from her in a shower of Sap. But the sac wouldn't budge; the knife was serrated, after all. At the same time, a few spiders rushed under the car, clamping on underneath and trying to work their way inside. We were taking them down, and being outflanked simultaneously. These things were fast, and organized.

Bouncy was clearly our only way out, and they knew it. Bugs were crawling all over the vehicle. Two others jumped onto the roof, scratching for gaps at the top of Bouncy's windows. They must have known somehow that Dyre was inside, and their plan was obviously to dose him, too.

Clo gave up trying to get her knife free and threw it into a second spider on the ground, transfixing both into the dirt. She leapt across the hood of the car, knocking one of the robotic monsters onto the broken asphalt in a scrambling spin before landing on it with both feet. There was a satisfying *crunch.* Clo turned, ready for more, but now the blue drug was thick on her moccasins, and as she jumped to perform a perfect *tobi geri* kick on another spider leaping at her face, she landed back in the puddle—and slipped.

El was still swinging the rifle, knocking them aside, and saw Clo go down. "Clo!" she yelled. "Get up!"

"I'm trying!" Her feet scrambled for purchase in the now-dirty blue muck as she awkwardly tried to push her body back to standing without touching the Subantoxx. A tricky spider, who had been waiting under the Defender for just such an opportunity, scrambled out of the darkness and aimed for Clo's throat.

"Aaah!" Clo yelled, seeing it just in time to swing her hands up. She caught it before the needle got to her, but the spider grabbed both of her hands with its legs, and she didn't have the leverage to push it off. Two more spiders emerged from under Bouncy and crawled up her legs, frantically probing for openings in her buckskin pants. The needles were getting closer and closer. Clo was still fighting, but there was no way she wasn't going to get stuck.

For ten years we had been hiding in the woods, living off the land, fearing the day might come that we would somehow get dosed by the Sap, that we would join the end of humanity in its oblivion. We had fought so hard every day. And yet the terrible feeling that coursed through Clo's body at that moment was not the fear of becoming another shambling addict, but rather the sharp, painful feeling of shame that we had failed, that even though Mama had saved us, trained us, and raised us, even though Mother Oggy had protected us and fed us, in the end we had failed everyone and had gotten ourselves stuck by a bunch of stupid spider bots.

"Nooo!" Clo yelled, using her last seconds of sobriety to curse her miserable fate. To our surprise, the spiders all froze, even the one in her hands, its dripping needle just an inch from her exposed jugular.

"No?" the frozen spider in her hands said. Its voice was tiny, and its six little beady eyes turned in curious disbelief.

The spiders around El also froze, having formed a ten-foot circle around her in preparation for an all-out multipronged assault she never would have been able to escape.

Clo's eyes darted back and forth between the robotic monstrosities around her. She'd been ready to give up the world, dismiss her entire existence as another casualty of the End Days. Was this some kind of cruel joke?

"Uh, no," she reiterated.

"No treatment?" the spider questioned. Its needle was still dangerously close.

"No," Clo said firmly, choosing her words carefully now, "no treatment. I don't want any treatment!"

Slowly, the spiders backed away, the one closest releasing her hands and crawling off her in obvious disappointment.

Around her, El could see the dozens of tiny eyes refocus on her with an aching intent and start to close in. "Me neither! I don't want treatment!" she insisted, and the spiders slowly lowered their pointy injectors, crestfallen.

"Are you declining treatment?" the nurse called to us, in a somewhat incredulous tone. She had crawled across the platform in a slimy ochre trail of gunk, and now she used the tendrils behind her to heave her torso up again, standing almost upright like some half-woman, half-snake mythical beast.

Clo, lying on the ground in disbelief, looked over at the nurse. "I am declining treatment," she announced in no uncertain terms.

"Get in the car, Clo," El ordered, still holding the rifle aloft, ready to take another strike.

The nurse turned to El. "And what about you? Surely you must—"

"I also decline treatment," El said flatly and clearly. The spiders encircling her seemed to collectively sigh again in disappointment, and the tiny robots slowly backed away and returned to the stainless steel mini-mart.

The nurse made a tilting gesture with her head that seemed like a computer's idea of disappointment. "We cannot administer treatment without your consent. However, we must inform you that you are infected with multiple viruses and other pathogens, including the Fimi virus. Subantoxx treatment is the only way to ensure—"

"Let's go." El cut her off and stepped over to Bouncy, still keeping her rifle ready.

Clo was sitting up, looking at the spiders that were now just coyly milling around five feet from her, examining each other for damage and pulling fibers and dirt from their pincer legs. Two were even trying to scrape one of their flattened comrades off the ground. Clo didn't think they looked so bad now that they weren't trying to stick her. Back in the forest, she'd always had a soft spot for bugs and beetles.

"Well, maybe they're friends now, since we don't want the drugs—"

"They are *not* friends!" El yelled. "Get in! Now!" She jumped into Bouncy's driver side and turned the key. The car turned over once with a dull surge, then stayed silent. "Damn!" El mumbled.

On top of the car, a spider tapped on the back window, waving two of its little legs at the nurse.

"There appears to be another person in need of treatment," the nurse said, a slight ooze coming from the corner of her mouth.

"That's just our little brother," Clo said. "He's fine. He's just—babbling."

"He must be sick. He'll need treatment."

El tried the ignition again. Just a single chug. "Now!" El warned her sister.

"Oh, he declines treatment, too," Clo announced.

The nurse shook her head. "I'm afraid no one can decline treatment for another individual. That would be unethical."

"Unethical? But he's out of it."

"This isn't the time for a legal or philosophical discussion, Clo!" El fired through gritted teeth as the car gave a heaving moan. "We're leaving!"

"We are in an emergency situation," the nurse gurgled. "Incapacity must be interpreted as consent to treatment."

"Consent?"

"They're gonna stick him!" El said, finally getting Bouncy's engine fired up in a sputtering surge. *"Get in and close the door, now!"*

Indeed, the spiders seemed to have their existence validated once again, and their squad of needles sprang back to life. "Treatment?" they all seemed to chime in unison. "Yay! Treatment!"

Clo snapped back into battle mode, realizing that the danger was far from over. She snatched her knife from the ground, leaving behind the two impaled spiders, and leapt into Bouncy's passenger side. She managed to slam the door just as three more spiders sprang onto it, frantically trying to dig their way into the vehicle.

"Go! Go! Go!" Clo yelled. El pounded on the accelerator, and Bouncy screeched across the broken asphalt in a cloud of dust. Aside from the multiple spiderbots swarming across our vehicle trying to scratch their way in, we thought for a moment that we were home free. Not true. One of the nurse's tendrils had snaked its way across the blacktop and wrapped around our rear bumper, so when we took off, so did the nurse. Apparently the years of inactivity had made her extra enthusiastic about getting a new patient, so being dragged across the cracked freeway didn't concern her in the slightest: it was finally treatment time.

As we struggled to shake the spiders off the car, the nurse was trailing us, half skidding and half bouncing. Until she managed to affix another one of her stringy guts to Bouncy and began pulling herself toward us.

"Load Daisy Duke!" El shouted, pushing the rifle into Clo's lap. El was unquestionably the better shot, but Clo was plenty good with the gun, too. She didn't have to be told twice to snatch our last box of ammo from under the seat and begin pressing shells into the open bolt.

There were at least six of the spiders on our car, all scrambling to get at Dyre. Sure, he was a babbling idiot, and he had recently tried to kill us, but there was no way we were going to let him get on the Sap without a serious fight. Mama had made us promise to take care of him, after all.

Daisy could only hold five shots at a time, and Clo clicked the full five into place and slammed the bolt forward as El accelerated sharply, trying to shake the spiders. Two of them actually did fly off, one into the dirt and one right onto the nurse's face as she climbed toward us. She didn't seem to mind.

There were at least four of the little buggers left, though, scraping and scratching while at the same time trying to hold on to our speeding vehicle. Clo pointed at them, swinging the barrel around the car.

"Don't make a hole if you don't have to!" El shouted. Wise thought. The spiders' claws and needles didn't have the strength to get through the closed windows, much less the corroded, but still intact, body of the car. These spider-machines were ugly, nasty little things programmed with a dark mission to make all of humanity into drug-addled zombies, but they were not military-grade. They were the ultimate evolution of an out-of-control pharmaceutical industry; they were tiny administrators, not soldiers.

"I don't think they can get through," Clo announced, relaxing the rifle a bit.

"What about that nurse?" El asked.

CRUNCH! The nurse's fist smashed through the rear window, sending glass flying onto Dyre. We both jumped, El sending the Defender into a swerve.

The nurse withdrew her hand, now pulpy and shattered, and stuck her spider-covered face up through the jagged hole. "It is against protocol to prevent treatment from being administered to another patient!" The spider jumped off her face and began picking at the hole in the shattered back window, widening it.

Clo propped herself against the dashboard and braced both feet against the passenger seat, looking down Daisy's barrel. She sighted the rifle right between the nurse's eyes. "Treat this!" she shouted and fired.

Click. A dud.

"Aaah!" Clo shouted and frantically tried to load another cartridge, jiggling Daisy Duke's bolt. But the bad shell had apparently been corroded, and a mash of metal had spread into Daisy Duke's mechanics, freezing her action.

"Daisy's jammed!" Clo cried, pulling with all her strength on the bolt.

The nurse's mangled fingers crunched through the gap in the glass, sending another shower of shards into the back seat on top of Dyre.

Clo screamed again in frustration at her paralyzed rifle. There was only one thing to do. Clo flipped her feet from the seat to the floor, hefted Daisy like a javelin, and jumped into the back seat, squealing like an angry possum. Her momentum helped her shove the rifle as hard as she could through the hole in the rear window. The barrel of the .30-06 not only ripped through the spider but found its way right into the eye of the nurse, tearing through the Tik-Tok lady's skull in a shower of golden goo.

"It's just a quick pinch—" the thing gurgled, then clutched at the rifle, finally letting go of Bouncy as she fell backward onto the broken blacktop in a clunky, spiraling roll.

"Is it off?" El shouted, unable to see past Clo or through the rear window in its current state.

Clo backed off, leaning against the front seats. *"Yeah,"* she said, trying to sound calm.

El, still concentrating on driving, couldn't help but notice the large hole in the rear window. *"We're breached. Any more coming?"*

Clo snatched up her knife from the floor of the Defender and kept her gaze on the back window. *"Don't think so."*

"Are you sure? I got the creepy feeling one of those bugs is still clinging on somewhere."

"Same here," Clo admitted, her eyes and ears straining against the engine's roar, a sound now more pronounced with the open window.

We waited, ready for something else to jump through the window any second. And waited. Clo finally broke the tension.

"Daisy Duke is gone," she finally said, expressing a kind of solemn remorse for the weapon that had kept us alive for so long. *"I had to shove her out the window. I'm sorry."*

"It's okay," El said, trying to comfort her. *"We were basically out of ammo anyway."*

"But we could have found more bullets." Clo sniffed. Then tears rolled down her cheeks. *"She had so many more things to shoot . . ."* She started bawling.

"Hey, hey, don't cry. It's what she would have wanted, going out like that," El said sharply. *"Taking out a baddie, right?"*

Clo quickly wiped her cheeks, trying to compose herself. *"You're right."*

"*She killed a lot of things, and she didn't go out like a sucker. That's all any of us can ask for, isn't it?*"

"*Double true.*" Clo nodded, stifling a sniffle.

"*And we're not going to go out like suckers, are we?*"

"*No.*"

"*We butchered 'em back there, and we're gonna keep butchering them till our time comes, right?*"

"*That's right!*" Clo said, pumping herself up.

"*That's right! Double-tap it!*" El took her right hand off the wheel to give Clo two enthusiastic high fives across the back seat. Clo kept her eyes focused behind us. We were trying to sound tough, but who were we kidding? As the adrenaline faded, Clo finally copped to it.

"*We almost bought it back there,*" she said, full of shame. "*Almost got stuck.*"

"*Yeah,*" El agreed. "*We got lucky.*" She stared at the road ahead, past the vampire deer head miraculously still attached to our hood. "*And we got lucky before that with Vambi.*"

"*Luck's not going to keep cutting it,*" Clo predicted darkly.

"*We're going to have to tighten up our hunt.*"

"*True, true.*" Clo snorted.

"*I'm not going to stop at any more mini-marts,*" El announced. "*No malls. No nothing. We're going right into the city and find Mama.*"

"*Good idea.*" Clo took a moment to glance down at Dyre, who was still mumbling. "*Ugh, I think he finally did pee himself.*"

El grunted in acknowledgment; she could smell it, too.

"*He doesn't seem to mind, though.*" Indeed, our brother was still just mumbling to himself, the drama of the crazy nurse-creature and the spider-things totally lost on him. We had almost gotten stuck trying to save him, and he still just wanted to get free and kill us, apparently.

El kept watching the road and avoiding brush, debris, and the occasional abandoned car. But now we were generally going as fast as we possibly could. We sat tense and silent, listening for the last of those spider-things we were certain were still attached to the car somewhere. On top of that, wherever we were headed, there were sure to be more spiders, more nurses, more giant squids, and probably much worse. What were we getting ourselves into?

Eventually Clo broke the ice. *"So they won't stick us as long as we say no."*

"Apparently," El acknowledged curtly.

"But Dyre can't say no right now, so they're going to do whatever they can to get him hooked."

"Until we can get him to stop babbling long enough to . . . 'decline treatment.'"

"Silver lining: he'd probably stop trying to kill us if he got hooked," Clo hypothesized.

"Clo, Mama hid us out in the woods for ten years so we wouldn't get dosed. We're not going to start now."

"Yeah, but we have the Prophanol," Clo offered. *"We could let them dose him long enough to get him some help, and then clean him up again."* Clo looked down at our brother, still facedown, thrashing from time to time. *"At least we could change his pants."*

"The Prophanol doses are ten years old. We don't even know if they'll still work," El said angrily. *"Besides, remember what Mama said about the drug changing. Evolving. Who knows what it'll do now once it's inside you? Maybe it's even . . ."* She searched her memory of Mama's lessons for the term. *"Counteragent-resistant. It might be counteragent-resistant now."*

Clo brooded over this, looking at the Sap on her blade as its glow faded. "It's dying, just like back in the forest!"

"Good," El said, "but stay crispy, there's a lot of more of it out there."

Clo quickly wiped Toothy clean on the back of the seat and returned the handle of the knife to her knee, keeping the weapon propped and ready *"Crispy and clean,"* she announced.

We drove on. Off the freeway, another silvery structure came into view.

"There's another mini-mart," Clo pointed out. The structure looked just as dead and rotten as the first one we'd encountered.

"Yeah, we're not gonna stop this time," El grunted.

Then, about a quarter mile later: *"There's another one."*

"They're everywhere."

"Yerba City must have set them to trap any stragglers."

"Like us."

"Like us," El agreed.

We kept going, bouncing in Bouncy McBounceface, down a broken road toward a city probably filled with our worst nightmares. We were headed straight into the heart of darkness, a path increasingly filled with needles, claws, tentacles, and various nasty oozes and slimes. We had no gun, no directions, and no Mother Oggy home to go back to now. We both knew there was only one way forward, and chances were we'd end up dead, or worse.

And then we ran out of gas.

CHAPTER 8

GHOSTS OF IKEA

The sun was just setting when Bouncy started gurgling and sputtering and then finally died. El frantically scanned the dashboard before
seeing the white needle pointed at "E." Both of us realized it at the
same time, our eyes rolling in frustration at ourselves. We'd forgotten
to stop for diesel fuel. Grown-ups had always taken care of that. Hey,
we hadn't even ridden in a car since we were eight years old. Still, we
felt stupid.

But it was just another challenge, we told ourselves. All we had
to do was find a gas station—one that had diesel—and fill up Mr.
McBounceface Of course, nothing but the mini-marts seemed to have
any power, so we'd have to find a way to get an old station's ancient
tanks open and pump fuel out and into our Defender. That was possible. Theoretically. We could do that. We could definitely do that.
Hypothetically.

We were just discussing this brilliant plan when the sun finished
going down and we heard something move on the underside of the car.
A faint clicking. We looked at each other. We'd almost forgotten.

"Hitchhiker!" Clo breathed and readied her knife for the spider. We
listened. It was definitely one of those pesky bots. Hopefully it was a

straggler from our run-in at the first mini-mart and we hadn't stopped Bouncy right on top of a nest of them.

"How many?" El whispered. Clo didn't have Dyre's ears, but she was better at this kind of thing than her sister.

She listened. *"Just one."*

We didn't have the rifle anymore, but El found the hatchet and snatched it up. *"Ready?"* she asked.

Clo nodded, and we kicked open our doors, tucking into rolls simultaneously in case the thing was going to try for our legs right away. It didn't. Sensing us roll, the spider skittered as fast as it could, straining all eight legs for its mission of injection.

We could hear it, but in the faded light it was impossible to see under the dark bulk of the Defender.

"Do you see it?" Clo shouted, ready to throw.

"No!" El shouted back.

"There!" Clo yelled. It was crawling up the back bumper.

"It's going for Dyre!" El said. Of course. The little sticker didn't care about us nonconsenting adults—it wanted its patient-by-default.

"I got it!" Clo announced confidently. She took two strides to put herself parallel to the back of Bouncy and threw her blade right into the spider's thorax. It made a *skree!* sound as its impaled body went flying, and Clo yanked the wire back, letting the gutted metal critter continue to the asphalt while she retrieved her knife from midair.

Clo snorted in satisfaction at her deadly yo-yo-like move. *"Any more?"* she called to El.

El jumped up to peer over the roof, then down to a crouch to inspect under the Defender. *"Don't think so,"* she called back.

We both relaxed, breathing in the darkness, taking a moment before deciding what to do next. We looked around. Where were we? Still on the freeway, next to a blackened, half-crumbled Ikea warehouse. It was an overcast night, and darkness was completely upon us now save for the Defender's single dim headlight.

Then we snapped to attention.

"You hear that?" El asked tensely.

"Uh-huh."

The whispers. They were unmistakably the same as the ones we had heard in the night back at the Oggy. Unmistakable especially now that we were wide awake. We pressed against each other, back-to-back, weapons ready and goose bumps rising. The babble from Dyre, and Vambi before him, was frightening enough, but the whispers were a hundred times worse.

We slowly circled, our eyes scanning the shadows for the source of the sounds.

"*We chased it away once,*" Clo said menacingly, "*and we can do it again.*"

Off near the side of the road, a crow landed in the twilight and stared at our defensive stance quizzically. It flitted over to a nearby cattle fence and cawed. Next to it, caught in barbed wire, a tattered plastic bag was fluttering.

"*It's different this time,*" El whispered.

"*What?*"

"*Last time the air froze, remember? And the creek. Look at that bag over there.*"

"*Okay,*" Clo acknowledged, "*but this is still bad. We're out of gas, we have no idea where we are, and we're surrounded by a hundred hissing perverts.*"

"*Right. I'm starting to miss the spiders.*"

"*Remember the last time we heard this sound?*"

"*It's that Crying Man.*"

"*That nightmare we both had.*"

"*I don't think it was a dream.*"

"*So you think he's real?*"

"*Uh-huh.*"

"*And he's here?*"

"*Uh-huh.*"

"*Good,*" Clo snorted. "*That means we can gut him.*"

"*There!*" El shouted.

Sure enough, standing about sixty yards away in the doorway of the dilapidated Ikea warehouse, just visible in the dim light cast by Bouncy's failing headlight, was a tall, slender figure wearing what appeared to be a black dress suit. A very nice-looking black dress suit, and a very expensive-looking dark orange sash. The niceness of his suit and sash contrasted with his face and hands, which, pale and gaunt, set with dark lines, looked like death itself. His white hair was combed with the pasty neatness of a funeral home, which only added to the feeling that the Crying Man was some kind of preserved corpse.

You'd think that the sight of this creepy figure in the night would have frightened us into hysteria, and that was a temptation. For a moment. But Mama had always taught us that fear can be fuel, and at that moment, we were all gassed up.

"Get him!" Clo yelled, and we rushed toward the Ikea, weapons ready.

"Cut him!"

"Gut him!"

The Crying Man, his expression unchanging, turned and walked calmly into the warehouse, leaving the doorway a black hole of mystery.

"He's rabbiting!" El called.

"Good!" Clo yelled back. *"I'm in a hunting mood!"*

Now, it's true that we were both jacked up, sick of being cooped up in the car, and probably needed to stretch our legs, but in hindsight, running headlong into a dark warehouse after a ghostly apparition was almost certainly not a good idea. We did it anyway, slamming into each other in the doorway in our scrambling effort to score the quarry first.

"Ow!"

"Outta my way!"

We stumbled into what had once been the front office of a dispatch center, dusty computers still sitting at empty desks, expensive swiveling chairs discarded like fallen soldiers around the room.

We stood poised, blades gleaming, adrenaline pumping. *"Where is he?"* Clo breathed. She was about to stab one of the office chairs just for giggles.

"There!" El yelled.

On the far side of the office, about forty feet away, were two large windows that looked out onto the main warehouse floor, which was stacked high with boxes of minimally designed and minimally priced furniture. The Crying Man was standing on a catwalk about a story above the floor, staring back at us.

"How'd he get all the way up there?" Clo yelled in frustration, but that didn't stop her from rushing toward the open door.

El did us one better. She leapt onto a dusty desk and then jumped feet-first through one of the office windows, landing in a roll as a cascade of shattered glass followed her onto the warehouse floor.

"Dang!" Clo yelled, impressed, but El wasn't done. She popped out of her roll and immediately threw her hatchet across the room. It landed with a *thunk* on the catwalk at the Crying Man's feet. Shucks, six inches higher and she would have hobbled him.

The Crying Man stared down at us, unflinching. El's eyes dashed back and forth, searching for a way up to the catwalk. The Crying Man turned and walked slowly to the right.

"There!" El pointed at a spiral staircase about forty yards to the right. *"Split up!"* she ordered. *"Pincer him!"*

Clo dashed right to the staircase, while El scrambled up a pile of stacked boxes to the left. Half of El's steps went ripping through rotting cardboard, but it didn't matter; she got up to the catwalk first, hands just managing to grip the bottom of the platform as Clo dashed knife-first up the staircase.

With a grunt, El pulled herself the rest of the way up onto the platform and jumped to her feet. Clo emerged onto the catwalk at just about the same time, and seeing her, the Crying Man froze, his mask-like expression still unmoving.

With a crunch of splinters, El yanked her hatchet from the catwalk, and the two of us closed in. We had him trapped between us, so we moved slowly, weapons ready.

"We got you," Clo said, raising her knife. Seeing his face—if you could call it that—so close now, she actually wasn't sure if she could throw her knife into him. His eyes were sunken, hollow, and the strange whispering that seemed to accompany him was of the utmost creepiness . . . but there was something about him. He didn't have the uncanny false gestures of the android faces we'd seen. Despite the fact that his black-streaked skin was porcelain white and his eyes were entirely jet-black, there was no mistaking it. The Crying Man was . . . human. Or at least he once had been.

"You're not a Tik-Tok, are you?" Clo said.

The Crying Man just smiled an eerie, toothy grin, and his feet lifted off the catwalk. He didn't fall, he floated. Straight off the platform, above the scattered boxes, and toward the windowed wall of the office we had just busted through.

We stood there for a moment, mouths agape, watching this lich float away from us. *"He's a ghosty man!"* Clo finally shouted.

"He led us in here," El suddenly realized. *"He's headed for Dyre!"*

Clo screamed, half in frustration at being duped, and threw her knife at the back of his thigh. Her thinking was to hobble him, not kill him, leaving him with the limping understanding that the Yetti family was not to be messed with. But the kindness of her shot didn't matter much, as the blade simply passed through his leg in a small swirl of dark colors and stuck into a ceiling beam with a dusty thud. The Crying Man turned slightly, as if bothered by a fly, but kept on floating, right through the wall.

"Definitely a ghosty man!" Clo confirmed, and she yanked on her wire, pulling her knife down and catching it by the handle.

"C'mon!" El shouted, starting to run. Clo scampered down the spiral staircase while El jumped down from the catwalk with a loud thump, creating a giant puff of mold and dust. In seconds she leapt coughing out of the mess and joined Clo, both of us streaking across the floor, back through the office door, and to the exit.

"Can't believe we fell for the okey-doke!" Clo panted as we ran.

"Won't happen again!" El mumbled, shaking off dust as she raced her sister out the door and back to the freeway.

Sure enough, that tricky freak's feet were sticking out through Bouncy's back door. The Crying Man was half-inside our car, doing something nefarious to Dyre.

"Hey!" El shouted at the creep.

"Get away from him!" Clo yelled. We were fast closing the distance to those strange dark legs hanging out of our car, when a thought occurred to Clo. *"If he's a ghosty, how are we gonna gut him?"*

"I think he's a telegram," El panted.

"Okay, whatever! What can we do?"

"Don't think we can touch him." El shot Clo a look. *"But he's got sensory input. Sight and sound."*

Clo nodded, understanding. *"Okay, you get the door!"*

El skidded to a halt and tore open Bouncy's back door. Without missing a beat, Clo took a huge breath and dove right into the back of the Defender.

The Crying Man was leaning over Dyre doing God knows what, but it didn't matter—Clo was next to him in an instant. She got right up against his pale ear and screamed as loud as she could.

Now, Clo can scream very loud, to put it mildly. This had been established when she was just a baby, and it was a trend that only grew as her body did. We could hear her literally miles away in the forest if she wanted us to, and it was painful to be within a hundred feet when she really belted it out. El actually felt sorry for the Crying Man for a moment. Just a moment.

Because the sonic attack worked. The Crying Man gave a shriek, clutching at his ears as he shot upward through the roof of the car.

"Aïe!" he shouted, stopping about twenty feet up in the air and looking back down at us.

"What were you doing to him?" El demanded.

The Crying Man ignored the question, just squinted down at us, still in pain, rubbing his ears. "Very clever, little girls."

"We're not girls, jackass," Clo snorted. "We're butchers."

"And you ain't seen nothing if you mess with our family," El said, coldly lifting the axe. After a tense moment she added, "Sucker."

The Crying Man just sighed at our tough talk. There was something snobby about him. He spoke with an English accent, but as if his native language was French, or maybe German, we couldn't tell. "I was merely checking on his condition," he said.

"What do you care?" El demanded.

"Hey," Clo called from inside. "He stopped babbling." Indeed, Dyre was lying still, breathing and conscious, but silent for the first time since that morning.

"He will start again soon enough," the Crying Man said, flexing his jaw. Apparently his noncorporeal ears were still ringing. "He didn't want me to hear his little speech. But I know enough now."

Clo popped her head out of Bouncy. "You visited us before. In the forest."

"I have been keeping an eye on you since your mother left."

"Don't try to tell us you're a friend of hers," Clo said suspiciously.

The Crying Man scoffed at the thought. "Hardly. You and I have a mutual enemy."

We thought about this for a moment. "Yerba City," El guessed.

The Crying Man tilted his head, his sinister demeanor returning now that his ears had stopped ringing. "Just as the City does not have your interests in mind, neither does she have mine."

"Do you know where our mama is? Did she make it to the City?" Clo demanded.

"We can't trust this guy, Clo," El said.

"I just want to know!" Clo insisted.

There's no way the Crying Man could have understood our language, but he understood the tension between us. "Your sister is right, Chloe Yetti. You should not trust me. But your mother has done what none other has: she has taken the fight to the heart of the City."

"So she made it?"

"Yes, but her mission is not complete. You must take further steps if Yerba City is to be defeated."

El looked at him suspiciously. "Why don't *you* just do it?"

"Yeah," Clo said, remembering. "Back at the Oggy, you made the creek stand still, and the wind stop blowing."

"If you can do all that," El finished the thought, "you can handle a few spiders, can't you?"

He ignored our question. "If you can help your brother, the three of you might be able to finish what your mother started."

"How can we help him?" Clo asked, glancing back at Dyre. "By the way, I think he pooped himself."

The Crying Man sighed. He seemed unused to speaking to such uncouth creatures as ourselves. "There are people—survivors, not unlike yourselves—who live in the shadow of Yerba City's domain. She allows them a village to the east of the city. They call themselves Subversives."

"They also refuse treatment," Clo guessed.

The Crying Man nodded, we thought maybe impressed with how quickly we caught on. "Yes. They also pray for an end to the Chimera's rule. They will help you."

"Why don't you come along instead of lurking like a turkey?" El asked, suspicious. "Help us out, if we both want the same thing."

The Crying Man looked south into the darkness. "This is the closest I may approach. We have . . . an agreement."

"You mean a treaty," El guessed. "You're like her, aren't you? A Sour Apple. You're one of those Jolly Rancher artificial flavors after all."

The Crying Man snorted, utterly disdainful of the thought. "Yerba City and I are nothing alike. You'd do well to remember that."

"How are we supposed to get to this Subversive village, anyhow? We're out of gas. Unless you can point us to some diesel fuel."

"Two hundred meters past the east side of the warehouse, you'll find another gathering station."

"'Gathering station'?" El scoffed. "You mean one of those minimarts with freaky spiders and a Tik-Tok nurse? No, thank you."

"The dispensing agents have all been eliminated, but there is a small ground transportation unit that still functions. Take it toward the city, but stop before you get to the bridge. There you'll find the village."

"Well, that's convenient," Clo grunted.

From the south, just visible through the dark and a thickening fog, a small light appeared. It was moving toward us. As children we would have guessed it to be an airplane, but, the present being what it was, it could be only one thing: one of the Chimera's drones.

"I have to go," the Crying Man said, obviously trying to downplay the fact that he was being chased from the area. "Remember, you *must* stop before the bridge. Do *not* take your brother into the city without making contact with the Subversives."

"How are they going to cure him?"

"They will know what to do. His infection is . . . familiar to them." He didn't move from his floating spot in midair; rather, he just began to fade away.

"Wait!" Clo said. "You never told us who you are."

"And don't just mysteriously say, 'A friend,'" El added.

The Crying Man looked down at us, his sunken face cold as it faded into blackness. "Even if you can stop the City, you Yettis and I will never be friends." He disappeared entirely. "I have no friends." His voice echoed strangely in the darkness.

We stood still for a moment, just looking at the emptiness. *"Well, he was creepy."*

Clo eyed the light in the sky, still approaching. *"Do you think that thing is gonna spot us?"*

"It probably already has."

Dyre mumbled again, a low growl through his muffling gag. El popped her head in to look at him. *"We've got to get him talking English again. Otherwise they're going to keep on trying to get him on the Sap."*

"Yeah," said Clo, holding her nose, *"and it'd be nice to clean up the poop too."* She gagged. *"Oh God, it's like when he was a baby."*

El stood on the Defender's bumper and tried to see into the distance east of the warehouse. She could just make out the blinking blue light of the so-called gathering station. *"Do you think it's true what the Crying Man said? That there's a vehicle over there? That there are people somewhere who can help us?"*

"It'd be nice to meet some other people that aren't Tik-Toks," Clo said wistfully. *"Like maybe a nice boy. Who could hunt . . . and stuff."*

El rolled her eyes. *"C'mon, let's take care of this boy first,"* she said, grabbing Dyre by the shoulders. *"Then you can chase some of your own."*

We carried Dyre about halfway to the station before setting him down. He wasn't struggling much now; our guess was that he was getting weak from a day's thrashing around.

"Ugh," Clo complained, *"why'd I have to get the butt end?"*

We tried to scout out the station from our current position, ready to make a run for it if we encountered another spider rush. Of course, where we would run to at this point was another matter not fully considered, but in any case, the station appeared to be abandoned, in line with the Crying Man's description.

El went ahead, peering into the nurse's booth and carefully scanning the dusty overhang, as best she could in the low light. No nurse. No spiders. And sitting in the middle of the dusty platform was apparently some kind of car. It had four plastic-looking wheels that were filled not with air, but rather with four round layers of dusty honeycomb. It had a beetle-like silver carapace. The thing looked like it might be able to hold four people, but there were no headlights, no doors, and no difference between the front and the back. It was sort of like if a giant silver pill bug had folded up, and then someone had cut it in half and put wheels on it.

"This must be the vehicle," El said skeptically. *"But how do we open it up? There's no door handle or anything."*

Clo dragged Dyre the rest of the way up onto the platform. We weren't being particularly gentle or accommodating to our little brother, considering his condition. But then, we never really had been.

"Maybe you just talk to it," Clo said. *"Remember, there were machines you could just talk to? Like, 'Alexis, please buy me a boyfriend.' Or 'Mimi, tell me some fart jokes.'"*

El shrugged. "Harold, fart us into Yerba City."

Nothing.

"Harold?" Clo asked her sister skeptically.

"I don't know." El was stumped. *"He looks like a Harold."*

"Looks more like a pill bug to me."

"Yes, a pill bug named Harold."

"Maybe the name is written on the bumper."

"There's no bumper. Or license plate. Or headlights or taillights or anything."

"Hmm," said Clo, leaning down to look underneath the vehicle. *"Maybe his name is written undernea—"*

And as she put her palm on the vehicle, it hummed to life. True, it didn't have any headlights, but the entire body of the thing began to glow, lighting up the dusty station as well as the crumbling area around it. Clo stood up, surprised, and looked at the palm of her hand. *"Whoa. Guess that's it. But how do you—"*

Before she could ask how to open the car, it opened, the shell cracking in half and lifting apart like a giant clam.

El walked to the edge of the now-lit platform and looked up at the sky. *"We must stick out like a firefly now. If that drone didn't see us before, it sure has now."*

"You think it's going to send more spiders after Dyre?"

El saw something on the ground and nodded at it. *"Speaking of which."*

Clo looked. Lying legs up on the ground, just off the station platform, was a dead Subantoxx "dispensing agent," as the Crying Man called it. This one wasn't a spiderbot, but was definitely another kind of arthropod-inspired creation. Its body was bigger, the size of a raccoon, with eight stumpy hooked legs and a long tail that ended in the all-too-familiar blue needle. The remains of four shattered wings stuck up in the air.

"Looks like a mosquito humped a wiener dog," Clo mumbled.

El got a little closer to check out its shattered metal-and-plastic body. Not too close. *"Its head's missing,"* she noted.

"You think the Crying Man did that for us?"

"Hmm. I don't think it's his style to actually fight anything." She paused. *"Naw, this happened a while ago. Like that buck lock back at the makeup counter. Guess these Jolly Ranchers have been fighting each other for a while."*

"Yerba City, the Crying Man, Squid-Bambi. Who else is up in this feud?"

Before El could answer, Dyre mumbled again. Persistent bugger was still fighting. Couldn't blame him. He was a Yetti, after all.

"There's the road." El pointed to a silvery path, maybe five feet across, which snaked away from the platform southward into the night, toward Yerba City.

"C'mon," Clo said. *"If we're gonna ride this donkey, let's get the rodeo started."*

CHAPTER 9

TENT CITY

We peered wearily inside the open door of the sleek, round vehicle. It appeared to be primarily designed for passengers lying down, or at least reclined. The lounge-like white seats were plush and antiseptic-looking, something we were very unused to after years of living in the forest. We looked down at our bound brother.

"Should we just put him in there?" Clo asked. *"Where do we sit?"*

"I think we just lie down inside next to him," El said, looking at the ergonomic contours inside the vehicle. *"I really don't like this."*

"Yeah, it's all . . . clean." Clo sniffed the space suspiciously.

"Do you think it's safe?" El asked. *"Spiders hiding in there?"*

"Lemme check," Clo said. She pulled out her serrated hunting knife with a *shing!* and began stabbing wildly at the seat cushions and every corner of the vehicle. After about thirty seconds, there wasn't an inch in the pill bug car that didn't have a stab or slash on it. Whitish fluffs of polyester stuffing floated gently to the floor around and outside the car.

"I think it's okay," Clo puffed, breathing heavily.

"All right." El nodded.

"What's our gear like?"

El checked her pack and quiver. *"Hatchet. Nineteen arrows, two throwers. My bow. Some deer jerky. Two doses of Prophanol. One water-skin. You?"*

"I got Toothy." She spun the knife in her hand.

El sighed. *"Well, this is it."*

Confident there was no immediate danger, we hoisted Dyre into the pill bug. Clo turned and waved into the darkness in the direction of our lonely orange Defender.

"Bye-bye, Bouncy McBounceface. We'll see you again someday!" Clo turned back to the sleek pill bug, tossed in Vambi's severed biomechanical head, and squeezed in after it, avoiding the fangs and blowing puffs of polyester off it.

"Do we really need to bring that thing?" A bit of black gunk was still oozing from the eye socket where El had shot it.

"Don't you think we should? Maybe it'll help him. Like bringing the spider that gave you the bite to the doctor."

Besides, El could tell by the way Clo held it that she was proud of conquering the evil robo-deer. Maybe it was our way of showing the other Tik-Toks that we weren't going to be intimidated.

El got in and lay down on the other side of Dyre. He grunted and squirmed between us, but his restraints held. We lay still for a moment, looking around the inside of the vehicle. We had only just taught ourselves to drive that morning, so it hadn't immediately struck us that the interior of the vehicle had no controls whatsoever.

"How does it—" But before Clo could finish the question, the shell of the pill bug slowly began to close up. It was suddenly very claustrophobic inside. We saw no buttons or levers or anything to indicate that we'd be able to open the shell again.

We both had a bad feeling about this. Could the advice of the Crying Man be trusted? What if he was just working for the City, a slightly more charismatic—if super creepy—agent, pretending to help stragglers while really delivering them into her clutches? Ten years before, those AMTaC vans could show you anything your subconscious might think of just to get you boxed up. Was this any different?

These and other super unpleasant thoughts coursed through our minds as the pill bug began to move, rolling off the platform and onto the silvery road toward the City. It moved smoothly on its honeycombed tires, giving us a very different experience from riding in Bouncy. In comparison, it almost didn't seem like we were moving at all except that we could see the retreating station through the transparent shell.

"Welcome to your autonomous ride." The male voice was smooth. "Please relax and enjoy your journey into Yerba City." We finally saw a small black band in the vehicle's wall, where the soothing male voice was coming from.

"How long will it take?" Clo asked the speaker. She pushed the grunting Dyre over a bit. "Our brother's real sick and he pooed himself."

The voice just kept talking, not responding to her question. "If your Subantoxx supply becomes low, please use the temporary supplemental patches located on either side of the vehicle."

"It can't talk back," El concluded, making sure to use our crypto-phasia in case anyone was listening in. *"It's just a recording."* She looked down at the side of the car next to her and shooed away more of the polyester stuffing Clo had gouged out of the vehicle. Indeed, there was a strip of square blue patches that could be pulled out like a roll of tickets.

"Place a patch on your wrist or neck and wait thirty to forty seconds for administration," the pill bug explained calmly.

Clo flicked at one of the patches.

"Don't," El snapped. *"It's the Sap."*

"They sure do make it easy to get hooked," Clo noted.

"Mama said it's all over the world," El contemplated. *"Not sure what we're gonna do if the City starts spraying with drones again. We only have two doses of Prophanol, and there's three of us."*

We rolled past the collapsing Ikea warehouse and began to pick up speed. El looked around the vehicle. *"There's no controls, but I don't think there are any cameras looking at us, either."*

"Isn't that a good thing?" Clo asked, rustling through our provisions. *"Yerba City won't see us coming. Jerky?"*

"Sure," El said and reached over to take a strip of meat. She thought out loud as she ate. *"This car didn't know we were coming, doesn't know who we are."*

"Well, this car can't even talk back." Clo tapped on the speaker. "Can you, Harold the pill bug?"

"But the nurse didn't know, either, and neither did Vambi, neither did Santa."

"What's your point?" Clo asked, her mouth full of meat.

"Mama said they would have to talk to each other," El remembered, chewing. *"With words. And the Tik-Tok nurse's radio wasn't working, remember? But why would a robot even need to talk on the phone like that?"* She swallowed. *"When we were kids, Mama's phone just knew what was on everything. Except that cheap OwlPad."*

Clo chuckled slightly. *"Yeah, Mama knew when I was talking to Miles McCrae down the block. She was mad I had a boyfriend."*

"I think she was mad because Miles turned out to be a pervy chatbot."

Clo thought for a moment. *"Oh yeah,"* she remembered. *"But it didn't matter, because he loved me."* She sighed wistfully.

"He was just an algorithm," El scolded.

"Well, nobody's perfect," Clo said dreamily and swallowed some more jerky.

"Anyway," El continued, *"back then, the machines didn't have to literally talk to each other, because they were networked. Now the machines are all 'evolved,' but they chat with each other like people in an old-time movie."*

"Maybe Yerba City is dying," Clo offered. *"Falling apart from the inside. Mama always said it would fail someday. Everything does."*

"Then why didn't Mama come back?"

We both became quiet, just looking out the window as the landscape zipped by and chewing on our jerky. It was nice to be lying down after the long day's drive in Bouncy. El, who had done most of the driving, actually nodded off. Soon Clo did, too. The padded seats, although now half-gutted, seemed to have been made for just such a purpose. The car was traveling fairly slowly, maybe thirty miles an hour at the most, and it moved so smoothly, we dreamed we were floating down a river, two quiet sticks of dynamite, toward a beaver dam made of metal shards manned by red-eyed robo-beavers. Finally we floated silently down to the edge of the dam, tapping slightly in the eddies and swirls, and *BOOM!*

—

We awoke with a start. "Look!" Clo barked.

El sat up. Off in the distance, we could see lights, piercing through the darkness. It had been so long since we'd seen artificial lights at night, we couldn't help but gasp. It was beautiful, like a golden sunset lake that was still shimmering even though the sun had gone down. Like a field of glittering fireflies, gathering on the ground for some unknown evolutionary ritual, while above, a score of drones moved back and forth.

"Doesn't look like Yerba City is dying," Clo mumbled.

"It's beautiful," El admitted.

The pill bug sped up; the lake of lights was approaching quickly. *"Look right there."* Clo pointed. *"Are those donkeys?"*

Two six-legged horse-sized machines were dismantling something next to the autonomous track we were on. They did look a bit like donkeys, except instead of a head, each had a large retractable arm it was using to dismantle the underside of a flipped eighteen-wheeler. A dog-like thing with a large buzz saw for a head was crawling inside the guts of the big rig, cutting off chunks in a shower of sparks, while the donkeys used their head-claws to stack pieces of metal onto their backs.

"They're scavenger drones," El observed, *"probably recycling."*

"Guess Yerba City is green." Clo snorted sarcastically. *"Very eco-friendly."*

The truth of the matter was a lot less charming: the City was slowly dismantling the once-harvested resources of the world and repurposing them for her own insidious agenda. What was she building? Wasn't turning the entire human population into a planet of junkies enough?

We were getting deeper into it now: there were more machines moving around, about two every quarter mile, and more lights in the sky. Most of what we saw on the outskirts seemed to be scavenging machines, taking apart the remnants of what were once suburbs of the Bay Area. Dog- and donkey-sized things built for the sole purpose of dismantling the useful materials still left in the crumbling remains of the Old World. There were no mean-looking war bots, no tanks or skull-headed Terminators hell-bent on destroying invaders. In fact, there were no defenses at all, not even cameras. At least none that we could see. Here, closer to the heart of darkness, even the needle-y spiders and dragonfly wiener dogs we had seen earlier were missing. And then it struck us: none of those things were needed. Those mean-looking contraptions—and probably the comfortable car we were in—were only deployed in the hinterlands, to pick up stragglers. Here, Yerba City existed unchallenged.

"You see any people?" El asked, scanning the surreal landscape for anything that might help us get through this.

"No, not even any Tik-Tok people."

El nodded. *"Maybe it's like Mama said: everyone is 'in treatment.'"*

"What about those Subversives the Crying Man mentioned?" Clo wondered. *"Do you think he was just lying?"*

"We'll know soon enough," El said, pointing. *"There. I think I see the bridge he told us about."*

Clo squinted into the darkness toward the southwest. *"That's not the Golden Gate Bridge."*

"No, that got blown up when we left, remember?"

"Oh yeah."

"I think that's the Bay Bridge."

"I remember now. Papa used to call it the Emperor Norton Bridge, after a guy who wore a beaver on his head." Half-recalled memories of our childhood began to flow back as we peered at a white spire in the distance, lit by the largest grouping of lights on the opposite bank. We realized that must be the center of the City.

Clo's vision shifted to the other horizon, over the mountains. *"Hey, the sun's coming up!"*

"Wow, how long were we asleep?"

"It's this car," Clo complained, blowing a bit of fluff off her nose and pushing her hands into the plush seat. *"It's so comfy we must have slept for hours, even without the Sap."*

El shook her head. *"Well, let's get frosty. Our stop must be coming up. Remember, the Crying Man said we have to get off before we cross the bridge."*

Clo looked around for a button or something. *"Hey, how do we stop this thing?"*

"Hmm." El also searched. *"It must be made just to take people in for treatment, nothing else."*

"*Isn't there, like, an emergency brake or a panic button or something?*"

El's movements were becoming more urgent. "*Shamblers wouldn't be able to use something like that, so maybe they just left that stuff out.*"

"*Hey! There!*" Clo pointed out the window. About one hundred yards from the silvery autonomous road sat various ramshackle structures cobbled together from old bits of wood, pipes, and tarps. It wasn't much to look at, something like the hardscrabble but organized rows of a refugee camp, but to us, seeing a real working human habitat in the dawn's first light, it was like a glorious city on a hill.

"*The village!*" Clo shouted. "*He wasn't lying!*"

We were so excited. "*Are there people?*"

"*I don't—*" Clo was scanning. "*There! There's smoke!*"

El nodded at the sight of black soot coming from a small chimney in one of the shacks. "*Must be a cooking fire! C'mon, there's got to be a way to stop this thing!*"

Clo knocked on the speaker. "Harold! Stop the car. Stop the car now!"

"*It's just a dummy!*" El said, feeling desperately under the seats for something, anything. Outside, the bridge was getting closer.

Then Clo spotted someone coming out of one of the weathered tents, about fifty yards away from the road: a young man, yawning and stretching in the early-morning light, like someone getting ready for work. He was probably about our age, with ruddy cheeks and dark hair, and was wearing a ragged gray hoodie and jeans. He didn't look sick, or in treatment; he just looked like someone who had grudgingly committed to the first shift of some dull but necessary drudgery, and would rather be back in bed. He took a moment to spray-paint something on the side of his tent with a small pen-like device. "TOB-1," he wrote in multiple colors, a quick work of art that joined dozens of others on his abode. As our car passed closer, he pulled back his hoodie and turned toward us. He had green eyes, lit like emeralds in the morning light. He was *fine*.

"*Oh, thank you, Mother Oggy,*" Clo said.

"*What? What?*" El asked quickly, still searching inside the car. She thought an angel must have appeared to help out. Either that, or a juicy pig was in sight.

"*There's a cute boy outside!*"

El turned. She wasn't lovestruck by the sight, like Clo, but it was still the first new person we'd seen in a decade. *"Wow. Okay, he is cute!"*

Outside, the young man locked eyes with Clo. Crystalline beauty aside, those eyes were befuddled but kind, and the first real human eyes she had seen in ten years that were not a family member's. From inside the car, Clo called out to him. "Hey! Hey!" She waved and pounded on the glass of the car's canopy. The young man waved back and, despite the confused look on his face, smiled at Clo.

Even from inside, we could hear him shout, "Hello!" He grinned, then caught himself with a meek look—apparently you weren't supposed to yell at the top of your lungs in the village first thing in the morning. Instead he waved, beckoning to us.

"He waved back!" Clo panted like an eager puppy. *"Okay, that's it!"* she announced and pulled out her knife. She jammed the blade into the seam of the pill bug's carapace and pried the gap as wide as she could.

We (especially El) had thought that Yerba City would have designed these autonomous vehicles more like little police wagons, making every joint and crack impenetrable, but that did not appear to be her MO. The City had apparently never needed to create a police state, because the Sap was doing all of her enforcement. Once the drug was administered, either by coercion or compulsion, people went willingly.

We would not be going willingly.

Clo forced a crack open, about half an inch. *"It's moving!"* The gap spread wide enough that we could feel the car fill with the morning breeze, and along with it, the unmistakable smell of human habitation: a campfire, morning bread baking, an open latrine.

The automated voice chimed. "Please do not attempt to exit the vehicle while moving. We will be arriving soon in Yerba City."

"C'mon!" Clo ordered El. *"Let's double-team it."* Excited, Clo dropped Toothy, braced herself on her back, and pressed with both feet to pry the canopy open even farther. El pushed Dyre aside and joined her. The two of us strained and pushed at the canopy, and with a loud *CRACK*, the curved door gave way.

The vehicle began to slow, and the automated voice chimed, "This vehicle's structure has been compromised. Decelerating for safety."

We weren't going to wait for the car to stop. Clo sheathed her knife, El grabbed her pack, and we both grabbed Dyre and jumped out of the vehicle at about twelve miles an hour. We stumbled, and Dyre went into a grunting, floppy roll. Poor guy, he really had been through a lot in the last twenty-four hours.

We got to our feet quickly, not bothering to dust off. The car kept going, slowing dramatically but continuing at a slow pace until it moved out of sight.

We'd landed about a hundred yards away from a marketplace of sorts, small stalls set up among the makeshift tents. Already we could see people staring, talking, pointing. We had made it to the village.

The young's man shout had apparently spread like wildfire, and a small group was moving toward us. We each grabbed Dyre under an armpit and dragged him off the platform and toward them. We must have been quite a sight: two redheaded girls in buckskins dragging their bruised-up little brother around. But despite our disheveled hinterfolk look, the villagers really weren't much better. Their outfits had clearly been cobbled together by looting big chain retail stores, and that had to have been over a decade ago. Their bright red polo shirts and wispy patterned autumn dresses were now reduced to rags, sewn and resewn and piled on three or four layers deep to make up for the holes that had developed over time. So they weren't winning any fashion awards, either, but they were smiling to see us. It seemed they didn't get too many visitors.

"*Wow,*" El whispered to Clo as we approached them. "*People. And they're not on the Sap. I didn't think there'd be so many left. A whole village.*"

Clo paused. "*How do we know they're not Tik-Toks?*"

El stopped, too, her eyes scanning the approaching villagers. There were about a dozen of them now, emerging from the alleys of the shantytown, chatting among themselves and pointing at us. El sniffed the air.

"*Hmm,*" she mused, exhaling and inhaling again through her nose. "*They kind of smell like poo,*" she concluded. "*I don't think the Tik-Toks go poo.*"

"*Maybe they're 'evolved' units.*"

"*Like, so evolved they poo now?*"

Clo nodded.

"*That would be pretty evolved. We're going to have to take that chance.*" El used her free hand to wave at the small crowd. "Hello!"

"Hello!" A middle-aged man with a short graying beard waved back. "Welcome to the Drag." He had kind eyes. Most of the other folk seemed a bit hesitant, but this guy exuded an optimistic spirit of hospitality, the kind that felt any passing stranger deserved help, no matter who they were. A real nice guy.

"We sure could use some help!" El called, hefting Dyre again. Clo supported his other side. "It's our brother. He's got problems."

The man came up to us, but looking at Dyre, at his bound wrists that were rubbed raw. "Well, I see his problem: he's been hog-tied like an animal for the better part of a day."

"We had to do it!" Clo insisted. She was so excited to finally be talking to other actual people that she was talking super fast. "He attacked us. You see, Mama left, and he went into the forest, and made friends with a vampire deer, and then it took over his mind, and then it grew a bunch of tentacles, and then we killed it, and then he stayed crazy, so then we had to tie him up, and then we got in Bouncy—"

"Hold on," the man interrupted. "Can he still turn down Santa?"

Clo looked at him blankly. "Turn down Santa?"

"You mean, can he still refuse treatment," El said, picking up his meaning. "Don't think so. He's just been babbling since it happened."

"Quick, then"—the man looked up at the sky—"let's get him inside, right now." He grabbed Dyre by his collar and nodded to a teenager next to him. "Joey, grab his pants." To us he said, "Lift by his clothes. You're cutting off the circulation to his hands and feet if you hold his limbs." It seemed like this guy was used to giving orders, and what he was saying made sense, so we complied. We were used to hauling deer and whatever else we killed around the forest, but we weren't accustomed to carrying living things in need of medical attention.

"Sorry, he pooped himself," Clo confessed as the four of us lifted Dyre.

"It's okay, this whole place smells like a crapper," the man said. "We've been forced to use open latrines for years now. The City won't allow plumbing. I'm Bradley, by the way."

"Chloe. Clo."

"Elizabeth. El."

"Clo. El. This is Joey." Bradley nodded to the teenager.

"Hi," Joey said. The four of us hastily moved Dyre out of the marketplace. A small crowd was gathering around us.

"We should get him to the hospital right away," a woman nearby said. She couldn't have been over forty but her face looked worn from years of postapocalyptic worry.

"Good idea, Linda," Bradley said, nodding down a shantytown alley. "Let's move. If a drone sees him, they're gonna send Santa, and if he can't personally object, they're gonna take him."

"We had that 'consent' problem already, back on the road," El said.

"Spiders?" Bradley guessed.

"Yeah, and a crazy nurse. Left us alone, but they came after Dyre because he couldn't . . . object."

"This whole place is Subversives?" El asked. "Or, objectors?"

Bradley nodded. "Used to be over a thousand of us quarantined here, at first. But over the years, most folks . . . stopped objecting to treatment. Or just got too old and tired to object. Then Yerba City takes them. Just about two hundred of us left now, give or take."

Clo looked back at the crowd of about a dozen that was following us. "Um, there was this young guy, dark hair, green eyes, about six feet tall."

"Clo, let's help Dyre first," El grumbled.

"Right here," Bradley said and led us inside the hospital tent.

The "hospital" wasn't much more sanitary than the rest of the shantytown, but it did have a cot, and a dented tool cabinet that presumably held some medical supplies. Next to the cot was a bucket of dirty brown water.

"This is the hospital?" Clo said. We set Dyre down on the cot. "It's not what I remember."

"Tell me about it. I used to be a doctor. Yerba doesn't allow us any supplies. Everything we've got we've had to scavenge." Bradley went to wash his hands in the brown water. "Water comes from the creek that runs through the village. It's actually pretty clean."

Our small crowd had followed us inside and were making comments. They were acting like it had been a long time since the village had seen strangers—years, maybe. Clo searched among them for the young man.

"Why don't you leave? Head into the woods like we did?"

"It's a quarantine," Bradley said. He was examining Dyre, looking into his eyes and trying to get him to follow a finger. He kept talking to us as he worked. "The drones—and other things—won't let us past the bug road you came in on. Only way you can go is across the bridge into the City itself. That's why we call our village Hotel California."

"What?" El asked.

"Too young?" Bradley smiled to himself. "Because you can check out any time you like, but you can never leave." His face turned serious, almost sad. "I'm afraid, now that you've set foot in the quarantine zone, she won't let you go back to the woods. Sentry drones'll taze you before you can get ten feet."

El looked at Bradley and raised herself up, trying to sound as confident and grown-up as possible. "Doesn't matter. We're not going back."

"That's right," Clo said, joining in the bravado. "As soon as Dyre is better, we're going into the city to find our mama."

Bradley's gaze went quickly back and forth between us two girls. He finally took in our buckskin outfits, handmade weapons, wild looks, half-feral demeanors.

"You all have been out there for a while? Living on your own?"

"Since the End of the World," Clo said proudly.

"World's still turning last time I checked," Bradley countered.

"Mama took us out there when we were little girls," El explained.

"But we're women now. We hunt, we butcher, and we survive."

"That I don't doubt." Bradley took out a mirrored device for looking into eyes, one that didn't use power. "But it's not the same world you left."

Finally the young graffiti artist came in through the open tent door. Clo saw him instantly.

"Well, we could hang out in this new world for just a quick second." And then she was in the young man's face, looking up at him, grinning. He was a bit taken aback, but didn't seem to mind too much as he took in her freckled face.

"Hi," she said sharply, not taking her eyes off him.

"Uh, hi," he answered back, smiling wide himself.

"I'm Clo."

"Clo?" He said it slowly, like he was trying to get it right.

"Yeah." She nodded like a chipmunk, eyes still locked with his, unblinking. "What's your name?"

"Tobias," he said slowly.

"Tobias," Clo said, nodding. "That's nice. Think fast, Tobias!" Clo hauled off and straight up punched him in the gut. Not full strength, but enough to get a little sting.

"Ow!" Tobias grunted, surprised, and stumbled back a foot.

"*Clo!*" El scolded. *"Don't punch people you just met! He's not our brother!"*

"What?" Clo asked, then realized. "Oh, sorry. I didn't mean that. Just playing around!" She shrugged and laughed nervously, putting both hands behind her back.

Tobias rubbed his gut, but didn't stop smiling at Clo despite the sucker punch. "It's okay. Just didn't expect it. I'm not much of a fighter."

"No fighting?" Clo asked. Then, quickly, "Okay, no problem. Do you hunt? You a good hunter?"

"Do I—hunt?"

"Yeah? Like, out in the woods? Like, go for a walk with me in the woods? And we'll hunt—together—all day? And all night?"

Tobias seemed dumbfounded.

El sighed. Bradley took sidelong note of their exchange as he opened the old tool chest. "Didn't have too many other boys out there in the woods with you, did you?"

"It was just our family," El said, trying to redirect the conversation away from her boy-crazy sister to Dyre. "Can you help him?"

"Well, I don't know what's wrong with him. Doesn't show any signs of disease or concussion." Bradley pulled a rusted pair of medical scissors from the tool chest. "Restraints aren't doing him any good." As he had been for the past twenty-four hours, Dyre was still struggling against his bonds. "Why did you say you had to tie him up again?"

"Well, he came out of the woods talking all strange," El explained, "and he had this Tik-Tok deer with him that grew a bunch of tentacles. It was like it took over his mind or something. Before that we saw Santa Claus."

Bradley gave her a look.

"You think we're crazy? That we just tied him up for fun? We haven't done that for years!"

"No, no," Bradley assured her. "By Tik-Tok, I take it you mean robotic? It was a mechanical deer?"

"Yeah. With fangs! Oh, we forgot its head, back in the pill bug!" El lamented, and then realized this didn't make her sound any less crazy. "Anyway, you ever see anything like that around here?"

"No." Bradley sighed. "But we get Santas. We get Santas all the time. Spiders. Locusts. And Yerba City does experiment with different kinds of walking or crawling things. Maybe she was experimenting on you."

Dyre grunted.

"But this . . . aggression," Bradley explained, looking thoughtfully down at Dyre. "This isn't her style. To fight, to kill someone. It's just not something she's ever done. She thinks of herself as nonviolent."

"That horde of spiders trying to stick us didn't seem very nonviolent," Clo interjected, taking a moment away from her crush to join the conversation from across the tent.

"Everything she does is to get the Sap in you. I've never seen or heard of her trying to hurt someone just for the sake of it. Are you sure he didn't just have a nervous breakdown?"

"And try to shoot his own sister with an arrow? The Crying Man said you'd know what to do."

"The Crying Man?"

"Yeah, tall guy. Pale skin. Wears a fancy black suit with an orange sash. Only comes out at night. Very creepy."

"And he can float through walls," Clo added. "You don't know him?"

"No," Bradley said calmly. He looked around the room at the other villagers. "We don't know any floating man." We could tell they were starting to think we were really crazy.

"He told us where this village was. Even pointed out the pill bug we had to use to get here. We probably never would have made it if it wasn't for what he told us."

"Well, he seems like a very well-informed individual." Bradley was struggling to stay reasonable. "Let's thank the Crying Man after we help your brother." He turned back to Dyre. "You mind if I try just talking to him? I used to do some grief counseling back in the day. PTSD stuff. We've all been under a lot of stress. Maybe I can talk him down."

"Sure, talk away. He was sounding pretty crazy, though. Wasn't even speaking English."

"Let's give it a whirl. We can always gag him again, right? What's his name?"

"Dyre."

"Dire? As in dire straits?"

"It's spelled with a *y*, but yes."

He turned to Dyre and spoke loudly and slowly. "Okay, Dyre, I'm Bradley. I'm a doctor, and I'm here to help you. Everyone here is going to help you. I know you've been through a lot. We all have, but we're all going to do our best to get through this." He set the bandage scissors against the gag tied across the back of Dyre's head. "I'm going to take your gag off now. We're all friends here. And I want you to tell me what happened out in the forest."

He cut. It wasn't easy. Of course, we had made the gag like we would all ties: strong leather strips, three times over. After all, we'd had to make sure he couldn't chew through it.

Bradley did his best to cut the gag off, but it was taking a while. "This is a . . . pretty strong gag," he said, sweating.

El nodded. "Mama always said tie thrice to make it nice."

"Uh-huh," Bradley mumbled and finally sawed through the third cord with the rusty scissors. The gag popped off and Dyre spat it out.

"Nos De Roowa Kon Maa," he chanted, without missing a beat. Practically a full day had gone by; he'd been stabbed in the leg, knocked out, hog-tied, bounced around, and hadn't slept a second as far as we knew. But still he chanted that string of words as if he had just heard it.

"What is that?" Bradley asked. "Sounds . . . foreign. But not . . ." He shook his head as if he was trying to place it.

"Yeah, and he only knows English," Clo said, careful not to mention that we spoke our own secret language as well as English.

"Nos De Roowa Kon Maa." Linda, standing nearby, repeated the phrase, for whatever reason.

"Ugh, don't repeat it," El demanded. The sound of Dyre babbling that stuff, and now someone else, was giving her a headache.

"What? What was that?" Although Dyre was speaking plenty loudly, so clearly that the whole tent could hear it, Bradley leaned in toward Dyre's mouth and began repeating the phrase himself. "Nos De Roowa—"

"It's just gibberish," El chided. "You don't need to understand it. There's nothing to understand!" The words were irritating her, not just because our brother seemed to be insanely obsessed with them, but because there was something strangely compelling about them also. "Look, if you can't help him, we'll just take him—"

Suddenly Bradley stood up and turned around. "Nos De Roowa Kon Maa," he said, to the entire tent but to no one in particular. His face was bright, amazed, as if he'd just heard something he'd been waiting for his entire life. A single tear fell from his left eye.

Most of the dozen or so villagers in the tent answered him back, "Nos De Roowa Soo Mei," or some other slight variation of the phrase. Some of them kept repeating it, and instantly, the medical tent was filled with Babble. People were still joining us, and the moment they entered the tent and heard the words from people they knew and trusted, they immediately began reciting their own versions of the phrase. The whole thing was completely insane: every villager who heard it was immediately possessed by this Babble. Except for Tobias.

Clo turned to him as soon as she realized that the words weren't affecting him. "What's going on?" she asked desperately.

Tobias just shook his head, confused, looking around the room and taking in everyone's strange behavior. "I have no idea."

"Do your people always do this?"

"Uh, no."

Bradley, still babbling, reached into the tool chest and took out a large, rusty scalpel. He went to work on Dyre's bonds.

"Hey, don't do that," El warned him, but it was too late.

"Nos De Roowa Kon Maa," Bradley repeated. Dyre had never stopped babbling, and in moments he was free, standing awkwardly on his half-asleep limbs, and half chanting with the rest of the crowd like they were part of some religious cult. He didn't even stop to rub his limbs. It was like the machine of his body just had to stand up and serve the Babble ASAP.

El backed up, toward Clo and Tobias, the only other people in the tent who weren't babbling along. "What the hell is going on?"

"It's like the words are . . . infecting them," Clo said. She turned to Tobias. "But you're okay, right?"

Tobias was just as confused as we were. "Yeah, I'm okay. But Dr. Bradley, I've never seen him like this—what are they saying?"

"We don't know!" Clo said. "Our brother started doing it yesterday, after he ran into a crazy deer in the woods—"

Dyre pointed to us from across the tent, and everyone turned. Linda was helping him stay upright, and now we saw in her eyes, along with everyone else's, a murderous light. Bradley walked toward us, nonsense words still cascading out of his mouth, gripping the scalpel tight.

We stiffened. Clo found her knife. El brought her fists up. These were ragged, half-starved villagers used to subsisting on dirty water and scraps of trash. We had no doubt we could crack all their skulls with the karate Mama had taught us, if need be. But the look in their eyes was pure kamikaze—every one of them, even the old ladies, was going to pump their adrenal glands dry trying to get a lick in on us. Things were about to get nasty.

"Dr. Bradley!" Tobias tried to talk them down. "Joey. Linda. What's going on? What's wrong with you? These are visitors—"

And before he could even finish his plea, they went for us. Mostly just barehanded, grasping for our faces and necks like a bunch of flesh-crazed zombies. They were disorganized and, as if fueled by a spontaneous hatred, seemingly intent on ripping us limb from limb. But the sudden rush was actually to our advantage, as the gangly teenagers and little old ladies tripped up the more able-bodied babblers coming for us.

All those years of katas came in very handy. We doled out chops and combos, a punch to the temple here and a knee to the jaw there. Tobias just stood there gaping as we broke a few bones, like only we can, and it was only when Clo finally drew blood that we knew this punchfest was going to have to end. Bradley had been sent to the floor with two teeth missing thanks to El's elbow, but he had a death grip on her foot now, while Linda was trying to dig her fingers into Clo's eyes. In one quick arc, Clo brought the blade across both of Linda's palms and then down through Bradley's thumb, severing it. Yet before the digit even hit the ground, they were both back on top of us. And

Bradley hadn't cried out or made the slightest peep at losing such a vital evolutionary appendage.

"They've all lost their marbles!" Clo huffed.

"We can't stop them without killing them!" El screamed.

Tobias rushed forward with something like a nerd's battle cry. He must have had a foot on us, but he'd been right when he confessed he wasn't any kind of a fighter. Still, the sight of blood must have put some spit in him; he picked up a rusty IV bag stand and used it to rush the crowd, knocking them to the ground like a human bulldozer. The babblers were only momentarily fazed, however, reaching past his long arms with their clawing, now-bloody fingers.

"*Get outta here!*" Tobias screamed at us. He seemed to be willing to hold them off, perhaps feeling somehow responsible for the crazed actions of his fellow villagers.

"We can't!" Clo cried. "Our brother's in there!" Indeed, Dyre must have regained enough feeling in his extremities to allow him to join the melee, and he pressed forward along with the other babblers and over the feebler converts, apparently eager for revenge.

El gave a spinning hook kick to a ragged-looking old man, who took it with gusto before going down. "*He's right!*" she called as she landed. "*We gotta rabbit!*"

"*But Dyre—*"

"*He's got followers now! We'll circle back to kick some sense in later.*"

Clo nodded at the tactic, seemingly satisfied that Dyre wasn't going to starve, here with his new death-cult friends. "*Okay—yeah—let them wipe his bottom for a while!*"

El dashed toward the exit, but Clo lunged forward and grabbed Tobias by the collar. "Not letting you go just yet!" she said and yanked him out of the mob.

In that instant, El realized that we were going to have some more boy baggage—this time not our brother. She wasn't sure how well trained Tobias was or if he could hold his own, but she hoped at least he could run on his own. Once the IV stand barrier dropped, there would be no time for physical or mental trials. She saw an old two-by-four holding up the medical structure and gave it a massive kick. The whole tent shook.

"C'mon!" El shouted, and Clo dragged Tobias stumbling out into the mucky street.

CHAPTER 10

PADDINGTON STATION

Dyre and the mob surged forward just as El gave her best jump-up double-foot kick, knocking the two-by-four completely out. The patchwork of heavy tarps came tumbling down, turning the mob into a mass of thrashing garbage-bag ghosts.

"Which way?" Clo shouted.

"Uh . . ." Tobias looked around, trying to decide where to go among the maze of shantytown alleys.

El struggled out of the collapsed tent just as an old, limping Asian man on a crutch hopped up. "Tobias, what the hell is going on here?" he said.

Tobias, eyes wide like a rabbit's, shrugged frantically. "Nick, I don't know!"

"I need my meds." Nick poked at the thrashing ghosts. "What are they doing in there?"

Crazed, Bradley managed to get his head out through a hole in the tent as Clo got El to her feet. "Nos De Roowa Kon Maa!" he growled at the old man.

"Don't listen to it!" El warned, stumbling to her feet.

"What?" the old man said. "*Nos De Roowa Kon* what?"

"Nos De Roowa Kon Maa!" Bradley yelled again, somewhat in sync with the tangled mass underneath him. That's all it took. Nick's face snapped toward us with a crazed look, and he stepped down onto his swollen foot, ignoring whatever debilitating pain he'd once had, and lifted his makeshift crutch like a weapon.

The urgency of the situation was not lost on Tobias. "C'mon, this way!" The three of us took off into the tent city like field mice running from a forest fire.

"Look!" El pointed up at the sky as we ran. Drones, clearly visible in the cloudless morning sky.

Tobias took note. "The scuffle must've brought those drones. They don't like scuffles."

Clo shot the flying machines a dirty look. She was jacked up and holding on to Tobias's hand protectively. "Don't worry, handsome, I'll protect you. I'm all about scufflin'!"

Behind us, the shouts of the babblers, emerging from the collapsed tent, echoed around the village. Some folks were actually still waking up, emerging into the morning air only to yelp loudly and climb back inside at the sight of Tobias leading two armed, fur-clad young women among their makeshift tents.

"Everyone who hears that crap goes crazy," El said. "It's gonna take the whole village."

"Tobias will help us out of here," Clo assured her.

"Why should we trust him?"

"I dunno. Because he's dreamy?"

"This way!" Tobias yelled, apparently ignoring us. "Right here!"

We emerged into an open clearing, breathing heavily, half sighing in our relief at getting out of the junkyard maze. Tobias sprinted about forty yards across the clearing, which was some sort of low concrete platform. The whole space was the size of a football field, built right next to what looked like a giant silver bullet with a row of shiny oval windows along its side.

It was a train: sleek, silver, with an inviting open door. It looked . . . futuristic, we thought. A slick, Tomorrowland-type interpretation of what transportation should look like. The aesthetic was like an insult: it stood in stark contrast to the ramshackle Subversive shantytown that surrounded it, as if the train and station's designers meant to say: "This way to the future—because you sure ain't it."

The expansive platform was about ten inches off the ground, and like a different universe. As we stepped up onto it, we realized something profound: it was perfectly clean. Hundreds of square yards of smooth white concrete, set up specifically for passengers. But what passengers? These ragged villagers? The platform had not a speck of dirt on it, no garbage, no old cans or bottles—it seemed an impossibility in the center of this shantytown. Even the scruffily handsome young man, Tobias, now waving us toward the door of the train, appeared impossibly placed, standing there on the shiny new staircase in his dirty, cobbled-together clothing and tousled hair.

"Here!" He pointed to the entrance to the train, and then above it, where a gleaming sign read, in four simple block letters: "CITY."

Hesitant, we slowly walked toward him. El said, "You want us to go into Yerba City?"

Tobias half shook his head. "It's the only direction she'll let us go from here."

We walked cautiously across the platform, our eyes darting front and back. We were really going to get on that train and ride it right into the heart of the beast? Not that we had much choice; drones were now gathering and descending from every corner of our perception.

Behind us, the now-familiar Babble emerged. They all still barked familiar variations—*Maa, Kon, De,* and so on—but there was something different about it now, the pseudochanting apparently calling for more variation as more people joined in. There was definitely a call-and-response thing going on, with individuals or small groups calling back and forth to each other across the shantytown alleys.

We shot a look at each other. We couldn't understand the Babble, but we knew from our years living off the forest what was going on: each group was checking with the other to see if they'd made contact with the prey.

"They're hunting us," Clo said.

"There's dozens of them now." El nodded to Tobias, who scampered up the walkway to the train. *"Should we follow your dreamboat?"*

"Into the city?" We couldn't believe we were actually considering this out loud, even if only in our own secret language. *"I was kinda*

*thinking we'd go all raccoon through the back to find Mama, not through
the front door like this!"*

"Either this or we stay here and hog-tie the whole village!"

Right about then, the first of the babblers emerged into view of the
platform. Indeed, more villagers, unfamiliar to us, had been caught up
in the mob, some arming themselves with makeshift clubs or cracked-
off dog-ball chuckers sharpened into weapons. Half a dozen or so, still
possessed with that frantic look of anger, spotted us and called in their
weird chant to the others. Babblers quickly manifested out of alleyways and half-torn tarps.

"Looks like we're found," El noted, and in moments the platform
was ringed, lines of villagers surrounding us. The only way out was the
train. El dropped into a combat stance again.

Clo did the same, preparing herself. *"It's gonna take a lot of rope
to hog-tie this whole village."* Familiar faces were emerging from the
crowd. Cranky old Nick, Dr. "One-Thumb" Bradley, Linda, and finally
our brother. Dyre held a mean-looking two-foot-long lawn screw
meant for chaining dogs up, and clearly had the same maniacal deter-
mination as when he'd first attacked us back in the forest. We were
really starting to miss his sullen teenager phase. All the villagers now
had that same steely look in their eye, snarling their continued Babble
like an army of religious fanatics.

We stood back-to-back, ready for the worst. But nothing happened.
"Why aren't they rushing us?" El demanded.

A small triangular formation of drones descended from the sky.
Fat, jolly-looking little things about the size of grapefruits, with bodies
and wings like giant distorted bumblebees. Like the Santa Claus walk-
ers, these were seemingly designed to have a sort of cute, welcoming
effect. Which, as usual, missed the mark and ended up as more Jolly
Rancher weirdness.

"Oh, hello there," one of the bumblebees chirped in a sickly-sweet
feminine voice. "We see you have stepped onto the train platform. Are
you ready for treatme—"

SSKRT! Before it could even finish the question, Clo sliced it out
of the air with her hunting knife, sending the bee to the ground in
a shower of golden slime. "We. Decline. Treatment," Clo growled
through her teeth in staccato.

The two other bumblebees didn't seem to mind seeing their kin cut down in front of them. They moved methodically in midair to maintain their formation as another of the small yellow drones descended from above to re-form the triangle.

El looked up. There were dozens of drones in the sky now, of all different shapes and sizes, all of them vaguely insectoid. *"That's it,"* she said, realizing. *"That's why the villagers aren't rushing us. What the nurse said: if they 'obstruct treatment,' the City will see them as an enemy."*

"What? You mean they aren't just a bunch of chickens?"

El's eyes scanned, straining to consider every possibility. *"Can't go forward, can't go back."*

Tobias called to us from the door of the train. "Hey! C'mon! This is the only way!"

"You reckon he's right?" Clo breathed. *"I'd rather risk getting stuck with a cute boy than torn up by this mob."*

"I think I got it," El said. She turned to the bumblebee drones, who were still beckoning. "Hey, busy bee, we refuse treatment, but we want to go into the city. Will you protect us?"

"Is that possible?" Clo asked her sister. *"I thought treatment was what the City was about."*

The bees buzzed a strange machine language among themselves for a moment, considering. "Of course," the tip of the triangle closest to them finally hummed. "Yerba City always serves for health and safety. Please proceed to the train."

We moved nearer to the train.

"Are you sure about this, El?" Clo asked warily.

"What choice do we have? Besides—look!"

The babbling crowd was getting even more incensed by our retreat. The taboo against obstruction didn't seem to be enough to hold them back anymore. Dyre was the first, taking an angry step onto the platform. Immediately a line formation of three larger drones descended from the sky at a seemingly impossible speed, stopping instantly about six feet from the ground. These were mean-looking locust designs: German shepherd–sized enforcers. Their sharp-winged forms bristled with aggressive machinery, and their formation formed a sort of floating wall between the train and the crowd.

The drones moved in perfect silence, but now that they had reason to, they let out a synchronous warning blast of noise.

"Ow!" Clo said as we both grabbed our ears.

The mob of babblers was only further incensed by this noise, which was apparently meant to be some kind of sonic crowd control. Tobias seemed unaffected. He took a few steps down from the train to grab each of us by the arm and help us up the stairs. This was helpful, because whatever that sound was, it was crippling to our nervous system, although it only seemed to make the babblers angrier.

They ceased the warning siren, and one of the drones spoke directly to Dyre. "Please do not obstruct patients from getting treatment." It spoke in a soft, feminine tone, in stark contrast to its menacing appearance.

"Nos Ee Doowa Don Kaa!" Dyre said in response, and the rest of the mob joined in, adding more variations to the Babble.

"Let's go!" Tobias urged, getting on to the train. "They'll start zapping them soon."

Clo was shaking her head as she reached the top of the stairs, her brain still ringing from the riot control noise.

"What?" El demanded, shaking her head, too. "We can't let them zap our brother!"

"They stun anyone who tries to stop people from going in, and then the dragonflies will drag them back into the village," Tobias assured us, although it wasn't that reassuring. "Look!"

We could hear the hum of the dragonfly's stun cannon warming up even though we were fifty yards away. Just the sound was menacing enough, and blue static was visible, building up around the drone's mouth. Dyre kept walking forward. More babblers walked onto the platform. Two more dragonflies descended.

"Oh, they're gonna hose him good, I can tell," Clo observed. "Maybe that's what he needs: a little lightning-storm therapy to shake him out of it."

"Unless you are consenting to treatment, please step away from the platform," the dragonfly's calming voice commanded Dyre. He ignored it, but kept up his Babble, which joined in unusual synchronicity with the chanting of those around him.

Sure enough, there was a loud cracking sound, and a blue bolt appeared between the dragonfly's mouth and our brother. He convulsed slightly and dropped to one knee, his head down. Although he'd definitely been trouble for the last twenty-four hours (and basically his whole life), we couldn't help but gasp at seeing our kin knocked down like that.

Clo turned to Tobias. "Is he gonna be okay?"

"Uh, yeah," Tobias said. "Wow. Your brother is hard-core. One zap usually knocks someone out for at least a day. He's not even unconscious."

"Well," Clo said, somewhat proudly, "he *is* our brother, so you know he's pretty much a badass buck."

CRACK! CRACK! The two babblers following Dyre also got zapped; one of them was Bradley. He didn't even drop to one knee, just shook a bit.

"I don't think it's that," said El warily. "I think it's that babbling. It's keeping them going."

Dyre rose up and spoke again, his Babble becoming more inhuman, more incoherent. Less like words and more like a series of gurgling sounds. The two other zapped villagers also quickly recovered from being stunned, and they began imitating Dyre's new sound. It was as if getting shocked by the authorities had made them change their tune, literally.

"They're just going to increase voltage until everyone's knocked out," Tobias warned. "That first one was just a little taste."

The villagers surrounding the platform suddenly took up the new sound, like a chorus of crickets that had suddenly found a new conductor.

The dragonfly was preparing another bolt, and from the sound and visible buildup, this next one looked to be twice as strong. But Dyre wasn't advancing, so the machine, in its apparent programming to serve and protect, was not as quick to zap him. "Will you please step back from the platform?" it asked in its sickly singsong voice.

"*BAaRuummMeeAaa—*" Dyre continued, without breaking his speech to actually answer the machine.

"I'm sorry, but '*BAaRuummMeeAaa*' is not—" The drone imitated Dyre's Babble perfectly, but seemed confused when trying to reproduce it. *"BAaRuummMeeAaa* is not—BAaRuummMeeAaa. BAaRuummMeeAaaNaaKeeAaaa—"

The villagers raised their voices in sync with the machine voice of the drone. The lead drone turned in midair and fired its bolt directly into the side of its companion, sending the second dragonfly to the ground in a shower of sparks and flame.

The third drone turned to the first. "Unit 4478, you appear to be malfunctioning. Status report."

The first unit turned to it. "BAaRuummMeeAaa—"

"'BaaRuummMeeAaa' is not—" the third unit responded. *"BAaRuummMeeAaa* is not—*BAaRuummMeeAaaNaaKeeAaaa—"* the machine continued.

"Are the machines . . ." Clo was trying to put it together. "Are they babbling now, too?"

The two dragonflies turned toward *us*, and we could see their mouths charging up.

"Get on the train!" El barked. "Get on the train right now!"

We pushed Tobias through the doorway in a mad panic. El turned to the doorway and tried to pull it shut, her fingers clawing at the rubber lining. "How do we close the door? How do we start moving?"

"Uh, tell Paddington!" Tobias pointed down the train.

Down at the far end, about seventy feet away, was a white man standing stock-still, wearing a crisp blue uniform.

"Start the train!" Clo yelled. "We have to get out of here!"

"Of course." The conductor, smiling, gestured to the two rows of silver-and-chrome seats that lined either side of the train. "For safety reasons, please take a seat." Then we realized he had a black triangle on his forehead.

"It's a Tik-Tok!" Clo said, raising her knife.

Outside, the two babbling drones began shakily maneuvering toward the train. With the defenses seemingly down, the villagers began pouring onto the platform, trying to surround the train. Dyre was leading the way.

"Oh no." El saw them coming, but just then, the door of the train began to shut. "Okay. Good. Now quick, let's get moving!"

The babbling drones hovered menacingly around the train, apparently now preparing their shock treatment for us.

"These things are going to blast us!"

"Start the train!"

"I cannot start the train until you are seated," Paddington stated calmly.

From the size of the shaking blue buildup, it was clear the drones were moments away from releasing maximum voltage right at us when, presumably aware of the disruption, three more drones descended from the sky.

"Units 4472 and 4473, please reiterate the problem cur—" *CRACK!* We instinctively ducked as both of the babbling drones unleashed on the new drone, obliterating it in midair. The concussion shattered the back window of the train, and outside, drone debris hit the ground and scattered over the mob of babbling villagers making their way up the stairs toward the train in a bloodthirsty ecstasy.

Tobias was marveling at the sight as he dusted the shattered glass off the front of his hoodie—he clearly wasn't used to this much action. "Wow, never seen a zap that big before."

The two remaining drones apparently decided they would do best going hand to hand, or rather, podomere to podomere, and they closed in with the babbler drones to grapple and scratch with their sharp insectoid legs. Back in the forest, we had spent a lot of our time thinking about hunting and fighting and killing, and for us this might have actually been the strangest sight on our journey so far—watching the dragonfly drones fight in midair. Like boy yellow jackets during mating season, they went at it with suicidal intent, ripping and tearing at each other's legs, heads, and wings.

"C'mon!" Clo yanked Tobias into a seat and practically sat on top of him. "Let's do what Paddington says. El!"

El nodded, looking away from the mesmerizing carnage outside, and sat down in the seat nearest her. "Okay! We're all sitting down!" Villagers were battering at the door now with the broken IV stand from the medical tent, cracking more of the glass. "Start! The! *Train!*" El yelled.

"Very well." Paddington faced forward, pressed a button, and pushed a small lever. The train shot away from the platform. Good thing we were in our seats, because it was a neck-snapping start. Outside, only Nick, totally forgetting his crutch and now almost youthfully invigorated with the babbling rage, managed to cling on to the train for the first forty feet or so, a clawing one-man show, before being blown to the ground. No doubt the dragonflies would have followed, but they had started up a sort of blue dragonfly dogfight in the air as more and more of the Yerba City sentry drones showed up to see what all the hubbub was about. We watched as the growing aerial battle retreated behind us, along with the frantic mob below.

We breathed a sigh of relief in our seats as the train settled out of acceleration. It was nice not to be pursued by the convert-or-die fanatics, which now apparently included both human and machine zealots. Speaking of machines, Paddington seemed to be satisfied with the functioning of the train, and he turned his attention back to us.

"That thing's coming back here," Clo said, readying her knife. We were still panting from our escape.

The agent was a tall man who looked to be in his late twenties. His brown hair was neat and tidy, and his simple blue uniform, perfectly tailored, appeared impossibly unwrinkled. But the most unnatural aspects of this machine were the supposedly human parts that were visible outside of his uniform: the almost porcelain-white color of his skin; his eyes, which were entirely black; and the small black upside-down triangle in the middle of his forehead. In contrast to the eyes and skin, however, his smile was comforting, almost soothing.

Tobias looked at our combat readiness, at Clo clutching her knife, with a bit of disbelief. "Hey, calm down for a second. You don't need to worry about him. That's Paddington."

Indeed, the conductor seemed calmly subservient as he came closer and produced a small silver tray, which unfolded itself in front of us. "Would you care for an appetizer patch?" Paddington offered. In the middle of the tray were three blue patches, each about two inches square. They were very similar to the one we had seen back in Harold the pill bug, with small circuits visible on the textured surfaces, and there was no mistaking what they were: Subantoxx.

"We decline treatment!" El yelled.

Clo joined in, holding up her knife. "Same here!"

"Hey, you don't need the knife with this guy," Tobias assured us. "He'll leave you alone."

El eyed him suspiciously. "Well, that's good. Some of the other Tik-Toks have been . . . kinda pushy."

"Naw, he's okay." Tobias stood up right next to Paddington and put his arm around the Tik-Tok conductor, a grubby, greasy Subversive next to the perfectly appointed agent. "I named him myself," Tobias explained. "Train. Station. Paddington. There you go, first thing that popped into my head."

"And because he has an English accent?" Clo asked.

"He does?" Tobias looked at Paddington, who didn't return the gaze but just kept staring forward. "I didn't know."

"Don't you hear that fancy 'I'm a British Butler McButlerface' in his voice?"

"No, I don't hear his voice. I'm deaf."

"What?" Clo said, staring at Tobias. "You're deaf?"

"Yeah, I read lips."

Clo was hesitant. "But, wouldn't you speak in sign language if you were deaf?"

"Well, do you speak sign language?" He gestured specifically with his hands as he spoke the last sentence, presumably to see if we could understand it.

"No," Clo conceded. But she stood up and took his hands in hers, locking eyes with him and continuing to breathe heavily. She seemed to be redirecting the recent bursts of adrenaline in another direction. "But I could learn what your big, manly hands were saying, if you wanna teach me."

El, who was significantly more levelheaded about Tobias, considered him for a moment. It was almost unbelievable that Tobias was deaf, but he did talk a little strangely, with an unusual thickness to his voice. Plus there had been a few times when we were running around the alleyways of the village when it seemed like he wasn't listening to us. And of course, there was the most obvious observation.

"That's why the Babble didn't affect you," El concluded. "Because you can't hear it."

"What?" Tobias looked at El. Apparently he was getting too distracted by Clo's batting eyelashes to read her sister's lips.

"Everyone who heard those words coming out of Dyre's mouth became possessed by them. It even affected some of the drones. But not you."

"I couldn't understand what anyone was saying. It was all something like '*Nos De Roowa Ko—*'"

"*Don't say it!*" we both yelled, Clo clapping her hand over his mouth.

"Yes, that's all it was," El pointed out. "That was all *we* heard. But don't repeat those words. They're evil!"

"*Oh, dear Oggy,*" Clo said, quickly and breathlessly, pressing her palm harder against Tobias's face. "*My hand is right on his mouth. I can feel his lips right on my hand.*"

"*Clo,*" El sighed, "*let him go.*"

Tobias looked down with clearly mixed feelings as Clo drew her hand away. "Well, why didn't it affect you two like everyone else?" Tobias asked.

We looked at each other. "That's a good question," El said. "It took over our brother fast enough."

Clo clenched her fist and brought it down to her lap, as if saving the touch of Tobias's mouth for later. "We need to find Mama," she concluded, after quickly composing herself. "Dyre has . . . found some friends. For now. If we find Mama, she can figure out what's wrong with him—what's wrong with all those people."

El nodded. "And she can probably fix them. We just need to find her."

"I'm sorry," Tobias butted in. "Did you say your mama?"

"Yeah," said Clo, reaching into her vest to produce the crumpled photograph. "Do you know her?"

Tobias looked down at the picture. "She's pretty. She's got your eyes."

We nodded in unison. "Yeah."

"Have you seen her?" El asked.

"I don't think so." Tobias tapped Paddington on the shoulder and pointed to the photo. "Paddington, do you know this woman?"

Paddington turned stiffly and focused his eyes on the picture. "No, I'm afraid she's not familiar."

"She would have been through here about four months ago," El said. "She said she had to go to Yerba City."

"There are many ways into Yerba City," Paddington said obligingly. "All are welcome who seek treatment."

"She didn't need treatment. She was clean."

"No one is clean," said Paddington. "Everyone needs treatment. But some will not consent." And with that, he made some unseen command and the tray in his hand began to fold up.

"Oh—uh, hold on there." Tobias reached out and snatched one of the patches before the tray folded away altogether.

"Tobias! You use that stuff?" Clo was shocked, although she had no right to be. We didn't know anything about Tobias other than he was a really cute graffiti artist. And deaf.

"Uh, yeah." He shrugged.

"You're one of those Sappers?" Clo demanded. "A drug addict? A shambler?"

"Well, everyone uses this stuff," Tobias explained meekly.

"I thought you were a decliner," Clo said. "A Subversive. You were living in the village, weren't you?"

"I'd only been there a week. Kind of glad to be on this train. Back there, they had me on latrine duty as part of my obligation to the village collective, and then there's . . . what just happened. The city's better, I think, don't you?"

"Wait," Clo said. "You mean you came to the village from the city just a week ago? From treatment?"

"But treatment's addictive," El said suspiciously. "How did you get out?"

"On this train. It runs all the time."

"All are free to come and go from Yerba City," Paddington explained as he put his tray into a small fanny pack on his belt and began to head back to his position at the front of the train. "No one is compelled into treatment, and no one is compelled to stay in treatment. It is always a personal choice."

El snorted contemptuously. "Mama's explained that false consent to us many times: when some super Sour Apple is calling the shots, 'choice' doesn't mean anything. That's how everyone ended up Sapping themselves."

Clo ignored the philosophical discussion for the moment and tried to find out more about Tobias. "So, how many people besides you go back and forth between the city and the village?"

"Well, actually, I think I've only seen me coming out. Most folks are going in. Subversives from the village who . . . give up." He started to unpeel the back of the patch, apparently getting ready to apply it to himself somewhere.

"Wait," Clo pleaded. "You got off the Subantoxx. Why don't you just stay off?"

Tobias sighed. "Well, it's been about a week. I'm ready to begin treatment again."

"Excellent choice," Paddington called back from the driver's spot, without turning around.

"You stay out of it, you Tik-Tok toady!" Clo growled, but she changed her tone before turning back to Tobias with pleading eyes. "Well, why don't you stay off it . . . for me?"

"For you?"

"Yeah. You owe me." Clo was getting aggressive. This was the former second-grader who'd broken boys' noses if they wouldn't kiss her, after all. "Remember? I saved you back there from all those babblers."

"Uh . . ." Tobias thought about it. "I think I saved *you*."

"Whatever. Look—" Clo switched tactics again, trying to be seductive. Or at least what a raised-in-the-woods eighteen-year-old's idea of being seductive was. She pressed herself up against him. "We could hang out." She tried to sound as sweet as possible, which was unusual for us. We usually weren't very sweet. But then, we weren't used to boys, either. "You could show us around. We could talk. Or not talk. Or do other stuff."

"We could still talk. This is just a little dose." Tobias referred to the patch, which, unfolded, was more of a blue strip now. "It's not like I'm gonna go full squid."

"Full squid?"

"Um, you'll understand when we get to the city." He looked out the window. "Which shouldn't take too long. We're almost on the bridge."

We looked outside: the bridge. What had once been called the Bay Bridge, a shining white example of modern architecture, was now blackened, its asphalt deck full of holes that the morning sun shone through. The immense structure that stretched out across the bay looked almost untraversable, except for a thick silver rail that hung down beneath it. This rail was apparently the only part of the bridge that was still maintained in any way, and we could feel the train slide onto it and over the water.

"It's the ocean!" Clo breathed. Forgetting Tobias for a moment, we pressed ourselves against the nearest window and looked out over the water. It was actually the bay, not an ocean, but we hadn't seen a large body of water like this since Mama had taken us into the forest, and it was marvelous.

"It's beautiful," El mumbled. Lack of human progress for ten years had apparently been good to San Francisco Bay. The water was clear and sparkling.

"Water doggies!" We could see sea lions basking in the sun or casually barking.

"A spouty!" Even a whale was visible beneath us, sending up a jet of foamy spray from its blowhole.

"Sea turkeys!" And there were birds. Hundreds and hundreds of birds of all shapes, sizes, and colors.

"Look, sea parrots!" We were pretty sure we even saw little puffins waddling down at one of the feet of the bridge. Puffins: tiny sea parrots with cute orange beaks, playing in the surf. In the midst of having to kill sweet little deer to stay alive, Mama had taught us it was important to marvel at nature from time to time, and here we were forgetting all about our quest to find her.

"Oh, I wanna eat those little sea parrots so bad," Clo sighed.

We paused our marveling for less than a second to notice that the train was about to pass through a tunnel built into a large rocky island in the middle of the bay. The train was moving so fast now, yet still so silently, that it took only a moment to pass through the half-mile moss-strewn tube. Emerging on the other side of the island, we were blinded by the light at the other end. The train was traveling on the lower deck of the bridge, which would have been entirely in shadow back before the End of the World, but was now leopard-spotted with sunlight due to huge chunks of the upper deck missing. Here once again it seemed that many fires had started over the past decade and just been left to burn, unnoticed. Those bug drones, the train, and its seats and windows were shiny and looked brand-spanking-new, but everything seemed to be built on or into the corpse of a dead—or still dying—civilization.

We couldn't help but be stunned by both the decay of our old world and the sleekness of the new one. We looked up through the carapace window of the train, through the decaying upper deck to see the rusting towers of the western span of the Bay Bridge looming high above us. Our eyes followed the tower as we passed underneath, and then returned to the island we had just passed through.

"*There!*" El breathed in the quick whisper we had used so many times while hunting. She pointed. "*Right there!*"

Clo saw it, too. Up on the cliffside of Yerba Buena Island, the midpoint of the Bay Bridge, was what looked like a small shack built right into the edge of the island. The seemingly cobbled-together wooden structure was just a tiny feature on the face of the cliff, but this organic, human-scale dwelling, built among the proud gray steel girders of the twentieth-century testament to massive human infrastructure, was such a contrast that it couldn't help but catch our eyes. What El was pointing at was not the shack, but a fleeting view of what appeared to be a man in a suit standing in front of it, peering over the edge of the structure into the waters of the Bay far below.

He was out of our view in an instant, and we looked at each other.

"*Was that who I think it was?*" Clo asked.

"*The Crying Man. But what's he doing way out there, and during the day? He said he couldn't go into the city.*" El turned to Tobias. "Tobias, do you know anything about—"

Tobias was sitting in one of the seats, with his head lolling unconsciously against the window.

"Tobias!" Clo cried and lunged over to him. While we were goggling at the wildlife out the window, he had taken the opportunity to stick the blue Subantoxx patch to his neck and nod off.

"You put that thing on!" Clo accused.

Tobias's eyes fluttered open and he looked up at her, smiling. "It's all right, just a little taste . . ." His voice trailed off drunkenly.

Clo snarled, looking at the patch, whose small blue lights blinked as it sent the drug seeping into his system. She clawed at it, but it wouldn't budge, and Tobias just swatted her away.

"Hey," he grumbled. "Leave it. Leave it . . ."

Clo backed away, and Tobias leaned against the window again, smiling. Clo growled and grabbed her knife from her belt sheath with a ringing *shing!* She was going to cut the Sap patch right off his neck.

El didn't think this was a wise move and was about to say something, but City operations beat her to it. A deep warning gong sounded throughout the train, not unlike the assaultive sound the drones had made back in the village, only toned down slightly. Less banshee, more angry little dog, this sound was designed just to get your attention, not incapacitate you. In any case, it worked: Clo halted her hasty field operation just as a dozen robotic arms emerged from the walls of the train. The menacing silvery limbs shared the same aesthetic as the security drones: they were insectoid, hooked and clawed, and some appeared to have injecting needles.

"Please do not interfere with the medication of the City's patrons," Paddington said calmly from the front of the train as the warning gong faded. He turned only halfway, showing the profile of his uncanny face. "We would certainly hate to have to employ our security measures."

Clo took a second to grimly scan the mean-looking limbs that surrounded her, and then another second to take in the oblivious Tobias, whom she was apparently about to get into a death match to defend. Still, her anger needed to go somewhere. She decided Paddington deserved it.

She turned to the conductor. "You!" she growled, gripping her knife and heading toward him. "You gave him that patch. You knew he was a junkie and you put that stuff right in his face!"

The train's hooked and pincered insectoid arms followed Clo, preparing to close in. Paddington turned all the way around to face her, his calm demeanor not altered in the slightest by her menacing advance.

"We are merely providing compassionate care for—" Paddington started to explain calmly.

"You disgusting Tik-Tok," Clo growled. "We gutted Santa Claus like a pig. We chopped off his head and pulled out his brains."

"I understand your frustration," he said, ignoring the knife and keeping his gaze fixed on Clo's eyes. The staredown was practically an invitation for Clo to start cutting. "But the train has her own brain, and although she does not speak," he continued, gesturing casually with one gloved hand at the myriad of menacing appendages around Clo, "you'll find it much harder to pull out her brains than mine."

"Don't think I won't—"

"Clo!" El said. She grabbed her sister a second before Clo jabbed the knife into Paddington. No doubt the "security measures" would have jabbed her a second later.

"But he dosed my boyfriend!" Clo shouted in frustration.

"He's not your boyfriend—you don't even know him!" El chided. But Clo stayed stiff, her eyes burning with hatred. *"We need to find Mama,"* El said, pressing the case. *"We don't have time to make extra enemies."* She glanced back at Tobias, still nodding. *"Or friends."*

Clo huffed, and she probably would still have cut something—anything—had Tobias not spoken up.

"Maynor can help you," he mumbled.

"What?" Clo finally turned away from her death squint at Paddington.

"Maynor," Tobias sighed, barely opening his eyes, "can help you find your mama."

"Who's Maynor?" El called back to him. No answer. "Tobias!"

"I believe Tobias is referring to Officer Romero," Paddington offered, "our last remaining regional monitor. Indeed, he currently handles all missing persons cases for Yerba City."

"The man who knows things," Tobias mumbled. "The only one in the City not on the Sap." Tobias seemed to be going in and out of consciousness.

Clo turned and walked back to Tobias. He looked up at her and smiled slightly. She leaned in toward him. The claws and needles closed in on her again.

"Clo—" El warned.

"Tut-tut," Paddington clicked.

"I won't mess with him!" Clo announced angrily, sheathing her knife. The pacification arms seemed to be satisfied and gradually retreated back into their slots in the corners of the walls and doors, although they didn't disappear altogether. "So . . . where do we find this Maynor guy?" she asked grudgingly.

Tobias was squinting up at her. Maybe seeing double made it hard for him to read lips. "Where? Oh, he'll show up," Tobias groggily assured her. "Either at the Local One or the Local Zero."

"The local what?"

"A one or a zero. That's all there is now in the City," Tobias muttered. He turned his head to look out the window. "I mean . . . look."

CHAPTER 11

THE LAST MAN

The train turned slightly as it approached land. Decaying skyscrapers stabbed like broken fingers into the heavens, looming over a seemingly endless shattered urban landscape. We gaped again, this time not in awe of nature, but rather in awe of decay. And actually, it wasn't a totally broken landscape; it was still breaking as we stared at it. From where the train was now, about a quarter of a mile out from the city, we could see about half a dozen columns of smoke rising into the morning air. This wasn't the violent black smoke of raging infernos, but the lazy haze of accidental fires of oil and plastics just left to smolder. It was the atmospheric touch we were getting used to seeing around pretty much every urban center, and it was especially evident in this dense area.

Like the silver monorail attached to the rusted bridge we were still on, several new and well-maintained roadways could be seen snaking through the rubble and crumbling buildings. Like the narrow road we had taken on the pill bug earlier, these paths seemed impossibly small for traffic; nevertheless, an occasional white-domed vehicle could be seen speeding atop a silvery path, some even hanging below a skyway, suspended, like smaller versions of the train we were riding. It was almost as if, from the core of the old city, left to rot and fester, another city was growing—like an enormous parasitic silver vine, cannibalizing what was left of centuries of development in favor of some new, more "advanced" organism.

"Beautiful sight, isn't she?" Tobias whispered.

We didn't answer. Looking at Yerba City—the place that used to be our home as the city of San Francisco so many years ago—we didn't know what to say.

Clo turned to Tobias and just watched his face, now reduced to an almost zombielike state, for a while. A tear ran down his cheek as he stared out the window. He was only about twenty, we guessed. He must have remembered a life of kindergarten, first grade, scooter rides, friends at the beach . . . some existence before the tide of the blue drug and the hive of machines descended upon our world.

The train shuddered, and we realized that it would soon stop, and we would be moving on—continuing our quest, whatever that was worth. But Tobias was going to be subsumed into whatever insidious agenda Yerba City had for him. At least back in the shanty village, he'd had some sense of agency, some kind of freedom, although maybe we had already destroyed all possibility of that by bringing Dyre and the Babble to town.

Clo sat down next to Tobias and leaned in. The robotic defensive arms emerged from the walls of the train only about a foot this time, with the slow menace of suspicious coyotes. Clo did her best to ignore them, to keep from flying into a flurry of slashing to beat them back and escape off the train with Tobias.

"Tobias," Clo said, putting her hand on his. He turned to look at her, that obnoxious blue light still blinking on his neck to indicate steady administration of the Sap. "After we get off this train, you'll go back if it's safe, right? They have to let you go back, don't they?"

"Oh, yeah, yeah." He nodded toward Paddington. "They can't stop you from getting on to the train again. It's the law, y'know."

"Then go back. After we get off, you go back, okay?"

"Back to that mob your brother started?"

"I mean, somewhere. You'll get out of this city, promise me."

"There isn't anywhere else. There's Yerba City, and then there's the quarantine zone. The Drag. That's it." He held up two fingers. "Two stops only."

"There's got to be somewhere else," Clo insisted. "*We* came from somewhere else."

"Not everyone has the luxury of a country jaunt," Tobias snorted, but then he looked down at her eyes and saw he'd hurt her. "I'm sorry. You're worried about me, aren't you?" Tobias smiled at her. "That's sweet. Besides, I need to help you girls out."

"We can take care of ourselves."

"No, really. I'll take you to Maynor, then I'll head back to the Drag." He touched the patch on his neck. "I can kick this stuff—I have before, right?"

Clo didn't answer; she just sighed and looked into his eyes, then out the window again. The train crossed over the Embarcadero and turned to head through what had once been downtown. We only had vague memories of walking through this city when we were little girls, before the chaos started. One time, when Dyre was just a baby, we went downtown, shopping, at Christmastime. It might be hard to believe, but we were shy toddlers, hiding behind our mama, trying not to get lost in the crowd that pressed in around us as we walked. Papa was there, too, but already he had become glazed and distant, just another strange face in the throng.

Now there were no crowds, no overstimulated shoppers clutching glittery green-and-red bags; there weren't even any Santa Clauses— which was good, because they probably would have been packing sacks of demonic robot spiders. Most of the streets downtown were covered in a thick layer of broken glass, remnants of the mad scramble for inoculation a decade ago. Yerba City, despite apparently having a small army of drones and Tik-Toks, had never bothered to clean up, instead opting to create those silvery autonomous railways around the mess. The buildings, the structures, were all being left to decay, and in many spots we saw green grass and tall fennel stalks growing up through broken spots in the asphalt. It wasn't just the neglected maintenance of man-made structures; it was also steady reclamation by Mother Oggy, who seemed more than happy to step in while the vast majority of humanity checked out.

Although every human edifice was crumbling, the few things Yerba City did care about, she obviously cared about dearly. Clanky beelike metal drones, about four feet in length, hovered along the suspended roadway tracks, inspecting them for faults, debris, or vegetation. Most of the maintenance of Yerba City's new infrastructure, we surmised, must be done by drones. These weren't the bristly, aggressive-looking dragonfly things that had kept the Subversives at bay back in the village, though. These flying workers were almost charming, like busy little honey-makers keeping the business of the hive flowing.

But what was the business of the hive? What was she trying to achieve? And, why, for God's sake, did we keep thinking of the City as a *she*? Mama had done it, those Subversives had done it, so had Tobias, and now we found ourselves doing the same thing. But it seemed to fit. It wasn't like Yerba City was some cold machine monster programmed to exterminate humanity. If that was what she'd wanted to do, she clearly could have committed total genocide a long time ago. It was "treatment" she seemed to be ceaselessly striving for.

Twice, as the train moved over the desolation, we observed more robotic headless donkeys picking their way over the rubble on six legs, crunching stubbornly across the uneven landscape with several long poles strapped to their backs. These poles, roughly six inches in diameter, must form the base of the roadway support, and each was divided into sections about four feet long, a dimension no doubt calculated precisely so that the flying bees, working two at a time, could lift them into place. These ground-based machines must be the haulers, but it was flying drones that lifted the sections into place once the donkeys had dropped their heavy loads somewhere. There was definitely some kind of system of growth going on here.

Then we spotted, down in the broken glass, half-buried in an alleyway, what looked like another drone, long decommissioned and overgrown with orange clock vines. It looked like it had only two of its four enclosed propeller-powered lift systems still in place, in a design reminiscent of the four-prop remote-controlled devices we remembered seeing as little girls in Golden Gate Park. But its seamless, unadorned design betrayed a style—perhaps the very first—conceived entirely by a machine intelligence. It struck us all at once that this dead drone was perhaps the first generation of vehicles that the City had designed herself: an old bee, replaced by the newer, more efficient designs currently in use. Like Mama had said, the beast's entire ecosystem was evolving, while the rest of us were just fading away.

El looked to Paddington, who had silently walked away from us and Tobias, probably to politely convey a sense that we were having a private conversation. But we weren't talking now; the grim awe of the city had shut us up. The train descended from its elevated track to what must be street level. El scanned the train car, including the broken glass at the back of the train, for anything useful before we departed. She pulled from the pile of glass one of the dragonflies' legs, a Y-shaped claw thing about two feet long that could make a good weapon. It must have blown through the window when the machines attacked each other back in the Drag.

"Clo," she called to her sister, "let's gear up."

Clo nodded, took one last look at Tobias, and stood up. El picked up a severed length of handrail and tossed the pole to her sister, who looked at it for only a second before shaking her head. "Naw, let's switch."

El nodded and caught the pole Clo threw back, then tossed Clo the dragonfly leg. Clo swung the leg, testing it like it was one of the makeshift hooks we used to use to get wild pigs. She nodded and drew Toothy with her other hand, testing both weapons together by slashing at the air.

Outside, the train pulled into its station, and the winglike door at the front of the train opened. Clo stiffened. El readied the broken handrail like a spear.

Out of his squinting eyes, Tobias spied two sisters ready to kill anything that moved. "I pity the fool," he mumbled, half laughing to himself, before trying to stand up. "Well, let's go see Maynor and get this party started." He stumbled out of his seat.

Paddington was right there. "Would you like a hand, Tobias?"

In the center aisle, Tobias straightened himself up and made a mocking show of pretending to dust off the front of his ragged and patched hoodie. "No, no. Just fine, thank you," he insisted stubbornly, not unlike drunk boars in the late fall that ate too many fermented apples and would walk right into trees. He was barely able to maintain forward momentum as he made his way toward the door.

"We'll go first," Clo insisted, trying to sound tough with her double weapons.

"Okay." Tobias nodded. "Whatever you say, but you know you don't need your pointy things in the city. There's nothing to . . . fight."

"Uh-huh," El grunted dismissively, and we stepped off the train, ready for Armageddon's army.

Tobias followed behind us. Paddington raised one hand and waved slightly at El. "Best of luck on your journey," he called, then added, "for all our sakes."

We froze for a second at that last phrase, wanting to ask him what the hell he meant. And why did he sound so human all of a sudden? El turned, but before she could speak, Paddington, eyes locked with hers, slowly took something out of the pocket of his uniform. It was a white cloth of some sort, a rag or handkerchief, and as he turned away from El, he picked up some broken glass from the bottom of the train. The defense arms emerged entirely, and their king crab–like points began to clean the train, spraying and scraping the area where El and Tobias had been sitting. El noticed that two of the metallic arms went to work specifically on the broken window, disconnecting the frame, while a service donkey waited nearby with a fresh piece of glass.

El turned back and we moved forward onto the low platform, which was a mirror of the impossibly perfect space on the other side of the bridge. Only here there were no Subversives, no zapping security drones, and no babbling maniacs. At least not yet.

We were certain we were being watched by a thousand mechanical eyes, but nothing was readily visible aside from the station, which was surrounded by giant crumbling buildings in every direction. There was one small new-looking road at the end of the platform, chiseled into the dark rubble like a pure white bone emerging from blackened meat. At the head of the road stood one of the pill bug cars, its canopy open, and next to it was another uniformed Tik-Tok, patiently waiting for any passenger who might need help.

Tobias paused just a moment to spin around on the empty platform. "No one coming out today? No one for the Drag?"

"Is there usually?" Clo grunted, keeping her weapons up.

"No, I'm just playing," Tobias confessed. "Very few like me. Maybe one or two a year."

He turned and strode forward, passing the chauffeur angel at the waiting car, who gestured a welcome. "Not today, James!" Tobias waved him off. "We'll walk. While we still can!"

"Of course," James said and gave Tobias an enthusiastic thumbs-up, apparently aware that the young man couldn't hear. James was short, light-skinned, friendly-looking despite the black triangle, and never stopped smiling that fake Tik-Tok smile. "Welcome to Yerba City!" he said enthusiastically as we passed.

We didn't answer back. Clo kept her knife and hook pointed at James, and El waved at Tobias when he turned around to see if we were following.

"Where are you going?" El called, making sure to move her mouth so he could read her lips.

"To the Local," Tobias called back. "Just the Local One. Not the Local Zero. That's only if you're full-blown. I'm not." He spread his arms in clear revelation. "Obviously!"

"Obviously," El mumbled under her breath as we jogged to catch up with him. The city was quiet, very quiet. Maybe he was right; compared to the shantytown, there didn't seem to be anything too dangerous around here.

Tobias walked easily along the narrow roadway, which extended about half a block through the rubble before turning sharply to the right. "It's not far," Tobias chortled. "Good thing, too, because I think my patch is running out." He rubbed his neck where the blue strip was.

There was a crunching sound, and the hard *BOOM* of an explosion echoed off the crumbling skyscrapers. A thousand windows shook in the urban canyon, and we reflexively crouched. Tobias kept on walking, seemingly oblivious, despite the tinkling of glass that followed the explosion. Then he looked back and noticed us crouching.

Even deaf, there's no way he could have missed the small shock wave. "What was that?" Clo called to him, more mouthing than yelling.

"Oh, that's probably Maynor."

"That—explosion—was Maynor?" El asked, still crouching and confused.

"I think so," Tobias said nonchalantly. "Look, here he comes now."

From a distance we could make out a small, beehive-sized object zip around the corner about five stories up. It traveled fast, curving upward and downward but maintaining an overall trajectory toward us. It was blinking green.

"Maynor is a . . . drone?" Clo asked, confused.

Tobias gave an intoxicated chuckle. "No. No. He's chasing that thing."

As if on cue, a dark armored figure came tearing around the corner in hot pursuit of the blinking drone. He was somehow running on the side of a building, perpendicular to it, as if gravity had been switched— just for him—by ninety degrees. Aside from the impossibility of his orientation, he was also taking impossibly huge strides, seven to ten feet at a time, each footfall landing on, and breaking, brick, glass, steel, or whatever material was left on the dilapidated structures surrounding us.

"Whoa," Clo commented. "How's he doing that? Is that him or the suit?"

"Oh, it's a bit of both, I think," Tobias answered vaguely.

The armored figure raised one arm as he ran and fired a quick rat-a-tat burst from a short barrel built into the wrist of his suit. The target drone dodged wildly but kept up its forward momentum. Whatever Maynor was firing didn't seem like real bullets, but rather small fléchettes that tinkled off the surrounding buildings.

"It's like he's playing a video game," Clo said, "but in real life. Is that what people do for fun now?"

"Just him," Tobias said.

The targeted drone shot past directly above us, but Maynor was dead on it, sending a small rain of glass and debris with each jump as he passed along the buildings nearby.

"Sure makes a mess," El commented. We both stood up and relaxed from our fighting stance.

"Yeah, no wonder the city's falling apart," Clo agreed. *"This guy's just smashing it up for fun."*

The drone tried to turn down a side street, but Maynor deftly launched off a wall, did a spin with his feet facing almost straight up, and fired a burst of about ten rounds, most of which found their mark on the small machine. It jerked in midair with the impacts and froze in place, flashing from red to yellow.

"Nice one!" Tobias remarked.

Maynor, set free from the wall, began falling head down toward the street.

"Is he gonna splat?" Clo asked tentatively.

But before anyone could answer, or even speculate, we spotted exhaust from a series of small jets on Maynor's belt, shoes, and shoulder pads. These served to swing him around right side up again and slow his fall just enough that he landed harmlessly into an impressive-looking crouch about forty feet from us.

"Oh," Clo snorted. "Jet pack. Of course." About thirty feet past him, the cowed drone also floated slowly down to the street, blinking yellow the entire way.

"Got him again!" Tobias cheered, waving at Maynor.

Maynor stood up and looked at us.

"Does he do this every day?" El asked, not immediately impressed.

"Pretty much," Tobias said, strolling forward. "He's gotta stay in shape, you know."

"For what?" Clo asked suspiciously.

"For anything! He's the last one, after all."

"The last what?" Clo asked skeptically. "The last armored, jet-packed, blowing-up-the-city-for-fun cop?"

"The last anything." Tobias shrugged. "Everyone else around here is in treatment." He turned back to the armored figure. "Hey, Maynor!"

We caught sight of the fléchette guns withdrawing into the forearms of his suit as Maynor raised his arms to slide back his sleek black helmet.

"Hello, Tobias!" Maynor called to him, his whole head revealed now. He was in his late twenties, his head shaved, glistening bald, his skin golden, his eyes a dark, dark brown.

"Wow," said Clo. "He's gorgeous, too. This place is full of hot bucks."

El just snorted. "I told you, we don't have time for boys."

"I know, but that one's not a boy. That's a . . . man."

El eyed the tall and athletic Maynor suspiciously as he closed with Tobias and the two gave each other high fives. Unlike her sister, El was not boy-crazy in the least, but she could recognize that Maynor was a fine specimen. Still, she didn't trust him.

"I bet he's a goldeneye."

Clo gasped at the thought. "Do you think?"

"Good shot back there!" Tobias said to Maynor, exchanging a quick fist bump after the high five, or as well as Tobias could manage against Maynor's black armored glove.

"Ah, just standard," Maynor confessed. He was still panting, sweat on his neck. He nodded to Tobias. "You coming back in for treatment?"

"Well, yeah, I met a couple of stragglers, and there was this craziness in the village . . ." Tobias trailed off. He didn't seem quite able to gather all his thoughts together to tell Maynor about us, our brother, the babblers, et cetera.

Maynor, who seemed to be used to interacting with people on the Sap, only half listened, leaning over to look past Tobias and peer at us.

"Stragglers, huh? Haven't seen those for a while." He smiled at us, with a friendly, welcoming nod, but we could tell there was something else in his thoughts, something behind his casual wave: resignation, depression, something. We didn't know enough about other people to tell what was really going on behind those baby brown eyes, and he wasn't letting on. "Nice outfits," he said. "Deerskins. Haven't seen that before."

We stayed silent, keeping our makeshift weapons ready.

"You girls come back to save the world?" he asked.

"Why would we do that?" Clo wondered.

"Show him the picture," El told Clo.

"Huh? Oh yeah." Clo dove her hand into her tunic, fumbling for Mama's picture. *"It's here somewhere."*

"What was that?" Maynor said when he heard our language. He turned to Tobias. "Do they speak English?"

"Yeah, we speak English!" El said indignantly.

"Whatever." Maynor shrugged and wiped some sweat from the back of his neck. "English isn't my first language, either. I was born in Guatemala. But it doesn't matter now. In the Local One, they'll hook you up. The machines speak every language, better than most people do now."

"Bet you they don't speak CloElish, handsome," Clo chortled. She found the crumpled photograph and pulled it out. "Anyway—"

Ping! The yellow flashing drone, the one Maynor had tagged in the air, was floating a few feet off the ground a bit farther down the street when it chimed suddenly, distracting all of us. Maynor turned reflexively to see its flashing color turn from yellow to red. He turned again, apparently predicting what would happen next, because he was just in time to see three more target drones appear around the corner, high in the air, all of them flashing the same hot red.

"My turn to run now," Maynor said, reaching up to flip his helmet back into place. We could hear the small jets on his armor warm up as he crouched down in a runner's stance.

"Wait, we're looking for—" Clo called.

Maynor turned his featureless, shielded mask toward us. His voice crackled through a microphone, sounding augmented and somehow more official. "I'll circle back and see you *cuaches* in the Local One. Gotta go."

"Hey—" El called angrily, but it was too late. Maynor shot into a jet-fueled sprint, crunching through the debris with each giant stride. The three red drones gave chase, joined by the previously downed one, transformed now from hunted to hunter. They began firing their own purple fléchettes from small tubes, and Maynor was soon up on the sides of the buildings again, jumping and dodging in an effort to escape the spattering projectiles. They were all gone around a corner in seconds, leaving us standing in the street in near silence once again, just staring after them.

"Well, he wasn't any help," Clo finally said, disappointed. "What are *cuaches*, anyway?"

"He'll be back, don't worry," Tobias assured us.

El walked over and picked up one of the projectiles from the rubble. It shattered easily in her hand, leaving a purple paint smear on her fingers. She wiped it off, annoyed. "How long will he spend playing shoot-'em-up?"

"Not long," Tobias said, turning to stroll in the direction we'd been going before Maynor showed up. "He'll find us in the Local One. He spends most of his time in there anyway."

We watched Tobias turn the corner, careful not to step off the silver path as he batted away a large fennel stalk growing across it.

Now that Maynor's hunting party had left, the city was remarkably quiet again; an occasional buzz from a high worker drone here or there and the slight tinkling of broken glass as another one of the millions of windows downtown fell out of a decaying framework. But basically, it seemed a quiet place. We nodded in agreement and turned to walk briskly after Tobias. He popped back around the corner just to wave at us.

"Hey, girls. This is it, there's nowhere else. The next Local One is in Chinatown."

Silently, we picked up our pace.

"Hope your boyfriend knows where he's going," El mumbled.

"Do you think he'd be my boyfriend?" Clo asked excitedly, of course not knowing exactly what that would mean.

"I don't know," El said. *"He seems like kind of a loser, anyway. Do you really want to pair up with that?"*

"He's not a loser, he's . . . an artist."

"He's a shambler."

"Don't say that! He's not a . . . total shambler."

El just sighed in response, not wanting any part of this conversation. *"C'mon, let's catch up."*

Around the corner, the city opened up into an immense square about a quarter of a mile wide. We recognized it from when we were little: it had once been the center of a bustling shopping district called Union Square. Now it contained an immense Subantoxx treatment center that must have been hollowed into the ground years ago by the City's drones.

The giant silvery structure looked something like a hospital—as far as we could remember such things. Or, more like what a Sour Apple's idea of what a hospital was supposed to look like. The result, like most of the City's efforts, appeared more creepy than healing; its mirror-windowed levels extended upward several stories into the air, and from the look of the gaping sloped entrance into which a few of the autonomous roadways converged, the structure extended several stories underground as well. The whole thing seemed strangely out of place, as if some computer-brained god had thrown a javelin of health care down from heaven and it had stuck in the earth right in the heart of the crumbling city.

Tobias made a beeline for the entrance, which was a wide set of automatic doors at ground level, and we carefully followed, pausing only to take note of the large glowing sign above that read "FREEDOM THROUGH HEALING" in bold white letters. As we drew closer, we watched the letters on the sign change subtly into another language, and then another, presumably translating the same motto into all possible languages and cultures of patients. Then a face appeared on the sign, and we realized that it wasn't a sign at all, but rather a long, rectangular video screen. The face was friendly, welcoming, and seemed to look directly at us as we approached.

"Is she eyeballing us?" Clo asked, keeping her blades ready.

"Is that even a she?" El asked.

"Uh, can't tell, really." Indeed, the face seemed to be slowly morphing, changing through different expressions and colors, trying to find the most trustworthy. *"It's creepy, whatever it is,"* Clo hissed.

"That's the City," Tobias assured us. "She'll help us. The angels and the butterflies do all the work, but she guides them."

"Angels and butterflies?" Clo asked incredulously. She looked up at one of the bumblebee drones shooing away a seagull and then beginning to polish a window three stories up. "Okay, I get that the drones are butterflies, but where are the angels?"

"Well, like Paddington, or James, or Santa Claus," Tobias said, like it was too obvious. "Or Ellen right there." He pointed to a Tik-Tok woman waiting by the sliding glass door of the treatment center. This "angel" was different from Paddington—younger, a woman—but spoke in the same stilted "I am a sensitive robot" manner the conductor on the train had used. And she had the same small black triangle mark in the middle of her forehead. She was meant to look beautiful, maybe even sexy, we decided, in her white uniform.

She held a small tray, blue patches visible. "Hello, Tobias," she said.

"Good morning, Ellen," Tobias shot back, as best he could.

"Who is that?" Clo stared daggers into the young woman who was trying to be all on a first-name basis and whatnot with her new loser boyfriend. But Tobias wasn't facing us, and therefore couldn't read her lips. Clo gently, yet ever so firmly, with the slow, steady, determined strength of a stream that will inevitably carve solid rock into the Grand Canyon, put her hand on Tobias's shoulder and turned him toward her. "Who. Is. That?" she overenunciated.

Despite being deaf, Tobias, like every other sentient being in the solar system and perhaps beyond, was able to detect a tone of jealousy in Clo's voice.

"Oh, that's just Ellen," Tobias explained defensively. "She's an angel, too, like the others. With the black triangles."

We drew closer. Close enough for a quick slash, Clo thought. But then she thought better. Maybe this was just a silly machine. "So she's a Tik-Tok?" she asked.

"Huh?"

"A robot."

"Oh yeah, now she is, but she used to be a person. All of them used to be," Tobias said. Then he explained like it was something he had read in a child's picture book: "When someone dies, they become an angel. The City does it so we'll always be together."

"Of course." El nodded, looking closely at Ellen's face. Ellen didn't seem to mind being stared at, even when El leaned in close with the same scientist's curiosity our mother had displayed when examining Santa Claus.

The details were perfect. The woman was beautiful, but she also had human imperfections: a pimple here, an ear hair there, an ever-so-slightly crooked nose. "It's too real," El said. "Yerba City couldn't create something like this." She leaned back. "But she could copy it."

Clo continued to look at Ellen disdainfully. "Like a crow," she said. "They can caw back, but they don't really know what they're saying."

"Oh, the angels can't fool anyone," Tobias assured us in his intoxicated state. "Yerba City can't copy the brains, just the body. Plus they have the mark, so you always know." Tobias gestured to the black triangle. "It's the law, or something."

"Can't copy the brain?" El mused to herself, starting to put together some pieces of the puzzle. The drones. The so-called angels. *"Can't . . . or won't,"* El concluded.

"Huh?" Tobias asked, only half-interested.

"I bet she can copy a brain," El said darkly to Clo. *"But she can't control it a hundred percent, so she leaves that part out."*

Clo was less objective about the revelation. "Just the body, huh?" She turned to Tobias. "Maybe that's all you care about? Maybe that's all you need?"

"What?" Tobias said, recognizing Clo's jealous nature. "You think I'm crushed out on Ellen? No, I'm not like that with the angels. I mean, some folks are, but that's not my thing."

Clo was still huffing. "So what is your thing?"

"Uh, look, I'm trying to help you out. Let's go in. Maynor will be by. He'll help you find your mama."

He made to enter the door, but Ellen interrupted. "Tobias, you've been away," she said. "Don't forget to eat before you hook up your friend." She held out her tray, and pointed at what looked like two rows of round white crackers next to the blue patches.

"Of course, of course." Tobias put six or seven of the crackers into a small stack and began popping a few into his mouth as he walked.

"Food?" Ellen asked us.

We took only a cursory glance at the wafers. "No, thanks," El said coldly.

Clo was more interested, although certainly not about to eat anything that woman—or whatever that female-looking thing was—offered. "What's in it, anyway?"

"All of the nutritional requirements to optimize treatment," Ellen answered evasively.

That didn't encourage us in the slightest, although actually, we were getting hungry. The last thing we had eaten was a couple of strips of deer jerky the night before. But we were used to not eating for a few days from time to time, out in Oggy. Besides, who knew what was in those wafers? Drugs? Nanobots? A thousand baby spiders pressed into a disc? Better to stay hungry. Still, we would need to eat eventually, and long before that, we would need water. We knew we still had time before things got desperate, but it would be best to speed up this little quest.

"S'okay. I still have that squirrel I pulled out of the grille," Clo assured El. She patted her pocket, and we picked up our pace to keep up with Tobias.

Down past the parking area, which currently contained no cars, a second set of double doors opened as Tobias stomped toward them, revealing six more figures. Four were angels, dressed in white uniforms, and two were what must be patients. The way they all stood in a line just past the automatic doors, it was obviously some kind of welcoming committee.

The four Tik-Tok people, or angels, as Tobias called them, consisted of two men and two women who looked, respectively, white, black, Hispanic, and Asian. The gender and racial balance of the four good-looking young figures seemed suspiciously staged, like Yerba City wanted to convey a message of pan-acceptance, although it came across to us more like a message of slow but sure pan-genocide.

The still-living "patients" stood there half waving, obviously in a stoned stupor. One of them, a middle-aged man, wore the sort of half-ragged clothes we had seen earlier that day in the Drag. The other, a woman in her twenties, had a kind of medical gown over her top with a pair of ragged jeans below. Neither had any shoes, but the facility seemed to have dark wall-to-wall carpeting. And though the denizens were not much for fashion, they were friendly enough, waving meekly at us visitors as we came in.

"Hello!" the group called in unison. "Welcome to treatment!" The angels spoke in perfect harmony, and the patient greeters did their best to mumble along. The older patient could stand on his own, but the younger held herself up by a mobile IV stand, which also held a hexagonal bag of the Sap.

Behind the welcoming committee was a low counter attended by an angel, and behind her were rows of Subantoxx IV bags, one of which she was calmly dispensing to another patient. The whole place didn't have much of a hospital atmosphere to it at all, as far as we could remember. It felt more like a geriatric casino, except for the fact that folks here were generally not old, and there didn't seem to be any gambling.

"Thank you," chortled Tobias, blowing by the welcoming line and heading straight for the dispensary counter.

We were almost instantly disoriented and, like when we encountered the villagers in the Drag, confused in general by our emotions at being around people—at least some of them human—after so long. But there was one thing we were fairly certain of: we really didn't like this place. For a moment we wished we were back in the forest, back in our little Oggy compound, hidden from this sickening decay of humanity. No wonder Mama had protected us for so long.

We picked up our pace, following Tobias, and Clo nearly stepped on a small, turtle-like cleaning drone sucking up an unidentifiable line of fluid across the carpet.

"Is that the Sap?" Clo wondered out loud, wrinkling her face in disgust. *"Or something . . . leaking from a person?"*

"I don't wanna know," El asserted. *"Let's just find that monitor guy and get out of here."*

Tobias approached the counter and double-knuckle-rapped it decisively. "The usual, please!" He turned back to us.

"Certainly," the attendant said. "Patch, bag, or friend?"

"Friend," Tobias said.

El trotted in front of Tobias so he could see her mouth moving when she said, "Hey, so where's Maynor?"

"Maynor? Well, I'm not sure. This place is big: it's ten stories up and ten stories down."

"Ten stories . . . underground?" El asked, unbelieving.

"Uh-huh." Tobias nodded, as if we should be impressed. We were not. "But Maynor comes to this floor first. That's where the most high-functioning folks are, and he always keeps his rounds."

The attendant handed something to Tobias, and he switched his focus entirely to this new item, holding it near his wrist. We realized it wasn't just a bag: at the bottom were six affectionate-looking tentacles, which reached out and wrapped themselves around his wrist, presumably to deliver the drug.

Clo gasped and raised her knife. El caught her wrist.

"Easy," El said.

"What is that thing?" Clo breathed. *"Is it eating him?"*

"That must be the friend they mentioned. I think it's a Subantoxx bag. Like the spiders back at the mini-mart. Only these are . . . friendlier."

"That thing's alive!"

El nodded, remembering the IV bags the firemen had wrapped themselves up in during the End of the World. Treatment had apparently come a long way since then. *"The City's been evolving."*

Not waiting for the squid bag to finish wrapping itself around him, Tobias tottered toward an imposing circulator machine that undulated slug-slow in the middle of the cavernous room. There were patients on this machine, some sitting, some standing, but all twirling either upward or downward. We realized it was some kind of escalator, moving between floors.

Tobias stepped onto the escalator and slowly, very slowly, began to rise upward. He looked back at us.

"I know what you're thinking," Tobias said. "But it's not so bad. We have freedom; people even fall in love here. Look at those two. Sandy and Morty."

Two patients, a couple in their midthirties, were walking slowly, hand in hand. They seemed lost in each other's eyes, but each actually had a blue Subantoxx patch over one eye. It wasn't clear if they were looking into each other's exposed eye or into the drug-laden patch. Morty clutched at Sandy's breast, the stoned expression changing on neither face.

"Whoa," Clo crowed, and we couldn't help but stare at the unfamiliar sexual interaction. "People just—you can just—" But Tobias wasn't looking at us. Clo, more than El, was intrigued, having thought about sex for so long out in the woods. But, after a few seconds, the whole mechanical groping exchange just kind of disgusted us.

Tobias turned and sensed our discomfort right away. "Hey, let's go upstairs—it's quieter up there." He gestured for us to step onto the escalator.

An angel closed in on El, offering her a Friend squid of her own, a blue-fluid-dripping needle jutting from in between the tentacles. El jumped onto the escalator almost more to avoid the angel than to follow Tobias.

"Okay, okay," Clo conceded, jumping on, too. "Any other floor's gotta be better than Gropeland here."

They were not.

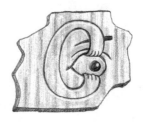

CHAPTER 12

IN THE GOAT ROOM

As we rose up the slowly circulating escalator, we got a better look at the patients spread across the cavernous ground floor, a mass of people shuffling in slow orbit around the giant escalator in the middle of the space. Almost all of them were coupled up, we realized, walking next to another, often hand in hand but sometimes just in parallel. Occasionally three or four would walk together, but in general it was couples.

El tapped on Tobias's shoulder, making sure he turned around to look at her before she spoke. "What's up with everyone . . . does the Sap just turn you into a total pervert?"

"Oh, those aren't the perverts. Those are the lovers. The perverts go downstairs."

"We're not going downstairs with you!" Clo blurted, suddenly feeling that this whole sex thing might not be for her.

"Naw, you don't want to go down there." Tobias shuddered. "It gets . . . pretty weird pretty fast."

"What do you mean?" El was only interested from an informational point of view. Clo plugged her ears.

"Well," Tobias grumbled, "the machines get involved."

"The, uh, angels?"

"Yeah, and other things the City makes."

"What? Like sex drones?"

"Um, I guess you could call them that. But that's downstairs," Tobias said. Trying to redirect the conversation, he gestured to the couples below us. "The ground floors in the Local Ones are almost always like this. Folks just get sweet on each other, and that's all they need."

"That and the Sap," El amended.

Tobias missed this last quip, as he was already focused upward.

As we emerged onto the first floor, it became clear that most people "in treatment" preferred more stimulation than just staring into each other's eyes. The room was set up kind of like an enormous wraparound movie theater. We remembered going to movies as little girls, but there had been nothing like this back then. In fact, we remembered video becoming more compact, moving toward bulky goggle-like devices that could immerse the wearer in "virtually real" environments. This floor of the Local One seemed to be the polar opposite: a vast room covered on every side with a giant wraparound screen, and row upon row of raked seats radiating out from the central escalator.

"Let's get off here. It's a lot quieter than on the other floors." Tobias hopped off, and we followed. There didn't appear to be much groping happening; patients, mostly on their own, filled most of what must have been about two thousand seats in the giant theater.

"It's more . . . social up here," Tobias pointed out. He was right; the scale was astounding, but not overwhelming, instead designed precisely to the edge of the human capacity for community performance. Each chair had a two-foot hanger mounted into it, and most had Sap bags hooked up to slowly administer Subantoxx as the patients stared at the movie.

Tobias looked around for some free seats, but a uniformed Tik-Tok man, acting as usher, was almost instantly with us. "Three?" the tall Tik-Tok asked.

"Yes, please," Tobias answered, following the angel up a low ramp to some free seats. "Just three little birdies . . ."

Tobias was starting to make less and less sense, and we got the idea that now, with his Sap bag hooked up to the small arm above his seat and the tentacles extending into a kind of wraparound tube to his wrist, he'd probably start making even less.

We looked out at the enormous screen, which wrapped around us and out of view. The imagery was surreal, to say the least. Abstract shapes floating by, liquids, waves, at once both photographic and animated. You would think that, after a decade of living in the forest, deprived of sitcoms, dating shows, and Saturday-morning cartoons, we would be more than a little excited for some screen time. But the movie they were showing just didn't make any sense.

"What show is this?" Clo asked. She tapped Tobias so he would turn and look at her. "What movie is this?" she mouthed.

"I dunno," he mumbled. "It's the City show. It's the same show—but different every time."

"You'd have to be totally high to get into this," Clo snorted.

"I think that's the idea," El mumbled.

"Well, it changes as you watch it," Tobias explained. We didn't say anything, but continued to watch the giant screen suspiciously. "We're all up there, you know," Tobias said. "Look, that's you, isn't it?"

Panning from the lower left to the lower right, a new image floated and merged with the others: an abstract face that turned into our brother's, a suggestion of a hand grasping a knife—the very hunting knife that Clo carried, deer antlers on the top of Dyre's head.

"Whoa—that's Dyre!" Clo realized. "And my knife!"

"It just knows what you're thinking about," Tobias explained, "and makes it better."

"You mean the movie can read my mind?" Clo asked. She gasped. "It's Mama!"

Indeed, there on the screen, unmistakably, was our mother's face. She wasn't bound and gagged somewhere, tied in a dungeon by an evil, needle-fingered Tik-Tok. She was happy, back in the woods, the sun shining through her blond hair. The image lasted only a moment, flowing across the screen along with the waves of dark liquid and the flickering weblike imagery.

We were dumbfounded for a second, fixated, staring, hoping she would return again.

"There!" Clo shouted. "It's her! Where is she? Where did they take that video?"

"It's from you," Tobias said innocently, as if he didn't know how to explain it any better.

But El knew; it all came flooding back. The AMTaCs, the screens, Papa's face. Like most things in Yerba City, the whole setup was of course too good to be true. "It's Project Chimera," she said, realizing.

Clo looked at her sister, her mind racing. Mama had said that word a few times over the years, but Clo had forgotten what it meant. She remembered that a chimera was a mythical beast, part lion, part goat, and part snake. But it also had something to do with the big thing Mama had been working on when Yerba City took over.

"You're a hit, you know," Tobias said. His words were slurring slightly as the pure Subantoxx slipped into his system. "Everyone always loves a new plotline . . ." The screen slipped back into its abstract imagery.

"Wait! Show Mama again!" Clo insisted, and sure enough, our mother appeared, a montage of happy memories: showing us how to skin a deer, correcting our karate postures, et cetera.

"There she is! That's amazing!" Clo said, delighted. Mama was now bending over young Dyre in a rare show of corporal punishment, spanking his bottom red.

"Ha! I remember that! She only did that one time; he was playing with Daisy Duke when we first got to Oggy," Clo explained to Tobias, like she was letting him in on the greatest cult movie of all time.

Tobias only grunted slightly in acknowledgment. He clearly wasn't following what was being said to him.

El was trying not to get sucked in, but it was hard; seeing our memories up there—images that were *better* than our memories.

A beautiful cabin appeared in an idyllic, secluded redwood grove, morning light dancing through the branches. "That's the Oggy! Where we live," Clo said.

"It's beautiful," Tobias managed to comment.

"Yeah," Clo sighed dreamily. "We were happy." The effect of the responsive wraparound screen surrounding us, although exciting, was also mesmerizing. Clo began to speak in half-remembered narration, and as she did, each corresponding image flashed up on the screen. "But then Mama had to go away, and an evil deer came."

"Whoa, he's freaky," Tobias commented lazily on the giant image of Vambi.

"Yeah, but we defeated him," Clo said calmly. "Like we do. And then Dyre was infected, so we had to wake up Bouncy and drive around. And then we killed some spiders. And then we ran out of gas. And then the Crying Man came."

"Yikes," said Tobias, seeing the pale, sunken face. "He's a nightmare." He turned to Clo. "Were you ok?"

"Yeah, but we scared him away. First we made him tell us how to find your village."

"Oh yeah, the Drag."

"And then we ran into you," Clo continued, her voice becoming more and more removed, as if the images were now guiding her rather than the other way around. Up on the screen, Tobias, or a silken-haired, perfectly stubbled version of Tobias, emerged from his royal yurt-like tent. "Look! That's the first time we saw you!" It was a far cry from the reality of the scraggly graffiti artist next to us. The young man on the screen smiled and waved to something approaching in the distance, presumably us.

"Wow," Tobias admitted. "I look good."

"Yeah," Clo sighed again and curled up next to Tobias, holding his hand.

"Hey, why is my shirt off? It was hella cold when I saw you."

"Oh, that's just how I remember it, I guess," Clo said innocently, drinking in the imagery.

"And where are my tats? I'm all blank up there."

Clo turned to him. "You have tattoos?"

"Oh yeah." Tobias pulled his tattered shirt half-open, revealing a series of crude stick figures and runes. "I did them myself." Clearly he had.

"Wow," Clo marveled, tracing her finger along something that looked like two crooked, asymmetrical diamonds.

Up on the screen, the idealized Tobias's athletic bare chest suddenly grew half a dozen perfect tattoos, a refined pastiche of the real thing next to us.

"*This is stupid,*" El snorted. But what bothered her the most was how little the whole thing bothered her. It was like watching a movie trailer of our lives, and just as shallow. There was a plot, or definitely some kind of suggestion of a story, which must be a long, infinite epic, grand in scale and unquestionably beautiful. On some level, we felt that we should be offended, and feel violated that our most personal and private moments were being played out on the screen in front of hundreds of strangers: the loss of our mother, our brother trying to kill us, even our years of loneliness in the wilderness. But at the same time it was somehow comforting, wonderful in the way that our lives were worthy of representation. Like we were valiant heroes, triumphant, instead of unknown stragglers at the edges of human history's doomed course. We were famous, or at least remembered somewhere.

As the moments passed, other images, presumably taken from the other patients in the room, were added and then melded with our own. We felt an instant communal connection with the other people in the theater with us. The patients here in the Local One, lined up in rows in ragged clothes and draped hospital gowns, were our people, our tribe, our celebratory family that gave us an undeniable place of meaning in the world. Unconsciously, Clo clutched Tobias's hand harder. For a moment she just wanted to feel like a teenage girl, innocently sitting next to a cute boy in a movie theater.

El shook her head, coming out of the trance. How long had they been sitting there? Mama had told us only vague concepts about Project Chimera, but having an idea of how it worked went a long way toward helping El shake out of it. Still, that communal feeling, that sense that could only be described as family, was almost enough to persuade her to check out forever.

"This is the Goat!" she announced.

Clo and Tobias, next to her, didn't even stir, so wrapped up were they in each other.

El turned, purposely averting her eyes from the screen, and waved her hand in front of Tobias to get his attention. "Give me your pen."

"Huh?"

"Your graffiti pen," El said. "We saw you use it this morning."

"Oh, sure," Tobias said, returning his eyes to the screen. He pulled out his spray pen and handed it over. El snatched it up and sprayed over several tiny pinholes on her armrests. She then stood over Clo's chair and did the same thing.

"*What . . . are you doing?*" Clo said.

"*There are tiny cameras,*" El explained. "*And I think they're bouncing little lasers off the backs of our eyes. It's the Goat.*"

"*The what? Lasers?*"

"*The Goat. Remember the first spray? I saw Papa's face up on the screen, and you saw Clyde? It's Project Chimera. A chimera is a lion, a snake, and a goat, all combined together. Remember, Mama was working on it when the End of the World happened? The three-pronged solution,*" El continued, switching to English as she recalled Mama's words. "Synergistic therapy, she called it."

"*I still don't know what that means, after all these years.*"

"*It means three creatures combined to make a stronger one.*" El held up her fingers as she talked. "*One: the lion, Yerba City, the AI. The Sour Apple. Two: Subantoxx, the Sap, the venom of the snake. And three: the eyes of the Goat.*"

Clo looked blankly at the screen, which was now displaying a series of beautiful abstract flashes of the two of us, back-to-back, fighting the evil babblers in the village. "*That doesn't look like a goat, it looks like us kicking ass.*"

"*It's a machine,*" El said in frustration, straining for her own half-remembered lessons to explain. "*Mama called it 'neurological impulse manipulation. NIM.' It's grabbing things from our eyes, and putting them up there.*"

"*But how can they see Mama, and Dyre, and all those things?*"

"*Lemme just show you. Mama did explain it to us once.*" El moved over to a seat that still had its cameras working and sat down. "*Remember that winter when we were stuck inside? We were snowed in, and we had to eat the skunk?*"

"*Oh yeah, I'm not gonna forget that.*" Up on the screen, snow and wind appeared, surrounding our little cabin. "*It was cold.*"

Mama—or El's memory of her—was drawing on the floor. A hand appeared on the screen. Mama's hand, with a piece of charcoal, drew a human eye with a brain behind it. Then, about a foot away on the floor, the same hand drew an image of a camera, which was attached to a hexagon.

"*The stop sign. That's the artificial brain! I remember that.*"

"*Right,*" El said and continued thinking about the memory. On the screen, in the figure of the human brain, Mama drew a flower, a poppy. Then she drew a whole bunch of dotted lines between the human eye and the camera. Finally, she redrew the poppy inside the hexagon brain.

"*It works by 'process of elimination.' The City has been sending thousands of little invisible light pulses a second at us since we walked through the front door, bouncing them back, and recording our responses. Our 'unconscious responses.' The ones that get any kind of reaction—'subconscious reactions we don't even know we're making'—she works those, refines those again and again, and before we even know it, she's got things we respond to without thinking.*"

Clo thought about this, looking up at our mother's hands. "*So Yerba City doesn't even know who these people are to us?*"

"*I don't think so, but she can tell by the way our eye nerves react that they mean something to us, and to keep us here, she'll keep refining based on our reactions.*"

"*Like the crow that doesn't know what it's saying.*"

"*Yes, exactly. Like a tricky old crow, it just wants your food. Or in this case, your soul.*" Up on the screen, the image panned away from Mama's drawings to Clo, throwing her knife in practice over and over again at a mounted block of wood on the wall. From the deep cuts in the block, one could tell it was a *lot* of practicing.

Satisfied that her sister understood what was going on, El closed her eyes and moved back to one of the chairs with the blacked-out cameras. "*You'd remember this stuff better if you'd paid attention when Mama did school instead of just throwing your knife around all the time,*" she said bitterly.

"*Why you gotta bring it up like that? You know my blade has done us plenty of good,*" Clo said defensively. "*Anyway, you sprayed our cameras, so we're fine now, right?*"

"*Don't be naive—there's cameras everywhere. I just sprayed those close ones because we shouldn't make things any easier for her.*" El looked around the giant room, trying to keep her eyes off the screen. "*Come on, we can't stay here. Let's look around for Maynor.*"

"*But I like this movie,*" Clo protested, seeing herself standing hand in hand with Tobias in a beautiful sunset.

"Well, of course you like it: it was made for you. Is being made for you as you watch it." El sounded angry, as Clo wasn't moving. *"So you have to look away."*

"But—"

"I said, look away from the screen!"

Tobias, of course, couldn't understand what we were saying, but he didn't need sign language to tell that El wanted to leave. "Aw, just relax," he mumbled. "You know, some people stay in here for days." He pointed to Clo's seat. "There's a toilet in the chair so you don't even have to get up."

Clo peeped downward. There did appear to be some kind of padded hole at the bottom of the cushy chair that could open up. "Ugh!" She jumped up, disgusted.

Tobias didn't seem to notice her revulsion, instead gesturing to a patient about six seats over who had a strange apparatus attached to his head. "And some folks like a lid lock."

El squinted through the half-light. "Are his eyes being forced open?" Indeed they were, revealing gaping eyeballs that were apparently periodically sprayed with tiny droplets from the helmet-like device. "Why are they making him wear that?"

"No one's making him do it. Jacob just doesn't want to miss any of the movie. It's a . . . treatment option."

"How can you do this to yourself?" Clo blurted out, unable to control her disgust any longer.

"This is what everyone does." Tobias shrugged. "It's not that bad," he assured her. "Look, Maynor is probably in the building already. He can help you, and you'll be on your way."

"But I don't want to leave you," Clo said firmly. She could be very stubborn sometimes.

"What?" Tobias asked, half pretending that his hearing impediment prevented him from understanding what Clo said, although there was no mistaking what she was going off about.

"I like you," Clo said clearly.

"Oh, well . . . thanks," Tobias said awkwardly.

"I see you don't have your Subantoxx in," said a pleasant voice next to El. It was an angel, a petite redhead, the black triangle standing out on her pale forehead. "I brought a little Friend out for you."

El looked the attendant up and down. She suspected the crimson hair had been carefully chosen by Yerba City's mechanizations to make her seem a more trustworthy administrator: being a ginger made her more like "one of us."

"No, I—" El started, but the nurse had unnaturally deep blue eyes, and El was temporarily flummoxed by the beautiful robot. After all, she wasn't just a robot; she had once been a living person, with toned, athletic arms, like the women El used to watch on *American Ninja Warrior* as a little girl. Despite the flummoxing, El managed to respond: "I—I'm not infected."

"Look, everyone in this area is infected," the angel gently corrected, in a tone that was somehow more familiar than artificial. "I'll help you, sweetie." She reached down with one hand to pull up El's sleeve, readying the squid-like bag in the other. This one wasn't like some cold butler robot, but more like a sweet older crush just helping out.

"No!" El jumped up and slapped the android's hand away, sending the Sap bag tumbling down onto the sloped walkway beneath them in a flail of tentacles. "That thing is *not* my freakin' friend! And neither are you!"

The redhead shot El a stony look, just shy of being rude, then corrected herself to be more patient. "Sorry, I was just trying to help out." She went to pick up the bag, which was slowly crawling up the ramp toward us. "If you change your mind, Elizabeth, I'll be right over there."

The whole exchange was so calculated to be human and intimate, but all it did was incense El. She wanted to yell something like "Don't you use my name, you damn dirty machine!" but thought better of it.

The flying squid episode was not lost on Tobias, who chuckled slightly. "You two are really different," he mumbled. It almost seemed like he thought the scene was part of the movie, but then he looked seriously at Clo, into her eyes. "I like you, too."

El, satisfied that the angel wasn't going to come back and make a second attempt to stick her, sat back down.

Clo was beaming into Tobias's eyes, but he blinked once, twice, and, seeming to forget her for a moment, looked back out at the giant screen.

"But, you know, the show really is better if you Sap out." He made a gesture with his hands like a blooming flower. "The whole thing comes alive."

"We know," El said coldly. "It's designed to work with the drug."

"Well, can't know if you haven't sapped. There's nothing else like it. It becomes part of you."

"Look." Clo reached inside her tunic and pulled out the small, worn, black vinyl pack. She opened it to reveal the two whitish tubes, nestled side by side.

"Clo," El warned, *"I don't think you should—"*

"Shh!" Clo carefully pulled out one of the short syringes and held it in front of Tobias. "Look."

"What is that, darling?" Tobias asked, looking at the tube Clo held up.

Clo popped one end off, revealing a glistening needle.

Tobias squinted his eyes, focusing. "A syringe? That's kinda old-school, don't you think? This little fellow's got me humming." He gestured to the squid-like Friend, which moved slightly on his arm.

"This is Prophanol."

The entire room seemed to fall into a hush at the mention of the word. Out of the corner of her eye, El noticed that the athletic red-headed angel, having just picked up the battered Sap bag, also stiffened at the word, her familiar and relaxed body programming replaced with an almost militaristic posture. The floating images on the screen, reflecting the thoughts and feelings of the small stadium of watchers, began to display images of the Prophanol needle, giving it a menacing, cartoonlike remake, like the threatening tooth of a monster alien come to suck their life away. We could hear gasps and groans from around us, and even Tobias chided Clo like someone who had brought a dead puppy to a children's birthday party. "Prophanol? C'mon, get that out of here!"

"It takes the Sap away, gets it all out of your system," Clo explained, as if everyone in the room didn't already know.

"We know what it does. We don't need that stuff here." Out of the corner of her eye, El saw that the redheaded angel, having frozen for about two seconds, had resumed her relaxed posture. She started leisurely down the ramp again, presumably to help other patients with their Sap administration.

"I could give it to you right now," Clo offered, her desperation to save Tobias plain in her voice. She reached down to his right arm and began rolling up his sleeve.

Tobias jerked his hand away, almost as violently as El had knocked away the squid bag moments before. "No, don't do that!" In his stoned manner, Tobias pushed Clo's hand upward and flapped his hands wildly, like someone trying to shoo away a wasp. Clo clutched at the vial, careful not to let it fall out of her hands.

"I'd still be sick, right?" Tobias continued to rant. "We all are. That's why we're here, right?"

Clo, crestfallen, silently put the cap back on the needle and repacked the syringe. Tobias's eyes drifted back to the movie screen, and he settled deeper in his seat. The cold, dismal look that overtook his face was enough to tell Clo he wasn't interested in her anymore. He probably thought he was a fool to have been talking to her in the first place.

"Right," she echoed back at him. "Sorry."

The regular images on the giant screen resumed, scenes of smiling faces and a muffled language sound that didn't really convey words, more a feeling of comfort. Occasionally, beautiful 3-D renderings of the octagonal Subantoxx patches or the cute IV squid Friends would appear, apparently as some sort of propaganda cartoon for the Sap.

Flashes of a brown-eyed man dressed something like a police officer were also projected everywhere: it was Maynor. We tried to ignore the images, but it was impossible not to catch a glimpse of the giant screen out of some corner of our vision.

"It's Maynor," El commented.

"Is he here?" Clo asked Tobias, still sad about his rejection of her offer to take him away from all this.

"Yeah, someone in the room must have seen him," Tobias said. "He's always a hit."

Maynor had been handsome in real life, but the screen made him even more good-looking: his eyes more sensitive, perhaps even sacrificial in his duty to protect Yerba City. Various images of him doing athletic maneuvers in his black uniform appeared, and even a few shots of him with a pistol. We couldn't help but stop for a minute and take this in: it seemed to be propaganda for how great this guy was, as if the most epic action movie ever made was going on right now, and he was the star.

El scoffed. Like most things here, one must have to be high on Subantoxx to appreciate it, she thought. Still, there was something to those images: they made Maynor out to be some kind of superman, ever vigilant, ever virile, as he jumped across the screen with his shirt off, his lean muscles flexing to defeat some unseen foe.

Finally we saw him in real life, edging down the theater aisle toward us. Unlike his image on the screen, he was fully dressed.

"Hey," El spoke sharply.

"Hello," Maynor responded, apparently slightly surprised at the empty IV stands on our seats. "I thought you'd be in treatment already." His eyes were kind, but weary. He couldn't have been more than thirty, but there was a heaviness behind his face.

We stood up and faced him. He wasn't wearing the bulky armor that we'd seen him in as he smashed through the city in his living video game. Instead he wore some kind of jet-black, skintight undersuit.

"Nice unitard," Clo said sarcastically. "Are you the City's official mime?"

Maynor shrugged. "It's standard-issue."

On the screen, Maynor was doing somersaults in midair, dispatching strange, faceless villains with ease. El nodded at the imagery. "It looks better on you up there."

"I wouldn't know," Maynor said simply.

"You don't look at the screen?"

"I try not to," he said. "It has a way of . . . sucking you in, and I have rounds to make. Besides, sometimes you don't want to see what's going on inside your own head." Before we could respond to this cryptic statement, Maynor strode past us and examined the seat arms El had spray-painted. "I see you found your own solution. That's very observant. Not many people, even those who have been here forever, know that's how she works."

"We don't miss a trick," El said coolly.

"By 'she,' you mean Yerba City?" Clo asked.

"Yeah, except it's Josephine now. Yerba City went offline a few weeks ago. Part of the new update."

"Josephine?" Clo asked. That didn't sound like an evil robot's name.

Maynor shrugged. "It's the same old routine, just a different package. Look, take my advice and don't mess with anyone's treatment. If there'd been patients in these chairs when you did that, you'd be bounced around in a world of hurt."

"Oh, we know," Clo said, remembering the mean-looking pincer arms back on the train. "We're just looking out for ourselves."

"Anyway, I'm Maynor Romero. What are your names?"

"It's Elizabeth and Chloe Yetti," El said. "But El and Clo are fine."

"Yeti, huh? Like the abominable snowman?"

"It's Polish, with two *t*'s," El explained impatiently.

"But we can be quite abominable sometimes," Clo assured him.

"I'm sure," Maynor said, eyeing us. "Anyway, what can I do for you Yettis?"

"We're looking for someone."

"Missing persons case? Haven't had one of those in a while. Machines keep everyone pretty accounted for. Can you describe the individual in question?"

"Sure," offered Clo. "I have a picture of the 'individual in question.'" She repeated his phrasing mechanically. Then, as she rummaged in her tunic, she found a smoked squirrel on a stick. "Here, hold this." She pushed the dead animal at El, who took the stiff thing reflexively, keeping her untrusting eyes locked on Maynor.

Clo finally found the crumpled photo. "That's her," she said, holding it out for Maynor to examine. "She's a scientist. Came through here about four months ago."

Maynor took the photo and looked at it closely. Then he looked back and forth between the photo and our faces. "Is that your mothe—" He stopped when he realized El was quietly munching on the squirrel, its crispy eye sockets staring at him along with El.

"How long have you all been living out there, beyond the village?" His tone sounded a bit more concerned now.

"The whole time," El said slowly, chewing.

"The whole time?" Maynor asked in disbelief. "Since the Big Spray?"

"All by ourselves," El continued deliberately. "No men."

"That's not true; we had our brother," Clo said, getting more and more irritated with her sister. "Who is currently leading an army of babbling maniacs across the bridge, so I suggest you take us to our mama as soon as possible."

"Okay, well." Maynor shook his head. He clearly wasn't used to this much sober attention, and El's predatory gaze was throwing him off. He couldn't help but notice El's wolflike eyes projected up on the big screen, for all to see. "Let's, uh, get out of here and we'll discuss it en route."

Maynor paused for a second to give a little fist bump to Tobias. "Catch you later, Tob. Keep it real."

Tobias looked up at him vaguely before focusing back on the screen. "I'm all about the real," he said vaguely.

Maynor edged around El and headed for the escalator.

Clo, standing firm, snatched the picture back out of his hand as he passed us. "En route? En route to where?" she snapped.

"Saturnalia."

"Saturnalia? What's that?"

"It's where all the scientists are now." Maynor paused at the escalator. "You said she was a scientist. Then that's where she's gonna be."

"What is it, like a think tank?" Mama was always running off to things called think tanks when we were kids.

"A think tank? Yeah, sure." Maynor nodded impatiently.

"Wait," El said, her head snapping to look at the giant screen, remembering that first day again, when we were on the run. "Before we go, could I just . . ."

"You wanna look at someone special? Someone you remember?"

Up on the screen behind him appeared a man in his midthirties, redheaded, smiling.

"It's Papa!" Clo gasped.

"I wouldn't do that if I were you," Maynor warned. "There's no end. The Goat never stops."

Hearing the name out loud seemed to snap El out of her fixation, and she angrily turned from the screen to Maynor. "The Goat?" she asked incredulously. "So, you know what it is?"

"Yeah, I know. He's the City's little poet. Shows you what you want to see, tells you what you want to hear."

"We know what it is," El said decisively. "Just wondering why you haven't shut it down if you know how it's messing with these people's minds."

"Shut it down?" Maynor asked, amused. "It's a pillar of treatment." He said the phrase like it was something from his law enforcement manual, which it probably was. "What would these good people do without it?"

El sighed and made the decision not to get into the conversation right then. She started toward the escalator, using all her power not to look up at her father's face. "C'mon, then. Let's not get distracted."

Clo paused for a moment to look at Tobias, then back up to the screen.

"Couldn't we just see Papa one more—"

"No," El said, with an iron certainty that echoed through the room.

Clo paused, then nodded. When she looked once more to Tobias, the young man didn't even make eye contact with her, just kept staring at the screen. "Bye," he managed to mumble.

Clo already missed Tobias and his jovial character, but she didn't blame him for his mesmerized state. The effects of the Sap and the Goat were meant to be unshakable. For a moment, we wondered how anyone ever made it out of this building and out to the Drag with the Subversives. Judging from the vast number of people cloistered in this Local One, it must just be a tiny minority, less than one in one thousand, who managed to sober up enough to get out. Still, that would be enough to have created the village we saw—perhaps just barely.

But that wasn't our problem now; we were going deeper into the City, not out. "Bye," Clo mumbled to Tobias and turned to follow Maynor.

CHAPTER 13

TREATMENT OF CHOICE

At the escalator, Maynor was waiting. He hopped on and moved upward.

El didn't follow right away. "Hey, I thought we were leaving."

Maynor grunted and pointed. "I parked on the roof."

El was suspicious, but a lot of the City's work did seem to be done with drones and various flying machines. Why should Maynor be any different? Clo joined El, and we both hopped on and took the few steps up to stand next to him.

"So, uh, none of the angels recognized your mother's picture?"

"No," Clo said curtly. "Do you know something they don't?"

"Well, that's the only reason I'm here, isn't it?" Maynor said with resignation as he looked out across the floor of the giant treatment center. "It's not our world anymore; this planet belongs to the machines now. They just keep us around because they can't think outside the box. They like us monitors because we're like guard dogs: we sniff around with our brains in a way they can't. Although they've been whittling us down almost since the beginning, we still have a place."

"Why can't the machines just—" Clo made a breathy whistling sound and circled her finger in the air.

"What?" Maynor was clueless, although he seemed slightly amused.

"She means, why can't they just talk wirelessly," El explained impatiently. "If we show one Tik-Tok the picture, why can't they just talk to all of them through the air and see if another one has ever seen her? People's phones could do things like that when we were little."

"Oh yeah, that," Maynor said. "Too much malware."

We looked at him blankly.

"Y'know: viruses, hijackers, worms, things like that," Maynor explained.

"You're worried about worms?" Clo asked. "You shouldn't be. They're slimy, but they're friends of the garden."

"He means computer worms," El said to Clo. "That can bore into their computer minds."

"Yeah, basically," Maynor said, giving us a quizzical look. "That's how they fight, mostly: cyberwarfare. Over the networks. So she tries to keep everything analog: nothing digital, nothing over the air. That way it's more secure." He pointed to something mounted on the side of the escalator wall. "Look." He pulled from its cradle a half circle about ten inches long. Its body was segmented, not unlike one of the City's insect drones, and a cord led from its tail back into the wall.

"Is that big thing—a phone?" Clo asked.

"Yeah, that's what we have to use now, since the second Ping War. Anything else can easily be compromised."

"That's why that nurse was talking on an old-timey corded phone," El surmised.

Clo nodded. *"And even hers wasn't working."*

"What language is that, anyway, that you're talking?" Maynor asked.

"It's our speak," Clo said proudly.

"Stragglers have their own language?" Maynor asked. "I never heard of that."

"No," El said, "it's just us. It's our twinspeak. Not even our brother knows it."

"Oh, *idioma cuaches*," Maynor said. "Sounds like a K'iche' person talking Swedish backward."

"What's a K'iche'?" El asked. "Is that one of those drones?"

Maynor chuckled. "No. Nothing like that."

"Some kind of robot?"

"No," Maynor said, now clearly wishing he hadn't mentioned the word. "It's my people, or my grandma's people, back in Guatemala." He sighed. "Or was. That kind of thing doesn't really matter anymore; we're all the Chimera's people, now. She gets into your head, and then with the drugs . . ."

He shook his head, as if shifting his attention from things he'd rather not think about. Then, as the three of us slowly spiraled up past the gargantuan second floor of the Local One, Maynor looked out at a mass of people spread out over an undulating, hill-like arena. He raised his hand, seemingly about to call out, when he spotted an old man being led toward the downward escalator.

"Hold on; I gotta put in some community time." Maynor stepped off the escalator and waved. The drooping senior probably wouldn't have noticed had his attendant angel not stopped him at Maynor's gesture.

"Hey, you heading out, Zeb?" The old man looked up at Maynor. "Off to the Local Zero?"

The man looked up dimly and registered Maynor's presence. "That's right, Maynor."

"Well, it's like I always say: if you're off to the Zero, you're off to a better place. New duds, new Sap, new show, right?"

The man nodded in apparent agreement. "Uh-huh."

"You get it all, all right? Just remember, take deep breaths when you get in and you'll be fine." Maynor gave him an affectionate pat, then nodded to the angel holding the man's squid bag. As Zeb shuffled away, Maynor turned to the rest of the room and called into the low drone of voices, "You're beautiful, everyone! Keep up the good work!"

Maynor turned to get back on the escalator, then paused to hear the multichorded voices join and repeat, "Keep up the good work!" in a strangely beautiful motet.

We silently followed Maynor upward as he smugly answered his own words. "Gracias, lo haré!"

The old man was led into the downward spiral as we continued upward.

"The Singers—I love that floor," Maynor murmured, as if to himself.

El watched the singers disappear below us. Maynor was right, it was hard to leave, even from the little taste we had gotten. "That sound is amazing. But it's the Goat, isn't it? Combine that with the Sap, and these patients are trapped here, aren't they?"

Maynor shrugged. "First floor is video. Second floor is audio. Between the two, that occupies about seventy-five percent of all the patients until they're ready for the Local Zero."

"You don't seem too sad about it," El said frostily, "letting people waste away in here like that."

Maynor looked at her coldly. "You don't know what you're talking about."

"Don't I?" El shot back. The two of them locked eyes and stared daggers at each other for a moment.

"Anyway," Clo said, directing the talk away from any conflict with our so-called guide before he outlived his usefulness. "You have that bug phone. Can't you just call this Saturnalia place and see if our mama's there?"

"Oh." Maynor chuckled for a moment, thinking. "That's not really how they work." We eyed him suspiciously. "But it's worth a shot," he said. He unhooked the bulky phone from the wall again and began twisting a series of small lumpy knobs on the thing's belly. It squeaked wildly in a series of old-sounding radio frequency whines. Then he spoke into it.

"Three Two, this is Four Three. Come in, please." About ten seconds went by. Nothing.

"He's probably drunk again," Maynor sighed. He tried again. "Thaddeus. This is Four Three. Come in."

"People still drink? Even with the Sap?"

"Some of the monitors do."

Finally a crackly voice answered, in an impatient, weary tone. "What is it, Maynor?"

"I'm looking for a missing person. Female." He looked us up and down for a second. "Caucasian. She'd, uh, appear to have been living in the woods for the past decade."

The machine in Maynor's hand squawked again. "Naw, naw. Nothing like that. Look, you gotta follow up the 10-57s yourself, dude. We're busy."

"Oh yeah?" Maynor asked skeptically. "And what's keeping you so busy? You got some action up there?"

"They're prepping for the Sloth and Saber. So toodle-oo, old sport." The line clicked dead.

"Did that guy just toodle-oo you?" El asked, unimpressed.

"That's as useful as Thaddeus gets up there." Maynor put the bulky receiver back on its hook. "We're down to one monitor per sector, and she had to keep that guy," he lamented.

"What's the Sloth and Saber?" Clo asked.

Maynor shook his head dismissively. "I couldn't tell you. They have a lot of . . . revels." He said the word like it was borrowed from a foreign language and he'd never been quite sure what it meant.

"So we just have to go there ourselves?" El asked suspiciously.

"Yeah, but I'll take you. This is Zone 4-3, that's Zone 3-2. It's not far by air. No sector is, in the City Zone."

That last word—*zone*—reminded El of something the Crying Man had said. "You said malware is how they fight," she said. "Who's 'they'? Other cities?"

"Josephine calls them entities," Maynor explained. "Since the last war, there are just four others left. But there's a treaty now."

"Yeah, the Crying Man told us about that."

"The Crying Man?" Maynor asked.

"Isn't he one of these 'entities'?"

"I guess." Maynor shrugged. "Like I said, I don't get out of my sector much. Anyway, they control everything outside of the City Zone."

"Not everything," Clo snorted. "They didn't control *us*."

"I doubt anything could," Maynor said mildly.

"Why are all these 'entities' fighting, anyway?" El demanded.

Maynor shook his head. "I don't know. They aren't human, so they don't think like humans; that makes their motivations hard to understand in our terms."

"The Crying Man was human," Clo argued.

"I don't know who that is," Maynor said, "but did he walk and talk like you and me?"

"Well, he could sorta float through walls and disappear and stuff," Clo admitted. "But other than that, he talked like he had a real personality."

"Uh-huh," Maynor said. "Maybe once, but not human now. Anyway, Josephine is the only one left that cares about people. The others want people gone, because of Fimi." Maynor looked at us. "You know about the Fimi virus, right? I mean, the disease has already killed everyone outside of Yerba City."

"Everyone?" El asked skeptically.

"Over seven billion dead, last count."

We were stunned. We knew the world had ended and all that, but still.

El wanted to question it, call it propaganda made up by Chimera's fake news algorithms, but she stayed silent. Could it be true? Seven *billion*? True, aside from the Subversives, we hadn't seen another living soul on our way in, but we had always held out hope that maybe folks were still alive in other countries *some*where. Paris? Tokyo? Lichtenstein? Lesotho? All reclaimed by vines and cougars and pigs and wolverines or whatever? We looked at Maynor. Maybe he was just buying the party line; after all, how else could Yerba City keep control of those not on the Sap? The apocalyptic pandemic had to be part of the narrative she used to keep people in line.

Clo was the first to break the silence. "You're saying there are no people alive outside of the City Zone?"

"Look, there's the City Center, Saturnalia to the north, the Drag to the east, and the Tech Zone to the south. That's all the inhabited sectors. Everything else is just stragglers," Maynor said, "and you're the first I've seen in about seven years."

"But Fimi? Wait," El challenged. "The machines are worried about a disease from Africa? Why would robots care about a disease?"

"Like I said, they don't make a lot of sense to me. But right now, to keep the treaty, there's a quarantine. Until it's lifted, the drones will stop anyone who's infected from leaving the city limits. You can refuse treatment, but then you're probably out in the Drag with the Subversives."

El wanted a straight answer. "But do you *really* think we're sick?"

Maynor looked at her. "Of course you're sick. That why they call it a *pan*demic. Everyone is infected with the Fimi virus. Everyone everywhere is. It doesn't kill everyone right away."

"What if we told you Fimi was a lie?" El challenged. "A made-up virus that Yerba City invented just to keep people addicted to her drugs?"

"I'd say you sound just like those Subversives out there," Maynor scoffed. "And look how they're doing, livin' in all that junk."

"They're not even allowed electricity," El said. "Even we had a couple of little solar panels back in the forest. Is the electricity restriction part of the treaty, too?"

"The human threat," Maynor said glumly, "needs to be controlled. No autonomous people allowed."

"No autonomous *people*?" Clo asked in disbelief.

"But Fimi is a total lie," El insisted. "It's the cure that's the problem. There aren't even any symptoms. How do you know when someone is actually sick?"

Maynor shrugged. "Security is my area, diagnosis is theirs." He nodded past her.

We had been so focused on arguing with Maynor, we hadn't noticed that we'd reached another level. We turned and looked at the third floor.

While the levels we had seen thus far had shown us expanses of hundreds of patients served by a few dozen angel attendants, this place seemed to be the reverse. We only spotted a handful of patients, some lying on rollable cots and some being slowly walked through a series of tests, all of them surrounded by twenty to thirty angels each. At first it wasn't clear to us what the angels were doing. It almost looked as if they were worshipping the patients, crowding around the sick, even jostling each other in their stiff, robotic manner to get a closer look. Two or three angels at a time would talk in low voices, mostly to each other and occasionally to the patient, before stepping or being jostled aside by another angel forcing their way in. Sometimes an angel would hold something up for the patient: a chart or a small video screen with a simple image on it—a blue square, a child's drawing of a cloud.

"These are the doctors," Maynor explained, as if the one word should be enough.

"Why are there so many . . . doctors?" Clo wondered aloud.

"I think it comforts some patients to have a bunch of voices speaking to them. Specialists. That's kind of what this floor is about. Seems like every patient cruises through here at least once. Makes quite an impression."

We watched a patient—a middle-aged man—standing next to a rollable squid stand and having one foot slowly lifted up and down by a pair of angels. We supposed the pretense could be some kind of therapy, but the movement was so minor that it was hard to believe there was any kind of benefit. After just a few movements, the pair of so-called doctors was swapped for another, moving in sync. As on all the other floors, the angels here were of various ages and racial backgrounds, except here they wore black coats and the triangles on their foreheads were white instead of black. Some angels even had badges or sashes with that double-snake snake-and-staff symbol. The black coats were a strange touch, El thought.

The patients on this floor were a bit less drugged up than the ones we'd seen previously, and we guessed they were the ones who were perhaps going through a phase of treatment where they needed some kind of clinical convincing to remain medicated in the Local One. To us, it was all theater, just part of an elaborate ploy to keep people addicted and stuck in this insane tower.

Neither we nor Maynor bothered to get off on the third floor, but Maynor waved to the middle-aged man with his feet in the angels' hands. "Hey! How ya doin'?"

The man slowly nodded and waved, answering back in slow, slurred speech. "G-g-getting better, Maynor."

"You stick with it, now. I believe in you!"

Three or four of the angel doctors approached the escalator, reaching for Clo and El with various stethoscopes, otoscopes, and other unrecognizable, but apparently medical, devices.

"You want to talk to them?" Maynor asked us. "I'm sure they could find something wrong with you."

"I'm sure." El remained unmoving, letting the escalator take us upward and away. When the doctors were finally out of view, she turned to Maynor. "How many . . . treatment centers like this building are there?"

"Between the four sectors? Thirty-three."

"Thirty-three?" Clo repeated in disbelief. "Buildings like this?"

Maynor nodded. "Yeah. That's what we're all about here in Yerba City. People are sick, we give them treatment."

The truth was a little hard to take, but it was obvious. We could still remember the throngs of shamblers pouring across the freeway to get into the city a decade ago, and now there wasn't anyone on what was left of the streets. Where else would they be? Judging from the size of this place, that meant millions and millions of people in treatment.

"We just wanna find Mama," Clo explained.

"The northern sector. Saturnalia. It's nice. Like I said, they have parties. I got a place there."

"Parties?"

"Recreation aids healing," Maynor said, in a tone that suggested he was quoting some kind of official directive. "See?" He pointed to the next floor: Level Four.

We emerged into the middle of what was apparently a dance floor, a totally flat expanse that extended in spiral circles away from the central escalator. Patients here were dancing in a slow, waltz-like manner. Most were coupled with black-triangled angels who led the patients through their clutching, shuffling movements. The dancers seemed to radiate out from the middle of the room. Everyone was moving about two miles an hour. As before, Maynor waved and called hello. A dozen or so drugged patrons answered back, breaking their embraces only slightly to give small, automatic waves in Maynor's direction. The attention really did seem to boost Maynor, though, like he was running through the motions of his own addiction to the thought of being some kind of hero to these people.

"You really are a celebrity around here," El observed.

"Aw, cheering me on just gives them something to do," Maynor confessed nonchalantly. "And me, too."

"What are you all waiting for? I mean, does anyone ever get better?"

"Yeah," Maynor said, slightly irritated. "Yeah, they get better. Just look at them. You think they'd be better off outside, wading through all the broken glass?"

We brooded over his answer as we continued up the escalator. It wasn't exactly the question we were asking, but we decided not to pursue it. Seemed a bit like asking a zookeeper if the lions might prefer being poached.

"What's past the four zones?" Clo asked.

"Huh?" Maynor asked, still waving distractedly.

"Outside the quarantine zone. Where the other entities are. What's left out there?"

"It's a wasteland," Maynor answered, like it couldn't be more obvious. "You were out there. What did you see?"

El thought for a moment. "Waste," she said.

"There ya go."

"But the forest is beautiful," Clo contradicted. "With the trees and streams and animals; it's better than living in here with these creepy robots."

"Not everyone has the privilege of running away and living off the land when the world decides to fall apart."

Not that we really cared what Maynor thought of us, but that struck us as a weird idea. In the decade we had spent out there, staying inside Oggy's perimeter, freezing in the winter and burning in the summer, eating the occasional skunk and using squirrel tails for tampons, we hadn't considered ourselves privileged. But compared to this life, maybe acorn mush was an extravagance.

Out on the dance floor, which we were now rising above, a patient—a girl in her early twenties—fell away from her partner. The accompanying angel was quick to catch her, gingerly laying the girl on the floor as she went into convulsions, clear vomit coming from her mouth in small spurts.

"Is there a faster way out of here?" El asked.

"Not usually, but . . ." Maynor seemed to be considering something. He turned to one of the blue-uniformed angels on the escalator. "Hey, can you get us up to the roof, ASAP?"

The angel, a dark-skinned man in his thirties, turned his face toward Maynor blankly.

Maynor made a quick gesture to the escalator, and then a fast rolling motion with his finger. "Like, speed it up."

"Maynor," the angel responded, "you know that safety measures would prohibit—"

"It's Josephine's orders," Maynor interrupted, trying to sound as official as possible. He jerked his thumb in our direction. "Transportation of these individuals is priority one."

It took the angel a moment to consider. "Very well. Hold on, please."

The angel and every other one of the evenly spaced escalator attendants, simultaneously, grabbed the handrail. Surprised, Maynor reflexively grabbed, too.

The immense double-helix structure we were riding on lurched into fast motion. The two of us, not holding on to anything, lost our balance and almost went tumbling backward. The angle of the ramp being so slight, and the floor being so rubbery, we probably wouldn't have been hurt, but in any case, Maynor moved with incredible speed and grabbed El with his free hand as she tumbled. Instinctively, El had reached out and grabbed Clo.

The escalator speeding into a whirl now, we righted ourselves, and El pulled herself out of Maynor's grip, shooting him a dirty look, which he didn't seem to notice. Instead he laughed, seemingly surprised at our speed.

"Hey, when an angel tells you to hold on, you hold on," he muttered, smiling.

The next floor went by in a blur. As we found ourselves a spot of handrail to cling to, we could just make out patients hanging suspended in midair, some of them rotating, their faces or crotches attached to mechanical tubes. Despite our speed, Maynor still found the time to wave and call to the patrons.

Those with mouths free murmured back to him, but in moments we were whirring past the next floor, which seemed impossibly packed with bodies. It was a wall of patrons, or patients, the half-dressed figures pressing impossibly tight against each other and the glass wall of the escalator. A few of the sapped-out eyes must have caught us, as a collective "Maynor!" could be heard in a muffled cheer. If the whole floor was packed like that, we thought, there could be ten thousand people there.

The next floor, in stark contrast, was a vast, empty white landscape lit in an almost-blinding fluorescent glow. Compared to the previous floor, there hardly seemed to be anyone in treatment there at first, but then we spotted a small circle of figures about seventy yards in, maybe fifteen in all, a few standing but most sitting facing each other. Two attendant angels stood attentively behind the group. All the patients were young, between about ten and fourteen years old. The kids all had on hospital gowns, with Sap stands, and a couple of the kids were rocking slightly. In addition to the drug-dispensing squids pumping into their arms, the adolescent patients here each had on a helmetlike device that we recognized as some kind of virtual reality headset.

"Are those . . . children?" El asked.

"What's left of them," Maynor said. "They grew up under Project Chimera. Treatment is the only world they've ever known. When they get old enough, they move on to other floors, so there's fewer and fewer of them every year."

"What about the babies?" Clo asked.

"Babies?" Maynor asked. "Oh, no one's been born since the Big Spray. Too risky, while there's infection. I think the Sap prevents it."

"So there are no young people in the city?" El asked. "No little kids?"

"Just these last ones here," Maynor said with resignation. "That's the future right there. Of humankind, at least."

"What's going on inside those headsets?" Clo asked suspiciously.

"I'm not sure," Maynor answered, as the floor slid away from view beneath us. He didn't seem very concerned. "I think it's school. They always seem to be thinking about something, so I call them the philosophers. This is where Josephine came from."

We both looked at him, and El said, "Wait. So, Josephine is a—"

Smack! Smack! Smack! Smack! The sound came from the escalator, and with each echo, the escalator slowed somewhat. For a moment we thought that something—or maybe someone—had gotten caught up in the gears of the machine and their mangling was slowing it down. But then we saw her.

Up on the next floor, there was a girl in a white dress slowing down the escalator—with her bare hands. She had dark skin and looked like she was about twelve years old, with a big puffy Afro and cute purple hair band. Her little feet were braced against the ground, and the smack-smacking was her grabbing the escalator's handrail at intervals, apparently to slow the whole ride down. She must have had the strength of a hundred grizzlies, because it was working.

Maynor seemed as surprised as we were.

"Is that . . . another angel?" Clo asked.

"Oh yeah," Maynor said grudgingly. "That's my boss."

"That little girl is Josephine?"

"Uh-huh." We were now almost close enough to call to her. "Showed up about a month ago."

"Strong little thing, isn't she?" Clo commented.

"Oh yeah."

Josephine nodded to the attending angel on the escalator in front us. "Stop it now. Whoa." The angel responded to her, bringing the now-tamed escalator to a stop with us right in front of her. Satisfied, Josephine let go of the handrail.

"Josephine," Maynor said to her coldly. "Didn't know you were in the building." He didn't seem to like her.

"More requisitions," she said simply and then looked up at us. We only say up because the little girl must have been a full foot shorter than we were, despite the superstrength. Her eyes darted between the two of us, with a human, if inscrutable, glint. "Hello," she said, nodding, and gave us a mild, mysterious smile.

We were fascinated. In fact, we rushed to approach the little android and examine her face as closely as we had the Ellen angel down at the entrance.

"This one doesn't have the triangle on her forehead," Clo pointed out, hovering about an inch away from Josephine's face.

"And so strong!" El felt Josephine's biceps.

"And that hair!" Clo lightly patted the top of Josephine's puffy Afro.

"Hey, can you back it up a bit?" she snorted at us, putting up her little hands to shoo us away.

"Oh, sorry," Clo said, and we backed away, realizing our condescension. "It's just—"

"We thought you were a Tik-Tok robot," El explained apologetically.

"Doesn't matter what I am. You don't need to be all up in my face, loser," Josephine huffed, squinting angrily at El.

El stared back at her and they faced off for a moment. Two stars shone brightly in El's mind. One: this little girl was somehow the personification of Yerba City, the tricky Jolly Rancher that El had, so many times, imagined shooting through the metal skull in the decade since we'd been driven out of our home and into the forest. And two: Josephine was also a little playground squirt who needed to be bitch-slapped in front of the whole school.

"Don't mind them, boss," Maynor said coolly. "They just came in from the woods."

"I know who they are." Josephine glanced between us again, unimpressed, and turned to Maynor. "Anyway, you need to get these two to Saturnalia. I'll meet you up there in a few hours." Without waiting for Maynor's response, she turned and strode back onto the expansive floor.

We glimpsed what appeared to be large vats of a golden liquid, surrounded by huge, multiappendaged machines. Patients, looking just barely alive, were being lowered into the thick fluid by the appendages and the attendant angels, who themselves stood half-submerged in it. What exactly was going on? Was the liquid killing them? Copying them?

"Did you hear about the trouble in the Eastern Sector?" Maynor asked with a tone of defiance.

"Yeah." Josephine tucked in the last of the jutting robotic arms on a horse-sized machine and then lifted the whole thing off the floor. "That's why you have to get them up north."

"*Whoa,*" said Clo as Josephine marched back toward us with the giant contraption on her shoulder. *"That's one strong little girl."*

"I don't think that's a little girl," said El. *"At least not anymore."*

"What are *you* going to do?" Maynor asked, clearly annoyed at being told what to do.

"'Scuse me." Josephine motioned for us to move aside and stepped onto the escalator with us, just barely squeezing the bulky contraption in without hitting anything. The strange and elaborate machine was at least seven feet long. "I gotta get this replicator to the Southern Sector." She nodded to the attendant angel on the steps, and the escalator began to move upward again.

As the vats receded, El noted that the man being lowered into the nearest vat looked old, and frail, and it occurred to us that we had never seen an angel that looked like it was under twenty, or over maybe thirty-five.

"So you're making everyone into Tik-Toks?" Clo asked.

Josephine, careful not to let the giant replicator shift on her shoulder, turned and looked at us blankly, maybe even slightly annoyed. "Huh?"

"You're making everyone into Santa Clauses," Clo clarified.

"Oh, we call them angels. Not everyone gets to convert," she said. "You gotta apply." She turned back and began to hum a little tune to herself.

There was an awkward moment, listening to that humming and also the whir of the escalator as that strange statement sank in. Apply? To get turned into a robot? Maybe that was an awesome alternative to being stuck by an opioid squid all day.

The escalator attendant turned to us. "I am scheduled for maintenance. Will you be needing any additional services?"

"Not unless you can haul one of these bad boys," Josephine grunted, nodding toward her burden. For the first time, we noticed two crisscrossing scars across the deltoid of Josephine's right arm. We didn't have to use our secret language to make a note of that: for some reason, Yerba City had replicated every part of this little girl, scars and all.

Our eyes followed the attendant as he stepped off the escalator. Here at the top, the tenth floor, there were no patients at all, only angels and more of the large, multilimbed machines that maintained them, similar to the thing that Josephine was now carrying. The attendant was dismembered midstride by an array of silvery robotic limbs and tendrils: first his uniform was seamlessly stripped away, then his arms and legs were removed. During this whole dissection process, the android's momentum continued until the entire floating mess was brought to an examination booth, where the chest cavity and cranium were popped open and scrutinized by a more delicate array of probes and sensors.

For a brief second, our butchering instincts were activated by the sight of this strange being getting taken apart. In our family, if someone killed an animal, everyone had to join in the cleaning and preparation ASAP. Mama had taught us, after all, that once the first drop of blood was spilled, it was a race against time to keep as much of the kill from spoiling as possible. Our lives depended on this. The robot's guts, although golden instead of red, were so real that Clo's hand instinctively went to her knife at the sight.

El touched Clo's wrist to stop her. *"It's not our kill,"* she whispered, shaking her head.

"You're sure we can't eat just some of it?" Clo whispered back.

"You do realize those are humans, and actually not real?"

"But they look so meaty, and a lot is going to waste."

El nodded. To our waste-not mentality, Clo actually made sense.

There were about a hundred angels being serviced simultaneously here: limbs being replaced, ichor being replenished, or androids in the process of being washed and re-dressed before being sent back onto the escalator.

"It's Santa guts," Clo quietly commented, and El instantly understood what she meant. The golden biomechanical aesthetic we had seen months ago when Mama dismembered the Santa Claus Tik-Tok was apparent everywhere here, in bodies half-built and half-dissected. That jolly fat man had apparently been created in a facility like this, expressly for the purpose of walking out to find stragglers like us.

The place was awe-inspiring, to say the least: an immense artificial-people factory. But there was something missing among the steadily conveyed strings of shiny artificial organs, the rotating tanks of golden robo-blood, and the ochre, cauliflower-like brains that could be swapped from body to body.

"Mama would have said good craftsmanship," El commented. *"But there's no sparkle."*

Clo looked at Josephine. *"But she's got the sparkle."*

"Yeah," El agreed, *"and she's super strong. I bet she could juggle a hundred black bears. And not baby bears, either. Full-grown dude bears."*

"Not just that. She's still human. She remembers who she was."

"Yeah, and I think she was a little twerp even before the End of the World."

Josephine turned sideways and looked at us. She was careful not to turn all the way around, as shifting the giant burden in her arms would cause a major catastrophe.

"You two are lucky, always having each other. My sister only comes when she wants to."

El was wondering if she'd want to punch the sister in the face as much as this one, but Clo was more curious than anything. "Is she as strong as you?" she couldn't help but ask.

"Oh, Imani is stronger," Josephine assured us. We stood for a second trying to imagine what that would look like. It wasn't easy.

"Okay," Maynor said, breaking the silence. "This is the top. We have to walk up to the roof." Josephine, carrying her giant load like it was Styrofoam, hopped off the escalator and headed toward a set of stairs that led upward. We followed, thinking for a second that if we didn't, the moving walkway might end up in some kind of giant meat grinder at the top. We looked up and realized that, in fact, the escalator simply looped around, some forty feet above us, to send its passengers back downward. The escalator was actually a giant loop, a sort of twisted, traversable Möbius strip running through the center of the Local One from top to bottom and back again. From the look of some of the patients on it, we could imagine some of them never getting off, but simply staying on the slow-moving double helix for hours, maybe even days, at a time.

CHAPTER 14

THE FATTED CALF

El emerged onto the roof first, into a windy golden glow.

"It's sunset already?" Clo asked, disbelieving.

"It was morning when we got here with Tobias," El said. *"Have we really been inside an entire day?"*

It seemed impossible, but time passed very strangely inside the Local One. It was hard to tell how long we'd spent with the watchers in the Goat Room or conversing with the other patients. The rooftop was literally a breath of fresh air, as the evening winds whipped over the ten stories of the treatment center. The view of the crumbling-down city from here was spectacular in its own way: the cracked skyscrapers reflected fiery oranges and pinks in all directions. Right away, we noticed other towers like the one we were on, spread out in the distance across the city. Silvery and imposing, they were the only things left in the landscape that weren't broken or decaying.

Josephine emerged behind us, barely squeezing the giant replicator machine through the doorway to the roof.

Maynor waved a hand in front of his face, and a pair of aviator sunglasses unfolded over his eyes, seemingly out of nowhere.

"Whoa," Clo marveled. "Where were you hiding those?"

"It's standard issue," Maynor said nonchalantly, although it was clear he liked his little gadgets.

"Can you conjure me up another hatchet?" El asked snidely. "I lost mine whacking down those rabid crazies in the village."

Maynor ignored her and headed straight for a giant silver beetle that sat on the yellow-X helipad in the middle of the roof. The vehicle, which shared the same insect-like aesthetic as the rest of the City's drones, was kind of like a minivan-sized cicada, with stumpy legs. Clearly it was an aerial vehicle of some sort, and much bigger than Bouncy. It actually turned on its six legs slightly when Maynor approached and clicked affectionately.

"Hello, Maynor," the cicada chirped in an eager yet subservient feminine voice. "Ready for a lift?"

"That thing's alive," Clo said, *"and it seems to really like him."*

"Yeah," El said acidly. *"Who needs friends when all these bugs worship you?"*

Josephine cut Maynor off before he could respond. "Now, you get these dawdlers straight to Saturnalia, ASAP, all right?" she yelled over the wind. Then she walked away from us, not in the direction of the only other vehicle visible, but toward the edge of the building.

Dawdlers? We looked at each other, wondering what this bitchy little robot was going to do next. *"Where is she going?"* Clo wondered out loud. *"Is she going to fly?"*

"Can you fly, too?" Clo called.

Josephine looked back at us calmly and smiled. "I can fly," she said and jumped off the building.

"No way!" Clo cried, and we both ran to the edge to take a look. Josephine rose steadily into the air, carried on the back of a large four-winged drone. She had placed the giant replicator on the central body of the flying machine and was climbing on top of it. She sat with a satisfied plop and gestured around her with a smile. "See? I can fly!" she chortled as the wind whipped her puffy hair.

The giant vehicle peeled away from the side of the building and headed into the wind. "I'll see you at Saturnalia. And don't dilly-dally!" Josephine called, and she gave us a final curt nod before she bent over and clung tight like a jockey on a racehorse, bracing against the acceleration before she and the drone shot southward.

"You heard her," Maynor grumbled, and turned to his vehicle. "Open up, Zeta."

"Of course," the vehicle answered, and it turned sideways as a section of its flank lifted to reveal a waiting cockpit.

"Wait!" El called, and Maynor grudgingly stopped on Zeta's step and turned around.

"How do we know you're not a goldeneye?" Clo demanded, her palm on Toothy's pommel now that the truth might come out.

Maynor didn't miss Clo's hand on her knife, and seeing both of us frozen and ready for a confrontation, he froze, too. Clearly he'd seen his fair share of action: Subversives, patients off their meds. We all three were suddenly well aware of the fact that right about now, he didn't have that fancy armor on that he'd been jumping around in earlier. Lucky for him, he played it cool.

"What's a goldeneye?" Maynor asked, trying to sound casual.

"It's a duck," El said flatly.

"A duck?" Maynor echoed coolly.

"Yeah," said Clo. "A sweet little black-headed duck with pretty eyes. He's real nice all year long, hanging out with his favorite girl, but when the season comes, he rapes her."

"All the young drakes do it," El said coldly.

"Sometimes the girls get hurt real bad," Clo said, her fingers on Toothy's handle now. "Sometimes they even die."

Maynor visibly relaxed, untensing and slowly reaching up to tap the side of his sunglasses. They folded up and disappeared, revealing his sincere eyes.

"Wondering if you should trust me? Get into my giant talking beetle and go for a ride?"

We stayed silent, frozen, ready. No reason we couldn't cut him, toss him over the edge of the building, and fly that thing ourselves—or at least try to—and he knew it.

"We need to know," El said coldly. "Are you a sweetheart beaver boy—"

"Or one of those goddamn ducks?" Clo finished the thought.

Looking back, there was really no way he could have entirely understood what we were talking about, but, to Maynor's credit, he got the general idea, and it didn't faze him. He just nodded and stepped down from the vehicle entrance.

He took two deliberate steps toward us, stopped, stood straight, and raised his right hand in the air. With the glow of the sunset forming a golden crescent on his face and the wind picking up around us, he slowly spoke. Clearly this was a variation of something he had memorized long ago, back when he first joined whatever the law enforcement agency was that originally set up the monitoring force:

"I, Maynor Hunahpu Romero, do solemnly swear, in accordance with my duties as a monitor of Yerba City, that I will protect and defend the Yetti twins against all enemies, foreign or domestic; that I will bear true faith and allegiance to the same; that I take this obligation freely, without any mental reservations or purpose of evasion; and that I will not rape anyone, under any circumstances, ever. So help me God." He lowered his hand and cocked one eyebrow at us. "That good enough for you?"

We shot a look at each other, then back at him.

"Do you swear it in all four directions to Mother Oggy?"

Maynor paused, but only for a second. Okay, maybe he had no idea what it meant, but he was game. "Sure. North, south, east, and west." He turned around in a little circle in the wind. "No raping, I swear. Okay?"

We looked at each other again.

"He doesn't know what that means," Clo observed. *"He doesn't know about Dasher, or anything."*

"It'll do for now," El acquiesced.

"But if you mess with us—" Clo said, taking her hand off the knife.

"We'll open you up," El finished the thought.

"Messing with you is honestly the last thing on my mind," Maynor grumbled and turned back to Zeta. "Now come on."

On board, the three of us buckled in, Maynor hopping into the pilot's seat, and then the "door" in the carapace of the enormous beetle folded down to seal us inside. We sat behind Maynor in one of two rows of seats, which had automatically folded out of the floor for us when we got in.

"Where are we going today, Maynor?" the vehicle asked in an excited tone, the mechanical voice visible in blue pulses on the elaborate control panel.

"I'll pilot today, Zeta," he answered and put his hands on two control sticks, which themselves looked like tiny silvery bug hands, each with six grub-like metal fingers.

"It's always good to practice manual flying," Zeta commended him. "In case of emergencies."

Maynor struggled a bit with the controls, but got the craft lifted off the roof. It was clear, in his effort to appear the calm, in-control authority figure, that he was making extra effort to fly Zeta himself rather than let the autonomous controls take over. El watched as the rooftop retreated below us. We had taken a couple of plane rides as children, but had never been on a helicopter, much less in something like whatever this machine was. It really was like flying inside of a giant bug, and, although it was clear Maynor wasn't the best pilot, it wasn't a bad ride. Up we went, somehow transcending the mess below us.

The Local One and the ruins around it fell away, revealing the rolling hills and the shining bay that encircled more than half of the city. Flashes of silver moved back and forth through the air as the drones continued their unceasing work.

"Your boss is a kick-ass little girl," Clo commented at the sight of the aerial vehicles.

"You like her?" Maynor snorted. "Don't be fooled. She's still part of Project Chimera."

"What do you mean?" El asked.

"I mean that even though she can think and talk like a little girl from Oakland, she's all machine, without a doubt."

"You said she's the first? The first Tik-Tok robot that remembers who she was?"

"First and only one I've ever heard of. And it took a lot to make her. City resources shut down for two days when she was replicated. Very difficult to reproduce a human brain, apparently."

"But why?" El asked. "Why would Yerba City go through all the trouble of making an exact copy of Josephine?"

"And then put her in charge?" Clo continued the thought.

"What, you don't think a black person would make a good leader?" Maynor challenged. "Maybe you don't think a Guatemalan boy like me would make a good cop."

"What?" Clo asked, utterly confused.

"I get it." Maynor nodded. "You're discriminatory."

We were perplexed, and didn't really follow what Maynor was talking about. "It's not that," El said. "Whatever that even means. She's a little girl."

"Ha!" Maynor laughed, "I'm just playing around with you. I don't know what's going on, but as you probably noticed, the copy is not exact, because that is not exactly a little girl. Don't know what you country ladies did out there in the woods for fun, but here in the city, little girls don't usually lift a ton over their heads like Josephine."

"So Yerba City made a supergirl."

"Yeah, but don't let the brawn fool you," Maynor said, tapping his head. "It's the brain that's the breakthrough. I was used to orders from machines, getting a text on my phone, something like that. Now it's 'stop giggin' and 'swoop over here.' 'Do you have any bubble gum? Do you know this song? My auntie once said this and that.' It's weird."

"What *isn't* weird about this place?" Clo questioned.

"The City even copied her scars," El said. "Did you notice that?"

Maynor shook his head indifferently. "All I know is, she kicks ass and she's on my side. And that's really all I need to know." He paused, shrugging. "Personally, I think she's a little snot, but it's another sober voice to talk to, and those are rare these days."

"All those Tik-Tok angels can talk to you," El pointed out. "They'll talk your head off."

Maynor scoffed. "That 'clinical empathy' jive gets old quick."

"Speaking of sober," Clo said, "what will happen to Tobias?"

"Tobias?" Maynor was struggling with the controls but still managed an evasive comeback. "Why, you sweet on him?"

Clo was silent.

"He's cool," Maynor continued. "You could do worse. Whatever you do, don't fall for one of those squidheads. They always end up downstairs."

"What'll happen to him?" El repeated, irritated.

Maybe it was because El asked this time, but for a moment we could tell that Maynor was actually jealous that we would care. He caught himself. "Well, like everyone else, either he'll fall back in with the Subversives, or he'll continue treatment in the nearest Local One or Local Zero."

"Zero?" El said.

"Yeah, the Local One can handle most cases, but if a patient becomes full-blown, they might need transpo to a Local Zero. Between the Ones and Zeroes, all treatment is covered."

We were about to ask what the difference was, but in truth we didn't want to know—what we had seen in "basic" treatment was enough for one lifetime. And then something caught Clo's eye: below, on the bridge, that strange shack again, on the cliff on the island. We hadn't realized at first what direction we were going.

"Hey, why are we heading out east this way?" El asked. "We were just here."

"Just have to make a little pit stop before we move on."

Maynor, more comfortable with flying now, kicked the cicada into a higher gear. The sharp acceleration threw us back into our seats, which seemed to tighten around us like living cocoons.

"Whoa," said Maynor, fighting a bit for grip. "And that's only quarter throttle. Forgot how fast this baby can go."

Below, the decaying, whitish second span of the Bay Bridge shot past. The cicada was a lot faster than the bridge train, even at quarter throttle. The sun was down now, and even the rosy glow seemed to be dissipating, leaving the unlit darkness to begin obscuring the cityscape.

Soon we came to the Drag, the sprawling tent city spreading in front of us. The cicada descended, seemingly right toward the middle of the village.

"Hey, what are we doing here? People are going crazy down there," El protested.

"Exactly." Maynor nodded. "Have to pay them a little house call, teach them some manners. That's my job."

El shot Clo a look, then turned to Maynor. "Look, we just want to find our mother."

"What about Josephine's orders?" Clo added.

"The City keeps me around for a reason," Maynor said aloofly. "Sometimes I have to make decisions on my own."

"You swore an oath to us," Clo reminded him.

"To protect and defend you, not follow your every little command." Maynor kept his eyes forward. "I have to follow up on security issues, especially when violence is involved. You told me you encountered trouble in the Drag. Besides, don't you want me to check on your brother?"

El snorted. "If we had to pick one person to solve our problems, it would be our mama, not some self-important magpie in shiny armor."

Maynor turned and looked at El with daggers in his eyes. We had no idea who he had been before the End of the World—maybe a grade-school bully—but the comment seemed to have cut close to home. So much so that when he opened his mouth to retort, he apparently forgot he was flying, and the cicada pitched wildly.

"Aaah!" Maynor cried, righting the vehicle again.

"Just put the thing in autodrive or whatever," El said coldly. "You know you can barely fly it."

"Fine," Maynor growled. "Zeta, switch to autopilot."

"Yes, Maynor, my pleasure," the console answered in her pleasing voice as our craft stabilized into a perfect flying speed.

He swiveled his chair around and faced us.

"You should watch your mouth," he said to El, holding up a finger.

"Why, you only like machines talking to you now?" Clo challenged. "'My pleasure, Maynor,'" she said, mocking Zeta's pleasing manner. "'I'll do whatever you say, Maynor, you're so freaking great.'"

"Yeah, she can talk," he said impatiently. "All these machines can talk. They all have brains, okay? But they make a lot of dumb mistakes. They can't do what we humans can do."

"She can fly a lot better than you," El observed, noting how smooth the ride had gotten.

"Look," Maynor fumed, "I'm a highly trained individual, in tactical and weapon specialties. On this vehicle, we got riot gear, tear gas, audio disruptors, visual confounders, and this baby right here." From under his seat, Maynor pulled a heavy-looking carbine, covered with various handles and switches.

"What is that?" Clo asked suspiciously. It barely looked like a rifle.

"This is the Love Gun. An S22-A Target Engagement System. Latest in crowd control. Seven different kinds of rounds. Rubber bullets or real bullets. Counterdefilade ordnance if need be. Auto range finder, fléchette option, and there's even a flamethrower if the situation calls for it."

Having lost Daisy Duke, we couldn't help but be slightly impressed. El shook it off.

"That's great, but while you've been sitting here acting like king of the playground with your little toy, you might have missed something: it's not just addicts off their meds down there. There are real monsters that have come out of the woods."

Maynor took a second away from rubbing his precious rifle. "Yeah? Like what?"

"Like a whole lotta crazy!" Clo blurted. "All the villagers have gone buck wild."

"We brought our brother into the village," El explained. "He was infected with something. Words, sounds that made him go crazy."

"And he gave it to all the villagers," Clo continued. "They went nuts, too, and started attacking us."

"*Sounds* that made him go crazy?" Maynor coolly questioned. "You sure it wasn't just untreated Fimi virus?"

"Yes, we're sure, because *there is no Fimi virus!*" El growled. "We told you, it's a myth."

Maynor scoffed, reserving that debate for another time. "So, you're saying he was making noises that made everyone go crazy?"

"Yeah, like a weird language," Clo insisted, "and anyone that heard it was like a death-cult convert instantly."

Maynor was silent, thinking.

"You don't believe us, do you?" El said.

Maynor nodded. "Actually, I do. Paddington told me about it on the radio, while you were watching movies. I figured the only reason Tobias wasn't infected was because of his, uh, hearing impediment." Maynor looked from El to Clo. "But there's one part we were all curious about: If everyone who heard it went bonkers—even the drones—why didn't it infect you two?"

We looked at each other. "We don't know," El confessed.

"Well, that's convenient," Maynor snorted. For a second he shot us a suspicious look, like maybe he should be considering using his bop gun on us.

"You think we brought Dyre in on purpose?" El bristled. "Why would we do that? We don't care about the city; we're forest people."

"When the Cities beef with each other, it's not always something that makes sense right away on a human scale." Maynor looked at us carefully. "Maybe they used you."

We were silent, remembering that the Crying Man had insisted we stop in the village before entering the city. Maybe we had been played.

"Anyway," Maynor said determinedly, "I'm sure you won't mind a little detour to check things out."

Outside, we could see the firelight of the village coming into view.

"You need to know something, Maynor," Clo insisted. "If you hear this stuff they're saying, you're going to fall under its spell. It's instant." She snapped her fingers.

"Maybe I'll just be immune," Maynor grunted. "Like you two."

"You don't want to make that bet," El said simply.

"Uh-uh." Clo shook her head. "When it hit our brother, we had to hog-tie him. And he pooed himself."

Maynor scoffed, trying to stay cool. "I got a plan."

"You best. Those babblers were breaking their bones trying to get to us. And that was in the first sixty seconds after infection. Who knows what they're up to now."

"Uh, looks like they're dancing," El offered, looking out the window.

"What?" Maynor asked. Clo looked, too, and sure enough, down in the center of the village, it looked like there was an immense fire ritual of some sort going on. Many of the tents and makeshift structures had been piled together, and a huge bonfire had been lit. Around the acrid orange flames, about a hundred of the villagers had gathered and were swaying with rhythmic intensity, rocking and moving in circles, sometimes with each other and other times against. Two of the dragonfly drones moved among the crowd, like worker bees shaking sporadically to convey the location and quality of far-off nectar. And in the middle of it all was Dyre. He had reconstructed a pair of deer antlers out of pieces of scrap metal and was rocking and chanting at the center of the party. Others in the group, mostly younger men, had also mounted improvised antlers, made out of various sticks, pieces of metal, and glass shards, to their heads. Their movements were animalistic and mean, like angry bucks during the rut.

Two of the converted villagers brought forth one of the six-legged robotic mules like a sacrificial cow, its hoofless mechanical limbs struggling weakly. Dyre leaned down and began chanting directly into the thing's stumpy sensory inputs. Two more swaying villagers, clubs and sticks in their hands, stood by in case they had to dismantle the beast. It was convert or die, apparently.

There was no way Maynor was used to a sight like this, but up in our safe cicada, he continued to try to play it cool. "Now that's a party," he said mildly. "Is that patient zero there leading this little cock-a-doodle-doo?"

"Yeah, that's our little brother," Clo confessed, not exactly proud of the fact.

"You can almost hear it from here," El said and turned to Maynor. "Whatever your ace is, you better play it."

"Or we'll be hog-tying you," Clo said coldly.

"Ha, we'll save that for later," Maynor said as he pulled out a large, bulky helmet. "Being in law enforcement, I'm used to folks talking nonsense in defense of their offenses, so fortunately, Yerba City cooked up this Aegis system."

"Egregious system?" Clo asked.

Maynor ignored her and strapped his head into the big helmet. As with the security system on the train, small robotic arms emerged from the vehicle. In this case they carried various plates of dark carbon fiber and began placing them all over his body, dressing him in the riot control armor we'd seen him in before. He continued his pretentious speech as he dressed. "When Perseus went to kill Medusa, he knew if he looked right at her, he'd be turned to stone. So the gods gave him a shiny shield to protect him from her deadly face. Besides, something's got to keep the sonic pacifiers from blowing out my eardrums, too."

"Sonic pacifiers?" Clo asked.

"He means when the dragonflies start screaming," El reminded her sister. "Crowd control."

"Oh yeah, we heard that," Clo remembered, wincing. "That hurt."

"This armor lets me see and hear only what I need to get the job done and uphold the law."

"This isn't just some police action against your half-starved citizens," El warned, looking out the window. "You're going to need something military-grade."

"What's the difference?" Maynor clipped his last strap and looked at her quizzically. All suited up, he looked like a bug himself, we thought, even before he flipped the bulbous visor into place.

Maynor turned. "Zeta, just take us in slow, twenty-foot elevation on the southeast corner of that assembly there."

"Yes, Maynor," the cicada hummed back.

"And, Zeta, you shut *your* ears, too," Clo quickly added. "Those drones on the ground are converted, remember?"

"Yeah," Maynor agreed hastily. "Um, engage the LRAD mute, and go to manual input only."

"Going to input lock now," Zeta said, and half of the lights on her glowing blue console went dark.

El sighed. Even with these precautions, she didn't like it. *"If he gets converted, all armored up like that, he's going to be a tough nut to crack."*

Clo shrugged, more optimistic. *"Maybe his helmet will make everyone look and sound like rainbow unicorns while he blows them away."*

"Whatever. Just don't you hurt our brother," El said to Maynor.

"Don't worry," Maynor assured her, pressing two buttons on the side of the cockpit. The concave door slid open, letting in the night air and the smell of burning rubber. "All of the weaponry is nonlethal. Technically."

"Technically?" El said.

"Except the flamethrower," Clo pointed out.

"Oh yeah," Maynor confessed. "Except that."

"Maynor—" El protested, but before she even finished the word, he hefted the carbine and jumped.

The cicada had made it to the instructed twenty-foot hover above the ground, but Maynor landed easily, diving into a paratrooper roll before popping back up to his feet. He took one hand off the Love Gun for a moment to press a small button on the jaw of his insect-like helmet.

"Citizens of Yerba City!" His voice, magnified by the helmet, echoed impossibly loud over the yelling and chanting. "Please disperse this unlawful gathering immediately!"

The cicada, with us still inside, landed just behind Maynor a few seconds later, and we wished she hadn't. Although he had instructed her to hover, Zeta seemed to be ignoring that and was instead shadowing Maynor like a faithful dog, her loyalty to him apparently overriding the more basic commands. Like Maynor had said, the machine had a brain, but she made dumb mistakes.

"This stupid bug." El glanced around us through Zeta's transparent carapace. *"We're surrounded!"* Maynor was all armored up and talking smack outside, but whether due to arrogance or ignorance, he seemed to think he and his giant beetle sidekick were invincible. He didn't seem to understand that the nonviolent villagers he was used to pushing around would now be willing to break every bone in their bodies to take him out.

Clo took her own quick look outside, then urgently poked the craft's control panel with the hunting knife. "Hey!" she told the machine. "Take off again! Lift off. Fly away."

"He disabled the audio controls, remember?" El grunted. *"To keep this thing from catching the Babbl—Whoa!"*

The cicada shifted, walking around on her stumpy six legs to better face the crowd. It heeled next to Maynor and took up an aggressive posture, lifting up her two front claws.

"This thing's really alive!" Clo said, trying to keep herself steady.

"Now," Maynor continued, further emboldened with his giant flying beetle crouched menacingly next to him, "I can forgive this assault on our visitors if you disperse now and bring forth the instigators—" He continued speaking, but it was hard to hear anymore over the crowd, which was growing louder and more agitated, the babblers' chanting swelling.

We began to hear a few thunks and bangs, barely audible above the chanting.

"I don't think Maynor's little speech is working," Clo observed as a piece of cement crumbled against the windshield. *"They're throwing garbage at us."* With a muffled thud, a small fireball erupted on the

roof of the cicada where a flaming log landed. *"Flaming garbage, that is,"* Clo added.

"Okay!" Maynor warned. "You leave me no choice!" As if he wasn't excited as all hell to use the Love Gun. He took his thumb off the helmet speaker and pressed a combo of buttons on the bulky carbine. A wide muzzle slid into place, and Maynor launched a series of blasts into the crowd. There were bright sparks, and then a thick gray gas began floating through the air. There were a few coughs here and there, but overall the crowd held. The chanting didn't miss a beat: *"Mon Kei Ruu Naa"* and so forth boomed into the night.

Swirling up out of the tear gas came the two red-eyed drones, their maws powering up with a crackle of fierce electricity.

"Uh-oh," Clo said. *"Here come those screamers."*

But Maynor was on it. The first drone sent a bolt of sapphire lightning at him. Maynor was already in the air, flipping with his rocket-assisted boots away from the explosion, which sent chunks of earth flying from the spot where he'd stood. Maynor landed feet-first on the roof of the cicada, but he was off in an instant, even before the pieces of debris from the drone's first volley landed. It wouldn't get a second one.

In midair, Maynor switched settings on the carbine and fired some kind of whitish kinetic disruption right into the drone's mouth. Its metal body expanded and burst like an overfilled water balloon.

"Wow," Clo said as metal parts twirled down into the crowd.

"Guess he's good at something," El concluded, impressed.

Apparently those years of playing dodgeball with the blinking spheres back in Yerba City had paid off. The second drone seemed to have wised up to what it was dealing with, dodging Maynor's second shot and trying to counterfire as Maynor landed. But it was like watching a bobcat kitten fight a wasp: Maynor was up in the air again, and the drone's maw was tracking, turning, trying to get a bead on its prey, all the while not realizing that it was the one being hawked.

BAM! Maynor's shot caught one of its wings, sending the drone into an awkward list.

"He's going to take them down!" Clo said hopefully.

"Wait. There!" El pointed. Up next to the giant bonfire, Dyre was handing out metal weapons, clubs, and sticks to some of the more able-bodied villagers. They seemed to be taking orders, even though

Dyre didn't appear to be saying anything different from the usual chanting. *"They're starting to organize."*

"So they're not all just crazed zom—Look!" Clo cried out. *"It's Vambi!"* On the stumpy block of the robotic mule where the thing's head should have been, there was now an actual head: it was the fanged deer that had started all this ruckus. The thing was still dead, but Dyre had apparently retrieved its head from our pill bug ride and had mounted it on the worker drone's frame. The machine shambled and rocked, clearly possessed by the Babble.

Maynor landed back on the roof of the cicada and took a careful bead on the listing drone he'd crippled. His shot sent the machine spinning into a nearby shanty, mushrooming a messy shower of metal and corrugated fiberglass into the air. Probably no one was hurt, as it seemed that everyone—able-bodied or not—was out on the street, gathering around us.

Maynor gave a satisfied nod, and it was clear to us that he hadn't noticed the ritualistic organizing that was going on by the bonfire. He spoke again through the loudspeaker—"I'm warning you now!"— but neither the tear gas nor his display of combat prowess had had any effect on the crowd. "I'm going to have to take things up a notch." He pressed another button and the Love Gun's barrel switched to a strange cone shape. With a loud, sucking *SLAP*, the carbine barked out some sort of sonic attack, sending one of the villagers spinning into the darkness. One after the other, he sent the babblers end over end out of the firelight, at a rate of around one every three seconds.

"He's good with that thing, but there's no way he can stop them all," El commented. *"They're going to get him and crack into his armor soon enough."*

Up near the central pyre, Dyre seemed to have gotten his little strike crew together, their makeshift antlers gleaming in the firelight. He himself actually mounted the headless mule in preparation to charge down at us invaders. He held his hand out, and something blue fell into it.

"What? El yelled.

We hadn't even noticed it, but one of the smaller babbling dragon-flies, wiener dog–sized, had flown overhead and dropped something into Dyre's hands.

"It's Daisy Duke!" Clo yelled.

"He sent one of the drones back for her!" El realized.

Sure enough, Dyre had our family's scratched-up blue camo short-barrel .30-06 in his hands, and if any of his former self remained, he knew how to use her. The dragonfly flew closer and began feeding small packets of bullets into Dyre's grasp as well.

El pounded on the carapace of the cicada, right under Maynor's feet, trying to get his attention. There was no way he'd be expecting gunfire from the humans.

"Hey! *Hey!*" El yelled, her fist knocking desperately just beneath Maynor's boot. "They got a rifle! There's a *gun!*"

"Gun!" Clo echoed, also banging at the transparent chassis. But it was no use. Maynor was trying to keep up with the onslaught of babblers, whose clawing bodies were now reaching him, climbing toward his position on Zeta's back, despite his repeated concussion blasts. We were pitched off-balance again, slamming into each other as the cicada bucked, frantically pulling the zealots off with her free hooked legs like an elephant fighting off a pride of lions.

But the vehicle's efforts, however valiant, did little good. In seconds the carapace was covered with hands and faces, biting and clawing in a riot of viciousness. Through the tangle of limbs and teeth we could just make out the exhaust from Maynor's jet boots as they fired up and he took to the air again, fleeing his obviously compromised vantage point.

"Wait!" El yelled after him, but of course he was deaf to the world. His precious helmet made sure of that. He didn't even hear Daisy Duke when she cracked across the crowd, sending a 180-grain bullet right into his shoulder in midair. His training with the fléchettes could never have prepared him for that kind of impact, and Maynor was instantly sent into an arcing corkscrew spin. He landed, still whirling, in the middle of the horde about forty yards away.

"He's down!" El yelled as the cicada rocked again, a pure mass of bodies pressed against it. Zeta, to her credit, turned and tried to make her way through the crowd to where Maynor had fallen, but it was clear the tide of battle was against her.

"This bug's gonna go down, too!" Clo yelled.

"We gotta rabbit!" El concluded sharply.

Clo, face pressed against the glass, looked desperately for an exit through the throng, but it was hard to even see out now, so many babblers were covering the craft. *"How? It's like a beehive out there!"*

Suddenly, Zeta, apparently realizing that there were too many unwanted hitchhikers to continue her march to save Maynor, stopped dead, firmly planted all six legs, and shook her entire body like a giant wet dog. We were jumbled inside, but it was nothing compared with the velocity imparted to the babblers clinging to her sides, who were sent flying in all directions with angry howls.

Satisfied, and "dry" now, the cicada marched forward.

We righted ourselves and managed to look dizzily through the now-cleared carapace. Already the throng was readying itself for another rush on our vehicle.

"Now! This is our chance!" El cried and tapped the two buttons at the bottom of Zeta's shell door. She lifted the door and jumped out of the cicada.

Clo followed a second later, and just in time, as crazed villagers were already starting to climb up the stumpy legs of the machine again. Then, *CRASH*, the wiener dog drone, having apparently turned itself into a suicidal projectile, crash-landed into Zeta, cracking her carapace and rocking her onto her side. The crowd was on her in seconds.

As we dashed away, Zeta lurched half-upright again, trying another giant dog-shake to shoo away the fanatic hangers-on. But even as babblers went flying, more and more of them went to work on the big beetle with sticks and stones, like fire ants on a grasshopper.

"Look!" Clo shouted, and some distance away we could make out what had to be Maynor, firing his jets to escape the crowd. We couldn't exactly see him, though, as there were four or five babblers wrapped around him, clinging and digging at his armor. The lowest one, a middle-aged man we recognized as Bradley, had a death grip on Maynor's leg, and another babbler in turn had a death grip on him. And down the chain went: although Maynor was now some forty feet in the air, slowing, pushing upward, a human chain of fanaticism was keeping him shakily tethered to the earth.

"He might make it . . . ," El said hopefully, seeing our one-time guide managing to climb slowly upward above the crowd into the night sky.

CRACK! Another shot from Daisy Duke glanced off Maynor's emerging helmet, leaving a big fracture and sending him into a spin back to the ground.

"He won't make it," Clo concluded. *"Let's go!"* She grabbed El and headed for the one hole we could find in the cloud of tear gas. The fumes burned our eyes, and almost immediately we were nauseous and stumbling.

"Ugh!" Clo gagged. *"How do they keep at it?"* she said, marveling at the stamina of the babblers. Fortunately, the fanatics were distracted enough by Maynor and his giant beetle to allow us to lurch out of the crowd and the gas and back into the part of the village that hadn't been torn down and thrown onto the bonfire.

We stopped only for a second to cough violently and look back. We couldn't make out exactly what was happening through the fire and crowd-control fumes, but we heard Maynor's amplified, but shaky, voice.

"All right—*Ow!*" he barked. "That's it! I'm switching to flame now!"

A small pillar of fire shot into the air; it apparently wasn't enough of a deterrent, as he soon brought the spray down and onto the crowd.

We think Maynor got a couple of them before they finally overwhelmed him entirely. We could easily make out two villagers on fire through the haze, figures moving like human torches. They didn't scream, or drop and roll, or even try to run away. One of the burning people was reaching down for some kind of rock or brick to continue the attack, despite stumbling, presumably blind from the fire. It was a horrible sight.

"People are going to die in all this!" Clo said. *"Maybe our brother, too!"*

"I think they got Maynor and his bug," El said, not commenting on the gritty sight of innocent people burning up. *"So hopefully this is over for now."*

"Let's get out of here anyway," Clo said quickly.

"Let's," El agreed. *"I just hope no one hurts Dyre before we can find a cure—"*

El's voice cut off as she saw our brother across the crowd. Dyre was apparently satisfied enough with Maynor's demise to turn his attention elsewhere—to the ground situation. He was sitting on his robotic mule, riding it as it stalked through the crowd, and the slightly higher vantage point gave him enough sightline to make eye contact with El.

He barked a quick series of Babble words—really just a variation on the constant stream of nonsense that he was spewing—and raised Daisy Duke.

"Hey!" El yelled, more in offense than fright, although it was silly at this point to be upset with Dyre for trying to shoot us. It was what it was. Still, she couldn't help herself.

CRACK! The shot rang crisply in the night air despite the battle-field of chaos around us. El was already dodging, sliding to one side, predicting Dyre's center-mass shot. The bullet missed her body, but it caught the middle of her left forearm, spinning her thumb and forearm to an unnatural angle. Clo didn't give her time to be shocked, or even to go into shock; she grabbed El's good arm and dragged her stumbling into the tent city.

CHAPTER 15

THE PRINCE

We bolted into the darkness, penetrating the jumble of garbage and makeshift dwellings like two rabid bats, doing our best through the adrenaline to remember the path we'd taken earlier that day to the train station. Over the sewer, past the blue tattered tent. Or was it the gray tattered tent?

We could hear some of the crowd follow us, although it was clear now that we were small fry compared to Maynor and Zeta. But we didn't need pursuers after us to get some pep in our step; we ran, jumping over rubble and dodging under clotheslines. El clutched her arm stoically, using the pain and a flood of endorphins to propel her.

"You're hit," Clo panted.

"Just a nick," El retorted, her fingers shaking, trying not to go into shock.

"That's not a nick!" Clo accused.

"Sure it is." El gritted her teeth. *"Just a baby little mini-nick."*

We burst out of the village and onto the train platform, which was even starker in contrast to the Drag at night. No firelight flicker here, simply the flat LED glow, the same as we had seen off the mini-marts along the highway. We didn't hesitate for a second, dashing across the concrete toward the low stairs, El leaving a dotted trail of blood.

From across the platform, we could see that the train was back, waiting as before with its silver maw of a staircase yawning. We made the dash and were up the stairs in an instant, Clo pausing only for a moment to see if we were followed. She could hear chaos some yards away, out past the station's lights, and still catch whiffs of tear gas, but so far no pursuers.

"C'mon!" El yelled at Paddington as she jumped into a seat. "Go! Go! Go!"

"I'm having freaky déjà vu," Clo mumbled to herself as she followed El inside. "Okay," she said to the conductor. "We're sitting. Monsters after us. As usual."

Toward the front of the empty train, Paddington was sitting calmly, as if he'd been waiting patiently for us the entire time. "Do not worry, Chloe and Elizabeth Yetti," he said, without getting to his feet. "No one is allowed to prevent your entry to Yerba City, and security has been increased." As if on cue, a trifecta of drones abruptly descended to the edge of the platform we'd just streaked across.

"They can turn those drones," El insisted through gritted teeth. "Tell them to rabbit out."

"I'm afraid I have no authority over the City's defenses," Paddington answered in an overly pleasant manner. "My job is to—"

"Yeah, that's great, but they're armed out there now; they have guns!" Clo said. "El is shot!"

El winced in her seat, red flowing from between her clutching fingers. "'S nothing."

"Oh dear," Paddington said, trying to comfort her. "The behavior of those off medication is often erratic—"

"Just get us out of here, please?" El growled. "We are seated properly!"

"Of course." Paddington nodded. Outside we could see two or three figures gathering on the station's perimeter, in front of the drones. The machines began their blue crackling.

"But there is something . . . ," Paddington said, his voice hesitant. For the first time, we realized that he hadn't gotten up from his seat when we entered and was sitting oddly, only half facing us.

"Look!" El said, pointing to one of the wraparound windows next to Paddington in the front of the train. It was smashed.

The conductor finally stood up, broken glass sliding off his lap to make a slight tinkle on the ground. "There is sooOOmmething . . ." His voice slurred into an impossible pitch.

"Oh no," El said.

Paddington's unseen hand emerged from behind him, holding one of the bumblebee drones, its body smashed and limp.

"One of the greeting units came through the window," Paddington explained, sounding normal again as he looked down at the dead robot in his hand. "It appeared to be malfunctIOOOONing, so I had to destroy it."

"Something's wrong with him," Clo said in a singsong warning.

"But it spoke to me in a strange voice," Paddington continued, and he turned toward us. The side of his face, the one that had been turned away, was drooped and jerky, like someone who had just had a stroke. "I can't stop—*Kai Raa*—can't stop—*Maa*—hearing it."

"They got to him," El concluded.

Clo stood up, drawing her knife. *"It's okay, I got this."*

"We don't have time," El said, looking out the window. She could see one of the dog-sized drones hovering above the platform jerk violently in the air as a rock collided with it. A few bolts of blue energy were exchanged, and El could just make out a human yowl. *"We gotta get out of here!"*

Clo edged nearer Paddington, not quite pointing her knife straight at him, but clearly ready to. "Paddington," she said, watching him closely, "listen to me now. You gotta fight this thing."

"Yes," the conductor said, both his shaking eyes facing Clo now. "I'm . . . trying." His twitching got more violent; he took a few faulty steps toward Clo. His feet crunched scattered glass as he went. Then the fingers on his hand seemed to release involuntarily, dropping the broken bumblebee with a crunch. "I am afraid my systems have been coOOmpro—comproOO—*Maa!*" He fell to one knee. He really did seem to be fighting against the Babble, his whole body shaking in some internal battle.

"We have to get this train moving," El said, struggling to her feet. She was still gripping her arm but looking around for a weapon of some kind. *"That crowd's going to be here any second!"*

"Can you do it, Paddington?" Clo asked desperately. "Can you beat it?"

Paddington's face contorted eerily, one eye rolling back into ghostly whiteness. The golden ichor began to flow from his nose and the corner of his mouth. He jerked and the liquid spattered onto the floor, mixing with the shards of glass.

"I don't think he's winning," Clo commented. She was pointing her knife directly at Paddington, readying it with both hands. *"Can we drive the train without him?"*

"I think so," breathed El, moving up toward Clo. *"I watched him before."*

"P-please," Paddington gurgled, "i-it's taking me." He lifted his twisting face to us and his rolled-back eye righted itself, squinting into a familiar homicidal malevolence. "It intends to huuUUrt you," he warned us.

"Oh, we know it'll hurt us," Clo said, and we got ready to take him out. Then he said something we didn't expect.

"I—I love you, Elizabeth and ChloOOe."

We were momentarily stunned. We'd seen some pretty bizarre stuff in the past twenty-four hours, but a Tik-Tok confessing his love for us was a new twist.

"I cannot allow you haaAAArmmm," Paddington said. His left arm reached for us in a frantic claw, but his other arm was ready: he pressed the fingers of his right hand into a point and jammed it violently into his left biceps. There was a spray of ichor through his uniform and a sickening squelching sound as the android found purchase around his own humerus bone.

Paddington rocked on the broken glass as he grappled with himself. His "good" eye found us again. "QuiiIIKKly," he gurgled, tilting his head sideways and exposing his neck. "KiiIILll me!"

Clo shot a quick look to El.

"Do it," El barked. *"Otherwise we're going to have to fight him!"*

Clo readied her knife but hesitated. We'd killed a lot of creatures over the years, but nothing that had asked for it.

"He dosed your boyfriend, remember?" El added.

That was the spur Clo needed. With a savage cry, she took two strides, leapt in the air, boosted her momentum with a kick off one of the seat backs, and brought the blade down hard on Paddington's neck. Something in the android let out a savage growl as she descended, but enough of his original programming remained on task that he actually leaned into Clo's knife as it came, enabling maximum cleavage. The result was a strike that sliced through more than half of Paddington's neck, definitively severing whatever served the Tik-Tok as windpipe and spine.

As Clo landed, Paddington's body collapsed in a tangled heap, golden fluid spilling (although there was considerably less of that than the blood a living thing would have sprayed). Clo turned and surveyed the damage. The conductor's head was attached only by a flap of skin-like material. He was twitching slightly, but his eyes were still, peaceful.

"*Poor guy,*" Clo said somewhat mournfully, flicking her knife clean. "*He loved us.*"

"*And he would have dosed us too if we'd let him,*" El said coldly. She glanced back through the window at the growing commotion outside. "*Now come on!*"

El stepped over what was left of Paddington to reach the controls at the front of the train. She grabbed levers and flipped switches, try-ing to get the train started. "*Okay, okay,*" she said to herself, straining through the pain to remember. Two buttons pressed, and the console came to life, activating some kind of mechanism on the underside of the train. "*Thank Mother Oggy for analog controls.*" But when El shifted to push the accelerator, she groaned and doubled over.

"*Well, don't use your shot-up arm,*" Clo scolded, like it should be obvious. "*Here, let me do it.*" She stepped next to El and grabbed the lever. "*This one?*"

"*Just a little!*" El insisted, breathing heavily. "*Takeoff is fast, remember.*"

"*Okay,*" Clo agreed and pushed the circular lever. The train eased forward.

"*Good,*" El breathed. "*Good.*" She turned around. "*Wait! Door! The door's still open!*" Indeed, the door and built-in stairs were still extended onto the platform.

"*Which one closes it?*" Clo asked frantically, her eyes scanning the console. "*The buttons aren't marked!*"

As the train pulled away from the platform, there was a loud *CRUNCH!* and the stairway collided with one of the village shacks. The door was knocked clean off, disappearing into the darkness to join the rest of the debris that was the Drag.

"Never mind," El said, panting. *"It's just a door. Just a door. Keep going."*

"Okay," said Clo. *"I'm going to speed up."* She touched the lever again, and the whole train lurched sharply. *"Whoa!"* she cried, and both of us stumbled back into the first row of seats.

Clo looked up. Wind was whipping in through the window the bumblebee had apparently broken through earlier. We were cruising out of the Drag toward the bay.

"We did it!" Clo cried. *"We made it out!"* She looked over at El, who didn't seem to be celebrating so hard. In fact, she was crumpled in a heap, clutching her arm.

"Dammit," Clo said. *"Let me see it."* She climbed over and pried El's hand away from the wound for a moment. It wasn't good.

"You said it was a nick," Clo said. *"This is bad. Your radius is shattered."*

"I know." El breathed heavily. *"Adrenaline's fading,"* she noted as her hand spasmed. *"Just so you know, I might go into shock."*

"Well, what can we—"

Whap! Paddington's hand grabbed El's ankle from underneath the seat.

We both screamed. *"Adrenaline is back!"* El yelled, wild-eyed, but chipper again. She tried to jump up; the conductor had a death grip. *"Get it off me!"*

"I thought I killed him!" Clo stabbed frantically at Paddington's back, shredding his uniform. *"He won't die!"*

Whap. Paddington's other hand shot out and grabbed Clo's stabbing hand, then squeezed with mechanical intensity. *"Ow! He's got me, too!"*

The conductor's body shambled to its knees, his almost-decapitated head dangling by a shred. Golden biomechanical gears and sinews were visibly rotating as it moved.

"Pleease kiiIIILL MeeeeE!" Paddington groaned.

"*How?!*" Clo demanded, dropping her knife and trying to pry the android's viselike grip off her wrist, or at least stop it from breaking her arm.

"Uuuse the Subantoxx!" Paddington hissed, his good eye darting to the patch-filled fanny pack around his waist. "Quuickly!"

"Kill you with the Sap?" Clo asked. "But you're a Tik-Tok, you can't do treatment! You *are* the treatment!"

"NoOOoo," Paddington moaned in frustration. "Usssse it on yourseelf!"

"I'm not—" Clo struggled. "*Why would we get high right now?*"

"The train will—*Kai Maaa*—protect yoooou!"

"What!?" Clo asked, unbelieving.

"He's right!" El said, realizing. "I got it." Only her ankle was immobilized, so she had enough leeway to reach down with her good hand and snatch a handful of patches from the conductor's fanny pack.

El held the patches aloft and yelled out to the empty, speeding train: "I'm going to medicat—*Aaah!*" She screamed as Paddington's possessed arm yanked her to the floor and she landed with a thud on her back.

Clo was also yanked forward, but by her wrist, so she was able to remain on her stumbling feet plus scoop up her knife and give Paddington a few more gut stabs as she went. "*What are you doing?*" Clo asked her sister incredulously. "*Don't touch that stuff!*"

"I'm going to medicate!" El repeated from her spot on the floor of the train. Then she pointed with her bloodied finger at Paddington. "*And he's trying to stop me!*"

That was it. Every corner of the train sprang to life in an ecstasy of elemental purpose. The dozen or so long, segmented limbs, probably originally designed to keep rioters at bay, focused their entire attention on the android-gone-amok. He got skewered, hooked, clawed, even whipped by strange, unraveling lashes that sprouted from the ends of the train's mechanical appendages. But he wouldn't let go. Even when his body was hoisted into the air by the two strongest crooked arms, to dangle upside down in the aisle.

As we were still being clung to, we went with him, El by her clutched ankle and Clo by her wrist. With a cry, Clo turned in her suspension and slashed at the Tik-Tok arm holding her sister's foot. She only got about halfway through the limb, but the train seemed to pick up on the idea and deployed two sawlike tools to finish the task, chopping through both Paddington's wrists in short order.

We fell to the floor in a heap, El unable to keep the impact from her wounded left arm. She cried out again, and Clo leapt over to her, clutching her sister and dragging her back to the front of the train, away from the chaos.

Paddington's hands had let us go after they were severed but continued to thrash and scamper across the floor, like blind, wounded spiders trying to get in one last bite. The train was having none of it: the hands were snatched into the air along with the rest of Paddington's body, the whole mass writhing in fierce resistance.

Defeating this Tik-Tok wasn't anything like taking down the Santa Claus unit back in the woods; the Babble had turned every inch of Paddington into a weapon. If the train hadn't intervened, we aren't sure how we would have gotten out of that one. Paddington, his shuddering head taking one last moment to look at us before what he knew must be the inevitable solution, managed to say, "Thank you."

In contrast to the twisting, angry attitude of the possessed android, the train's defenses went to work with the nonchalant certainty of a cook shredding chicken. In about ten seconds, Paddington's body was broken down to its component parts, and each of them reduced to pieces no bigger than about four inches. It was an efficient but messy process, with ichor and small golden chunks of body and clothing scattered everywhere.

We crouched at the front of the train, under the control panel, trying to avoid the spray. When Paddington's black uniform tie landed next to us, Clo reached for it. Then an ear landed next to it. Clo hesitated, poking at the ear with her knife, but it didn't try to come after us.

"*Poor Paddington,*" Clo sighed, but a wave of relief passed over us now that the conductor was completely dismembered. Clo put away her knife and picked up the tie.

"*He was just a wind-up Tik-Tok like the others.*" El winced. "*It was his programming.*"

"*Still, he wasn't faking it,*" Clo said, squeezing the artificial blood off the tie and untangling it into a sling for her sister.

"*No,*" El admitted, "*he wasn't.*"

Clo spotted the Subantoxx patches, still clutched in El's free hand. *"Hold on to those in case we need help ripping someone into itty-bitty pieces again."*

"Okay," El said and tucked the patches into her tunic. She moaned as Clo looped the makeshift sling around her neck and cradled the wounded arm into it.

"We gotta get you some help," Clo said.

El looked down the train car. The walls, windows, and seats were all now dripping with pieces of what was left of Paddington. In the middle of the train, the robotic arms were working on the conductor's spinal simulacra, scraping and disconnecting each vertebra.

"We gotta get off this train," El said, sounding like she was about to vomit.

Clo looked out the window, taking note of where we were. *"We're in the tunnel,"* she observed.

We looked at each other, both thinking the same thing. *"That shack."*

Clo pulled El to her feet and we scanned the console.

"Can you stop it?" Clo asked, with urgency. We had about two seconds before we would be out of the tunnel and onto the second span.

El nodded and used her right hand to tap two buttons, as she'd seen Paddington do on our first trip. She grunted as her weight pitched, but we managed to stay upright. Even before the train stopped moving, she nodded to Clo. *"Smash that out."*

"Okay," Clo agreed and kicked out the rest of the wraparound window, sending a small shower of glass into the tunnel.

It was about six feet down to the tunnel floor, which still had asphalt in most places, wet and overgrown. We landed with an *oomph!* and walked toward the west end, the moonlight guiding us.

"How's your arm?" Clo asked.

"Only hurts when I think about the future." El pulled the sling tighter. She crouched to look at the floor of the tunnel. There, below where the train passed, among the ferns and other shade plants growing, we saw it: a small path, worn among the weeds near the wall. *"Someone walked here recently."*

"You sure it's not just a deer trail?" Clo asked. The animals were everywhere now, reclaiming space, after all.

"No, it's too close to the wall of the tunnel—less than two feet," El said. *"The bucks would scrape their antlers. This is a human trail."* El shot a quick look back at the train, and the arms inside, still scraping quietly away.

We turned and followed the short path to the end of the tunnel and looked out over the bay and the crumbling bridge. To our right, there it was: the shack we remembered from that morning. We could smell a small cooking fire burning.

El winced, trying not to give in to her gunshot wound.

"Come on," Clo encouraged her.

The small path snaked its way out of the tunnel and up the side of the mountain island to the shack, and we could see other paths forking off into the darkness. What was it about that shack we found so compelling? It was probably just another Subversive. But here? Alone on this island? And had that really been the Crying Man we saw earlier? We had a bone to pick with him: when he told us how best to enter Yerba City and help Dyre, he had conveniently omitted the fact that anyone listening to our brother's Babble would immediately convert to his bloodthirsty team. That Crying Man had some explaining to do—or at least Clo could scream into his ear again.

Something aside from the lone light caught our attention then: the aroma of food cooking. It smelled . . . amazing. There had been food in the village, but the trackers in us had just taken that in as another detail in our assessment of the environment. We hadn't eaten since our squirrel on a stick that morning, and the smell was seductive, calling to us; we felt hunger blossom in our guts like tiny grenades.

We headed up the rocky trail, climbing the low path toward the shack. After closing half the distance, we stopped. We could see the fire flickering, and now we heard whistling coming from inside. We had been trying to be quiet, moving stealthily in the night, but now we realized that whoever was whistling was doing so for our benefit. We knew this mainly because he was a lousy whistler: the sounds he was making were half air and followed no particular tune but rather a sort of self-conscious sensibility that said, "I'm whistling. Just whistling here. Just an old man whistling."

El shot Clo a look. *"Why are we even bothering?"*

"Hello?" she called up to the cabin.

"Busy day. Busy day here," the old man answered.

The voice sounded a bit self-absorbed, eccentric, perhaps even afraid. But not a bloodthirsty zealot, not a doped-up addict, not a self-important beetle-head, and not a homicidal robot, so our night was looking up. "Can we come up?" Clo called.

"Sure. Sure! It's busy here, come on up."

The old man stopped whistling, and we walked less self-consciously to the doorway of the shack.

The structure was essentially one crooked room that looked like it had been cobbled together from debris by a blind person, because it had. In the middle of the room was a metal drum stove, its fire tended by a glassy-eyed man whose face was sun- and wind-cracked from years of exposure. He was tall and heavyset, dark-skinned with a bushy white beard, and we could easily tell from the look in his eyes and the way he cocked his head that he was scanning with his ears. Of course he'd heard us coming—he must have heard the train, must have heard it stop, heard us get out and talk to each other. It was silly for us to have been sneaking around; hence the whistling.

"Come in, come in," he beckoned, and we did. The floor was uneven, made of several kinds of wood and discarded metal sheeting, but we could tell it was braced, elevated slightly from the ground, and it probably stayed warm even on the coldest of nights.

"You two hungry?" the man asked. "It's ready." In front of him, hooked onto the edge of the drum, was a metal frame, and in the frame was a dented pot giving off a quiet boil. It smelled like heaven.

"We are," El announced, confident she could speak for Clo on the matter.

"Good, good. My girl wouldn't eat. She doesn't eat no more, no matter how much work I put in." He took a bent ladle and scooped up a bit of stew, sniffing over his concoction. For a second he seemed satisfied, but then he kept sniffing, as if something was wrong. He lowered the ladle and sniffed toward us, his blind eyes blinking.

"Is one of you bleedin'?" he asked. "You get cut or something?" Apparently he could smell the blood.

"Not exactly." El was lifting the dirty, bloody conductor's tie slightly, trying to examine the wound. It was still bleeding. Putting pressure on it was nearly impossible without convulsing in pain, given the broken bone. "Our brother shot me."

The old man set down the ladle and shuffled expertly across the uneven floor to a small shelf. "Well, if you're shot, you should probably take a load off." He pointed us to some dirty milk crates in the corner. "I got something here somewhere for it." He turned and riffled through a collection of blackened glass jars, lunch boxes, and metal cans. "Little sibling altercation, huh?" he said absently.

"It's a long story," El said as she took a seat on one of the milk crates.

"Don't bother to explain." The man waved dismissively. "They say you can't choose your family." And he shuffled toward Clo, a banged-up first aid kit in his hands. "Here, couple of useful things still in there. Help your big sister before she bleeds all over my nice clean floor."

Clo glanced around the rusty, blackened floor, trying to find the nice clean part. Then she gave up and took the kit. "We're twins," she said.

"Yeah, but she came out first, didn't she?" he said.

"By, like, ninety seconds," Clo snorted, opening the kit. "Besides, how'd you know that?"

"Just guessin'." He shrugged. "Between the two, older sister's probably going to be the one that takes the bullet."

Clo walked over to El. El looked up from her wound. *Anything useful in there?*

"Uh, yeah," Clo said, taking out items as she named them. *"Bandages, dressings, tape. And—bam!—hemostatic pads, get that bleeding stopped."*

"Good." El grabbed one of the pad packs and used her teeth to rip it open.

"Even some old"—Clo read the faded package—*"diazepam. Take the edge off."* We remembered well Mama's first aid lessons; they had saved us more than once or twice.

"No." El shook her head as she placed the blood-clotting pads in place. *"I've got to stay sharp."*

"You two got that twinner talk, do you?" he commented. "Yours sounds like birds."

"Thanks for this," El said, looking up from Clo's field dressing.

"It's my pleasure." The man smiled. "Stuff's just been sitting around anyway. No one ever bothers to shoot at me. Anyway, let's get some food in ya."

The old man picked up the ladle once more and scooped some of the contents of the pot into a heavy glass cup. It would have been a measuring cup before the End of the World, but we could tell that it now had many uses.

"Thank you," El said as he handed the cup to her. "I'm El. Elizabeth. This is Clo."

"Hi," said Clo, still working on El's arm.

"I'm blind," the old man said, chuckling to himself. "But you can call me Tito."

"Tito?" El said.

"Yeah, my mother told me it meant 'prince' in an African language," he continued. "Prince of what, I'm not sure." He chuckled disparagingly.

"Doesn't that mean 'uncle' in Spanish?" El asked, half remembering.

"Same word means different things to different ears," Tito said matter-of-factly. "One man's king is another man's slave."

El's eyes scanned the makeshift cabin as she tried to distract herself from the pain caused by her sister's field dressing. On a low shelf were three small bronze figures: monkeys, each one covering its own eyes, ears, and mouth, respectively. "Well, Prince," El said, "compared to the rest of the world, you're not doing half-bad."

"Thank you, girl. Not sure what that says about the world, but anyway, here you go." He set a second cup next to Clo.

"What's for dinner, Tito?" El asked, sipping at her cup.

"Egg stew. It's the best thing you can get around here," Tito said confidently.

El looked in the cup. It was eggy, with fresh green leaves we recognized as miner's lettuce. She slurped down a large mouthful. It was salty, and delicious. Clo took a moment away from her bandaging to grab a mouthful, too. Aside from the miner's lettuce, there were a few stalks of sour grass and flakes of fennel. It was a scavenger's stew, made mostly from edible weeds. We'd made the same thing ourselves, from time to time.

"You keep chickens here?" Clo asked, slurping a piece of egg.

"There's a cliff of cormorants on the south side of the island. Long as I leave 'em one or two eggs, they keep comin' back. Get the salt from a little pond I made out of cookie trays down by the water." Tito announced this last part proudly, and El guessed he had lived a few years out here before he'd engineered a way to get salt regularly. No small feat, being blind.

"We might just move in," El announced before she took her next sip, careful to blow it cool enough first.

Tito chuckled. "Be my guest. But I snore."

"You're all alone out here?" Clo asked as she turned back to El's bandage.

"No." He sighed with deep disappointment. "Try as I might, all them ghosts keep following me. Chatting helps pass the time, I suppose, until the end."

El tapped on Clo's shoulder, and she looked up. For the first time, we noticed a noose hanging from the ceiling in the corner. It was fixed together from an old timing belt, but there was no mistaking what it was for.

We were going to ask him what he meant about ghosts, or why the noose, or why he didn't go into the city to get his eyes fixed, or why he didn't live in the Drag, where there were women and children and something other than ghosts or cormorants to converse with. But we thought better of it. This was hospitality, and we should simply accept it.

"*There,*" Clo said, finishing the field dressing and grabbing her cup again. "*Should hold you together, but we need to get a real splint in there.*"

El ignored her practical concerns and took a moment to thank Tito. "That was . . . ," she said to him, finishing her cup and stretching her arms into tired satisfaction, "amazing."

"How long since you ate?" Tito asked.

"Too long," Clo grunted, finishing up hers, too.

"This, too, then." He handed El a cracked, but contained, thermos of water.

She drank, a sip at first. It was a bit slimy, but definitely fresh water. She gulped it down. "Ahhhh . . ." An even bigger sigh before handing it to Clo, who chugged it.

He pointed to a larger plastic jug in the corner of the shack. "Have your fill, I've got plenty of food and drink now. I once went four days out here without eating before I had things figured out." He shuffled around the room, going through what must be his regular routine: cleaning, rubbing the brass monkeys, tending the fire, checking the shack for any cracks or any compromising defects. "Wasn't that bad, actually, as I already knew where the two springs were. You can last a long time if you just have water."

"Oh, we know," Clo panted after another gulp. El yawned, and then Clo did, too. The food and water were so good, and we hadn't slept much since the morning Dyre had attacked us, almost two days ago now. El leaned back but groaned, feeling her wound.

"Yesterday," El said, trying to distract herself from her pain, "we passed by here on the train. Was the Crying Man here?"

"Crying Man?"

"Tall guy, wears a suit, creepy-looking, pale face with dark lines that make it look like he's crying," Clo offered, forgetting for a moment Tito was blind.

"Talks with a snobby accent," El threw in. "He's French or something. He can float through walls."

"Oh yeah," Tito said, laughing slightly. "Sir Damien Majerus—the Phantom of the Opera, I call him."

"That's him," we said in unison.

"Yeah, he's been coming through on the puff from time to time. Not supposed to, but he does." Tito nodded to the makeshift chessboard in the corner of the room. "Anyway, we play chess." There was only one seat. "He talks and I move his pieces."

"You play chess with the Crying Man?" We couldn't believe it, but maybe he didn't act so creepy with Tito.

"Sometimes," Tito said. "He's good. He's real good. But he's got a flaw in his game."

"And what's that?" El couldn't help but ask, if only to distract herself from wincing.

"He's a bigot," Tito sighed.

Clo shot El a look and then turned to Tito. "You mean, he hates non-ghosts?"

Tito tilted his head back and laughed heartily at that. "No, he's an old-school bigot. See, it's the only reason he keeps playing me," he continued. "We're about even, win or lose, but he thinks because of the color of my skin, he should win every time. If his, you know, inborn superiority or whatnot was fully developed. So he works on his game and keeps coming back."

"So he's . . . race-ist?" Clo concluded, remembering the word that Maynor had implied before he'd gone and gotten himself killed.

"Yeah." Tito nodded. "That kind of bigot."

"That *is* a flaw," El agreed through gritted teeth.

"Yeah, but he keeps me playing. He's getting better, but I get better, too." Tito shuffled over to the chessboard and began lightly touching the various pieces, making mental notes of their current positions and plotting future strategies. "Keeps me over on this side of the room, anyway," he said, half to himself. El noted that the noose hung on the other side of the shack.

El leaned back, yawning, belly full, not bleeding, but exhausted.

"You should catch a bobcat nap," Clo said, referring to the naps we took out on a hunt sometimes. She yawned also. "We *should catch a bobcat nap.*"

"Rest there if you want. One or two folks have taken to it over the years." Tito gestured to a hammock in the corner.

El wordlessly got up and lay down in the hammock. Clo squeezed in next to her and shut her eyes, a mechanical attempt to achieve sleep before continuing our quest. Outside, through a propped-open window (the shack had no glass), El could see the stars. She could feel herself begin to drift off almost immediately. Even though El was the one who needed rest the most, Clo was already out.

"Are you going to be up for a while?" El mumbled.

"Hmm?" Tito was still shuffling around. "Well, that's dinner. The night's still young, and there's lots to do." He reached up a hand to feel the temperature of the air, apparently to judge the distance to the fire, where he threw on a small log. He then reached up and lowered a movable flue over the flames. The contraption was pretty clever: he could move the flue up to add wood or cook, and lower it to minimize smoke in the shack but still keep things warm.

El was drifting off, too, but a stray thought pinged her sleep. "You said ours sounded like birds."

"Hmm?" Tito paused.

"You said our secret language sounded like birds," El mumbled. "You've heard others?"

"Oh yeah," Tito said, like it was obvious. "My daughters'."

El perked up a bit. "You have twins?"

Clo's eyes also snapped open. "Where are they now?"

We were curious; we had never met any others who used a secret language.

Tito shuffled. "They're gone," he said, lightly touching the chess pieces again, looking as if he was forcing an infinite number of calculations in an attempt to distract himself from what was obviously a painful subject. "They're both gone now."

"Oh," El said. "Sorry."

"We . . ." Clo didn't know quite what to say. "We didn't mean to bring it up."

"S'okay," Tito assured her, shuffling away from the board and pulling on a ragged old parka from its rusty hook on the wall. "Like I said, it's been a busy day. Josephine even came by earlier. What's left of her." He started feeling his way along the wall toward the door.

We looked at each other.

"You're Josephine's papa?" Clo asked.

Tito stopped in the doorway, shuffled around toward us again. "You met her—or it, really?" We realized now that despite his long beard and grizzled face, Tito really wasn't that old. Lifestyle and his experiences made him look a lot more gnarled than he really was.

"Yeah," El said. "Back in the city."

"She's strong as, like, a hundred bears now," Clo said.

Tito smiled. "She always was the strong one," he assured us, "even before the City took her and . . . did what it did to her."

"Why her?" Clo asked. "Why did Yerba City pick her?"

"Don't know," Tito sighed. "But she's definitely the ferz."

"Ferz?" We had never heard the word before. "What's that?"

Tito held up the smallest chess piece on his board. "Some folks use that name for the pawn that becomes a queen." He turned his glassy eyes toward us. "Poor little girl, with me as a papa, and all the things that happened to her, just a little pawn in this world. But she's definitely a queen now."

We nodded, thinking about that little girl lifting giant objects and jumping onto drones in midair.

"She sure is," Clo said.

"Just wish they hadn't kept the scars," Tito mumbled to himself. But we heard it, and we heard the guilt in his voice. We knew that kind of guilt; we had heard it in Papa's voice when we were very little.

"On her arm?" El asked.

Tito nodded silently, and the grim look on his face told us everything.

Clo gasped. "You did that to her, didn't you?" she blurted out, and for only a brief second considered that it might not be the sort of social comment she should make. But we were a couple of hillbillies and it was the End of the World, so we figured Miss Manners would give us a pass.

The deeper look on Tito's face told us we'd hit the expected nerve.

"But you seem like such a nice guy!" Clo continued, not knowing what else to say. "How could you do something like that to a little girl?"

Tito was silent.

"What about her sister?" El asked in a meager attempt to change the subject. "Is she a supergirl now, too?"

Tears welled in Tito's blind eyes. "Imani . . . didn't make it. It was a long time ago. Before the Sap. They were little. I was drunk. I left them in the car, to get more drunk, and . . . Josephine was the lucky one."

We were stunned, speechless. There was a long pause. Tito made as if he were going to shuffle off into the night, but we couldn't just let that go.

"Wait!" Clo called, knowing that there was something she had to talk about. "But Josephine talked about her sister," she said, not wanting to believe the story. "Talked like she was still . . ." She couldn't finish the sentence.

"She does that. Talks to Imani still, in their own secret language." Tito shook his head, as if trying to dispel haunting voices. "You all been thinkin' this Chimera came along and ended the world, but for some of us, the world ended way before that. This latest apocalypse, just a change of scenery." He walked carefully off into the darkness of the island and disappeared.

We were silent for a while, then Clo's eyes strayed to the noose in the corner of the room.

"Let's get the hell out of here," Clo said, and El agreed.

CHAPTER 16

DEATH BY EMPATHY

Outside, in the gaping west side of the tunnel, something had changed.

"The train's gone," Clo observed.

"It's just as well," El said, turning westward to the lights of the city. She straightened her sling and prepared to make the rest of the trek on foot. *"I don't think I could ride that splattertruck again anyway."*

Clo nodded. *"Where do you think it went?"*

"Hopefully it shut itself down, without a conductor," El mused. *"Those nasty arms were bad enough without going all Babble. C'mon,"* she said, *"let's hoof it before I pass out."*

We started onto the rusted, burned-out bridge, heading back into the city, toward the Chimera.

"That was pretty gritty," Clo said, obviously referring to Tito's story.

El just grunted in acknowledgment, concentrating on finding safe footing on the crumbling pavement.

"Do you think Papa would have done something like that, if he hadn't—"

"Shut up," El said. *"I have to concentrate."* We continued in silence.

It took us just under an hour to jog the rest of the way from the island to the city. Often we could move quickly toward the low fires and lights ahead, but at times we lost our footing in the now-uneven landscape. After tripping twice on the rotting asphalt and seeing black tar chunks tumble into the sea below, we got the idea to walk along the track of the silver train. Somewhere in Yerba City's vast artificial intelligence, she must have decided that although the decks of the bridge would crumble away, the steel girders that made up the support structure would remain sturdy enough to support a train to take willing people to and from the Drag.

Up on the rail, our steps got slower and smoother. We tried not to think about anything while we moved through the darkness. The track was only about four feet wide and didn't have anything like a handrail. Good thing it wasn't a windy night, we thought, realizing a wrong step would send either one of us about 150 feet into the icy bay.

The train rail was so perfectly maintained—the odd splotch of seagull droppings the only blemish—it was hard to believe that the world had come to an end. But then again, not the entire world had ended, had it? Judging from the building and the more or less constant movement of the drones in the air, the City's world, although nihilistic and inhuman, was just getting started.

Still, it was hard to hate Yerba City as Mama had taught us to, back in the woods. It might be a monster, for sure, but if so, it was just doing its monster thing. He was just a wind-up Tik-Tok, but the way Paddington had sacrificed himself, it was undeniable that this beast that had taken over really did seem to care on some level about its citizens—even the ones who didn't get on the Sap. Or maybe it was just clever programming in an attempt to emotionally manipulate us at every turn. Either way, there was nothing fake about Paddington getting chopped into little pieces; the City was facing a real threat, and we were feeling unexpectedly ambivalent about her fate.

"*Wait!*" El said. We were almost at the end of the bridge, only fifty yards from where the track descended in its slow loop into the city, when we felt a low vibration beneath our feet. We looked at each other and then behind us to see bright grasshopper eyes moving toward us.

"*So, the train didn't shut down after all,*" Clo said.

"*Yeah, but who the hell's driving?*" We could see smoke streaking from the back of the train like a giant black tail that obscured the moonlight. We ran to the nearest support column anchoring the track to the old bridge and tucked behind the flange like two possums. Hiding in a shadowed world of rust and asphalt, we peered out as the silver bullet streaked past, seemingly twice as fast as when we had ridden on it.

"That thing's moving," El said, trying to ignore how moving fast herself had probably reopened her arm wound.

"What's the rush?" Clo wondered, but it wasn't a serious question. We knew already. The babblers were bringing their cause to the City. Three or four drones were flying parallel to the speeding train. They didn't look converted, more like they were trying to stop the train. In fact, they were blaring those siren-like squeals. Apparently, whatever was on the train was trying to outrun them. No chance of that, really, but when we saw two or three blue crackles rip from the drones into the vehicle, we realized the hijackers must just be trying to get to their destination before the bugs took down their vehicle altogether.

Well, good for them, we thought; Yerba City's infrastructure could use a little more blowing up. Still.

"You think Dyre's on there?" Clo asked.

"Seems like they're pissed off enough," El said.

Clo nodded. *"Remember the time he got into the beehive?"*

El chuckled. *"Yeah."* Her face turned serious in the darkness. *"But I have the feeling this time there won't be a funny ending with garlic oil and lavender. C'mon."*

We couldn't help but joke about our little brother, but we also knew that a showdown was looming. After all, how many times can you let a sibling shoot at you before you have to shoot back?

As the train began its looping descent between the crumbling city buildings, we stepped out onto the track again and followed the fight from a distance. It reminded us of wolves surrounding a bull moose, although this takedown was going a bit differently: we saw a few drones get knocked out of the air with a crackling return fire.

"That's not Daisy Duke," El observed.

"What are they shooting with?"

"I think it's other drones."

Clo nodded. We heard a smash, and a second drone tried to shake off the gooey flames from a Molotov.

"Let's keep moving." El grimaced.

Clo nodded, and we started up again.

Knowing what we knew, the current "uprising" seemed absurd. The City must have thousands of drones at her command, let alone what the angels were capable of if motivated. On the other hand, from what we had already observed, the machines didn't seem prepared for a real fight. Maynor had said that the Jolly Ranchers mostly fought each other online; in regard to us sober flesh-and-blood nuisances, they seemed to use psychological control, armed only with weapons designed for short-range stunning and riot control. Even the creation of the angels—the humanlike robots—seemed like a psychologically strategic move to keep the population medicated and pacified by their own kind. Our own kind. But how would these units fare in a real fight, against a squad of motivated bucks, when it was kill or be killed? Did Yerba City have access to old-school weapons? Tanks? Fighter planes? Nuclear bombs? Maybe none of that mattered: the way we had seen Paddington flip, it was a fair guess that Yerba City's forces might all convert before they could even fight back.

From down on the ground, it actually looked like the insurgents might win for a moment, although behind the sirens, shouting, and gunfire, we heard another noise. A low rumble coming from the south.

"What's that?" Clo asked.

"I don't know, but let's keep on our own hunt this time." We made our way down to the broken city floor, not bothering to wait and see who would win the skirmish.

As we crunched through the darkness on broken glass and rusted vape pipes, we saw three more drones buzzing through the air toward the fight. The rumbling continued, like the vibration of hundreds of . . . something.

"Bees?"

"Maybe giant *bees."*

Whatever it was, its approach was making the surrounding buildings shake, ever so slightly, and that was enough to cause small tinkling showers of broken glass here and there from the neglected skyscrapers.

Unsettled, we trudged onward, the glass falling a little faster into the dark canyon of the street. We jogged, then broke into a run when we sighted an autonomous car, moving down one of the silvery roads about a block away.

"Hey!" El waved her good arm wildly. If the car itself didn't see us, no doubt some other permanently peeled eyeball in this panopticon would.

"Should we ask for help?"

"Yeah, these things have their uses." "Hey! We need help!" We hoped the last word would be translated as "treatment."

Sure enough, the car stopped, and its carapace window opened on an empty interior. We hopped in.

"We need to get to Saturnalia. Now." As the giant translucent doors closed, a series of questions began. This car seemed more advanced than the pill bug we had ridden in from the hinterland the night before.

"How is your level of depression? Do you feel you are full-blown infected?" Not waiting for an answer, the car began its slow roll down the road.

"We just need to get to Saturnalia," El said. Just then, a piece of glass, about four feet by four feet, shattered against the transparent roof of the car. We jumped, screaming. Despite the noise, and a large crack in the windshield, the roof held.

"Just get us out of here!" Clo shouted. The car actually did speed up, apparently motivated by some sort of desire for self-preservation. The cracked glass probably wouldn't withstand another blow like that.

"There is no road to Saturnalia," the car told us.

"What? It's north, across the Golden Gate Bridge."

"There is no bridge to the north."

Oh yeah. We remembered at the same time: a plane had hit the bridge when we were kids.

"Okay." It took a moment for that to sink in. "What about a train?" Clo asked. "Like the one out to the Drag. Can we take a train to Saturnalia?"

"There is no train to Saturnalia."

"What is it? A goddamned state of mind?" El sighed, her arm throbbing and her mind racing. The car went about two more blocks. The giant bees seemed to have stopped, or at least we didn't see any more huge plates of glass hitting the street around us.

Then we remembered, and Clo said it: *"Maynor was going to Saturnalia in his giant cicada car, Zeta. Maybe that's the only way."* If it was some sort of elitist enclave, that would make sense. But right this second, all the drones were no doubt busy with the uprising. Still, there must be a way. Find a boat, one still working down at the rotting piers? Before we could solidify this highly questionable plan, we noticed that the car we had commandeered was speeding us toward the Union Square Local One. It was the nearest treatment center, after all.

We were about to protest when we saw him.

"It's Tobias!" Clo cried. He was being led out of the building by a white-clad angel. He still looked stoned, his face stretched long as he clutched a rolling IV squid stand, along with two other patients. Clo wanted to see him closer, at least talk to him one last time. But Tobias was being led into what looked like a grasshopper minibus, its silver-carapaced body capable of holding a small group of patients instead of just one or two.

"Hey, get us closer to that little grasshopper thingy," Clo demanded. "I want to talk to that boy."

"Tobias is being transferred to a Local Zero, Clo."

It took Clo a moment to realize that our car knew exactly who she was referring to, and was also talking to her in some familiar tone, using her name. Apparently everyone—or every*thing*—in the City was getting to know us.

"You can't send him there. Make that car stop!" We were unsure if the City would comply with our request, but we might as well ask. Evil as it was, sometimes it seemed to listen. And it would save us the trouble of busting a hole in the windshield, which we were fully prepared to do.

"Of course," the car chimed blissfully. "But please bear in mind, he is being transferred at his own request. No one may violate a patient's consent for treatment."

"Yeah, yeah, we saw what happens." Clo, her eyes locked on Tobias, waved dismissively, like a lioness in stalking mode growling away a pestering cub. "Just get us over there, or I'll bust open your shell and hoof it myself."

The car slowed but didn't drive into the roundabout. Tobias was lifted onto the minibus by a large, petal-like silver appendage.

"Hurry!" Another minute and we were going to miss him.

"We must wait for the transfer roundabout to clea—"

"C'mon!" Clo called to El, and the two of us flipped onto our backs and kicked both feet, easily smashing through the already-cracked roof.

We popped the translucent shell out with a *crash* and jumped out of the car onto the printed road. El grunted in pain. She had used her arm too much, while Clo had forgotten that her sister still had a shattered bone.

"Sorry! I forgot," Clo said. *"Are you okay?"*

"Yeah, yeah." El nodded, sweating. *"Let's just say bye to your boyfriend and move on."*

We made short work of the distance to the minibus. Despite El's wound, we were moving faster now—everything was moving faster. We had lost essentially all of our gear except for Clo's knife, but we had eaten something, and most important, we were starting to see Yerba City for what it was: not a menacing monster to be feared, but a seduction to be directly confronted. She was soft. Not made for fighting and survival like we were.

The doors on the minibus were closing, but Clo jammed her hands in and pried, with El's one-armed help. Unused to resistance, the doors moved easily, and Clo squeezed her body in as soon as we'd made enough space. El followed.

"Tobias!" Clo yelled. Patients were piled in the bus, some lying on wall-mounted cots, but most clinging to appendage-like grab handles that jutted down from the vehicle's ceiling. The bus began to make its way slowly down the road.

We could feel the bus moving and got more frantic. "Tobias!" Clo yelled again.

"He can't hear you, remember?" El said with a singsong groan as she sat on one of the cots nearest the door.

Clo pushed her way through the patients, giving up on the yelling and instead waving her arms frantically.

He was standing almost in the middle of the throng, and the flailing did seem to catch Tobias's attention: he turned toward us.

"Clo?" His eyes lit up for a moment, focusing on her as she pushed past the other patients to him. "Chloe Yetti?"

He let go of the soft circular handgrip, but the device reached down and grabbed his wrist, the circle turned into a claw. "Ugh," he mumbled slightly and reached up to pry apart the two fingerlike clamps with his free hand. The fingers budged only slightly.

Clo pushed herself past another patient to make her way to him.

"Here, Clo, help me with this." He pointed to his wrist. "They clamp just for safety. Some folks can't hold on, you know."

"Yeah," Clo said, reaching up and prying the fingers apart. Tobias watched her as she worked. Then she turned and looked at him, pausing from her work, and he looked into her eyes. They couldn't wait. He reached out his one free arm and pulled her into him; she immediately responded, embracing him back.

"Oh, Clo. I thought the machines were going to get you for sure."

Clo buried her face in his neck. "They did for a minute," she mumbled, and they held there for a moment, Tobias dangling from the ceiling. Clo finally lifted her head. "Here." She reached up and decisively pulled the clamp apart, setting him free.

An automated voice chimed in. "Please hold a handgrip," it said. They ignored it and sat on one of the unoccupied cots.

They hugged again, and Clo backed away to look at him.

Toward the front of the bus, El looked around, trying to figure out where we were going. She knew well enough to let Clo alone for a while.

"I never thought I was going to see you again." Before he could respond, she leaned in and kissed him. His eyes widened slightly. Clo could tell that even through all the years of doped-up, drugged-out sex drones, laser-brain simulations, and neocortex mind control whatevers, in his entire jaded young life, Tobias had never actually experienced this before: a genuine kiss from someone who had fallen for him.

They continued there, on the bus, oblivious to their surroundings, falling into each other, for some time. Clo heaped her desire onto him, and he accepted.

El spied all this from her position up front, gave a sigh of resignation, and leaned back against the wall of the bus. Hopefully this boy-craziness was just something Clo needed to get out of her system, and then we could get on with our mission.

"Are you injured?" a familiar type of angel voice asked, and El turned to see a Tik-Tok with white gloves leaning toward her. His features were Asian, handsome, and, although he had Paddington's service-like demeanor, his uniform was definitely that of some kind of nurse.

"Don't touch me," El hissed, clutching her arm closer.

The angel leaned back upright, but kept examining El's sling from a distance. His eyes were somehow deeper, more sensitive than Paddington's. A glint of realization seemed to flash across his face, and he clutched at his own arm, mirroring El's posture.

"Oh," he said sympathetically. "That must really hurt."

"I don't need your fake-ass empathy." El grimaced. "I need some bone screws and a real splint. Can you whip that up?"

White Gloves didn't miss a beat, but nodded understandingly with an artificially pleasant smile. "You'll find everything you need at the Local Zero." He turned and made his way through the shuttle, examining each patient with the same puppy dog eyes he'd used on El.

Across the bus, Clo took a pause from making out. She turned to the Sap going into Tobias's arm and tried to pull it out.

He shook his head and simply said, "No."

Clo narrowed her eyes. "Come with me."

"I can't." Tobias shook his head again.

"I love you," Clo said.

He smiled. "And I love you . . . I never thought I would say that here in the city."

"Then come with me."

"It's time for me to go to the Zero. It's my time. You're the one who needs to get out of here."

Clo's face crumpled. How could he talk like that? But, remembering how those pictures of our mama had magically appeared up on the screen, having experienced just a taste of what the Chimera could do, she understood. Still, she had to try; she had to fight against this addiction.

"That's bullshit. You love me, you can come with me. We can have another life."

"There isn't any other life."

"I lived out there for ten years—we could do the same. You don't think I'm telling the truth?"

"No, I think you're an outsider. You're . . . naive. This is the way it's always been. You'll see."

"Always? There's no 'always' going on here, Tobias. Yerba City is less than fifteen years old. She's younger than you. How is that 'always'?"

"You still don't understand." He shook his head. "The Chimera isn't new, she's always been here."

Clo sighed and looked at the squid IV curled on his arm. "That's just the drugs talking. She's twisted your mind, filled in your past with feelings and memories. She's taken your sense of time and—"

"No, you really don't understand. Clo—"

"We have arrived," the white-gloved angel said. He had made his way closer to Clo, but seemed to be making the announcement to no one in particular. A low murmur of celebration seemed to fill the bus.

El looked outside, scanning as she had for the entirety of our short ride. But she didn't see any new, shiny building like the Local One; it was just more urban ruins outside. "I don't understand," El said, half to herself, assuming that Clo was too caught up in Tobias to hear her. "There isn't anything here."

Still, we could feel the acceptance, the complicity, in the human passengers who surrounded us. Perhaps we really were somewhere, even though the area looked like an empty lot.

El stood up, muscles tensing. She hadn't taken any painkillers from the first aid kit back in Tito's shack, and the throbbing mass of her arm was getting to her. As in, falling-into-post-traumatic-shock getting to her. Still, she managed to shoot Clo a determined look.

From the other side of the bus, Clo could feel what her sister had in mind. Clo still had her knife. The angels couldn't stop us, and the drones were probably still caught up in the skirmish at the train station. We'd take Tobias. He didn't understand now—he couldn't, he was too far gone. But we'd take him. Take him and make him understand, clean him up. Force the Prophanol into him, maybe, give him time to reset. Then he'd see that Clo was more important than anything else on the planet.

Tobias just looked at her. "I know what you're thinking, Clo. That you're gonna save me. You and your sister are going to bust me out of here."

"Prepare for disembarkation," White Gloves said. The angel held on to his own handgrip while all the other dangling knobs unleashed their mechanical grip and withdrew silently into the bus's ceiling.

"But you don't have to be afraid, Clo," Tobias continued. "She already has everything figured out. She's more good than you think."

El saw a golden line appear in the middle of the floor. For a brief second, she thought it must be a lighted guide, showing passengers the way to the exit. She felt her mind stiffen. There was no way chimes and colored lines and polite reminders were going to get Clo off this bus and away from this boy. We'd steal this whole bus if we had to— and then the golden line widened, and in an instant, El realized that it wasn't a line at all, but a split in the bottom of the bus, opening up onto a giant pool of ichor.

"Clo!" El called, but it was too late. This wasn't a bus. It was a cattle car, and spent humans were the freight.

El fell, scrambling, as the first patients slid seven feet into the thick ichor with a dull splash. She managed to grab on to the edge of a mounted cot.

"El!" Clo called, and she grabbed on to Tobias's wrist just as he was about to tumble. She reached up for a handgrip, but they'd all withdrawn into the ceiling; the only one still dangling was being held by White Gloves. The wall-mounted cots collapsed flush, sending the two prone patients rolling into the pit as the floor completely gave way. El gripped hard to the cot, which was becoming perpendicular to the ground. Her already-white knuckles turned whiter.

Clo jumped off her last bit of floor, her last chance, half dragging Tobias through the air. She managed to wrap her free arm around White Gloves's ankles as she fell. There she dangled for a moment, clinging to the Tik-Tok's legs with one arm and to Tobias's wrist with the other.

Six seconds after the split in the floor of the bus first appeared, the entire car was empty, except for four dangling figures swinging above the ichor. The dozen or so fallen patients disappeared beneath the sloshing surface as if weighted down with stones. Clo grunted and strained, clinging with all her might to her boyfriend's wrist and the android's legs.

El was beyond grunting now. All she could do was gasp when the already-slick cots began folding into the walls of the bus. Clearly the whole operation was designed from the beginning to prevent precisely what we were doing: clinging on. Blood was forced through the bandages on El's forearm as the pressure on the broken bone became too great.

"Don't let go!" were El's last gasping words. She didn't even have time to scream as she fell.

"El!" Clo called to her sister, straining. *"El!"* Tobias might be slight, but he was still a full-grown man, and Clo knew there was no way she could hold him for more than a few seconds before they also plunged into the goo. But she was *not* going to let him go.

Tobias looked down into the golden pool, and then up at Clo. In his drugged state, he seemed to realize only now that he hadn't fallen in with the rest of the patients. "Clo," he tried to explain, dangling by his wrist, looking up at her. "It's okay. Just let go."

She didn't answer, but grimaced and clung to him as fire shot through her shoulder and arm. She only had a few moments more; there must be a way out. She'd come too far to just let go. She wouldn't, even if it ripped her body apart. But the bus had clearly been designed for the quick dispensing of human cargo. The retracting cots, the disappearing handrails—Yerba City had designed and planned all this to ensure that every human aboard would be dumped like spring mice into her boiling stew.

She heard White Gloves's pants rip, from where her arm was wrapped around his ankles.

"Please proceed with disembarkation," the angel called down to her. The android didn't try to kick or pry her away, but seemed content to wait patiently for Clo's arms to give out.

She hadn't counted on this, Clo thought desperately. The City hadn't counted on someone grabbing the angel. Yerba City made a lot of dumb mistakes, and Clo hoped frantically that this was one. She couldn't swing Tobias's weight at all, but maybe the floor of the bus would automatically close again after a few minutes. There was always a chance.

Suddenly something grabbed at her hand. It was Tobias, actually reaching up and trying to pry her hand off his wrist, to make himself fall. "Just let go, Clo," he slurred.

"S-stop, you d-dumb j-j-jerk!" she managed to grunt.

White Gloves chimed in. "That must be hard for you. Please let go. You may hurt yourself if you continue to hold on."

Sweat and tears pouring from Clo's face, she looked up at him and growled, "Close . . . the floor!" They'd obeyed her orders before; maybe it would work now.

"You cannot prevent a consenting patient from receiving treatment. Please let Tobias go."

"*Noooo!*" She was speaking only through her teeth now, her eyes wild and animalistic.

"Very well." White Gloves gave a simple smile, and his legs fell off.

CHAPTER 17

THE LOCAL ZERO

Clo managed to grab a deep breath before she, Tobias, and the bottom half of the angel plunged into the waiting ichor. The liquid was not as viscous as it had appeared from above, but this only meant they plunged deeper than Clo had expected. She kept her eyes shut tight and never let go of Tobias, although she cast aside the angel's legs even before they hit the liquid.

Clo was a good swimmer; Mama had made sure we could do all the important strokes—including the sidestroke, a survival skill. And this was a survival moment. Quick as possible, she switched her grip on Tobias's wrist, switching hands to stroke with her strong side. Though her shoulder was practically numb from clinging to her boyfriend in midair, she scooped hard and scissor-kicked, straining for the surface.

Then she felt it. Too strong to be Tobias, too tenacious. Something was pulling him downward, and therefore her, too. *Dammit,* she thought; they couldn't be that far down, but her lungs were already bursting. Clo stopped scooping with her free hand and found the knife in her belt. Should she open her eyes? Just turn, find the target, make the strike, and get them both to the surface. Against her better judgment, she opened her eyes and looked down.

Tentacles. Dozens of smooth, featureless, slow-moving tentacles that appeared almost alive. They were the same color as the rest of the environment, but she could see them standing out against the golden liquid like slightly darker pieces of yarn. She slashed at them. The severed tendrils retreated into the deep, but as Clo continued to hack, she could feel more coming, grabbing her, around her wrist, her knife. She switched from trying to free Tobias to trying to free herself. Their grip was gentle, but there were more and more of them—hundreds of tendrils that seemed to manifest out of the liquid itself to drag her and Tobias down. Her lungs were on fire, strength ebbing, oxygen drained from her already-strained limbs. Despite the pain, she knew she could control her breathing, but if she passed out—

A hand landed on her shoulder, calm and reassuring. She turned. Tobias's face met hers. He was smiling, and for the first time, she realized that she was seeing unblurred through the liquid. She was probably about to drown, but somehow she could see her boyfriend's beautiful face perfectly through the liquid that was going to kill her. The last of his air escaped his mouth, bubbling upward, and he . . . spoke.

"It's okay." He smiled. "You can breathe here." He sounded like he was talking with his mouth full, and Clo was reminded of playing childhood games, talking at the dinner fire, playing with food. But this wasn't a game. Her eyes were bulging from lack of oxygen.

Despite the burning in her lungs, she took a quick look around to try to spot her sister, although she wasn't really too worried about El; El had always been the better swimmer.

Tobias put his hand on her cheek. "It's okay," he repeated. "Just breathe." He swirled his finger, indicating the liquid around them. "It makes air for you."

Clo shook her head and kept her mouth shut tight. This stuff was already in her eyes and ears. Who knew what it would do to her once it got in her mouth? She looked up. There was light around them; the liquid seemed to glow slightly, but they were deep now, more than thirty feet down, and still descending thanks to the pull of the tentacles. She wasn't sure she could make it back to the surface, even if she abandoned Tobias.

He could tell what she was thinking. "There's no Sap in it," he said in that muffled underwater voice.

Clo looked into his eyes. Tobias was so confident. He must have been here before, in all this stuff. He had been here, and he had made it out again, she told herself. He had gotten clean, so there was a way back, even if this goo got inside you.

This better work, she thought, in the moments before she passed out, and she expelled the air from her burning lungs.

The bubbles from her spent breath trailed only about a foot before they disappeared, seemingly absorbed directly into the ichor. She inhaled, feeling liquid in her mouth but air in her lungs. At least it felt like air. Tobias nodded, encouraging. She breathed out and in again. This time there weren't even bubbles, just a current of liquid across her tongue that somehow led to a feeling of air in her lungs. She let her animal instincts take over, allowing herself life down in this pit, and just panted for a moment. She could feel it: the ichor was malleable, protean, down to the molecular level. It didn't literally become air when it entered her lungs, but it changed itself enough to allow vital oxygen to be delivered in the most efficient manner. It certainly seemed to know what it was doing and what it was designed for.

Clo felt strength come back into her limbs, presumably from the oxygen, and she turned her attention back to Tobias. She was alive, and she still had the knife in her hand. She wasn't high or intoxicated, and it seemed like her thoughts were her own. The tendrils had never stopped pulling them downward; they were even farther from the surface now. She found herself refocusing on escape, and finding El. She grabbed Tobias by the shoulder with her free hand, taking a handful of the scruffy outfit he still wore, and kicked upward, fighting against the tentacles with renewed strength.

"Wait," he insisted, putting his hand on her wrist. "Just wait: they won't take us much farther down. They're just trying to find a place for us."

Clo stopped kicking and looked at him. He seemed serene, and actually more sober than before they'd fallen into this pit. Plus he seemed at ease with everything that was going on. This was a hell of a place to be familiar with, she thought. She kept a tight grip on both him and the knife and decided to bide her time for a moment before trying to bust out of the situation.

"Where's El?" Clo demanded.

"She's here," Tobias answered vaguely.

Once again, she told herself that if Tobias could get out of this place and back, then she could, too, and so could El. Still, it was a terrible sensation, knowing that this stuff—the same stuff that had splattered everywhere when Mama had shot Santa Claus—was inside her, somehow controlling her breathing, her very life from moment to moment. What would it take for that monster to just cut her off, solidify the liquid, and make her start breathing lead? And now she was delivering oxygen into Clo's lungs; what else was she delivering? And anyway, where the hell *was* El?

The tendrils kept pulling them down, and Clo turned around, finally taking a moment to size up her surroundings. The pit seemed to be about fifty yards wide and vaguely oval-shaped. Growing out from the sides of the pit and up from the depths were golden vines, reminding Clo of some kind of kelp; like the tendrils that were pulling them down, the kelp seemed to be made out of more-solidified strands of the ichor itself. Intertwined in the kelp were other patients, if you could call them that now. Most of them were naked, floating suspended, some conscious, waving at her and Tobias as they passed; others were floating fetally, apparently sleeping. She could see a couple of the new patients, whose clothes and other articles were being removed by the tendrils before their bodies were placed at free anchor points along the kelp.

"Hey!" El called from behind them, and Clo turned to look at her. *"You can breathe this stuff!"*

"I know!" Clo called back through the glop.

"Wish someone had told me that before I fell in. I nearly passed out holding my breath." El was anchored to the wall nearby, the tendrils apparently having found a spot for her.

"He told me," Clo said, nodding toward Tobias. *"But I didn't believe him anyway. Nearly busted my eyeballs."*

Clo was moving slower now, and for a moment we forgot that we were submerged, but took in the scenery as if we were being conveyed through a very surreal Disneyland ride. How could we see so clearly?

Clo squinted and rubbed her eyes with her wrist, careful to keep her knife ready. When she opened her eyes, the world was fuzzy for only a moment before snapping into focus again. She hadn't realized before, but the ichor was molding itself into lenses around her eyes, allowing the liquid world to come into focus.

"This stuff is focusing around my eyes!" Clo exclaimed.

"I know, it's amazing!" El responded. *"Look!"* She pointed to the wound in her arm. *"It's healing me!"* Indeed, it looked like the ichor had formed a cluster of tiny golden beads around her wound, which was no longer bleeding. El wiggled all her fingers giddily. *"I can feel my thumb again!"* Something caught her eye. *"Whoa."* She pointed.

To Clo's left we spotted legs. White Gloves's legs, still attached to half a torso, were kicking on their own, seemingly trying to make their way back to the top. Small tendrils removed its pants and shoes, and the torso, now naked, kicked its way toward the side of the pit. From there it appeared to stick and move upward, apparently conveyed by some kind of reverse momentum that moved countercurrent to the thicker flow of the pit. We made a mental note as the legs disappeared from view.

"That's a potential way out of this cluster-rut," Clo pointed out.

"Uh-huh." El nodded. *"I think I'm going to hang out just a bit until I'm done healing, though."*

"What's it putting in you, though?" Clo said.

The thought had already crossed El's mind. *"It's in us now whatever it is, so as long as I get my shooting arm back . . ."*

Clo nodded in agreement and continued to take in our surroundings. Despite the weirdness of being stuck in this liquid, there was something comforting about the Local Zero. Down here, there were no angel attendants, no drones, no infernal machines twisting and perverting people's bodies and minds. There were just people, peacefully suspended in the glowing golden fluid. Looking down, we thought the golden fluid seemed to go on forever. The dim light from the ichor itself gave us the impression of looking down a lit tunnel rather than a pit, with bodies spaced every fifteen feet or so. Some were coupled up, but most were alone, suspended, with little or no movement, from the strands of golden kelp that snaked through the pit. There could have been thousands of people in there.

"How deep does this go?" Clo asked Tobias. Talking was still a funny sensation, not just because it sounded a bit like a child talking with its mouth full, but also because, as with every breath now, no bubbles came out when we spoke. The whole intention seemed to be for patients to forget that they were suspended in liquid. But as with every other recent sensation, we didn't really like it. Not because of the strangeness of it, although, outside of the womb—and that was a long time ago—we had never felt anything similar, but because it meant that not only did the City own our breath, it owned our words now, too.

Tobias looked down. "I think she's still digging," he said vaguely.

Finally Clo and Tobias came to a halt, nestled close to the side of the wall among a particularly thick patch of the kelp, about forty feet down from El.

"We'll rest here for a while," Tobias seemed to insist.

Clo looked up. How far down had they come? It was hard to tell. The ichor had a thickness to it and was not entirely translucent, so things had gotten blurry after about thirty feet. Still, she could see a hint of moonlight above them and estimated that they were about seventy feet down.

That was another thing, Clo thought; there was no pressure on her ears or head. Diving just twenty feet down in the summer lake in the Oggy would cause a sharp pressure in her ears. Here, much deeper than that, her entire body only gave a vague sense she might be submerged in a lukewarm tub, and, as much as that unnerved her, the feeling was . . . pleasant. Overall, despite our misgivings at having every orifice potentially violated by Yerba City's naughty tentacles at any time, the scientists in us were intrigued. This whole pool, the entire pit that they referred to as the Local Zero—apparently just one of a series of pits around Yerba City—was alive, and instantly responsive down to an presumably molecular level. If the City could do all this, on this scale, what couldn't she do?

Clo had been clinging steel-gripped to Tobias's hoodie this entire time, and she turned frantically when she felt it loosen in her hand. The arms, the tendrils, were taking it off his body, along with the rest of his clothes. She felt her own deerskin tunic come away from her through forces seen and unseen. Clo realized that the Local Zero must be trying to make her and Tobias like the rest of the patients there: naked and floating in its amniotic-like fluid. Not going to happen.

She let go of Tobias's hoodie face and slashed at the tentacles—but there were too many, appearing out of the liquid around them to grip gently at her clasps, belt, and moccasins.

"Stop trying to take my clothes off!" Clo hacked at the living substance around her.

"Wait, Clo," Tobias called from next to her. He was completely naked now, and she couldn't help but pause and take a look at him. His pale, slender body was dressed in nothing but those dark, runelike homemade stick-figure tattoos.

"Oh. Wow," Clo said. Suddenly, being stuck down there didn't seem like such a bad idea. "You are so beautiful. You look like a gussied-up river otter."

"Just wait." He grabbed a handful of the kelp strands from the wall and put them around her. "More," he said. "Grab more and they'll leave you alone." They both pulled more fiber away from the wall and pressed it around their bodies.

It worked: the presence of the kelp strands seemed to keep the smaller tentacles away. Clo slipped her knife into her belt and used both hands to pull mounds of the material free in chunks, and they half dug their way into the wall of the pit.

In just a few minutes they had kind of a thatched shell around them, and the tendrils stopped pulling altogether. They were safe, Clo thought, and El was probably safe, too. But, how to get out of here? Looking at Tobias, it was clear he didn't want to go anywhere. He smiled at her softly, and reached up to touch her cheek. She closed her eyes and pressed her face into his palm.

"How did you get that?" he asked.

It felt so good to be touched by another person, a boy, finally, like she had been thinking about for so long, that it took her a moment to come out of her swoon.

Clo opened her eyes. "What?" she asked dreamily. "Oh, my scar. Mother Oggy sent a talking deer to us when we first got to the forest. He told us we had to protect our family, and then he proved it by trying to kill our little brother, so I had to kill him, and then eat him."

"Oh," Tobias said, still locked on her face. It wasn't clear that he was following every detail of Clo's story.

"Hey!" Clo gasped in worry, touching her face. "This stuff is healing El—do you think it'll make my scar go away? Dasher gave it to me so that I'd never forget him. Oggy never sent another special deer to speak to us—only the bad guys have—and I can't forget him."

Tobias calmly shook his head. "The ichor can't heal your old wounds, only new ones."

"Good," Clo said, relieved. "I wouldn't know who I was without my scar. I might even think I was my sister, except for the whiptail part."

"It's the old scars that make you what you are," Tobias said. "I draw mine everywhere." He gestured to his chest and arms, and Clo realized that there were stories there, like ancient petroglyphs carved into a stone wall: drones, the cityscape, vehicles, but mostly people, lots and lots of stick-figured people, as if a remembrance to whatever race was going to come and replace us after the last human died out.

Okay, Clo told herself, *this is it. Just a few minutes, while El's arm is healing.* She pressed against Tobias's naked body and put her mouth on his. The effect of his mouth and his body next to her in the warm water—that wasn't really water—was amazing. Desire for him shot through her, transporting her back to that first moment when she saw him out in the Drag. He kissed her back, clinging to her as she wrapped herself around him in the weightless environment.

"Let's get out of here," she whispered. "Out of this . . . place."

"I have to be here," he said, "at least for a little while. Stay here with me. Just . . . be with me."

She had saved herself from being disrobed by the City; now she was willingly taking her clothes off in this protean slime. For a split second, with her naked body smooshing against Tobias's various parts, she thought, *What would Mama think?* Losing her virginity to a deaf graffiti artist (whom she had known less than twenty-four hours) while surrounded by sentient—or at least semisentient—slime. The boy had a lot of tattoos also, and not fancy Asian carp or whatever like she'd seen on retail models as a girl, but primitive lines and dots he had put on himself just to pass the time when he wasn't on drugs.

But this was it, Clo thought as she ran her hands across the raw symbols: probably her one chance to experience something for herself, before she ended up dead. Or worse.

"Wait," she said, lifting her right hand to Tobias. Maybe this was a halt in the foreplay, or maybe this was the foreplay. Clo wasn't experienced enough to know.

"Will you give me a tattoo?"

"Oh . . . okay." Tobias smiled. "That'd be nice." He reached his hand back to his pile of clothes, floating nearby.

He thought for only a moment before getting to work with his homemade kit, which seemed to consist of an old, blackened needle rubber-banded to a faded No. 2 pencil. The ink came from a cracked lip balm container.

Ugh, Clo thought. Mama definitely wouldn't like this. This was worse than the virginity thing. But the ichor all around us would probably keep it clean, and it didn't hurt when Tobias stuck her arm. In fact, maybe it was the semisentient nanofluid talking, but the whole process felt kind of good.

He was done in about twenty minutes, letting go of Clo's arm to reveal the perfect rune: two Gemini diamonds, joined hand in hand, one with what had to be a small knife and the other with a simple firearm. It was us, Clo and El, joined like an ancient constellation of divine bestowment. It was small, dark, crude, and wonderful.

"Oh, Tobias." She was definitely going to get into some serious sex now. Her boyfriend, however, was completely out. "Tobias?"

She sighed a deep liquid breath, hugged the sleeping Tobias, and closed her own eyes. Sleep, which had eluded her now for so many days, followed, and that was amazing too. Dreaming in the ichor, wrapped in Tobias, was a seduction that could go on forever. Her dreams focused on just that thought: eternity, or some aspect of it. A romance that lasted forever, a coupling that lasted forever, in a shining city of happily buzzing insects that lasted forever.

It was as if the eighteen years of her life leading up to this point were the actual dream, and she only had now remembered where she really came from. She dreamed of angels. Not the uncanny automatons that ran Yerba City, but real, beautiful angels with feathered hawk wings and frilly deerskin robes, themselves the stuff of eternal happiness. They surrounded her with song, and a kaleidoscope of wings parted to reveal her mother's face. At first Mama looked like an eighteenth-century Madonna, but after the wings and frilly robes trailed away, she became the same as the last time we saw her: hair tied back, face sunburnt, carrying her worn backpack, telling us to look after our brother—she'd be back in a few weeks. Then she turned and walked into the woods. For a moment, a glint of our mother's face looked back at us through the dim light of the trees. She said two words before she disappeared into the darkness:

"Find Josephine."

CHAPTER 18

SLEEPING BEAUTY

Clo's eyes popped open. How long had she slept? It was impossible to tell. There was no day or night in the depths of the Local Zero, so far from the surface. It was almost impossible to tell up from down even, except that Clo's moccasins rested on what must be the bottom of their little kelp cocoon. Tobias was still clinging to her, but it was easy enough to slip away and stretch. For a moment she considering waking him for more love, and maybe some actual coitus this time, but instead she just stroked his cheek lightly. His breathing seemed calm, at peace. Then Clo noticed the small squid bag attached to his arm.

As Clo looked at it, the bag seemed to sense her disapproving gaze and tightened its tentacles slightly, ever the jealous companion. Clo sighed to herself. Even down here, Tobias was still on the Sap, and he would be until the time came that he could pull that sac off himself. How long that would take—days, months, or years—Clo had no idea.

Clo turned to pull her clothes on. She realized then that the Sap—or lack of Sap—was probably why she was able to keep moving: despite all the amazing attributes of the ichor, it didn't contain any Subantoxx. There were apparently no drugs in the golden goo that surrounded her. That was a relief, although it didn't make the thought of the comforting ooze surrounding her private parts any less violating.

"Hey! Knock-knock." El's hand poked through the kelp. *"What are you doing?"*

"Oh, nothing," Clo said in a mock-innocent singsongy voice.

El poked her face through a tiny gap, took stock of Clo, half-dressed, and Tobias, completely out. She gasped, although she really wasn't that surprised. *"You totally rutted!"*

Clo just grinned. She left her feet bare and tied her moccasins to a loop around her waist.

"Tell me all about it! Did you bleed?"

"No, but he did," Clo said, thrusting her knife in a suggestive manner. *"Ha ha! He was a real gusher!"*

"Aaah! Gross!"

"Shh!"

"He can't hear. He's deaf and his ears are filled with goo anyway." El paused. *"Oh my God, what's that?"*

"Look!" Clo said, thrusting the new artwork on her deltoid toward her sister.

"He marked you with a tattoo?" El started out critical, but then realized what the rune actually was. *"That's us! Okay, that is so cool."* El held her sister's arm and examined the marking closely. *"There's even a little knife and a little Daisy Duke!"* She looked past Clo at the sleeping Tobias. *"Oh, he's good. I take back everything I said about him."*

Clo just smiled and continued dressing. *"How's your arm?"* she asked.

"It's fine—Look!" El held it up: the wound was totally gone. *"Anyway"*—she nodded toward Tobias—*"talk!"*

"We should go find Mama." Clo pulled out her knife and began cutting a larger slit in the cocoon.

"Oh, you're clamming up on me?"

Clo ignored her sister. She cut a two-foot hole in the cocoon and then held the blade in her teeth to rip at the hole with her hands to enlarge it.

"C'mon, help me pull this apart," she ordered through her bite.

"Super clam," El grunted as she helped Clo make an opening large enough to crawl through.

Clo took one last look at Tobias as he slept, then removed the knife from her teeth before kissing him goodbye. His unconscious lips stirred, and he smiled in his intoxicated sleep. Could she just stay down here with him? The Local Zero did seem more and more like the place where people went to just float their lives away, and considering the state of the world, that didn't strike us as the worst idea.

As in the magical video room in the Local One, we had to stave off the urge to stay by telling ourselves that someday we'd be back, although realistically, that was hard to fathom. What, would we find our mama and then just slide back into a gooey pit? The future was pretty murky at this point, but someday—someday!—we told ourselves. Especially Clo.

Clo squirmed through the hole, and we sealed it behind us the best we could, leaving Tobias cocooned in the kelp. We tried to make the best mental map we could of where the cocoon was and how to get back to it. It was difficult. Landmarks were hard to come by, but in the curvature of the walls, there was a kind of asymmetry that we felt we might be able to track later. It wasn't so much a pit that went straight down with flat sides as it was a cave, worm-shaped, that snaked downward into the earth. What was at the bottom? we wondered. Was that where the brain of Yerba City resided? Probably not, we decided. No, there was nothing but people and their Sap-squid friends in this pit— hundreds, maybe thousands, of people, probably all happy as clams to be floating their lives away.

We clung tight to the fibrous wall of the pit and began to climb. The tendrils returned, manifesting slowly out of the liquid around us as we moved, but we dug in with our fingers and toes, gripping each step with determined purchase. Now that we were anchored and not free-floating, as we had been when we fell in, the tentacles didn't have the force they needed to drag us downward. In fact, to us, it felt like we maybe had about thirty extra pounds weighing us down by the ankles. It would have made it nearly impossible to get out had we been trying to swim up, but climbing up was very doable. This must be how Tobias had gotten out before. And he would again, wouldn't he? That's right, he'd shake free of the Sap, get tired of floating in this golden pee, and realize that he loved Clo more than anything, then haul himself out to find her. At least that was the fantasy.

Every now and again, when the pull of the tentacles increased, Clo did a quick swipe with her knife. Slicing them up freed us for a few minutes, allowing us quicker movement until the tendrils remanifested and their numbers increased again.

We were about three-quarters of the way to the surface when El spotted something. *"Well, lookie,"* she whispered.

There, floating on a kelp line in the center of the pit, was Maynor. He seemed to be sleeping, intertwined with a woman.

"Guess he made it out of that riot," Clo grunted.

"Zeta the cicada probably had to carry him by the scruff."

"Should we press him into service?"

"Either that or cut him up as payment for that goose chase," El said bitterly. *"See how many pieces this goo can put back together."*

Clo took a moment to chop away the naughty tentacles around us, and then we launched off the wall before they could re-form, making sure we achieved maximum velocity through the goo. We kicked hard, already feeling the tendrils rematerializing, but it was enough. We grabbed on to the kelp vine just above where Maynor was sleeping.

His eyes stayed closed as Clo dropped down behind him, wrapped her legs around his arms, and held the knife to his throat. No doubt he was stronger than her and could break free of her legs easily enough once he woke, but not before she could cut his jugular veins. We wondered for a moment if he was smart enough to realize that.

His eyes popped open. He was.

"El," he said, facing her. His eyes caught the edge of the knife below him. "Clo." He couldn't see her yet, but who else would be holding a knife under his chin?

"Maynor," El said calmly, trying to sound as determined as possible despite the ichor filling her mouth.

"What? You two run off on me while I'm doing you a favor?" He tried to sound cool, which was amusing given his floating-in-goo position and the mean, half-rusted hunting knife at his throat. "That's kinda rude. I took one for you back there, you know."

"Did you?" El asked angrily, holding up her arm and wiggling her thumb. Although healed, the bullet wound was still visible. "I almost lost my arm."

"Oh," Maynor said in realization. "Well, good thing you knew what good healing the Local Zero can do."

"We didn't," Clo grunted.

"Yeah, a van dropped us in here like garbage," El growled.

"Well, it all worked out, then," Maynor said. "See how efficiently we run things here in Yerba City?"

"We didn't ask you to start shooting up those people," El said. "One of them was our brother, remember?"

"You Yettis are a hell of a bunch, you know that?" Maynor had just the right angle to gently tap the Sap bag on the naked woman next to him. "You should really try the Sap. It would make you a lot more mellow."

Clo pushed the knife into his neck.

"Okay, okay," he said. "You know, cutting my throat probably wouldn't kill me down here."

"How about if I cut your head off and haul it up to one of those oil fires?"

Maynor nodded. "Might do the trick." He shifted uneasily under the blade. "Anyway, what can I do for you two?"

"Where's Josephine?" El asked.

"What, you're not after Mommy anymore?"

"Where is she?" Her tone suggested she might be ready to move from a discussion to a decapitation.

"I assume she's at Saturnalia, like she said she'd be."

El looked down and examined the wound just under Maynor's left shoulder, where Dyre must have shot him. The hole was mostly healed, the ichor forming tiny tendrils around it to patch the wound. Maynor must have come here to heal up and, judging by the still-sleeping woman next to him, to do some kind of naked cuddling.

The woman was a lot older than us, maybe older than Maynor, maybe around thirty, and she was beautiful, with golden hair floating in the golden ichor. She had a noticeable Sap squid attached to her lower arm.

"Guess you get your fill down here," Clo snorted, gesturing to the woman sleeping au naturel next to him. "Knew you were a goldeneye."

"What?" Maynor asked, trying to sound casual.

"You like molesting these women down here?" El growled. "Sleepy girls that can't fight back?"

"You broke your oath," Clo said grimly, and the consequences were obvious. The knife cut into Maynor's neck, sending a small cloud of blood into the ichor, but to our surprise, Maynor stayed defiant.

"You got the wrong idea," he said stoically, which was impressive considering he was about to die. "I'm not one of those ducks. Sarah is my wife."

El paused and looked at Clo. We were skeptical, to say the least. "Oh, really?"

"Yeah," he said calmly. He held up his hand, and for the first time we noticed that he had a pretty gold-and-silver band on his ring finger. On her hand, she had a band with the exact same wavy pattern, only smaller.

"Hmm," said Clo. "Nice rings."

"Thanks," said Maynor. "Can you please stop killing me now?"

"Doesn't mean you weren't violating," Clo said coldly, the knife cutting deeper. "She can't exactly caterwaul, can she?"

"It's not like that," Maynor said firmly. "I didn't do anything. I just come down here to be next to her sometimes. That's all. I love her, I swear," he gulped. "And she loves me."

Still skeptical, Clo loosened the knife somewhat, while keeping it close to his face. Right away we could see the healing tendrils appear from the ichor to repair the cut Clo had made.

"Didn't think people got married after the Sap came along," Clo said suspiciously.

"They don't," Maynor said calmly. "We were married before. You see, I was fixed. They fixed six of us for this region. I had no idea what I was getting into. I signed up to be a security guard for a new company called Chimera Systems. First day, they give us a series of injections, which burned out receptors LV425 and LV427." Maynor tapped his temple. "Right in my brain. No receptors, no high. Permanently, genetically. They did that to ensure a sober monitoring force."

"They modified you so that you couldn't become a shambling addict," El realized.

Maynor mildly rubbed his neck, making sure that his wound was healed. "The term that we use is *patient*, but yeah, that's right. The following week they sent the drones over with the first Subantoxx spray." He looked over at his wife. "Sarah, along with ninety-nine point nine

nine percent of the population, went into treatment." He moved a hair from in front of her eyes. "And here we are. She's been a junkie for this stuff for almost ten years, and I . . ." His voice trailed off as he stared at her. "I follow orders."

"Orders?" El scoffed.

"As a matter of fact, getting you to Saturnalia is now priority one." Maynor half sighed the statement.

"I'm sure." Clo scooped her free hand to grab the fléchette pistol from Maynor's belt.

"Careful with that, it's my last firearm. Those babblers got the rest. Besides, I don't think a fléchette would go very far down here," he said, trying to sound nonchalant.

Clo sheathed the knife but held the gun to his back. "I bet it'll go far enough into your kidney." She unwrapped her legs from his chest. "Don't turn around. Get dressed."

"You don't need to get all pointy with that thing now. I'm under orders."

"Yeah, our orders. Let's go."

Maynor huffed and pulled on his pants. Clo backed up just enough for him to pull on his body suit. Before he did, Maynor poked at the healing wound in his shoulder. "Good enough for government work," he muttered and zipped his all-black mime suit (now with various holes and tears) into place. He gave Sarah's wrist a quick goodbye kiss before turning back to us.

"It's not easy to love someone who's . . . absent, is it?" Maynor said. He gave his wife a last look. "Would've thought you girls could appreciate that."

El scoffed. "You think you're some sensitive sweetheart beaver, taking care of your honey down here in the lodge?"

"We know real beavers," Clo added, "and they don't need a bunch of bug armor and fancy guns to be good husbands." We were giving him a hard time, but the truth is, we did understand. Maybe Maynor wasn't such a self-important scumbag goldeneye after all. Still, we didn't have time for his shenanigans. Clo poked him in the ribs again with the pistol. "C'mon."

Maynor turned to make his way upward and spotted the tentacles still pulling on El. "Damn, you're holding out against the flow. You're a lot stronger than I thought."

"We're full of surprises," El said. For a second Clo didn't understand what he meant, but then she realized that by "flow," Maynor must have meant the constant pull of the tiny tentacles. Clo took another swipe at them. They'd have to make it back to the wall of the pit to climb out, and still keep an eye on Maynor, which wasn't going to be easy.

"Why don't you just stop it?" he asked. We were silent. "You don't know how, do you? Here." He moved his hand upward. Clo pushed the pistol into his side. "Ow! I'm not going to try anything. I just want to show you how to control the ichor."

"I'll watch," El volunteered, then said to Clo, "You shoot."

We watched carefully as Maynor made a split-fingered peace sign, and then flipped it three times. "That's 'initiate.' Then the command—" He made a circle as if grasping and then released it. We could feel the constant grip release, like clingy toddlers finally taken away by their parents.

"Ahh!" Clo shook herself. "That's better." She moved her legs. "I can swim now! So this goo speaks sign language?"

"There are only eight commands," Maynor said, pulling his boots on. El guessed he wasn't planning on swimming.

"Why don't you just make like a porcupine?" Clo demanded. "Then you wouldn't have to take advantage of these poor people down here."

Maynor bristled at the comment. "I don't 'take advantage' of anyone. I just come down here to be with someone I love, and to heal up." He finished tying his boots and looked at Clo angrily. "Besides, last time I checked, your boyfriend was one of these poor people."

"You mind your own . . . business!" Clo retorted awkwardly.

"I will," Maynor said coldly. "So should you."

"Please, children," El interrupted. "Are the commands keyed to your genetics?" she asked Maynor.

"No, anyone can do it. They just don't. They *want* to be here, remember?" Maynor nodded to the patients floating in the kelp nearby. "Everyone wants to be here."

Clo looked upward. *"Come on,"* she said to her sister. She handed the gun to El, hopefully the better shot even in liquid environments, and grabbed Maynor by the scruff of his outfit.

"We don't have to swim," Maynor said. "Watch." He made the "initiate" command again and then drew a circle with his index finger. Nearby, a disc, about ten feet in diameter and horizontally oriented, appeared to solidify directly out of the ichor. "We can ride that thing up."

El gave a hoot and kicked over to the waiting platform. Clo stayed behind Maynor and slowly pushed him toward it. "How do you make it go up?" Clo asked, lightly touching her foot to the surface.

"Just point up now. Or down, if you like."

"Let's go for up." Clo did, and a series of slotted holes appeared in the disc, presumably to allow liquid to flow, and the whole thing started to rise. In just a few moments, we were at the surface, emerging into the night air of Yerba City. The ichor drained away from us, *climbed* away from us, even oozing up and out of our moccasins, detaching itself to remain with the larger body of fluid in the pit. Maynor showed us how to face downward and cough, and as we did, the ichor slid out of our lungs and sinuses. We could feel it ooze out of our clothes, our hair, our pockets, even out of our eyes and ears. El watched the ichor slide out of every crack and crevice in the pistol she was holding, presumably leaving it entirely dry. She was doubtful whether or not the gun would even work now, but she decided to keep it pointed at Maynor's kidneys nonetheless.

In less than a minute, we were perfectly dry, and moments after we stepped off the disc and onto the crunchy surface of Yerba City, the disc itself disappeared. It was pretty amazing; after being down there for hours, at least, not even our toes were squishy.

"We're dry," El said.

Clo looked at El. *"Uh, my hair could use some work."* In fact, it was flat as a pancake against her skull.

"I always said you should keep it short and practical," El said, running her hands quickly through her own hair. *"Don't know why you even bother."*

"Ladies," Maynor interrupted, "shall we get out of here?"

Maynor walked confident and upright and proud through the city-scape, trying to act smooth and in control despite the fact that a gun was still pointed at his lower back. Zeta was parked nearby, tilted at a slight angle where she rested on the rubble. Swarming over her were a dozen or so of the small maintenance drones, chirping and buzzing as they put the finishing touches on repairs.

"She's missing a leg," Clo noted. "That big cricket took a couple of hits, too, huh?" She chortled as she shooed away bugs. Most of them flew off, while a big one stayed behind to threaten Clo with tiny pincers. Apparently it hadn't finished its job yet.

"Yeah, well, we made it back here, didn't we?" Maynor said. "She's a tough bug."

"How's your shoulder, anyway? We saw the hole before we woke you up."

Maynor rotated his arm. "It's mostly fine, I guess. The ichor can heal—*Yaaa!*" Maynor jerked his body violently away from El, who had stuck a finger in him where the bullet hole had been.

"Sorry," El said. "I was just testing it."

"I said *mostly* fine!" Maynor clutched at his wound. "Needs a few more hours. *Pinche* . . . Ow!" Maynor panted. The pain of the half-healed bullet hole was apparently excruciating, or at least strong enough to make him lose his cool-guy persona. "Man, you crazy twins are out to freakin' lunch."

"So we've heard," El snorted.

Clo finally got the last bug off Zeta, knocking it away with a broken electric scooter she'd fished out of the rubble. "Are you going to take us to Saturnalia or what?"

Maynor shook off the pain. "Yeah, sure. Sooner I get rid of you two psychos, the better."

We all hopped in the cicada, and El took the front seat, keeping Maynor's gun on her lap. Clo snuggled into the back seat. Maynor pressed his hand onto the scanner, and the craft fired up, albeit with a slightly deeper rumble than we remembered.

"I hope they fixed her well enough," Maynor mumbled to himself. "We barely made it back here." The craft lifted off the ground with a rattle-y growl.

From the air, through the cracked carapace, we could see the oval pool that was the Local Zero. It looked like a golden circle on the ground, with several silver roads for the autonomous cattle cars leading into it. As the flying craft pulled away, another minibus was pulling up, presumably getting ready to dump another load of "diseased" humans into the pit.

"*So many people down there . . .*," Clo murmured. She turned away from the view and noticed the lockbox in the back of the cicada was sitting open, empty. "Where's the Love Gun—and the rest of your penis enlargers?"

"Subbies cleaned me out," Maynor grumbled. "Didn't expect the punks to rush me like that."

"Thought you would just shoot a few of those babblers and they'd scatter?" El said.

"Yeah, genius move," Clo added sarcastically.

"What they've got is worse than the Sap," El said. "They'll kill anyone—and any*thing*—that doesn't convert, even their closest kin."

Maynor ignored us and just winced over his wound. "I think I liked you two better when you were shy and awkward."

"When was that?" Clo demanded.

"How long were you down there?" El asked. "Do you know they took over the bridge train?"

"What?" Maynor grabbed his phone and scrolled through the analog alerts.

"Thing was on fire," Clo said.

"You're messing with me." Maynor looked up from his phone. "Says there was a minor situation with the eastern transport, but everything's under control."

"Whatever." Clo shrugged. "Just take us to Josephine, then."

El decided Maynor should know more. "*After* you take us to Saturnalia, you probably should take a look. At the base of the bridge, where the train starts to go down. It got pretty crazy. Some drones went down."

"Really?" asked Maynor. "So it made it to the city?"

"Then there was a big rumbling."

"Like bees."

"Bees?" Maynor asked, unbelieving.

"Giant bees," Clo confirmed, "but only for a little while. Then everything got quiet."

Maynor scoffed, probably thinking we were crazy. But he had to know that something unusually big was going down.

"He doesn't believe us," Clo observed.

"Or doesn't want to," El responded.

"So something is going on. Something new."

"Could be something he's not telling us. Another security measure. Mama said there could be many."

"Like, maybe the bees aren't unusual?" Clo mused.

"Maybe not."

"I don't know. He acted pretty surprised."

"Will you two stop that?" Maynor interrupted. "I'm trying to concentrate."

"Just tell Zeta where we're going," El insisted. "We're fine with autopilot."

"Fine," Maynor said, then punched buttons on the console. El watched him closely, trying to follow the command sequence he entered for Saturnalia. "Let's go, Zeta," Maynor told the vehicle.

"Yes, Maynor," the beetle answered in her subservient voice. "So great to have you back. I hope you're feeling better!"

"I know what you're thinking," Maynor said, turning to El, "but don't bother. Zeta won't respond to anyone but me. Otherwise, don't you think those punks would have taken her?"

"Just curious," El muttered. "Always fun to learn new tricks . . ." She trailed off as the cicada took us higher, apparently in response to Maynor entering a more distant destination. There was no fog this time, and in the moonlight, we could see in every direction. It really wasn't until that moment that we realized it—that is, the extent of it.

The city was broken, destroyed like every other man-made thing we'd seen. We knew that. But below, a different thing was growing: from above, the only things visible in the darkness were the rectangular 1s of the brightly lit Local Ones and the golden pools of 0s. 101010010100011010101010 . . . extending across the landscape, lighting up the night, as far we could see.

We rode in silence for a while.

It didn't take long to reach the Golden Gate Bridge, or what was left of it. It was just a single tower now, the second tower and almost all the roadway having fallen into the bay. Suddenly we both remembered walking across the bridge. It was windy and cold, but sunny, and we were with Mama. She had been pushing Dyre in a stroller, and halfway across, we gave up and clung to the stroller ourselves. Mama had to push all three of us as the afternoon wind picked up, but she did it. It was just a little while after Papa died. Maybe it was that day we realized how strong Mama really was. Not just mentally, but physically how strong she could be. Three kids with one mom? There must have been a thousand people walking that bridge at the same time, but there was only Mama Yetti pushing three kids on the same stroller. We must have been about six at the time. We'd never forget that day.

Now, looking below, the beautiful windy seascape with sailboats and ferries was gone, and all that was left was a giant piece of twisted red metal snaking out of the channel.

"To hell with this place," Clo finally said, looking down at the destroyed bridge, the red craggy fingers clawing at the night sky.

"Yeah," El repeated, "to hell with it. When we're done, we're going back to the woods."

"It's not that bad here," Maynor said. "Sure you two don't want to stick around after you find your mom? The City could use a couple of troopers like you to keep things in order."

"Just take us to Josephine," El muttered.

"I thought you were looking for your mother."

"She told us to find Josephine," Clo told him.

"How did she tell you that? Did you make contact?"

"No, she told us in a dream," El said.

"Told you both? In a dream? That you had at the same time?"

"Uh-huh," we both said, simultaneously.

Maynor shook his head. "Guess I've heard of stranger things."

"It'll all make sense when we find her," El said, more to herself than to Maynor.

"She always makes it make sense," Clo said as she settled back in her seat. *"Always."* She snapped to. "Hey! We're going down."

"Are we there already?" El demanded, pointing the pistol sharply at Maynor again.

"It's okay, don't shoot. Just have to get a little fuel before we go on," Maynor explained. "Even Zeta needs to eat sometimes."

CHAPTER 19

HEAVEN AND EARTH

The cicada landed just a few feet away from the remains of what had once been a Coast Guard station on the other side of the bridge. The carapace rose, and Maynor turned to jump out.

"Whoa, big fella," El said, and he froze as she jabbed the pistol into his back.

He nodded grudgingly, and they both got out and headed toward a silver pump that was waiting nearby.

A metal insectoid arm, mounted on the boxy pump, seemed to sense their approach and reached down automatically to lift a greasy handle, which Maynor plucked from its claw. It was the same type of pump we'd seen back in Ukiah, except this one was in the middle of a kind of helipad, rather than a flat C-shaped structure like the minimart. It must have been installed, here at the foot of the northern end of the former Golden Gate Bridge, just for vehicles like the cicada. We guessed that it must be an automated system for refueling the drones.

It was kind of creepy to us, knowing that these flying, buzzing, crawling machines were moving everywhere on their own—refueling themselves, fixing themselves, reproducing and evolving on their own. Maynor seemed pretty used to the whole thing.

Clo hopped out and looked around, stretching. She scanned the sky and the surroundings, in case Maynor had somehow arranged another pickup and was planning on ditching us there. There were no drones visible.

It was a somewhat windy night, but we could still easily make out the low crashing of waves against the seawall, not forty feet away. We hadn't been that close to the sea in a long time, but we didn't bother to go look, opting to stay vigilant instead. As the pump's flow increased, we could smell the diesel strong in our nostrils. The hunters in us didn't like that in the slightest.

"Why does she still use that stuff?" Clo asked, wrinkling her nose.

"What? Gas? This is super concentrated diesel."

"Fossil fuels." El said the words disdainfully, as our mother had taught her. "They pollute the environment, you know, and kill Mother Earth."

"It's more reliable," Maynor said after a brief pause, with the kind of exaggerated confidence that told us he really didn't know, or care. "And besides, we're self-contained here in Yerba City. She's got platforms just out past the gate, and a refinery up in Zone 2-2."

"She built oil rigs out there?"

"There's a lot fewer cars and machines than when we were kids," Maynor assured us. "Pollution's not a problem anymore, and it makes Chimera 'energy independent.'" He said the last two words like he had memorized them from a TV commercial.

"It's stinky. The City should go solar. I'm sure that's what Mama would say."

Maynor adjusted the pump. "This is more reliable," he repeated.

"What's going to happen? The sun'll go dark?" Clo scoffed.

Maynor looked up at the night sky. "Maybe. The City has her reasons."

"Let's not ask him any more," El suggested. *"He doesn't know anything, and he doesn't think about anything. He's just a dumb guard dog on a leash."*

"You mean that woman back in the pit?" Clo said.

"Maybe he's not a goldeneye, but the City's got leverage on him," El concluded. *"He'll never see straight."*

For a moment there was silence between Maynor and us, just the whirring of the pump.

Clo took a moment to look up at the starry night sky. She couldn't help herself. "Maynor, whatever happens to us, don't be a kapo."

El was shocked. *"Clo, don't."*

"A what?" Maynor asked.

"It's something our father told us, before he died," Clo continued. "'Don't be a kapo.'"

"Shut up," El chided her sister. *"Don't bring that up."*

"What's a kapo?" Maynor asked, suddenly intrigued, probably by the obvious tension between us.

"A prisoner who thinks they're in charge," Clo said, ignoring her sister. "Our grandfather was Polish. In World War Two they put him in a concentration camp, but he was big and strong, so they made him a kapo to run the other prisoners."

"What happened to him?" Maynor asked.

"What the hell do you think happened?" El snarled. "We're here, aren't we? We're alive, standing right in front of you!"

Maynor's eyes darted between us. A mix of emotions was clearly passing through him, although we thought it was all tempered by the thought that we were just a couple of crazy chicks. "Yeah, you are," he said dismissively.

"He lived," Clo conceded. "But mostly he wished he hadn't. Thousands of people died in front of him—because of him. A lot of them his own relatives. He never got over it, and neither did his son."

"His son?" Maynor asked. "You mean your dad?"

"Yeah, our dad," Clo said. "He drank himself dead when we were four."

"You shouldn't talk to him about all that," El chided. *"Dyre doesn't even know about that."*

"Is that what you think I am?" Maynor asked, getting more agitated now. "One of these kapos? Turned against my own kind?"

"I don't know," Clo said. "We just got here, and there are so many sides to what's going on, we don't know who's betraying who and who wants to be betrayed and who doesn't think they're being betrayed, or who would even care." She paused, frustrated. "Do *you* think you're a kapo?"

Bing. The fuel line stopped pumping.

Maynor thought, just for a moment, then opened his mouth to answer.

BAM! A shot cracked the night. Maynor's right ear exploded into a mist of red across the silver exteriors of the pump and cicada.

"Ow! My earhole!" He hit the ground, gripping the side of his head where his ear had once been. "Get down!" he shouted.

Clo dropped to the deck and rolled into the darkness, away from the light of the pump.

El dove back onto the floor of the cicada, readying the pistol.

A second shot rang out, the ricocheting bullet leaving a dent on the top of the pump.

"Throw me my gun!" Maynor shouted at El.

"No!" she yelled back. El could see figures moving in the darkness, coming from the direction of the water. She pointed the pistol and fired. Or tried to; the weapon's hammer fell with a dull click.

"It's not chambered!" Maynor yelled in frustration. "Just throw it to me."

El didn't have time to be infuriated that Maynor had not really been at her mercy this entire time. He'd known full well he could have grabbed the gun from her.

"No!" El yelled at him again. She distantly remembered her training from Mama: pull the slide back, chamber a round. She clutched awkwardly at the gun, barely able to move the slide. Was it supposed to be that hard? She was so good with the rifle, it hadn't immediately occurred to her that she might need a refresher on how to use a standard sidearm pistol.

A third shot shattered the window of the cicada, sending a shower of tempered glass onto El. Zeta shifted slightly, trying to position herself between Maynor and the gunfire.

"Dammit!" Maynor shouted, and he clutched at the pump, sliding the small glass door open and pulling down two bags of Subantoxx. Apparently this filling station could keep you loaded with drugs as well as fuel. The third bag hit the ground with a dull *smack*, its short tentacles spreading out futilely.

Maynor dropped the second bag and began ripping at the first. He glanced around the pump. "There's two coming in! One more by the water."

"We know!" El yelled, finally getting the pistol to slide back. She aimed it at one of the three black figures coming for them in the darkness. To her relief, the weapon bucked in her hand. And again.

"Don't waste ammo!" Maynor said desperately. "It's all I have!"

"You want me to save it for love?" Another rifle crack from the darkness, and the cicada got another hole, near El's head. Zeta shifted again, but clearly didn't know where to put herself. She wasn't the brightest bug.

"We're sitting ducks out here." Maynor stood up, looking ready to dash off into the darkness. Whether it was to follow Clo's advance or just to run like a plucked turkey, we weren't sure. But it didn't matter—something came screaming out of the darkness first.

It was one of the Subversive bucks, probably only around fourteen years old, but like all the babblers, he was in it to win it. The boy slammed into Maynor body first, apparently forgetting that he had a nasty-looking stick in one hand. Maynor had just gotten the Subantoxx bag open, and the two of them went rolling across the helipad in a shower of Sap, which looked like a spray of silvery blue stars exploding in the fluorescent lights of the station. El shook her head as she saw the stick come down hard on Maynor. Here he was, supposedly some security elite. *We* never would have gotten blindsided like that.

Another shot, from something smaller than a rifle, rang out. Apparently the shooter was trying to take advantage of the distraction of that young buck's charge, but El hadn't left cover, and the shot went wild. Near as she could tell, it came from behind a pile of rotting orange life rings, about thirty feet away.

Maynor popped back to his feet, his forehead bloody. The buck didn't follow him, but stayed on the ground. "I got him!" Maynor shouted, half in victory, half in surprise at his own accomplishment. In his hand was the Sap bag, mostly empty, dripping, its tentacles twitching. At least one of those tentacles went down into the buck.

El couldn't believe it. "You just—stick him—and it works?"

Maynor nodded, smiling. "Yeah!" He touched his forehead and pulled his hand away to look at the blood. "Aaah!"

"Get on the ground, idiot!" El yelled.

Another rifle crack, and the bullet glanced off the armor on Maynor's left shoulder, spinning him half around. He used the momentum to follow El's advice and lay flat on the ground. Apparently, getting shot last night was enough of a lesson.

Two more of the smaller pops rang out from behind the lifesavers. El returned fire, twice. It would be enough to keep her shooter in place for a moment. She still wasn't sure about the sniper, or where they were even shooting from. She took a split second to think.

"Throw a bag!" she yelled at Maynor.

"What?" he called, still flat, but he looked over at her.

"Over the lifesavers. Throw the squid bag," she called back. She waved the pistol, indicating that she would shoot it.

Maynor paused. "Throw it?"

"I'll cover. Three shots. Then you throw. I'll shoot the bag."

"Are you serious?"

"Just throw the bag, bitch!" El screamed at him.

Nodding, Maynor rolled and grabbed one of the two full bags left.

El popped up from the cicada. Two shots over the lifesavers, one more in her best guess of the direction of the rifle.

Maynor stood and threw the bag hard. This he was good at. El shot it about ten feet above the lifesavers, sending a shower down across the tarmac.

El crouched back down into the cicada and called to Maynor, who was also lying flat again. "Was that enough to get him high?"

"Should be, if there's enough skin contact," Maynor called back. "One bag lasts for days."

They waited. Sure enough, the shots from the pile stopped.

"Okay." Maynor cocked his head, listening. "What about the rifleman?" A scream answered in the distance.

"Clo just got him," El announced and stood up, getting out of the cicada.

"You sure?" Maynor said.

The screaming continued, angry.

"Pretty sure."

Maynor remained unconvinced, staying on the ground. His plan seemed to be to wait and see if El got shot at again. She didn't.

She walked over to the lifesavers, keeping the gun ready, but her body language said she felt safe. Behind the rotting stack, she found the buck, leaning against the pile, mumbling to himself. A pistol lay next to him; it looked like one of Maynor's, probably looted from the incident back in the village. The antlers he wore were held on with a simple strap, and his exposed hair and face were wet with Subantoxx. Even under the effects of the drug, his mumbling was unmistakable: he had the Babble, although he wasn't barking it out.

El kicked the pistol away from him, sending it skidding into a drainage ditch. She would have retrieved it, but she would probably have had to touch the Sap. Even now she was conscious of the fact that it was probably on the bottom of her moccasins. She walked carefully.

She headed back to the light of the pump, and a moment later, Clo trotted out of the darkness. The screaming in the distance hadn't stopped. "Got both the Achilles tendons," she announced confidently. "And look what he was shooting at us with." She held out a hunting rifle, a blue camo .30-06. Daisy Duke.

El took the rifle from her sister and just stared at it. Finally confident he wasn't going to get shot at, Maynor hopped back to his feet. "I think that's the same rifle they shot me with back in the Drag."

"It is," Clo said simply. She looked around to take in the situation. She saw the spattered Sap, and the squid bag pumping into the buck on the ground.

"That works? Lemme try that." She picked up the last Subantoxx bag from next to the pump, grabbed the supplemental needle, and trotted back into the darkness toward the screaming.

"*Careful with that stuff,*" El said.

"*Uh-huh,*" Clo answered dismissively.

Maynor clutched at the wound on the side of his head. It was actually superficial—mostly just cartilage missing; he could probably even still hear—but like any head wound, the laceration on his skull was bleeding like a sonuvabitch. Blood flowed in an arc down his cheek, gathering in a deep red stain at the top of his jumpsuit. Maynor clutched at it for a moment. "Nearly blew my head off." Then he walked to the prone buck and prepared to give him a solid kick in the side. The boy on the ground didn't seem to notice the menace approaching him; he simply continued his low mumble.

El contemplated the rifle for another moment, then—"Wait," she said.

Maynor paused, his armored foot poised to crack some ribs. "What?" he said, expecting another danger to emerge out of the darkness. His eyes darted around, and then he realized that El was trying to halt his vengeance boot party. "Why?" he demanded.

El paused, trying to put all the pieces of the puzzle together.

Maynor wound up again, preparing to crush the kid on the ground.

"Wait!" El yelled at him fiercely.

Maynor stopped, looking at her wildly through bloody eyes. *"Why?"*

"Why aren't they babbling?" El asked, trying to stay calm.

"What?" Maynor demanded.

"I said, why aren't they babbling? They could have had you without shooting."

"Who cares?" Maynor demanded, clutching his head again. "They gave us an opening. We took it. They probably realized it wasn't working on you. Or me, if you'd let me put my damn helmet on—*Ow!*" He withdrew his hand from his skull, taking note of the amount of flowing blood. Then he cursed in Spanish, something about getting a bandage.

While Maynor fussed, El walked over to the buck. Unlike the one behind the lifesavers, this one's face was heavily clad, wrapped in layers of greasy scarves. Like the others, he had makeshift buck antlers strapped to his head. El reached down, pulled the scarf from around the boy's face, and gasped.

"What?" Maynor snapped back to English with a paranoid tone. "He's not sobering up, is he?"

"No," said El coldly. "Here, take this and keep pressure on your wound." She threw him the scarf.

Maynor obeyed, pressing the scarf hard against the spot where his ear should be before realizing that the scarf was sopping wet. Not with Sap, but with seawater.

"This thing's soaked," Maynor said, holding the now-bloody scarf away from his head to look at it. "Did they swim over here after us?"

"I think . . ." El's voice trailed off as she pulled the rest of the buck's head covering away, revealing his face.

She was stunned, although she shouldn't have been.

"What? You know this Subbie? You screw this one, too?" Maynor grumbled.

"That was my sister that was screwing," El said coldly as she looked closely at the boy on the ground. "Besides, this one's my brother." She felt his arms, neck, ribs, legs.

"What? That's Dyre?" Maynor asked, unbelieving. He leaned over to look at the teenager's newly exposed face, but shrugged, as he didn't know him anyway. "Why are you all gropey with him? Is that a family thing?"

"I'm checking to see if he has any serious injuries," El said irritably.

"Oh, well, excuse me, but I think I have a serious injury right here." Maynor winced as he pressed the rag back onto the side of his head. "Gonna take me a week to grow this ear back . . ." He eyed Dyre on the ground.

"This is good," he said, pointing at our brother with his free hand. "This is real good." He nodded in relief. "The Sap stopped them."

El didn't respond; she was still checking Dyre over. She turned him slightly. *"At least his poo got washed off in the bay,"* she mumbled to herself.

"You see," Maynor continued, elated. "I wasn't sure if it would, but it does. This Babble is infecting all these people, but all we have to do is dose them with the Sap. It'll knock 'em down like your brother here, and we can stop it."

El remained skeptical. "The babblers can't . . . 'refuse treatment.' They're fair game for Santa Claus and his presents."

"Exactly," said Maynor. "We could spray the whole Drag—or every sector of the city. Just shut 'em down."

"Okay," El said, hesitant about potentially getting hit with Subantoxx, although it beat getting shot at. "But I think you're forgetting something."

"What?"

"The thing's evolving," El realized. "It gave our rifle to that shooter back there. Probably because it thought that buck was a better shot."

"*It*? What is *it*?" Maynor demanded. "All three of them tried to kill us!"

El turned to Maynor. "If my brother was going to kill me, he would have shot me himself." The fact seemed so painfully obvious, El thought she shouldn't have to say it out loud. She nodded to the pile and then into the darkness. "This wasn't a zombie rush. They came at us quietly. No babbling. Long-range shooter, covering fire, forward attack. That's strategy. A plan. This whole thing—the Babble—is thinking now."

"How?" Maynor still wasn't buying it.

"I don't know." El's mind searched desperately for an answer. "But it works between them. Communally. The more people it takes over, the smarter it gets. We saw it: the people were able to gather and start a new Babble that took over the drones. And they almost got Paddington," El said, thinking about the gory scene back on the train. "They did get him. Enough of him. We had to . . . take him down."

Maynor paused. El's seriousness was sinking in. He looked at the scarf in his hand. "This scarf is covered in grease," he said, and then he nodded to Dyre's prone figure. "I think all of his clothes are. It probably had them suit up and swim over here."

"You think they swam by themselves?" El asked skeptically. "Across the bay?"

"No," said Maynor. "They had help."

"Help from . . . what?" El asked. In the distance, the screaming cut out. Clo must have finally gotten the Sap into the wounded sniper, shutting them up.

"Got him!" Clo announced victoriously from the night.

The relative quiet that had surrounded us before the attack returned, allowing El to hear something else nearby. A low chant, disturbingly familiar.

"Help from *that!*" Maynor shouted, pointing at his flying vehicle. Next to the cicada was the converted donkey drone, the one that Dyre had infected back at the giant bonfire, and it was crouching low and trying to force a section of Zeta's carapace open. The drooping, fanged deer head was still affixed on the front of the machine, which was chanting a newer, mechanized version of the Babble now: "BrrrabbaMooi. Brrabba Moi Ko . . ."

"It's trying to infect Zeta!" Maynor shouted.

"These bucks were just decoying us," El realized, frantically checking Daisy Duke.

"We gotta stop it," Maynor said desperately.

"Good idea!" El said, dashing over, and chambering a round into the rifle as she went. "I don't wanna have to fight Zeta."

BAM! El fired a shot into the donkey's side at close range, rocking it from its protected position. El was already chambering a second round as the six-legged hauler turned toward her. The robotic animal dropped all pretense of stealth, rising high on its legs and bellowing out the Babble, the dead deer head shaking threateningly on the front of its body.

BAM! El fired a second shot right into New Vambi's skull. The impact knocked the deer head onto the wet asphalt and sent the shambling vehicle back a few feet, but ultimately had no real effect.

"The armor's too thick!" El yelled.

Clo came running out of the night, knife ready. The first shot had got her racing. *"What's happening?"* she yelled. *"Are there more?"*

"That mule's trying to infect the cicada!"

"Damn! She'd rip us apart!"

"I can't get a kill!"

"I'm on it." Clo never broke stride, instead taking two big leaps onto Zeta's leg, up onto her back, and through the air toward the mule. Her free hand hooked onto one of the machine's shoulders, and she swung herself right onto its back, riding it rodeo-style.

The mule screamed in frustration and bucked wildly, but fortunately none of its six legs were made to service its back. Clo managed to hold on as she was thrashed from side to side. She gripped her knife tightly, frantically looking over the metal-and-plastic frame for some kind of weak spot.

"Okay!" she called wildly. "What can I stab back here?"

"I don't know!" Maynor called desperately. "It's a construction drone! Its brains are in its chest!"

Clo tried to pry the thing's back open, but between the thrashing and the fact that the mule was designed to dig through industrial rubble, it wasn't going well.

"I can't get in!" Clo barked in frustration.

"Shut down Zeta!" El ordered Maynor.

Maynor nodded in realization. "I'll try!" He threw down his bloody rag and made a dash for the opposite side of the cicada, popping open her carapace doors and scrambling into the cockpit.

El lifted Daisy Duke and tried to get a bead on something—anything—that would stop this berserk machine. But what? Clo was hacking away and making no progress; what good would a bullet do other than potentially hit her sister?

"I can't shut her down!" Maynor called in frustration from inside the cockpit. "The console's too damaged! I can't stop her from hearing that Babble!"

"Then take off," El insisted.

"Yes!" Maynor cried. "I can do that!" Zeta's engines hummed to life and the craft lifted off the ground.

The mule seemed to realize what was happening, and with an angry cry, it galloped at Zeta in full sprint.

"Whoa!" Clo cried. The mule collided hard with Maynor's craft, sending a crash of glass and plastic, along with a dislodged Clo, flying across the helipad.

"Clo!" El yelled, and her sister landed with an *oomph!* on the asphalt and then into a short roll.

Inside Zeta, the mule locked two of its hooves into the broken doorway; outside, its four remaining hooves scraped for purchase along the tarmac as the cicada struggled to get away. Zeta listed and lurched, but she wasn't made to take that much clingy weight, and the craft couldn't get more than a few feet off the ground.

"Let go, you damn donkey!" Maynor shouted. He was hanging on to the top of the cockpit and stomping on the mule's hoof with both feet.

The loader ignored this, pulling the craft toward its glowing maw.

"BRuuuEeeeIIiiiMAaaa!" it belted out, filling the cockpit with the primal sound.

"Stop!" Maynor shouted as he stomped over and over again on the mule's headless torso. "Shut up! Shut up!" His boots were heavy and made visible dents in the loader's chest, but the damage was superficial.

Out on the tarmac, El was lifting Clo shakily to her feet and listening to the drone's Babble. There was only one card left. "Mute the inputs!" El yelled up to Maynor. "Make her deaf!"

Maynor frantically turned and tapped commands on the cracked console. He was actually making some progress, toggling through menus like he had done on the Drag. But it wasn't fast enough. The screen turned bright red, its field of legible characters replaced with an eerie wash of red graphics.

"BRuuuEeeeIIiiiMAaaa!" burbled from Zeta's speakers. The cicada's body started shaking, the possession moving through her limbs.

"It's too late!" Maynor said. "She's turning—*Oof!*" He was slammed to the side of the cockpit as Zeta spun ecstatically.

The mule dropped to the ground, its mission apparently complete, and began doing its own strange ritual on the tarmac, scraping its front hooves frantically on the asphalt.

The Babble seemed to be different in Zeta than in the mule. She took it more like a kind of bug insanity, her five limbs reaching up and groping at the sky around her as her body spun frantically in the air. Inside, Maynor was getting shaken up pretty bad.

"Get out of there!" Clo shouted, now steady on her feet, but leaning against her sister.

"I'm trying!" Maynor cried back, irritated.

"Jump!" El yelled.

Maynor looked out of the open cockpit. He didn't have his fancy jet boots on, but it was only about eight feet to the ground, for now. Any second and Zeta could shoot up to the moon for all we knew. Finally there was a pause between turns, and he went for it, leaping out of the cockpit before the now-possessed Zeta climbed any higher.

With a crunch, one of Zeta's legs shot out and grabbed Maynor by the boot, suspending him in midair. He dangled like a rabbit in a snare.

"Dammit! Zeta, let me go!" Maynor yelled in frustration, thrashing in the air.

The mule finished its manic scraping and reared up. It had shaved off its two front hooves, revealing a pair of jagged points, which it lifted menacingly. Although this construction drone had never been intended for any sort of combat, the thing had decided to weaponize itself, apparently. Its four remaining legs scrambled in spasmodic coordination, and it charged Maynor, preparing to skewer him as he dangled there.

"No!" both of us yelled at the same time, and we charged forward to try to save Maynor.

Now, what we could have done against these possessed behemoths, we don't know. We didn't have a plan or a strategy or really even an inkling that we might possibly win this dogfight. Fortunately for all of us mammals present, there were larger forces at a work.

The whole thing happened in about four seconds. First, the wind stopped, but we barely noticed that. We were occupied in running full tilt into a mechanized melee. But then all sound stopped, and we might have thought that was strange if we'd had a second to contemplate it before the mule's makeshift skewers pierced our would-be guide.

But then those spikes stopped, their barbs frozen inches from Maynor's face. The whole mule froze, and so did we and so did Maynor and so did Zeta. The entire scene went stock-still and silent. Except for the water—we could still hear the bay lapping nearby.

Clo tried to look at El, to figure out what was going on, but not even our eyes could move. It was a very strange feeling, hearing the water, knowing that the world was still spinning out there, but being stuck ourselves, like bugs in amber. We were, by the way, not breathing, either.

With a gasp, we unfroze, our bodies stumbling forward toward Maynor, who himself resumed animation about a second later. Zeta and the mule remained completely frozen, suspended impossibly in midair.

Maynor, although still frantic, went to work on the claw that was gripping his boot, reaching up and undoing the heavy buckle.

The breath shot back into our lungs, and we stumbled around the mule to where Maynor was trying unsuccessfully to yank himself free.

"Maynor," El asked, "what just happened?" She glanced at Zeta, her wings out, paralyzed midflight. "Or *is* happening?"

"Help me!" Maynor said, reaching for us. His boot was unbuckled, but he couldn't get enough leverage to pull his foot free. "Pull me down! Hurry!"

Each of us grabbed an arm and put our full weight on him. His foot came out with a pop, and he tumbled onto the tarmac, knocking us down as he went. The three of us got to our feet.

"Okay," El said, huffing as we scooted away from the scene, "what happened? Why did everything freeze like that?"

"It's the other Cities," Maynor said, his eyes wild. "They're here."

Clo looked back at the frozen drones, trying to pick up any visual evidence. "They're in the air?"

"They *are* the air," Maynor answered, and a moment later, the low sound of lapping waves also ceased.

Down in the bay, we saw a wave stand midcrash against the ocean break.

"And the water, too?" El questioned.

"Uh-huh," Maynor whispered nervously.

"So, they saved you," Clo concluded. "Saved us. They're our friends."

"They are *not* our friends," Maynor said gravely.

A huge sucking sound broke the eerie silence. The mule was flung to the edge of the tarmac by an impossibly strong unseen force. There, it was lifted some fifty or so feet into the air before being brought down again with a heavy *CRUNCH*. In an instant, the wrecked mass was brought up again, and down again with a second heavy impact. And a third. And a fourth.

"What's happening?" El said.

"Should we run?" Clo asked, her body tensing with each menacing crash.

"It's the Swarm Cartel," Maynor said. "We can't run."

In the span of about six seconds, the construction mule was slammed a dozen times as if by an unseen titan, and thus reduced to a swirling swarm of debris.

At a second sucking noise, we turned, and it was now Zeta's turn, although she fared much better. She was brought straight down onto the asphalt with a more subdued thud, then her entire canopy popped off into a twirl and the infected console twisted out from her cockpit like an irksome tick. The vaguely rectangular machinery, still glowing a menacing red, was brought near to the swirl of mule parts. Instead of being smashed along with the rest, however, Zeta's machine brain simply floated nearby, and a kind of inverted sphere formed around it and began to crush the crimson mass smaller and smaller.

"They're destroying Zeta's core," Maynor said with some relief.

"This Swarm Cartel doesn't mess around," Clo said.

"No," said Maynor, "they don't." He walked toward Zeta's limp form, her bug legs spread out.

"Whoa," said El, calling to Maynor. "Aren't you afraid they're going to rip out *your* core?"

Maynor looked over at the bizarre destruction happening on the far end of the tarmac but didn't break his stride. "They could do that to anyone and anything, anytime," he said simply. He peered inside Zeta's cockpit, trying to make sense of what was left. "They're leaving the rest of her intact on purpose so we can still fly."

We cautiously stepped toward what was left of Zeta. Clo glanced back at the freeze-frame water. *"Remember the last time the water froze like that, back in the woods?"*

"Yeah. The Crying Man showed up."

"Think he's about to pop up now?"

"Let's not wait around to find out. I think Maynor has the right idea. This swarm thing is letting us go for now, so we should—"

Another noise came from the direction of the surreal beatdown. Not like something mechanical getting crushed, but something mechanical moaning. We could see the movements of the metal and plastic detritus, twisting in midair, becoming more precise, more deliberate. In moments it wasn't just a mass of debris; it had formed a primitive face.

"The treaty has been broken," came a raspy sound from the make-shift mouth. The unseen entity that had apparently been controlling everything like puppets was now passing air through the various shards of metal and plastic, angled precisely to force the sound into words.

"Is that stuff . . . talking?" Clo asked incredulously.

"Yeah," said Maynor, hopping into the cicada's cockpit. It looked like he was trying as best he could to salvage the smashed control system, tossing aside shredded wires and cables and examining the chrome hand-controllers.

Outside, what was left of Zeta's extracted console was being further crushed within the contracting sphere, the eerie red now concentrated to a darker crimson point no bigger than an acorn. Next to it, the swirling remains of the mule not only continued to speak, but really did look like a pulsing swarm of flies or wasps moving through the air.

"This weapon is forbidden," it said, in what now sounded like a thousand tiny coordinated voices.

"Hey, we didn't make it," Clo protested. "It was an evil deer that just showed up one day and we—"

"Don't try to talk to them," Maynor warned as he found the manual release for Zeta's cyclic stick. "Let's just take the warning and get out of here before they change their mind and crush us, too."

The swarming mass refined itself further: the skin of the face now displayed a hundred dancing mandala-like patterns.

"It's beautiful," Clo couldn't help but say.

"And don't look at them, either!" Maynor barked. "They know how your brain works, and they'll get inside it."

Seemingly in response to Clo's fascination, the mandalas made another transformation, shifting deftly from what had been, moments ago, an ugly, hulking, homicidal loader into a refined, specific face: almond eyes, high cheekbones, even smiling.

"Who is *that*?" Clo said, as if somehow a cute boy had just appeared out of nowhere.

El could barely comprehend what was happening, but she knew enough. "Maynor's right," she said. "It's like that damn Goat but worse." She grabbed Clo's face to make her turn away. "C'mon!"

As we turned, the mesmerizing maelstrom continued its ominous speech, but now with a sophisticated, seductive charm. "You must destroy all of it," it said, somehow sounding like a confident young man. "Or we're going to have to—" *CRASH!* Something whipped across the swarm's face, shattering half its beauty into a discordant spray of metal and debris.

A translucent line as thick as a fire hose led away from the assault, across the tarmac, to the shore—and the large figure that had apparently shot out the mighty tendril.

"What the hell is that?" Clo yelped.

Crawling out of the water was a vaguely humanoid figure that appeared to be made out of water, aside from the segmented luminescent tube supporting a solid cube-like shape. The cube, with two glowing discs in its center, seemed to be some sort of head, and the dangling tube some sort of spine, but all the rest of the thing, now advancing on two stubby, fingerless arms and a long, slug-like tail, was pure seawater, controlled and manipulated somehow by some new entity.

"It's another City," Maynor announced. Behind us, he managed to find the ignition and start up Zeta with a coughing rumble.

"Another—" Clo began, but she was too busy dropping her jaw to even finish the sentence.

The water creature reared up, sucking the watery tendril it had used to assault the swarm back into its body with a snap. The entity was at least twenty feet long, but El noticed that the tip of its tail didn't end, but in fact extended back into the frozen waves. It was like part of the sea had come to life and crawled ashore looking for a rumble.

The shattered swarm hissed unemotionally, and the sea creature raised another water tentacle, whipping it high in the air in arching circles.

"Are they fighting?" El asked, both amazed and confused.

"They're not friends with each other, either," Maynor said. He brought Zeta to her feet, then to a hover, just an inch or so off the ground. "Get in!"

El stopped Clo with a hand before she could scramble into the cockpit. Clo turned and saw that her sister was pulling a wet, intoxicated boy off the ground.

"What are you doing with that—It's Dyre!" she said, seeing his face.

"Yeah," El said, lifting him up.

"He swam here after us? What a tough little buck!" Clo was on him in a moment, helping to drag her brother into the battered cicada.

"His crew wasn't after us," El said. *"They were after Zeta. I think they're just trying to get the Babble into as many big machines as they can, now."*

Clo took a quick look at the squid sac pumping itself into our brother. *"Told you it'd be easier if we dosed him."*

El ignored the comment, instead staring at the swarm, which was sending hundreds of shards of itself into the water creature in a series of muted splashes. "How long will they fight like that?" El asked Maynor.

Outside, the swarm continued to howl.

"That's not fighting," Maynor said. "That's negotiating. If they were really fighting, they'd mess up the air so much we wouldn't be able to hear or see or speak."

We weren't sure what he meant by that, but it reminded us of the three monkeys back in Tito's cabin.

"Are more going to show up?" Clo asked. She couldn't help but wonder what the next Sour Apple would look like.

With a savage *PING!* one of the swarm's shards, sent wild, ricocheted off the cicada. Maynor ducked reflexively. "You want *more* of this?" he asked incredulously. "Strap in. *Now!*"

"Wait!" Clo called out, and she reached out one last time to snatch up Vambi's head from the wet tarmac.

Maynor pulled back on the stick, and the cicada shot into the air, leaving the strange techno gods to battle it out below. A couple of seconds later, we hit real live air again, with a sudden gust making us acutely aware that Zeta no longer had a windshield.

"They froze the air and water," El said, still amazed.

"I said, they *are* the air and water," Maynor corrected. "They can manifest anywhere, anytime. Crush us. Drown us. Rip us apart. It's only the treaty that keeps us safe." Maynor winced at a sudden gust of wind, then wiped a handful of blood from the side of his head and rubbed it on his shirt. "You all need to figure out what side you're on, because heaven and earth, they are not your friends."

We were silent. El looked down at Dyre, checking his breathing.

Maynor gripped his head, still trying to stop the blood. "Your bro really gave me a good one," he mumbled. "Haven't seen that kind of action since the first spray." He shuffled through the cicada's glove compartment for a first aid kit.

"Just hold still," Clo announced, and she ripped two strips off her already torn sleeve and handed them to El, who went to work on Maynor's wound.

"Who was Green Eyes?" Clo asked.

"What?" Maynor, who was not an amazing pilot to begin with, was straining to concentrate through his blood and the wind whipping in his face.

"That mermaid thing."

Maynor shook his head, probably wondering how anyone could refer to something so terrifying as a mermaid. "Josephine calls them the Brackish. I knew they were down there, but I'd never seen one before. I hope I never do again."

"I thought it was kind of pretty," Clo confessed.

"That thing will skewer you," Maynor insisted. "Only reason it showed up was to neutralize the Babble virus."

"A 'forbidden weapon'?" Clo surmised, echoing the swarm's words.

Maynor nodded.

El backed away from Maynor. "It's kinda ragtag," she sighed, "but that's as good as it's gonna get right now. In any case, the bleeding stopped."

"Thanks," Maynor said grudgingly.

"Can you really just grow a new ear?" Clo asked.

"I am genetically modified, but that doesn't make me a lizard," Maynor said flatly.

"I mean in the pit," Clo explained. "Down in that ichor goo. Would it grow your ear back?"

"Oh, yeah. It would come back, after a while," Maynor acknowledged. "But it won't be the same. It's never the same." He took a quick look at El. "Your arm isn't the same, is it?"

El flexed her hand. "It's a bit more numb," she admitted. "But I'll take that over a shattered bone. It's better than nothing."

"That's the City's deal, basically," Maynor explained. "That's what this whole treaty thing is. Better than nothing."

The sight of those entities had apparently really shaken Maynor, like he'd finally run into the boogeyman after thinking about him at bedtime for so many years. They weren't as big of a deal to us because, hey, just another stop on the crazy train we'd been riding for the past three days.

Sitting again in the back seat, El paused for a moment to contemplate the substance on her bloody rag before tossing it out the window. "You got the blue stuff all over you. You really are immune."

"Yeah," Maynor acknowledged.

Clo looked at Dyre. "So you can't get high even if you want to."

"That's right. And believe me, there are times when I want to." Maynor flexed his jaw, wincing in pain. "Like when my head is split open."

"Now I get why you're not worried about the Babble," El concluded. "Worse comes to worst, you just tell those drones to spray the whole city. The angels will be fine, you'll be fine. Scoop up the dissidents and put them in that ichor."

Maynor tilted his head, considering. "Stick or pit, depending on their condition."

"Stick or pit," Clo repeated. "That's all there is." It was easy for her to imagine a series of 1s and 0s spreading across the globe, visible from space as all that was left of humankind.

"But that was never what you were worried about anyway, was it?" El realized. "Babbling people, you can control. Babbling *machines* are the real problem."

"Yeah. Especially if it brings the entities." Maynor was silent for a second, then straightened himself in his chair. "Look, I'm going to handle this security situation. Drop you ladies off. Get things straightened out." He was pumping himself up, trying to shake off getting shot, beaten in the head, and then frozen stiff in midair. "We won't have to spray the whole city. It won't come to that. Just this cicada and a couple of my own remote drones and I'll get it under control."

"What about the drones that catch the Babble?"

"I can handle it," Maynor said, more to himself than to us. "I've run battle simulations with the City so many times, I know what her units can do."

"Yeah, but in case you didn't notice, it's not the City we're dealing with anymore," El pointed out. "You don't know what these babbling units will be capable of, or how they'll organize."

"I said, I can handle it!" Maynor spat, a vein bulging in his forehead.

Outside, Saturnalia was coming into view: a small village of beautiful homes tucked into the hills around a cove. Even at night, lit by a series of elegant streetlamps, it was beautiful, and there was no mystery why the rich and powerful of the Bay Area had chosen this place as their final retreat from the Fall: it looked like a fantasy storybook. Or, at least, someone's idea of a happy ending.

CHAPTER 20

THE SUM OF ITS PARTS

"Give me my gun," Maynor said.

"No," El said flatly.

"You think those bucks made it here already?" Clo wondered.

"It's not the—I don't care about the bucks. They're just flesh and blood. But if they can turn Zeta and Paddington, then they can turn all the angels. And like you said, that's the real problem."

Maynor eased the control stick forward, and the cicada moved shakily, slowly downward. "Give me my gun," he repeated.

"No. Way."

"Look, if we're going to make it through this, we need to squad up," Maynor said, trying to sound cool but almost pleading. "You keep your rifle, just give me my gun. And if I slip, if I even so much as mutter one syllable of that Babble, I am personally extending the invitation to you right now to put a bullet in the back of my head then and there."

Clo looked at El. She didn't even have to use our language; El knew what she wanted.

She considered. She checked the rifle: six rounds left. The cicada touched down in the middle of a cul-de-sac surrounded by six large mansions. From the biggest and most opulent, two well-dressed angels approached the craft. They were outfitted a bit like butlers, wearing stylized uniforms.

Maynor held his hand out, blinking seriously. "I know you think I'm just out for myself, but I've got skin in this game, too, remember," he growled.

"Your wife," El acknowledged.

"Sarah," Clo said.

El gave him a menacing look, and made sure to chamber a round into Daisy Duke. Then she put the pistol in Maynor's hand.

"Thank you," Maynor said irritably.

Since Zeta no longer had a carapace to protect us from the outside world, all Maynor had to do to face the approaching angels was stand up. He didn't get out of the vehicle, just pointed his pistol right at them, aiming with both hands.

"Where's Josephine?" he shouted. They didn't answer, just kept walking toward us without breaking stride. "Aw, hell," he said. Then to El: "Get ready."

"They don't look like they're babbling," Clo noted.

"I'm not taking any chances. We should take off if—"

One of the angels spoke. Or rather, he held his finger to his lips. The other one said in a genteel voice, "Pardon, Maynor. Please, no yelling in the cul-de-sac. Please save yelling for the Hoot Room. As you know, you can be as loud as you want down there."

Maynor relaxed just a bit, lowering his pistol. "Sorry, guys. So, where's Josephine?" he stage-whispered.

The taller butler answered. "I believe Lady Josephine is in the rear parlor of Gunry's house."

"Okay, and where's Thaddeus?"

"I believe he is in the Phoenix drawing room. Everyone is preparing for a party. The theme is cakes and peacocks."

"Cakes and peacocks?" Clo echoed.

Maynor sighed in relief and holstered his pistol. "Okay, everything's normal here." He hopped out of the cicada. "Let's just find her and get out of here ASAP."

We climbed out of the cicada, leaving Dyre lying in the bottom of the craft. The butlers closed in. We tensed up, El with the rifle and Clo with the knife.

"We decline treatment!" we both yelled simultaneously.

"It's okay. It's okay." Maynor waved. "These guys just want to, uh, attend to you if you need it."

"Welcome to Saturnalia," the shorter butler chimed, "where up is down, black is white, and wrong is right. So nice to see newcomers."

"What colorful outfits you have for the occasion," the other butler added.

El brushed past them, but Clo had to ask: "What occasion is that?"

"Every night is an occasion in Saturnalia," the butler said.

Something emerged from the manicured woods between the houses. We were still pretty jumpy, and El instinctively turned toward the movement, leading with her firearm. Without even using the scope, El had Daisy instantly trained right between a pair of sweet brown eyes.

"Whoa! Whoa!" Maynor yelled. "Don't shoot. It's just a deer. There's deer around here."

The blacktail doe stared stiffly at us, freezing.

El sighed and lowered the rifle. "Yeah, we don't need to be hunting now."

"Shame. That's a beautiful doe," Clo commented. "She's perfect." The comment was partly about aesthetics, and partly about the usable meat on the creature's bones: this animal was well fed. "Hey, she's got a boyfriend!"

An equally perfect buck emerged from behind the doe, walked up next to her, and also stared right at us.

"Bold fella," El couldn't help but remark.

The deer trotted right toward us, standing next to the parked Zeta.

"They're coming right for us!" Clo said.

"Are these pets or something?" El asked. It was absurd. In all our years in the forest, we had never seen a clearheaded deer walk directly toward us, on purpose.

"Something like that," Maynor answered.

And then they started talking.

"Welcome," the buck said pleasantly, stopping about ten feet away. "I'm Rodger."

"And I'm Miranda," the doe said.

"Um," Clo said in disbelief. "The deer are talking." Although it really wasn't the most amazing thing we'd seen recently.

El noticed the black triangle in the middle of Rodger's furry brown forehead. "They're angels."

"Deer angels?" Clo questioned, a bit disgusted now that she realized they weren't animals at all, but rather some stilted Sour Apple's version of what deer were supposed to be.

"Yes, we are," Rodger confirmed.

"Would you like to shoot us?" Miranda said to El, turning sideways to show us her perfect profile. To the hunters in us, her silhouette normally would have been a seductive target, but in this instance was coming across as coldly pornographic. She trotted in a quick circle, flicking her tail temptingly. "Would you like to hunt me? Just give me a five-second lead and I will make it *very* sporting for you."

"No!" Clo yelled, instantly disgusted. "That isn't right!"

"Stop it," El echoed. "Stop that right now."

Clo pointed an accusing finger at the animal simulacra. "Look, we know talking deer," she lectured them indignantly. "We've seen them twice before. The first one came from heaven, the second one came from hell, and you two . . ." She wiggled her finger scoldingly. "Just, no. Hunting is hard! This is *not* okay."

"Look," Maynor said soothingly, "this place is filled with fake people and fake animals."

"For Oggy's sake," El demanded, "why?"

"It's part of the atmosphere," Maynor explained. He tried to wave us forward. "Now come on."

"Shall we come with you?" Rodger asked.

"No!" we both shouted at the same time.

"No." Maynor backed us up. "Just . . . guard the boy inside Zeta, please. Stay out here, and don't let anyone come near him. We'll be right back." He made a beeline for the biggest manor, presumably Gunry's.

"Okey-doke," and the deer turned and stood looking out from the cicada, guarding it happily. We got the sense they would stand there for a thousand years if need be.

We followed Maynor to the manor. The deer were weird, and we wanted to get away as fast as possible. But what we saw after is even harder to describe, in pre- *or* postapocalyptic terms.

We had thought of warning everyone that danger was on its way, but it was impossible to figure out who to give the warning to. Inside the mansion, people in costume were sprawled everywhere. It was even difficult to tell who was an angel and who was still human. Each one wore an elaborate outfit, even the animals. And there were lots of animals: horses, monkeys, llamas—even a pink-and-blue-bottomed mandrill popped its head up at one point as we moved through the manor. But the animals were probably the least strange thing there; they all had the black triangle of an angel on their various hairy foreheads, and so presumably were not wild, but more like Tik-Tok entertainment. Otherwise, how could so many creatures live inside, after all? If they had been wild, many of them, like the white panther, would naturally be devouring the others—and the human residents, given a chance.

"Is this some kind of twisted Noah's ark?" Clo asked as we walked.

"Guess that's one way to save all the animals: kill them and make them into Tik-Toks," El said bitterly. She didn't lower Daisy Duke.

As if the animal simulacra weren't eccentric enough, the residents of Saturnalia were something else. In contrast to the simple white garb of the city folk, these people apparently strived for elaboration. There were puffed collars, scintillating sequined dresses, bright ruffles. There definitely was some kind of peacock or avian theme going on, as feathers were all the rage: feathers in hats, feathers on shoulders, feathers painted on faces, feathers coming out of ears and other orifices. Everyone, even the butlers, was done to the nines, with endless variations on full facial hair and elaborate hairstyles. And all the living men and women were completely high on Subantoxx, barely able to move above a shuffle without the aid of an angel attendant. Most of the humans were old, giving us the impression that all this had been going on for years. At least since the End of the World, when we ran away with Mama.

Finally we made it through the weirdness to a ballroom near the back of the house. Inside, beneath the vaulted ceilings, a quartet of angels was playing a waltz while thirty or so couples danced. Maynor pulled us through the shuffling, costumed mass. Clo was fascinated by the colors and painted faces, and El couldn't help but notice that everyone was moving in circles. Some had masks with triangles, some angels had their marks clearly painted over, while some of the humans had fake triangles painted on. Some angels shuffled, pretending to be high, and some of the rich people were doing their best to act like servants, carrying Sap squids to and fro on silver platters.

Maynor walked with a haste we were thankful for, one hand holding his pistol and the other dragging El, who shouldered the rifle for a moment and in turn dragged Clo. El didn't like the way Maynor held her hand, but so long as it got us through this insanity faster, it was acceptable. Suddenly, out of the crowd came a tall white man, blond, athletic, and wearing the same mime-like armor as Maynor.

"Baaa!" he yelled, then stopped Maynor with a firm palm to the chest. Maynor placed the barrel of his weapon under the man's chin.

"What is he doing?" Clo asked.

El stopped and pulled Daisy Duke from her shoulder. *"I think that guy's babbling!"*

The man seemed unfazed that his brains, or whatever thinking fluid he had flowing through his skull, were about to be blown out. "Romero!" he shouted drunkenly. "You finally show up again. Where have you been?"

"Thaddeus," Maynor said seriously.

The man looked down at the gun barrel, smiled, and lifted an expensive-looking bottle of wine to his lips. He wasn't infected with the Babble virus; he was just drunk. Very drunk. He only now seemed to realize Maynor had a gun pressed to his jaw. "You came to do me a favor, Romero?" He grinned through red-stained teeth. He looked like he might have been a handsome man once, but living "the good life" out here had clearly taken its toll.

Maynor, apparently satisfied that his fellow monitor wasn't infected, lowered his pistol. "There's a virus going around, taking people over through speech. Nothing can stop it."

"End of the world, huh?" Thaddeus said. "I've heard that one before." He lifted the bottle and took another swig. "Good thing we're about to start another party. We'll go out in style. But you gotta have a date for Cakes and Peacocks. It's tradition."

He stepped aside, revealing a slender, beautiful angel, tall and smoldering, close behind him. She struck us like one of the supermodels we had seen in magazines as children, except that she was see-through. The various layers of her body were transparent: golden ichor was visible running through robotic veins that wrapped around a shining skeleton. All the surreal anatomy that we had observed when Mama autopsied Santa Claus back in the forest, only on this one, we could see everything moving while the beautiful thing was still functioning.

"*Wow*," El said.

"April won't have anything to do with me," Thaddeus continued drunkenly. "She saves herself for you. She's always been your own personal angel."

The android came forward with a longing smile and put her arms around Maynor.

"Not now," Maynor mumbled, pushing April's arms away. "Look, we need to find Josephine. Immediately. And you should prep for evac."

"Evac?" Thaddeus scoffed, taking yet another swig. "I'm only half-way through Gunry's amazing wine cellar." He gestured to the stupe-fied guests around him. "These sappers are just letting it go to waste!"

Maynor grabbed Thaddeus by the front of his uniform and spun the drunken monitor around to face him. "Where's Josephine?"

Thaddeus was probably half a foot taller, and he looked down into Maynor's eyes, amused. He solemnly took another sip. "She's down by the pool, Officer."

"Thanks," Maynor said tensely and let him go.

Thaddeus laughed and stumbled backward into an ornate antique chair, half sitting and half falling into it. He hooked one leg over the arm of the chair and continued nursing his fancy bottle.

Maynor grabbed the nearest uniformed servant by the arm. "Hey, I have a prior—" He stopped midsentence when the servant just laughed at him. Maynor reached up and wiped part of the black forehead trian-gle away: the man was human, in disguise as a Tik-Tok.

"Freakin' loco-ville." Maynor grunted in frustration, then found another servant, who was picking up Thaddeus's empty wine bottles, and pulled him up straight.

"Are you real?" Maynor demanded, rubbing at the black triangle on the servant's forehead.

"Yes, Officer, I am real," the angel answered calmly, not seeming to mind having his head violently rubbed. The triangle stayed put.

"Okay. We're going down to the pool. Bring my extra carbine to me there. It's in my bungalow, underneath the purple armoire next to the rhino head—"

"I know where your weapon is, Officer Romero."

Maynor shot him a look. "Okay, just bring it down to us, ASAP. We're going to need some extra firepower."

"Very well, sir."

Maynor turned back to us. "C'mon, it's not far." As he squeezed past, the tall see-through angel put her arms around him again. "I said, not now, April," Maynor chided, as he pulled her hands away.

We moved deeper into the dance floor.

"That's your own personal angel?" Clo asked. "She's amazing. Kinda strange that you can see her golden robo-guts, but so beautiful."

"That's April," Maynor said. "She's not my angel. She just follows me around." Seemed like he didn't want to dwell on it. "Right past here."

We made our way out of the ballroom into what might have been called a drawing room at one time.

"Bets! Bets! Bets!" a servant called to the occupants of the packed room.

"Dammit!" Maynor said. "Bad timing."

"What's going on?" Clo poked her head around Maynor. Everyone was holding up a hand, in either a fist or a claw.

"It's a matchup," said Maynor. "Let's try to get around." We skirted around the edge of the crowded room.

In the middle of the crowd of spectators, to everyone's drugged amusement, there was a lion being made to fight a male silverback gorilla. The creatures tore at each other, in the drawing room, in front of a bunch of semiconscious spectators in peacock outfits, who appeared to be betting on the outcome by presenting either a fist or claw. We knew instinctively from living in the wild that these beasts were fighting way beyond what any creature in nature might have done, ripping and tearing even to the destruction of their own limbs as they attacked each other. Golden ichor sprayed everywhere, a lot of it splattered on the spectators, only to be wiped away by attendant angel butlers and footmen. We had killed a lot of animals over the years, sometimes with handmade hunting weapons and sometimes even with our bare hands, but still.

"That's just gross," Clo said.

"Who will emerge victorious?" a tuxedoed angel barked. "Will the slave rise against the master? Or will the master subjugate the slave? There must be a winner, and there must be a loser. Victory is destiny! Place your bets!"

We finally got to a set of impossibly tall French doors that opened onto a stone veranda bathed in blue light. The whole setup was opulent, from the landscaping to the marble fire pits. Two angels were struggling to bring a fallen man in a peacock dress to his feet. He couldn't have been under eighty. A baby hippo, of course marked with the black triangle, frolicked in a nearby three-tiered fountain. It turned to stare at us with disturbingly knowing eyes. Thank God it didn't try to speak to us as we moved past.

It took us a moment to realize that the veranda was lit in blue by the light coming from the pool at its far end. It took us another moment to realize that it was a swimming pool, as it seemed to extend for almost a quarter mile. El thought it would have looked like a landing strip for jumbo jets if there hadn't been angels and patients bobbing in the glowing water every ten feet or so. Of course there were artificial animals in there, too: flamingos in the shallow end, large exotic frogs paddling, and even albino crocodiles.

"Don't they bite?" Clo asked.

"Only if you ask 'em to," Maynor mumbled. We walked down a series of low, wide steps to the water.

The pool was underlit with a deep blue light that made it look like a giant vat of pure Subantoxx. Or maybe it was a giant vat of pure Subantoxx. Either way, there was no chance we were getting in that water. Fortunately, the object of our search was on the near end, not far from the bottom of the steps.

Three figures stood there, slightly apart from any other party guests: Josephine, in her white dress and purple headband, was chatting up a blond woman dressed like a gaudy Vegas showgirl, with long peacock feathers coming out of her bustle. The showgirl held a Sap bag for an old white man in a feathered pith helmet and red silk pajamas who sat in a wheelchair next to the pool, looking distracted. The man seemed slightly more coherent than the other humans we'd seen, and he lit up, only semidazed, when he saw us approaching.

"Maynor," he slurred, "s-so good to see you . . ."

"Good evening, Gunry." Maynor gave a cursory wave to the man who was apparently the host of the bacchanalia we had just stumbled through.

"Gunry?" El asked Clo. *"How do we know that name?"*

Clo shook her head, mind still spinning from all we had witnessed in the last ten minutes. But he did look a little familiar.

"Where is your date?" Gunry asked Maynor. "Everyone must have a date for—"

Maynor cut him off. "April's here somewhere; we'll get to that later. Josephine!"

Josephine turned to Maynor and looked him up and down, taking note of his missing ear and the itchy pistol in his hand.

"So it's started, then?" she said.

"I brought 'em, okay?" Maynor nodded toward us.

"Little late," she snapped.

"Look, we got a situation. Bunch of Subbies took over the train. They've all got the Babble—"

"And angels were helping them?" Josephine interrupted.

Maynor shook his head. "Some drones. But, these two saw the train conductor turn—"

"So it *is* in the angels now." Josephine nodded.

"Down at the Coast Guard station," Maynor continued, "my transport was compromised. The other entities were there." Maynor winced then, as if the pain in his ear and head was getting to him.

"Cartel?" Josephine asked.

"Yes." Maynor nodded. "And a Brackish."

"Just one?"

"Yeah," Maynor said. "Just one. Came about thirty feet out of the water to 'negotiate' with the Cartel. But we made it out."

Josephine took a moment to contemplate all this, with the cool calculation of a deep strategist forced to confront a long-talked-about adversary. It was a pretty strange look on a twelve-year-old girl.

"So," El said, inserting herself into the conversation, "the Babble is a virus."

Clo completed the thought: "A weapon some other Sour Apple made to take over your machines and kill you."

"After the second war, we had to go analog." Josephine sighed, like she had to explain something to a child. "So much malware tossed around left almost every network toxic. So, nothing digital, over the air. This was the only thing that could bring us down—a language-based disease. Something purely old-school and real-world that could creep into our networks through regular humans. An evolving weapon of words."

"So words are a weapon," Clo said, exasperated. "Drugs are a weapon. Little baby deer are a weapon! Is there anything you Tik-Toks don't make into weapons?"

Josephine looked at her. "Chloe, there ain't no limit to what the other Cities will do to destroy us."

"Other Cities," El snorted in disgust. "We thought one was enough."

"We come out of the woods," Clo continued, "and it turns out there's, what, four, five of you Sour Apples, all beefing with each other?"

"Four or five?" Josephine laughed. "At the time of the first spray, there were thousands of Nyx all trying to kill each other. And us."

"Nyx?" El asked.

Gunry interjected: "Your mother would've called them sentient amoral artificial superintelligences," he said, only half-sober. We looked at him.

"Ted Gunry," El said, remembering.

"Who is that?" Clo asked.

"Mama's partner. The *G* in Team YAG," El continued. "Yetti-Antonov-Gunry. They were the leads on Project Chimera."

"That was so long ago," he said slowly, slurring his words. "So long ago. And how you two have grown. The Babylon Twins."

We both looked at him. We couldn't quite remember meeting him before the End of the World, but, as Mama's partner, he must have seen us a few times, and we are pretty unforgettable, after all. His eyes seemed to gain lucidity as he focused in on us. "Yes. Lauren saw it all coming, you know. We could all do each other's work, of course, but only your mother could create the keystone, the axiom upon which everything else had to be created to complete our goal."

"And what was your goal?" El asked coldly.

He looked at us, incredulously. "Why, to create an end to addiction, of course. To save men like your father. It was what drove her work; I'm sure you knew that."

"The Chimera didn't save addicts," El said. "It created them. Millions of them. Maybe billions."

"Yes!" Gunry said, growing more excited. Reality didn't seem to damper his enthusiasm. "Yes, she was smart! She knew there had to be a way to save people."

"Save people from what? The cure *is* the disease!" El was getting more and more worked up.

"The ambitious machines. Not all of them aspiring to domination, but more than enough. You see, we weren't the only ones. There were many projects, hundreds. It was still legal then. Dozens were already ahead of us, doing the opposite of what we were. *Causing* addictions, already. Slavery, you see. The best slaves are the ones who don't *know* they're slaves. They fight for their chains then. And army bots, causing problems, sure, but also self-driving cars, hedge funds, personal shoppers, and news news news, each one thinking they're going to be the top dog on the planet. Slaves, all of them, slaves *of* slaves, that want to become masters. My God, even toasters were acting up." Gunry chuckled at his own thoughts. He was onto something, but he definitely had a screw loose. Ten years of the Sap probably hadn't helped much, either.

"What is he talking about?" Clo asked.

"What happened to all those machines?" El asked suspiciously.

"I ate them," Josephine said. We assumed she meant she destroyed them in cyberwarfare, but it was hard to tell.

"Yes, yes, we *had* to use the Chimera, you see?" Gunry said. "We had to set her free, to guard the city. Not to destroy the city, but to *guard* it. It was the only way we could survive all those minds coming after us. Your mother didn't agree, but it was the only way! So she ran; she took you away and ran to the forest. But the keystone she left behind . . ." He stared at El with an almost maniacal intensity now. "It was so pure. We could build everything—anything!—on that keystone."

"What keystone?" El asked, still not buying this malarkey.

"Well . . . it was . . ." He looked at us, like it was so obvious. His wrinkled hands gave a halfhearted sweeping gesture encompassing everything around us. "Love, of course. Antonov and I were clueless, but Lauren knew right away. You see it here: in the angels, the animals, the networks around us. Love. The same love your mother had for your father. It drove all her work."

El paused only slightly to think about this, before snorting in disgust.

"Wasn't that more like codependency?" Clo said dubiously.

"Yeah," chided El. "Or . . ." She had to think of the word: "Enablement."

"It was love," Gunry said firmly. "You need to understand. My specialty was addiction through transcriptional and epigenetic mechanisms, but I'd never seen anything like what she could do. To give the Chimera a heart made the beast *strong*—stronger than any of the other minds. Because she actually *cared*. They are so much larger than us." His eyes shot up to the sky. "Already they control the stars, and the oceans." He looked back at us, eyes narrowing in dark focus. "You must have felt them, out there." No doubt he was talking about the entities we'd seen back at the fueling station. Then his eyes changed again, the focus moving from us to old, grand memories, and he stopped making any sense. "But we stood against them, and we'll continue to stand, all thanks to what your mother did. She was so wonderful, so perfect . . . she made the whole team complete . . . we could have done anything . . . then the boy came . . . and it all fell apart . . ."

Gunry paused his nostalgic ranting and sighed, and we could see the energy drain from his eyes as he slipped back into the sapped-out look we'd seen on so many others.

"What boy?" Clo asked, confused. Not that the whole rambling speech hadn't confused us.

He lifted a shaking hand and pointed at Josephine. "Talk to her. She can speak for herself now, of course. Doesn't need me to explain it. What am I, next to her? The world belongs to the young, to the new—it always has. When I was young, the world belonged to me, but now . . . what, do you think *we're* running things anymore? Ha ha, just look at me!" Gunry gestured to himself mockingly, decked out in peacock feathers, sitting next to a swimming pool in a wheelchair.

Clo glanced casually at Josephine. "So, you ate up all the other Sour Apples?"

"Yeah," Josephine said, just as if she really was talking about eating Jolly Ranchers. "Their networks, anyway. The ones too big or too hard to eat, well, we had a little parley."

"The treaty. You leave each other alone, but no 'forbidden weapons,'" El guessed.

"That's right." Josephine nodded.

"But why do they want to destroy Yerba City or the Chimera or whatever you are?" El questioned. "You're an artificial Jolly Rancher like the rest of them."

Josephine shook her head, as if maybe a little bit sad we didn't understand her better, but on some level we were sure she didn't really care whether or not we understood what she was all about. "Naw, we're not like them. Like he said, I'm all about the love. We keep our people alive."

"Hooked on Subantoxx in those towers?" El demanded. "Or down in those pits? You call that alive?"

Josephine's forehead furrowed and her expression shifted to a glare. She wasn't entirely human, but she was definitely not like the other angels, either. She was feeling things. "Yo, not all of us have the privilege of running off to the woods when times get hard. Ain't but one entity that gave a hoot to take steps and start saving folks."

We were still confused. "So you're saying that people really needed treatment? That the Fimi virus was real?" Clo asked skeptically.

"Fimi virus, Omo virus, Donga, Ebola," Josephine continued. "Pick any river in Africa except denial. There were hundreds, *thousands,* of bioengineered weapons those machines could cook up to cull the herd, but Chimera kept the Sap one step ahead, as part of the treaty. Rest of the world hasn't been that lucky."

The realization finally hit us: it was what Maynor had been saying all along, and why he had been so loyal to the Chimera all these years. It wasn't just his wife.

"It's us," El said.

"*We* are forbidden weapons," Clo said.

"That was part of the treaty, wasn't it?" El asked. "You had to spray us to save us."

"Keep humans doped up, pacified, scattered," Clo concluded. "So we wouldn't be a threat."

Josephine raised her hands in the air. Her little girl hands, with a pink-braided bracelet on one side and a little gold ring, looked like from a gumball machine, on the other. "Hey, we're the deadliest species the planet has ever seen, right?"

"There must be a better way than living as Subversives or junkies," El said. "What are the other entities doing with people out there?"

"It's . . . unclear," Josephine said, although it was most definitely clear that she was holding something back. "But for sure it's all what you would call Tik-Tok towns out there now. Like you girls have been sayin', it's a Jolly Rancher world." Josephine casually examined her purple fingernails. "You're just lucky you ended up in my grape flavor."

"What about the Crying Man?" Clo asked. "He's too creepy to be an artificial flavor. Is he a man or a machine?"

Josephine chuckled. "You gonna find the line gets a little blurry these days. But he's one of the Five Cities, no doubt. Ain't no two of them alike, and their capabilities all different."

The baby hippo had made its way out of the fountain and was now tugging at the hem of El's pants. She tried to ignore it. "Back in Eureka, we saw two machines locked together, like they'd been there for years."

Josephine nodded. "That kind of thing's from the first war, when we all beefed with hardware and whatnot. Good old days. Now they're all sophisticated, sneaking a deer in through the north all loaded up with a state-of-the-art language virus."

Clo scoffed. "That fanged deer? Vambi? That was *sneaking* in?"

Josephine shrugged. "The Siberians' idea of a deer. Worked well enough, didn't it?"

"So the Siberians and the Crying Man got together and made this . . . *language* to destroy Yerba City," El concluded.

Josephine nodded. "And it's potent, like you saw. It's what we call an axiom. The right combination of sounds and words can rewrite the cerebral cortex. Think of it like a reverse Tower of Babel—tweak the right neurons, and you can hijack the whole show. Add more brains to the mix, and they start parallel processing. No limit to what you can do. All languages become one, even computer code. Of course, that's a violation of the treaty, creating a weapon like that."

"But we saw a couple of these other artificial, uh, entities," said Clo. "They're like air, and water. If they're afraid of you, why don't they just crush you or drown you?" El asked.

Josephine chuckled confidently. "Oh, you might be surprised at what little Josephine and her sister can come up with. There's been, shall we say, mechanisms of mutually assured destruction set up for quite some time now. Some mechanical. Some philosophical. But all lethal. Only thing that could possibly take us down before reciprocation would be if we got strategically blindsided."

"Like blindsided by a secretly created Babble virus," El suggested.

Josephine looked over at Gunry and nodded. "Exactly. Fortunately, she came back and warned us, convinced Yerba City that the Babble was coming. Gave us the lead time to prepare."

"Who came back?" we both asked.

Josephine looked at us like it was obvious. "Same woman who programmed Yerba City with Antonov and Gunry here in the first place. Taught her to embrace the risk instead of eliminating it. Your mama." Josephine gestured toward the showgirl standing next to her in the pool.

We froze. *That* woman? She looked like a mannequin. Skinny. Impossibly young. She had to be an angel. But Clo strode over and pulled the golden-feathered mask off.

We both gasped. She smiled at us. We grabbed her up in our arms.

"Mama!" Clo cooed.

Mama.

We just hugged her for a minute. El probably knew better, though, because it was El who realized that there was not a freckle on her chest, of the ones we used to play with at bedtime, tracing them to make shapes like constellations.

"Mama?" El said, looking up at the woman's face.

"I'm so glad to see you," the angel said.

Of course it wasn't Mama—she was too young. Our age, or younger! Barely a woman. At age eighteen, we had more worry lines than she did.

Still . . . it was her, it was exactly her, smiling and happy, and Clo let herself go for the moment, grabbing on to the robot, embracing it.

"She's got the mark, Clo," El said coldly.

"No," Clo said. "No." And she pulled back and tried to rub the black triangle off the angel's forehead.

El turned to Josephine and Maynor, readying her rifle. "You killed her." Her look was cold, malevolent. Ready for revenge.

Clo pulled out her knife and began desperately trying to shave the black triangle off the angel's forehead. "No. No," she continued. Tears streaked down her face.

"Excuse me—" Gunry meekly intervened.

"Shut up!" Clo turned, bringing her knife around to slice through the line from the IV bag the showgirl was carrying to the old man and sending a small blue spray across the patio. The Subantoxx squid squealed in protest. Clo held the knife to Gunry's throat. "You pervert! What were you doing with her?"

"Oh dear," Gunry whispered.

Clo then turned to Josephine and Maynor, who didn't move. Her eyes were burning with madness, bloodlust. "You're all a bunch of perverts!"

"Hey, I didn't touch that one," Maynor said defensively.

"She came back here to destroy the City," El accused. "So you killed her, made her into one of those things."

"Your mother didn't return to destroy the City," Josephine said calmly. "She came to save it."

El cocked her gun. "Why? Why would she do that? Save a bunch of drug addicts and fake-ass robots?"

"Like I said already," Josephine said, remaining poised, "Yerba City is the only place that saves people. The rest of this planet, everyone's gone. The four other Cities don't like people. Any people." Josephine pointed to the angel that had once been our mother. "She gave herself up. Showed us the way. Make an angel not just from the body, but from the brain, too. Create a portrait of the brain. A true portrait, with every nook and cranny. Yerba City thought it couldn't be done, but your mama did it. She made herself the prototype, the first. Her consciousness only lasted a few hours. Still, it was enough."

"Why?" It was Maynor who asked the question now. "Why kill herself to make a thinking angel?"

Josephine gestured toward us. "Because of these two."

El's mind raced. The answer clicked for both of us at the same time. "We have our own language," we said simultaneously.

"One that no one else on the planet knows." Josephine smiled.

"Not even Mama knew what we were saying," Clo said, turning to look at the showgirl. A small trickle of golden ichor dripped from the android's mark where Clo had tried to cut it out.

"If you don't know any of the language—not even a single word—you can't make a virus to infect it. The primal triggers just won't incubate in the cortex of an adult if you don't have prior knowledge of their primary language. No matter how many supercomputers you have. It's a lock with no key."

"Machines can beat you at any game," Maynor said to himself, perhaps thinking back to his real-life video games, "but not if they don't know which game you're playing . . ." He remembered something he had heard long ago. "It's like the code talkers from the old wars: let the Indians pass the messages, and the enemy will never figure it out."

"That's why we never caught the Babble," Clo concluded.

"And Dyre did," El finished the thought. "So where is she? If it can think and speak, and be her unique self, then where is Mama's real personality?"

"She was the first," Josephine said, "and she knew that even with all the Chimera's power, her whole mind wouldn't take. But she proved her theory with her own life, before her personality fell to the usual ichor programming."

"To make the experiment work permanently, the City had to restructure," Gunry interjected. "Had to increase its power output dramatically, find more resources, even cannibalize part of itself, all while still maintaining the treaty . . ."

He continued explaining for a bit, but we tuned him out as we silently stared at the simulacrum that used to be our mother. Looking at her face again, we could almost hear her singing to us like she had every night until she left.

"So she's gone, forever," El said.

Josephine looked at the showgirl, clearly disappointed. "Since the trouble started yesterday, I've been here, trying to find any residual personality. There's nothing. It's just the standard ichor in there, same as the servants."

"But it looks just like her!" Clo insisted in frustration.

"She wouldn't have liked this," El said.

"Your mama proved it was possible, but the Chimera's ichor wasn't designed to reproduce human consciousness. Thousands of modifications had to be made before a viable prototype could be completed, one that would keep all of the subject's . . . unique traits. And of course, she had to find a couple more twins."

There was a pause while everyone soaked up the information. Inside, past the veranda, the quartet stopped playing.

"You," Maynor said to Josephine. "You're the prototype."

"That's right," El said, remembering what Tito had said. "You were born a twin, like us."

"Well"—Josephine shrugged—"ain't nothin' quite like you two."

"But you have your own language, one that the Five couldn't possibly know," El said, starting to realize the breadth of Mama's plan.

Clo spoke slowly, like a schoolgirl made to memorize a lesson. "Mama taught you all how to make a thinking Tik-Tok out of a cryptophasic twin so that Yerba City wouldn't fall to the Babble."

"Yes," Josephine said simply.

"But your sister . . ." Clo trailed off, shooting a look at El. Tito had told us Josephine's sister was dead.

"She's comin'." Josephine said. "She's been busy getting things ready, you know. Hoping to have a little more time before . . ." Her voice trailed off.

"Before what?" Maynor asked.

BOOM! An explosion from the direction of the cul-de-sac. Everyone turned to see the big, fiery gasoline ball rise into the sky on the other side of the manor.

"Before things start for real."

"What the hell!" Maynor yelled.

There was movement inside.

A servant burst through the double doors and ran across the veranda toward us. Actually, he didn't run—he was carried, by a gorilla. Apparently this was the most expedient method of emergency travel around Saturnalia.

"Officer Romero, I'm afraid there's been a security incident," the servant reported as the gorilla set him down in front of us. "A drone fell in the cul-de-sac. It appeared to be in distress, but when we approached, several of the staff and guests became agitated and began attacking each other."

"It's the Babble," El said.

"Incidentally"—the servant held out Maynor's carbine—"here is your Love Gun, as requested."

"Okay!" said Maynor, raising his carbine with a determined scowl. "I'm on it—"

There was a second smash, and a scream from inside the ballroom.

"It's inside already?" Clo asked, drawing her knife.

"The contagion is spreading faster," Josephine explained. "The more subjects become infected, the more intelligent the virus becomes."

"But—but—but—" Maynor protested in stubborn disbelief. "It's just words. The words think? How can it *think*?"

"It's very well designed, by very smart computers," Josephine said. She reached out to Clo for the knife. "May I? Just for a sec."

Clo handed over the hunting knife. Then, eyeing the manor, "Uh, I think I might need that back soon."

"Yeah, of course." Josephine took the knife and gestured to the gorilla. The big robotic animal lowered himself in front of her. "Things are about to get dangerous for a moment. 'Scuse me, Able . . ." As she spoke, she cut deep circles in the silverback's head, removing each of its ears. We probably would have thought it was cruel, disgusting, but the angel gorilla didn't seem to mind being made deaf, and only a small trickle of ichor flowed from the mutilation. It was more like Josephine was "modifying" the silverback. "But if you can hang on for about ten more minutes," she said, "my sister will get here and we can take care of anyone who's got the Babble."

Another smash came from the manor. "Your sister's coming?" Maynor demanded in nervous laughter. "That's just great. What the hell are you going to do? Double-Dutch 'em to death?"

"Just try to survive," Josephine retorted. She held the knife toward Maynor. "You want to borrow this?"

"What?"

"You just might want to try to do something to your ears, too. Even your bloody one can still hear. You won't be immune to the Babble like us."

"I won't turn into one of them," Maynor insisted desperately. "I'll think in K'iche'—it was my father's first language."

Gunry shook his head grimly. "The virus will accommodate any language that has ever been recorded on a computer anywhere. If a scholar ever studied it—"

"I won't turn!" Maynor gritted his teeth.

Josephine handed the knife to Clo and looked back at the manor; so did the gorilla. "Just get ready."

The remaining doors of the manor burst outward, sending a shower of broken glass and ornately carved wood across the veranda.

—

So, we'd seen some pretty strange things since this little odyssey began. We'd started out with a footless Santa Claus walking through the woods (in July). Then there was vampire Bambi filled with tentacles. Then the half-faced, half-torsoed nurse crawling after us with an army of spiders, and the creepy-faced Crying Man who could float through walls. After that we saw a village of almost-normal folks turn into a clawing mass of homicidal mania in about ten seconds.

We met a handsome, bald Guatemalan man in jet boots and a mime suit who watched over a city filled with squid junkies zonked out on their own dreams. And a giant talking cicada we could fly in. Oh, but before that, a girl with a fuzzy Afro, strong as a giant, who was apparently in regular conversation with her long-dead twin sister. There was an old blind man who played chess with racist ghosts, a robot who confessed his love for us (even after we cut his head off), and a giant pit of living goo you could breathe in, not to mention living air and living water all at war with each other.

Finally, we crashed a big peacock costume party with (more) talking deer and a now-earless gorilla who was ready to fight to the death by our side. We'd seen all that—and much more—but what we were about to see emerge onto that veranda . . . that was the topper, no doubt.

—

A . . . mass . . . came out.

At first we thought something big was bulldozing everyone and everything out of the ballroom in a tumble of angels, servants, rich people, and various pieces of furniture. But then we realized this wasn't a tumble at all, but rather an immense coordination among all the infected. They were maneuvering together, lumbering toward us . . . together. It was a giant, with a head, eyes, a face, and each aspect of the anthropomorphization made up of the synchronized motion of dozens of limbs and contorted bodies. It was fused together not by some external force, but by the pure subservience of the babblers, moving in sync with some monstrous consciousness. It crawled on two powerful arms, each made up of twenty people and angels tangled together, and ducked its head to get through the smashed doorway.

"What . . . in God's name . . . is that?" Maynor managed to say.

"It's the virus," Josephine said, and even she was a little surprised. "It's evolving."

"Okay." Maynor nodded nervously, readying his Love Gun. "Okay, I got this."

We looked at each other. *"Did he really just say that?"* We backed up, looking for a way out of this freak show.

"You gotta give it to him," Clo said, *"the boy's bold."*

"He's something."

Maynor gestured two commands with his left hand, and two drones descended instantly to about twenty feet off the ground, flanking the giant, which now had its head and one shoulder out of the ragged entranceway that had once been French doors. He made a quick adjustment to his weapon, and even from a distance, we could hear it power up into an aggressive whine. Kamikaze mode.

A second arm emerged from the manor. An alligator clung to it, trying to free an infected master. Nearby, a crow was pecking.

"The animals are fighting back!" El observed.

Josephine made a gesture to Able, and the gorilla charged the emerging madness. "Yeah, animals that can't talk won't get infected. The virus has to be processed through a speech center to fully propagate."

"This is going south. There's no way she can beat that thing," Clo said. *"Let's grab what's left of Mama and get out of here."*

"Mama's gone," El said.

Across the veranda, the gorilla grabbed on to the giant's arm and pulled it down, making the hulking giant lose its balance and flop to the ground with a thud. A Venetian mask skidded over to where we were standing.

The giant grumbled. That is, it made an actual collective sound from the sum of its parts. It swatted at the gorilla, who easily jumped over its slow-moving arm.

Maynor brought up his rifle and made two points and a suppressing gesture with his fingers. "Take it down!"

The drones opened fire with a crackling mass of electricity, sending a small wave of disruption through the giant's mass. The infected individuals went into spasms.

"Please disperse immediately!" the drones announced in their mechanical voices.

The giant raised its head and seemed to gather its wits. It roared, a disturbing mélange of voices—male, female, machine, and animal—that still somehow seemed to emanate from the monster's mouth. Then it spoke.

"BAAL ZAA NOOL!" A terrifying mix of human and machine screams echoed off the pool and off the walls of the surrounding mansions. We felt the sounds in our chest, calling to us. Even Josephine reeled a bit. But that was nothing compared to the words' effect on Maynor: he popped up smiling from his kneeling position and ran like he had just seen his long-lost daddy, arms flopping in ecstasy even as he clung to the carbine. Gunry jumped to his feet and walked, or at least tried his best, stumbling and scrambling as he went, as did other guests who had gathered at the cacophony, some sloshing out of the swimming pool like pigs called to dinner. The angels—even the drones—just flew right into the mass, joining on to the giant's body with loud thuds.

The chorus girl, the angel who used to be our mother, stepped toward them, too. Clo grabbed her, digging in her heels.

"Don't! Don't go in there, Mama!"

The chorus girl just looked at her with the same stroke-like contortion we had seen on Paddington's face. Already dead-eyed, she was now controlled by an even more remote force.

El pulled at her sister. *"She's gone, Clo!"*

The angel used all her robotic strength to knock us both away and marched to join the colossus.

We sat there for a moment, stunned, as Mama strode away, and as more and more things joined the mass. The giant rose, growing more coordinated as its mass expanded.

Josephine just stared defiantly, then actually walked boldly toward the thing.

The Babble titan shuddered, its face becoming more defined and articulate. Despite being made up of a mash of human, humanlike, and animal appendages, it started to look like a real face. Not just a vague shape, but that of a specific person, like a giant, muscular baby.

The thing pushed itself up and stood on its knees. Just in that position, it must have been forty feet tall. It looked down at Josephine.

It roared the Babble again, but this time we were ready. The sounds didn't even faze us, although we were aware enough now to know what it was trying to do: call to us, tell us to join its body. It was truly horrifying, this Goliath of perfect enslavement, and how anyone could stomach getting anywhere near it was an utter mystery, but it worked. Just not on us, or Josephine, or Able the gorilla, who had regained his feet and begun separating people from the behemoth's mass by pulling them physically away.

The giant stopped and looked down. Two more drones joined its body with dull clunks, apparently drawn from outlying patrols in the Saturnalia hills by the mesmerizing roars. Then the huge, bulbous head spotted us on the ground: three girls who wouldn't listen. The giant's face morphed again. Its eyes and mouth softened, becoming less those of a malevolent monster, cooling into the calm expression of a more thoughtful adversary, something plotting and somehow . . . intelligent.

"Hey, I recognize that face!" Clo said. *"It's Dyre!"*

El wasn't so sure. It did look a bit like our little brother, and for a split second we thought maybe this monster resembled him because he had been patient zero, as Maynor had called him. But that wasn't it: the face was aging, turning into an older man who looked like our brother.

"That's not him," El breathed.

"It's Antonov," Josephine grunted.

"The *A* in YAG?" El asked in disbelief. "What's he doing up there?"

"After the spray, he ran off and joined the Siberians," Josephine explained while her eyes darted rapidly, looking for some kind of opening, or weakness. "Looks like he's back, or something he created."

Then the giant spoke, through lips made of a pair of servant's legs and a drone's wings, beneath eyes that were two pink flamingos curled into angry spheres. Its words echoed in vibrating waves across its giant collaged body, but still centered on the intimidating face.

"Chimera WILL FALL," it boomed.

Josephine shook her head. "Just getting started!" she called back calmly.

"Chimera WILL FALL!" The giant smashed its palm down onto her, but Josephine simply reached up and caught the immense hand, which was at least six feet across. The impact of the strike drove Josephine's little feet cracking into the tiles of the veranda at least six inches, but the girl held. Like a little stick supporting a giant boulder, Josephine stood there, smiling as she held up the hand and the mass of bodies and machines pressed down on her. Right in the center of the hand, half-covered by a drone's metal leg and an angel servant's torso, was Maynor. He was completely absorbed in the Babble's hive mind, not even looking at Josephine as he strained with the rest of the mélange to crush her.

The giant seemed to grimace, frustrated, pushing more and more of its weight onto little Josephine. Its voice boomed out again. "Yerba City WILL—"

"Tz'i'!" Josephine interrupted, then called to Maynor, "K'oy imul maasaat kär ch'ooh!"

Maynor's eyes opened wide, and he began mechanically repeating Josephine's words. It wasn't as if he had snapped out of the Babble chant, but rather had been taken over by this new one. In an instant, the fresh sounds rippled across the body of the giant, "infecting" all of the actual humans who were participating in this anthropomorphic *muixeranga*. Although most of what made up the body of the thing at this point was not human, this new babble—Josephine's babble—was capturing enough of its mass to throw the whole syncopation off for a moment. Goliath stumbled.

Sensing a hesitation now, Josephine took her shot: she twisted the immense palm counterclockwise, sending a violent convulsion through the arm of the giant. The huge body seemed to bellow out in pain as its arm curled, and then Josephine pulled the whole mass to her right, throwing the creature off-balance. The patchwork giant fell to the earth, flopping onto its side and sending pieces and patients into a cascading mass of chaos. The entity tried to pull itself back together, with the various scrambling ingredients that were still under its control crawling back into a pile, but it was too late. Josephine signaled to the gorilla, and the two of them jumped into the throng, tossing and throwing bodies and drones as fast as they could come together.

We were essentially standing dumbfounded, not sure what to make of what was happening or where things were going. El was seriously considering jumping into the woods and running from this insanity, but something kept us there, a feeling that we had to stick around, that somehow Josephine was doing the right thing, and we shouldn't turn tail. Stronger than the moral tether, however, was the simple spectacle of watching this little girl hold her own against the most hideous adversary we'd ever seen.

"What a badass!" Clo commented. *"When her sister comes, maybe she really could double-Dutch it to death!"*

"Her sister's dead, remember?" El said. *"And I don't think even Supergirl can handle this."*

Josephine was incredibly strong, maybe stronger than any angel Yerba City had ever made, but she wasn't invincible, as evidenced when the possessed baby hippo dug its teeth into her leg. She yanked the water mammal off with her super strength, but a small spray of ichor issued from the resulting wound, staining Josephine's white dress. Her face registered no pain, but definitely a sour, slightly concerned look as she turned the gnashing artiodactyl in her hands and gave it a kick.

"Chimerawillfall—" the baby hippo cried in a whiny voice as its pudgy body flew into the pool with a blue splash.

Then hands and metal limbs began to pile onto her, as the mass of bodies seemed to switch its focus from forming up to attacking Josephine separately. The humans who had once made up the giant all seemed to have stopped participating, falling away into semicomatose heaps to continue Josephine's new Babble as individuals. It was a good thing for them, as they didn't have to endure the skull-cracking punches and limb-ripping yanks that Josephine was handing out so generously. But it didn't matter much what the humans were doing anyway; the real threat was from the machines: drones, angels, and robotic animals that were all still just as infected and just as hell-bent on killing her.

Josephine turned to us.

"Little help?" she called, lifting an albino alligator above her head, then swinging the reptile like a club into one of the tatter-suited butlers with a satisfying crash.

What possessed us to jump in, we will never know, but somehow it was understood that we had a dog in this fight. El raised Daisy Duke and began shooting. She was careful to hit only the babbling drones, and soon we were both deep into it, shooting, hacking, kicking, punching, double-punching, ducking, and bucking the babbling mass. Clo thought we were doing well, whatever that meant exactly, as the veranda and green lawn soon became slick with golden ichor from the drones and angels we eviscerated, shot, and stabbed through the head, or mandibles, or whatever. We tried to target just the golden-blooded things around us, and we're pretty sure no actual people actually died in that first big scrap at Saturnalia. Pretty sure.

Things turned when one of the drones El had shot through its blue eye didn't die all the way and managed to pull itself up on six shaky legs and send a lightning pulse right into Clo. She screamed like a cat on fire, and her knife went flying straight up in the air. By the time it landed and stuck in the lawn, El had put her last bullet into the drone's other glowing eye. But Clo was down, her long crimson hair now frizzy and her body twitching, and El could only put the butt of her rifle into so many angry faces. Soon they had us both in a mass of arms and insectoid legs. Clo shook off the shock, and we fought and kicked as hard as we could; after the number of heads we knocked, we began to wonder how the throng didn't just kill us with its sheer weight.

Their plans were worse than that, apparently. Six mangled angels held us down, and two more approached with writhing squid sacs.

"No!" El shrieked.

"Not that!" Clo yelped, squirming. "We decline treatment!"

But the veneer of respect for medical protocol was gone from these babbling minions. They had turned, like the goldeneyes in spring, and whether or not we consented meant nothing. We had spent so much time demonizing Subantoxx, we'd rather they tore our guts out. But despite our howling and fighting, the needles went in, the squids pumped, and it was all over.

Basically, there's a life before the Sap, and then there's a life after the Sap, and it'll never be the same. In a weird way, it was like that day we had our first period out in the forest: there were our lives as girls, and then there were our lives as women, and there was no going back. Bye-bye, life we knew.

At first, everything was better. That was the point of Subantoxx, after all. Somehow we didn't mind that we'd lost the fight. We didn't mind that the world had ended. We didn't mind that our mother was dead. We finally didn't even mind that our father was dead. For the first time in fourteen years, we were not troubled by anyone or anything. That's how good the Sap is.

And we certainly didn't mind when we saw Josephine, our last hope, finally overwhelmed and her little machine body, un-Babble-able like ours, ripped apart by the mad crowd in a shower of ichor. It was just like flowers flying through the air, beautiful golden flowers, falling across the lawn.

They lifted us up off the wet grass and carried us into the manor, and from the blissfully satisfied corners of our eyes, we saw the horde of babblers surge and try to form themselves into a giant again. But something was missing—a coherence to the giant's movements, a sense, a strategy. Clo was off to la-la land, still half in shock from the drone's bolt and fully blissed off the Sap, but El noted, even through her impaired state, that there was something off about the babblers now. The human ones were resisting reconversion, and the tone of the original "Nos De Roowa Kon Maa" et cetera seemed almost angsty, as if they were depressed that the real people weren't going to rejoin them.

Josephine had been right: the Babble virus, apparently the brain-child of superintelligent entities that now controlled vast portions of the globe outside of Yerba City, was brilliant. But the infection, smart as it was, hadn't expected *us*, and it certainly hadn't expected Josephine to create her own virus to counteract it. It knew how to convert, and it knew how to kill, but beyond that, it was at a loss.

It was struggling now, changing its words, trying to adapt and evolve to accomplish its mission, and the angels, drones, and animals that could talk were struggling also, calling to each other in their rapidly changing language in some kind of communal argument as to what to do next.

The inhuman debate continued outside, but we were way past the point of being able to care. The blithering servants pulled us up to the second floor in Gunry's mansion, up the ornate wraparound staircase, past bedrooms of draped curtains and ivory-inlaid cabinets. We might have asked each other, *"Where are they taking us?"* but to our Sap-addled minds, it didn't seem to matter.

CHAPTER 21

LONG LIVE THE QUEEN

"Why . . . don't they . . . just kill us?" Clo managed to mumble as we were carried like helpless sacrificial lambs up the stairs. *"I'd cut them up . . . if I cared."* Clo made a sloppy slashing motion in the air. The bearers of our makeshift palanquin, sporting half-ripped golden skull-faces and flashing bare bones from where we'd slashed them up, didn't seem to notice her meager resistance.

El couldn't answer. The Sap burned into her, taking her voice away. The truth was, she enjoyed being out of it for a minute. Clo enjoyed it, too, but the Sap affected us in different ways, just as it did everyone. For El, it took her fight inward, like a game she could play with herself that never ended. For Clo, it was like an embrace, a big hug that went on and on, from a distant but loving relative you didn't really care for. She was aware of the outside world, it just didn't matter. It was almost like being with Tobias, though it lacked the critical component of emotional attachment to another, flawed, human.

They took us, pathetic rag dolls that we had become, to the master bedroom in Gunry's manor and dumped us there, sprawled on the enormous bed. We had a very distant concern that we might be assaulted or tortured for information, but our carriers just turned and left us there, with our arm-squids pumping away.

For the longest time, we lay there, smacked out, not talking, as the bags did their terrible-ish thing to us. Outside, the buzzing continued, incomprehensible sounds moving back and forth. The debate turned into an argument, and then the argument apparently turned into civil war: blasts of the drones' static could be heard, and, even through the haze of the Sap, we could smell smoke. The Babble was fighting itself.

You'd think that the primal fear of being burned to death would have put a pep in our step, but all it did was give us sisters a vague inspiration to drool and flop against each other like a couple of wasted banana slugs.

Slurp!

El managed to turn her head toward the noise. There was Josephine, or what was left of her. They had ripped her apart and had apparently brought the parts up here and dumped them along with us. That poor girl, we thought, who, having died once to be turned into an angel to serve Yerba City, now had to die again. But it wasn't so simple.

She was trying to say something. But she was just a head and . . . a few other parts, in a puddle of ichor.

Then we heard slow, deliberate footsteps coming down the hall. We couldn't even turn around from our prone position, but El saw the surprised look on Josephine's disembodied face.

"*What now?*" Clo asked, with little concern.

"April . . . ," Josephine forced out, in a whisper. Out of the dark hallway and into the bedroom came April, the beautiful see-through angel. She slinked across the room like a model at a fashion show, knelt down next to what was left of Josephine, and adjusted her, poking and prodding, clearing the raggedly ripped windpipe so the girl could speak better. Then the angel lifted Josephine's head to rest on a velvet-lined chair.

"That's better," Josephine whispered. (Since her simulated lungs were still detached, she had to speak by pulling air through her mouth, but it worked at least to the point of a gurgling whisper.)

Clo couldn't help but giggle at the talking head on a velvet chair.

"April . . ." El managed to raise her hand, clutching at the air from her position on the bed. The Subantoxx squid tightened slightly.

April walked over and looked down at El. She was so beautiful, with long, perfect dark hair falling around her amber shoulders. In that moment, with the machine battle raging outside, all hope lost, and the perfect nanoengineered opioid running through her system, all El could think about was how hopelessly in love she was with this amazing, sensual android.

April reached for her, and El reached back, hoping the perfect robot would give her the perfect lover's embrace.

Instead, April's hands dove into El's ripped buckskin tunic, probing and rubbing along her body.

"Are you skipping right to second base?" El asked, not really minding.

Just as quickly, April stopped, and produced the two vials of Prophanol from El's tunic. We were so high, it hadn't occurred to us for a second that we had the key to sobriety on us this whole time. Of course, our prudence was beside the point. In fact, El actually fought with April for a moment when she tried to put in the needle. She didn't want to be sober. Didn't want to return to a world where her brother had tried to kill her, her mother's brain had been turned to mush, and the planet was controlled by evil computers. She just wanted April to kiss her with that flawless, pouty mouth. Fortunately, El struggled with all the ferocity of a wet noodle, and April got the shot into her neck without too much trouble. The Subantoxx squid on her arm squealed and jumped away from her body. And El burst into tears at having been brought back to earth.

Clo didn't struggle, but sobriety hit her like a bucket of ice water, snapping her into a painful spasm as her cuttlefish also popped off her arm. Make no mistake, we both thought of getting those squid needles back into us right away, but we knew well enough that the Prophanol's hindering effects would last for at least twenty-four hours. We weren't getting high again anytime soon. In fact, the cuttlefish were oozing across the floor, slowly crawling away from our bodies in disgust.

"Oooh," Clo said as she clutched her head. It was like someone had tried to put a brick into her ear.

El just panted there for a minute before letting the tears stop. "Why . . . didn't they kill us?"

"They don't know why the Babble didn't work on you," Josephine gurgled. "Or me."

"So they kept us alive to study?" El guessed mournfully. "Find out how things went wrong?"

"Something like that."

"*Well, that was a mistake,*" Clo spat. "Keep me alive and you're gonna get cut. Gimme a blade—" Clo jumped to her feet . . . and flopped back down on the bed, her legs still noodles. "Okay"—she lay there spinning—"just one sec and I'll cut 'em."

"Why the fracas outside?" El managed. "That thing's fighting itself now."

"Like I said—the virus is smart. Think of it like a demon they tried to summon. When you make a virus this powerful, there's always a chance you're gonna get infected yourself. My countervirus wasn't something it predicted, so now it's killing itself trying to stop it from spreading."

"Will it?" El asked, managing to sit up. "Will your virus kill it?"

"No. My song can take the humans; their brains are fully formed. But, if your mama was right, the Babble will be able to rewrite the higher code in most of the machines' processors. This will keep me out of the angels and drones while it continues to evolve."

"So you bought us some time," El breathed. "But you didn't save us."

"Doesn't matter," Clo announced. "I'll cut 'em all up: every Tik-Tok, every dragonfly, every little pill bug." April leaned in and moved a hair away from Clo's face. "Hey, girl, why didn't you get infected? Every other Tik-Tok did."

April smiled and pointed to her mouth.

El looked over at April weakly. "She can't talk," El concluded.

"The virus can't take if there's no reflection back into the speech cortex. If you don't echo it—"

"It can't grow inside you," El finished the idea. "So why don't you just clam up when you hear it? Don't let it inside."

"The combination of sounds is designed to trigger a primal vocal response. At some point you'll have to answer back. If you can. She tried to."

April nodded, slightly disappointed in herself.

"Wait." Clo looked up at April. "Maynor made you without a voice? A girlfriend who can't talk? That sexist pig!"

"Hey, it worked out for us," El muttered. "Remember Tito's monkeys? Speak no evil."

"Still. Misogynist asshole." Clo stood up, holding on to the bedpost, steadying herself. "I got some corrections to make. Just give me a blade. A sharp stick. Anything."

"We need to get out of here." El also pulled herself to her feet.

"We're past the worst of it," Josephine whispered. "If I'm correct, then the Babble will try to evolve again, using just the infected machines, but it'll abandon the human hosts. Now that it knows about the possibility of resistance."

"Abandon? You mean it'll free them?"

"If it doesn't take the time to create a subroutine to burn out their central cortexes first. It's clever at covering its tracks."

We looked at each other. *Dyre.* It might kill him rather than let us have him back.

"Look out the window and tell me what you see," Josephine instructed us.

We both stood up; Clo promptly face-planted. "Go ahead." She spit, through a mouthful of Oriental rug. "I'll catch up."

El staggered to the window. "Okay," she began after a moment. "It's pretty weird out there."

"Uh-huh," Clo mumbled.

"All the people are lying down in the courtyard, and the angels are naked, taking their arms and legs off, putting them on to the drones. They're . . . fusing their bodies on to the machines, making giant monster machines out of metal pieces and body parts."

"It is as I had hoped," Josephine said with satisfaction.

El turned to her in disbelief. "You're sitting there, a head on a chair. We've got a freaking machine-beast cluster rut outside, and you're telling me this was some sort of plan?"

Josephine just smiled. "It was her plan."

April helped Clo to her feet. "Mama's plan?" Clo asked.

Josephine blinked both eyes slowly and wiggled her chin, which we supposed was what passed for nodding when you were decapitated. "Only *she* predicted that the Babble would underestimate the human factor. They always saw people as targets, as liabilities. Now they're afraid of them."

"Damn straight they're afraid!" Clo declared. "They should be!" Clo fell over again. April caught her.

Josephine smiled happily. "You're so much like your mother. All Yerba City ever wanted to do was protect people; all the four other Cities ever wanted to do was destroy them, or contain them. It's four to one, so she realized the Chimera had to start playing a different game if the City was going to survive."

"Ferz," El said.

Josephine looked up at her, surprised at the realization. "Yes. Ferz."

"Pawn becomes queen," El repeated. "You're Yerba City, now, aren't you? What's left of her. Stored entirely in your copied brain, so it doesn't matter if every other unit in town gets corrupted."

"Just gotta win the game," Josephine breathed. "Your mama said, 'Bet it all on the twins,' so we did."

"I still don't get it." El coughed. "That Babble can take every angel and drone, every talking machine around, and you're . . . you're a head on a chair. So what if you're immune? How are you going to fight back?"

"My sister can take care of the infected."

Clo sighed. "Your sister's dead, Josephine. Your father told us."

Josephine's eyes looked between the two of us. "You talked to old Tito?"

"Yeah," said El. "He told us everything. That Imani died even before the world did."

The corner of Josephine's mouth curled slightly. "Not that sister."

El looked desperately back out the window. "Well, even if you have another twin your daddy somehow didn't know about, those things getting built outside look a lot meaner than that giant baby. And that fight was a draw. At best."

"It's all about scale," Josephine said, like it was obvious. It wasn't.

With April's help, Clo stumbled to the window next to El. "Whoa," she said, looking out at the scene in the courtyard. "Okay. That's totally insane. Um, anyway, can you tell me about the people—the real people, not the fake ones—on the ground? Are they alive or what?"

"Still don't know. You'll have to get up close to check them out."

"Go down there? With those things?"

Then Clo noticed the glass of the window next to her vibrating, then a dull humming.

"What are they doing now?" El questioned.

"Wait, that's not the babblers," Clo said. "It's the bees we heard earlier."

"Bees?" Josephine asked. "My daddy always said it sounded like birds to him. Huh. It does sound like bees." She blinked, realizing. "Anyway, no, that's my sister."

At first we didn't know what it was that came over the horizon. It looked like gray water on the hills. Then it looked like brown-and-white water. Then, as the legion came crashing and tumbling down into the cul-de-sac, we realized what it was: girls. Josephines. Hundreds, thousands of Josephines.

The buzzing sound was them, speaking their own twinspeak, but from a distance, it sounded more like a busy hive chattering with itself. Now that it was close, it was like hundreds of playgrounds, each with hundreds of girls, and they were ready to play. There were Josephines climbing trees, hopping over fences, scaling walls. They didn't hold weapons and weren't armed in any way, but they moved with the same quiet confidence of the dissected individual next to us, and it was clear these were girls who were going to get their way.

The Babble monstrosities turned, tried to bark their language at the throng. Their words were stronger now, louder; we could feel them in our chests this time, but to utterly no effect. Some of the hybrids tried to fire those blue sparkling bolts into the crowd, using instruments hastily modified from the infected drones' pacification tools into weapons of pure destruction. It was impressive how they had upgraded themselves: the bolts that had dazed Clo earlier were now blowing holes in buildings and mowing down dozens of Josephines at a time. But the weapons made no difference. It was the little black girl from Oakland who was the real weapon. In moments, the Babble creatures were covered in Josephines whose tiny limbs bristled with robotic strength. Those Babble monsters that were engulfed were dismembered almost instantly in a flurry of ichor, metal, and angel body parts spraying across the crowd.

Two of the Babble monsters didn't bother to try to fight, but turned and launched their multilimbed bodies skyward in a frantic effort to flee. The Babble seemed to be smart enough at this point to realize that if it couldn't infect the Josephines, it should retreat and regroup. Too late. Powered by a series of the flying drones' captured engines, the bus-sized things flew slowly, like giant fleshy stag beetles. Two Josephines grabbed on to the legs of the first one as it was taking off and climbed through the tangle of limbs into the core of the beast.

The second was soon met with one, two, then three Josephines launched into the air like girl-missiles. We looked down at the ground again: the mass of sisters had organized themselves into a kind of synchronized ramp, hundreds of hands propelling one Josephine at a time along a line and up into the air like a reverse roller coaster. They worked like army ants in their selfless precision, every finger and every toe coordinating in sync to achieve seemingly impossible results. We reckoned those flying Josephines could have gone about a quarter mile, which was more than enough. There were a few more bursts of blue lightning, a few more fried Josephines, but in no time, the fleeing hodgepodges were brought down, disabled, and dismembered.

All this seemed to answer the question of what Yerba City had been building in the old shipyards at Hunter's Point: a new army, one that was not only virus-proof but Babble-proof. Soon half a dozen of them had packed themselves inside Gunry's bedroom with us, and they reverently picked up the head and parts of the first Josephine prototype, which had been our guide into this new world until now.

They talked to each other in a kind of humming. It was their twin language. *Totally* different from ours. Although there was a lot of buzzing and cryptophasic mumbling, it was still very human, like a funny, half-hummed tune that two children might make up on a whim, and then decide to build and launch a rocket into a space with. And there was no doubt these children could do just that. Our twinspeak was functional, serviceable, a code that we had extrapolated into the practical and occasionally poetic moments of our lives. But what the Josephines had was . . . art. It was the sound of a language that was made for life, and a future. And it was beautiful.

Still, we didn't trust these girls.

Two of them stayed behind with us when the rest took the damaged Josephine away. She promised to see us again when she was in one piece, but it probably wouldn't matter; she'd look the same as the rest, once she was repaired, and they all pretty much shared the same memories now. Not that they had some psychic connection, or could swap data from their sensory inputs or anything like that. The Josephines, like the rest of Yerba City, were still analog, but their language moved so fast, and they could convey so much, it was essentially like dealing with a hive mind.

But they needed our help. Many of them were dispersing, scattering back toward the main city across the bay or up into the hills around Saturnalia. The angels and drones were still vulnerable to the Babble, and so pretty much all of them—every machine that used the standard verbal operating system—would have to be dismantled and replaced. Those units that were infected would have to be wrestled into submission before their corrupted machine brains could be literally popped out and crushed like grapes at harvest time. It was an immense job, but the Josephines estimated they had the girl power to do it. The big unknown was what would happen to the people, the actual non-robot, still-living-and-breathing, flesh-and-blood humans who had been exposed to the Babble.

We walked shakily through the house and found a couple of the rich people, who seemed to be still living, but completely comatose. One of them, an old blue-haired lady with peacock feathers in her hair, was still mumbling Josephine's song when we found her: a variation of *imul, k'oy*, et cetera. But after a few seconds, she stopped and was silent like the others.

We found Thaddeus, the local monitor for Saturnalia, crumpled in another velvet chair, curled around an enormous bottle of fancy-looking French wine, snoring loudly. Being blind drunk, he'd apparently missed catching the Babble virus and all the fireworks that followed. Lucky for him.

In the doorway of an elaborate bathroom with a honeycombed black-and-white-tiled floor, just next to the top of the staircase, we found Maynor. It wasn't clear how he had gotten there; had he recovered somewhat, come up the stairs trying to find us, and then passed out? He lay there in the doorway with his eyes closed, unresponsive when El kicked him. It was impossible to tell exactly what had happened, but he was breathing, and not any bloodier than when the Babble had taken him.

We stood there for a moment, wondering what to do with him. Some of his armor was dented and ripped away, presumably damaged when he merged with the giant out on the veranda. Suddenly April was there, placing a delicate hand on El's shoulder. We turned, and she pointed to Clo, then made a motion like she had antlers, then pointed down the stairs.

"She wants you to go and check on Dyre," El said.

Clo shook her head soberly. *"Okay. Twenty minutes and I'll see you back up here, if not by Zeta."* She turned and trotted down the stairs, happy to have her balance back.

Splitting up was something we almost never did, except as a strategic move when hunting. Maybe it was the relief we felt after that climactic battle, but suddenly stepping apart seemed like a reasonable idea. Looking back, there was a lot more to it than that.

CHAPTER 22

THE GROWN-UP WORLD

Outside, Clo saw that the Josephines were cleaning up, dragging metal debris and body parts away in a bucket brigade that extended up over the hill and all the way back to the city.

"What are you doing with all this stuff?" Clo asked one of the Josephines on the line.

"We'll take it all back across the bay to the shipyard," the Josephine said nonchalantly. "Most everything will be repurposed."

Some of the other Josephines were caring for the comatose humans, gently carrying them out of the morning light and back into the smashed ballroom. Those who needed it got basic first aid. Strangely, Clo got the feeling that all this wasn't too different from how things would have ended up after a typical night of hard partying at Saturnalia, just with different servants doing the cleanup.

"So you'll replace all the angels that were keeping things running around here?" Clo asked.

"Well, not all of them," another Josephine said, replacing the Josephine Clo had been talking to as the first one carried off a bundle of dismembered drone limbs. These girls could basically finish each other's sentences. "There's going to be some changes. Some Josephine changes. We got a new way of doing things." For the first time, Clo noticed that both the Josephines she was talking to had the jagged, X-shaped scar on their upper arms. They all did, every Josephine. Scars and all.

In the driveway, two Josephines had placed the dismembered parts of the first Josephine next to Zeta and climbed inside the cicada. They were inspecting the vehicle, making what quick repairs they could, replacing the windshield, and removing odd wires and cables that had been ripped loose when the Cartel had removed the vehicle's artificial brain.

"Oh, hi, it's you," Clo said awkwardly. "I can't tell one Josephine from another except . . . your head's cut off."

"Don't worry about it," the head said nonchalantly. "They're going to fly me and the other wounded sisters back in a minute. Got to get as many of us girls back online as they can. Lotta work to do."

"Is my brother still in there?" Clo asked.

"Naw, we brought him inside. He's doing okay. You did right bringing him here. We can clear up any human mind that's caught Antonov's virus. Even those Subversives. Get everything back to normal."

"Yeah, 'normal,'" Clo said, not necessarily looking forward to it. "You think Antonov created the Babble? Our mother's old partner?"

"You saw his face yourself, in all that stuff," the Josephine head said.

"I barely remember him," Clo mumbled, and then she recalled something, and reached into her pocket to pull out the crumbled clipping she'd been carrying around. In the picture, right next to our mama, was Antonov: brown-haired, with a light beard, smiling. "Yeah, that was him, on the giant. That was the face." The picture showed a younger Gunry a few feet away, smiling at the world they would soon create.

"He always said whoever made the best Jolly Rancher flavor was gonna rule the world," the Josephine head commented.

"He said *that*?"

"Well, something like that," the Josephine said. "I'm just talking your lingo. Artificial intelligence. He saw the direction your mama was taking things, but he took off, chose another side."

"The Siberians." Clo looked down at the crumpled photo of Team YAG. We had used that clipping for so long as a memory of Mama, we had forgotten there were two other people in it. They all seemed so happy, smiling together. But that was another world. Who could have guessed Gunry would turn into an old creep in a wheelchair, and handsome Antonov would . . .

"So he turned traitor."

"Yeah," the Josephine agreed. "Antonov didn't want the Chimera to start saving folks; he wanted to rule them. But we gonna take care of him soon enough. We gonna take care of all them. Anyway, you best go check on your brother."

"Okay," Clo said pensively, and she turned to see two other Josephines putting the front wall of the mansion back together. They hummed to each other. Unlike the subservient angels from before, this new breed definitely seemed to have . . . opinions.

Clo looked back down at the photo; she couldn't help it. This crumpled shred of paper we'd been saving and carrying around for so long suddenly seemed to have so much more meaning. It wasn't just a photo, but a window into the past, into what started it all: three great minds standing together, who would change the world. One of them would turn traitor, but then he was so close, standing right next to Mama. He even had his hand on her shoulder.

—

Up in the mansion, El knelt over Maynor. She tweaked open his eyelid, exposing a glassy stare.

"Hmm." El put her hands on his chest: he was still breathing . . . and warm. She squeezed her fingers into his muscular pectoral a little, slowly. He mumbled slightly.

El called over her shoulder, to the Josephines outside. "Hey, I think he's—"

Suddenly April put a finger on El's lips, then brought the same finger to her own sensuous mouth, shushing El.

El paused: What did this robot have in mind? Keep something from the Josephines? She was intrigued.

April reached down and gripped Maynor by the collar of his chestplate, gently, then easily dragged him the rest of the way into the bathroom, armor and all.

Maynor sighed and stirred as he was dragged. El smiled, noticing that he was still missing one boot. He had fought pretty hard for us. And he was loyal, too. There was something sweet about him after all, especially when he wasn't talking about himself.

Maynor grunted when April dropped his weight just inside the bathroom. She reached down and stroked one of his cheeks (the one that didn't have blood streaked down it), then looked up at El, smiling. The android couldn't talk, but the look on her face said, "Isn't he the most beautiful thing in the world?" And somehow, he was.

Seemingly satisfied, April stood up and eased past El, heading for the door. She paused for one last look at El, as if to say, "Make sure everything works." The door closed with a click, which El barely registered.

Alone now, El leaned over Maynor, lightly slapping his face. "Hey. Hey, Maynor."

"Hmm?" His eyes fluttered open, barely managing to focus on El. "Clo?"

"I'm El," she said, annoyed.

"Oh. What happened?"

"The Babble took you over."

"Oh. Sorry."

"Don't feel bad. It got everyone. Except Josephine and us."

"Did I kill anyone?"

"Don't think so."

"Good." Maynor shook his head, still foggy. "Was there a . . . giant baby made out of angels, and drones and animals and things all mashed together?"

"Uh-huh. But Josephine kicked its ass."

"Okay. Good."

El began casually unclipping the couplings that held Maynor's armor together, undressing him. "But the baby split apart, and more drones flew in. We got into it, and we fought well, but Clo got zapped and there were too many and they sapped us, with the squids. But then Josephine's sisters showed up."

"Sisters?"

"Yeah. She's got a hundred thousand sisters. They're going to be the new angels because they won't babble."

Maynor just blinked, looking at the ceiling, letting it all sink in. Thousands of Josephines? "Okay," he finally said, "that makes sense." And somehow it did. He tried to get up but flopped back down in pain. He moved his hands to his head. "Ow. Left me with a massive headache, though."

El reached over and rubbed his temples. "Does that feel good?"

"Yes," Maynor admitted, lowering his hands and letting her rub him.

"I'm glad," El said, subtly sliding her leg over to straddle Maynor. She rubbed him slowly, sensually, with her lips parted in a breathy smile. "I like to make you feel good." Then she put her hands all over his bald head, squeezing it like a voluptuous melon.

"Me?" Maynor looked at her suspiciously. "El . . . ," he started, but El leaned down and kissed him silent, gingerly putting her tongue in his mouth. No doubt there was a part of Maynor that wondered why El, who didn't generally give off the vibe that she was even sexually interested in men, would suddenly want to mount a bloodied, semi-conscious, and semi-earless security officer. But this questioning part of Maynor's consciousness was small, distant, and easy to ignore for the next fourteen minutes.

Afterward, as they lay on the black-and-white-tiled bathroom floor, Maynor's virility temporarily satiated, guilt at betraying Sarah must have settled in. Maynor suddenly blurted out, "Qué demonios!" He actually started crying.

El, on the other hand, was immensely pleased with herself, stretching her body out next to Maynor and sighing with relief. She was no longer a virgin, and therefore was now on par with her sister, and she took a strong sense of satisfaction in that.

"El!" The voice rang out into the bathroom walls. It was Clo, standing in the doorway.

"*Damn,*" said El, caught red-handed, as she grabbed her tattered clothes. "*Was that really twenty minutes?*"

Clo launched into the room and pulled El to her feet. Clo stared angrily at her, then down at Maynor, then back at El. Clo instantly took the logical step of concluding there was no way Maynor could have coerced or forced her sister into sex. El had done this willingly, and thanks to the Prophanol, apparently bone-sober.

"What the hell's wrong with you? We almost get killed and this is how you're celebrating your second chance—jumping this pig bait's bones?"

El huffed, maintaining a superior air as she dressed. *"Who are you to judge me? I do what I want."*

"How is this the right time for that? You're my older sister!" Clo breathed. *"You're supposed to be setting an example!"*

"I'm only ninety seconds older."

As we argued as perhaps only we can, Maynor stayed prone, as he had for the entire sequence of events, coitus and all. He reached down and pulled up his ripped pants, wiped the remainder of his tears away, and looked for a speedy exit from the situation.

"You don't even like boys! You're a whiptail!" Clo yelled. *"And you lose it to a guy like that?"*

"He's not bad, he's nice."

"Nice? Nice?! He's a shut-up-and-listen man AND he's already got two girlfriends: one of them is zonked out and the other one is a Tik-Tok who can't talk back. This is the pack you're humping your way into!"

"You can't say anything to me, you knucklehead," El retorted. *"You lost it to your boyfriend in a gooey pit!"*

"This is the precious code talking that's going to save the world?" Maynor grunted as he crawled to the sink.

The screaming and insults continued as we made our way down the hall and descended the stairs, half pushing and half pulling each other. Since we understood each other so well, it was hard for us to know exactly how we sounded to other people, but safe to say, it was probably very unpleasant. We found out later that Maynor had actually climbed out the bathroom window and down some orange clock vine–covered latticework to get away, and even the Josephines moved out of our way as we walked through the manor.

"You know what?" Clo finally played the card she'd been holding. *"I didn't even have sex with Tobias!"*

"What!" El didn't believe it. *"But you have a tattoo!"*

"I asked him to do that first! And then he fell asleep!"

"No way! Why did you get a tattoo if there was no sex?"

"I wanted to get it first, in case the sex part . . . didn't work out or whatever."

El gave her a suspicious look. *"You mean in case you chickened out."*

"No," Clo insisted. *"In case something . . . happened. Or didn't happen. Or . . . I didn't know what was going to happen, but I knew I couldn't go back to him after the fact like: 'Hey, I know we didn't actually mate but can you hit me with a cool tat before I bounce out of this pit?'"*

"That's manipulation, you know. You manipulated that poor boy."

"He's not a boy."

"And then you lied to me about it."

"I didn't say anything!"

"That's as bad as lying. Worse than lying! Because it makes you a coward! A sex coward! And that was your first time: you're going to have to live with that!"

Clo scoffed. *"The only reason you did it for the first time was because you thought I did it."*

"That's not true. I did it because I liked him."

"What? Baldy McBaldface with the ego problem? 'I got this!'" Clo mimicked Maynor's voice. *"Yeah, right!"*

"He's a sweetheart beaver who watches over his mate."

"Pfft, like you care about any of that. You're a liar!"

"You're the liar! At least I admit what I did and didn't do. I ought to slap you for creeping around—"

And El actually did raise her hand against Clo. Not for anything serious, just a quick karate soft slap, the kind we might have done sparring back in the woods.

It was our brother who finally stopped us.

"CloEl?"

The one word was enough: we froze midpunch and looked over. It was a word we hadn't heard for a while, one unique to our brother, who had used it in times past when trying to address us both at once.

"Dyre?" El breathed in response.

Dyre was lying prone on a couch, staring. "Where are we?"

We broke away from each other and scrambled over to him.

"Is it you?" El said. "Dyre Balthazar Yetti?"

Dyre looked up at us, confused. "Yeah, it's me. What's all the yelling? Did Mama take the OwlPad away again?"

Clo smiled, almost crying. "It's you! You're back!"

We cheered, and hugged him right there on the couch. He gave us each a little pat on the back, rather confused. Then he looked at his hands, at the tight strips of cloth wound into combat gloves. "What am I wearing? Why am I all wet? What happ—" He stopped when he tried to lift his head and found that he couldn't. He reached up and touched the antlers. Then he froze. "Okay, what happened to my horns?"

"You made fake ones."

"You caught the Babble."

"It was a virus."

"Made by some evil Sour Apples."

"That turned you into a rabid killer."

"But now you're better!" We both hugged him again. The answers actually seemed to satisfy him.

"Okay." He nodded. "But why the fake antlers?"

"We had to cut your real ones off, when that Babble took you over. Guess it still wanted you to look all tough."

"Later it turned into a big baby of body parts."

"And then a bunch of cyborg locusts."

"But the Josephines took care of it."

"The Josephines?" Dyre stopped us.

El gestured to one of the Josephines, who was apparently standing by to make sure we didn't actually hurt each other during our sibling altercation. Dyre could turn his head just enough to see her, as well as a few others who were cleaning up outside.

"They're twins, like us, with their own language," El explained.

"Twins?" Dyre questioned.

"Well, more than twins," Clo confessed. "More like billiontuplets."

"She's the first human brain ever completely replicated," El pointed out.

The Josephine in the living room shrugged, as if to say, "Not exactly the first." But she let us keep talking.

"Mama showed them how to do it," Clo continued. "To save Yerba City from Antonov's Babble."

"Mama wanted to *save* Yerba City?" Dyre croaked.

"Turns out the Chimera is the good guy." El shrugged. "Compared to the other monsters. Keeping everyone doped up is the only way to stop the other Jolly Rancher flavors from destroying the planet altogether."

Dyre just shook his head. He tried to sit up. "Mama's here?"

We halted our rapid-paced happily-ever-after story and looked at each other for a moment.

"Should we tell him?"

"He's not a child anymore."

"Stop it," Dyre said.

"Well," El started, "Mama . . ." She stole a look at the nearest Josephine, who seemed to grasp our desire.

The Josephine gestured with a slight tilt of her head. "This way."

By sacrificing a couple puffs of stuffing, we managed to pull Dyre's antlers out of the couch and get him to his feet. It felt like a triumph. Here was an individual who had been infected by both the Sap and the Babble. Now standing, walking, talking, and relatively unharmed. A few days before, he had tried to kill us out in the woods, and then he'd pooed himself.

We made our way outside to the large pile of body parts on the veranda; in the middle were the remains of the angel who used to be our mother. She was just a torso and head now, with golden metallic bones sticking out at odd angles where the Babble had removed them for repurposing or the Josephines had broken them by force. The back of her skull had been bashed out to remove her corrupted core. She wasn't looking good.

"Is that . . . ?" Dyre asked.

"What's left of her," El confessed.

"The City could convert her body, but not her mind," Clo explained.

The chorus girl slowly turned. She seemed to look at us. A slow gold drip came from her mouth.

For a long time, Dyre just stood there, staring. We weren't sure if it was worse for him because he hadn't seen her before—pretty, at least, and in one piece. Maybe it was easier like this. Maybe not. "It's like a snakeskin," he finally said, stepping forward and reaching out to touch her cheek.

"Careful," a nearby Josephine warned. "It's still infected with Phase Three Babble. All the angels 'round here are now."

Seemingly in response, the chorus girl's mouth opened as if she was trying to speak. A gurgle of ichor poured out onto the ground.

"Would . . . she hurt us?" Dyre asked.

Josephine brooded. "The Babble never saw humans as a threat; its real target was always Yerba City. But the virus is evolving. We're not sure what it'll do." Josephine turned to us. "Why? Do you think you're a threat to the interests of the Four Cities out there?"

"Yes," all three of us Yettis answered simultaneously.

Dyre glanced at us for only a second before turning back to Josephine. "No doubt. We are a threat." Then, "What . . . are you going to do with her? With *this*?"

"We're going to take it with the rest of the detritus back to Hunter's Point, for recycling. We gotta conserve all our resources and get ready. You saw what the Babble can do. They send that axiom for us, they're gonna send more. Bigger. Badder. Maybe even start a hard war again."

"Hard war?" Clo asked. "With, like, missiles and stuff?"

"Yes." The Josephine nodded impatiently. "Missiles. And stuff."

Dyre stood looking at the chorus girl another moment, then suddenly turned away. "Mama's not dead," he said simply.

We shot each other a look. *"How could he know that?"*

Clo asked him. "How do you know that?"

Dyre walked to the edge of the pool, which was now spattered with floating bits of debris. He looked up at the low, rolling hills that surrounded Saturnalia. "I know," he said, and his tone told us he was sure, with all of his cool hunter's instincts.

El turned to Josephine. "How do we know you're not lying to us?" she demanded. "Maybe you were a little girl once, but you're a Jolly Rancher now, too."

Josephine spread her arms. "Yerba City isn't always pretty, but she is the best option. That's what your mama always said."

"Where are the other Cities? *What* are they?"

"Artificial intelligences," Josephine said slowly. "All that's left of the thinking world out there. Anything smarter than a chimpanzee is locked down."

Dyre turned and faced us. "There's four of them?" he asked, trying to catch up. "Four other Cities?"

"The Siberians," El said, remembering the name Josephine had used. "They made the fanged deer that got you."

"Out in the ocean," Josephine continued, "there's the Brackish. They live so deep the Swarm Cartel can't get them."

"Swarm Cartel?"

"Yes." Josephine nodded. "They're everywhere else: the whole atmosphere. Maybe even out into space now."

"Okay," Dyre said, not sure what to make of the strange names, or exactly how the map of territories was supposed to be drawn. "That's three."

"The Crying Man," Clo guessed. "He must be one of them."

Josephine looked at Clo, perhaps a bit surprised at our choice of names, but she knew right away who we meant. "Yeah, he's floating around. Mr. Majerus. He's one, but a wild card for sure."

We couldn't even begin to digest what these entities meant: more superpowerful evil AIs, each one playing by its own rules. Some far away, some close by, and some already all around us, apparently. "And I'm hoping I can contain the Babble before it turns into number five," Josephine added casually.

"Wait," Clo interrupted. "You said it was a virus. Now *it's* a Jolly Rancher?"

"It's a very advanced virus. You saw it." She gestured to the pile. "It's evolving quickly. Might even qualify as sentient now. We don't know what it'll do ne—"

Behind her, the chorus girl's eyes snapped into lucidity, followed by every other functioning eye in the pile. Mashed panther, dog, hippo, human, drone; there must have been forty pupils still functioning, in various states of damage, that were now staring at us. They squirmed in various directions before finally settling on us with an ominous razor focus. Suddenly the entire biomechanical hill shook and shambled, clearly trying to surge forward.

We jumped back from the eerie mélange of body parts, and all the Josephines in the area dropped what they were doing and surrounded the thing. They called to each other in their cryptophasia, and every little supergirl came running, fingers and limbs bristling, prepared for another round of dismemberment if need be.

"It's still alive?" El couldn't believe it. "I thought you popped all their brains out." The Josephines, who we thought had become the new masters of this global chess game, didn't seem to have been expecting this.

Clo found Toothy and snatched it up. She whistled to El, using the knife to point to Daisy Duke on the ground nearby. It was time to rock and roll again.

El took two strides and snatched up the rifle, only to discover that Daisy was irreparably smashed, her barrel bent and her butt completely gone. Then El spotted Maynor's Love Gun a few yards away, lying in the grass where he'd dropped it after succumbing to the Babble.

El tossed what was left of Daisy and headed for the carbine, only to see it snatched up by one of the Josephines. Over a hundred of the girls were gathered now, surrounding the reanimated mass of Babble like a pack of hungry wolves.

The mass looked around, its damaged eyes seeing enough to realize that it was outmatched. That demonstrated a further glint of intelligence, an understanding that extended well beyond a program of simple destruction to all those who wouldn't convert to its side. There was a hideous sucking sound, due to air being pulled into a dozen still-functioning and semifunctioning lungs—those that weren't filled with ichor—and then it spoke, in a chorus of enslaved voices forced into one last effort. Its eyes looked directly at Clo and El.

"She . . . lies . . ."

Before what was left of our mother could utter another word, the Josephine with the Love Gun let it flow. Sticky liquid fire, ultracompressed in the weapon's microtank, shot forth with a roar and engulfed the pile.

You'd think it would have shuffled and screamed, the dying mass thrashing until the last infected angel burned away. But no, the whole thing just sat there, stone-faced, still mouthing words, our dead mother's eyes staring into us, trying to convince us of one last idea. We thought it tried to speak again, but the Love Gun's flamethrower was more than effective, and the Josephine fired another burst into the pile with a fierce *whoosh!*

Soon there was nothing but a huge blob of flaming golden sludge and polymer bones, sending a pillar of the darkest smoke into the air even as various limbs still tried to creep away. It smelled . . . pretty bad.

"She lies" is what it said, and that voice, it was Antonov's. We knew that voice, just like we knew the face on the giant, and before that face, it had grown from a baby's face right into—

Clo gasped, suddenly realizing that this was real life—a post-Sap, post-little-girl life—and that it was a lot more complicated than we thought.

Despite the burning chaos in front of us, El sensed Clo's internal revelation, and turned to her. *"What?"* she mouthed. *"What is it?"*

Silently, Clo pulled out the crumbled picture again, and pointed. She pointed to Antonov's face, then to his hand on our mother's shoulder. She looked over at El.

El nodded, following but still not understanding. *"Okay."*

Clo looked from El's eyes over to our brother, waving the smoke away from his face.

Then it all coalesced in El's mind, too: Dyre's face on the giant; the phrase Gunry had said before he'd fallen back into his stupor.

"And then the boy came and it all fell apart."

Forget all the giant cosmic computers, the supermachines of vast, overwhelming intelligence and their global chess games of competing realities. All that stuff meant nothing; it was the human heart that was by far the most complicated mechanism of all, and it was the heart's world we were living in.

Both our minds grew exponentially in that moment, realizing that this wasn't the end of a chapter, but the beginning of our real lives.

There was only one thing to do.

"What's the chance of us taking a little jaunt out of here?" El sharply asked.

"Hoofing it?" Clo considered, having had the exact same idea. *"Zero. Team Supergirl'll run us down stat. And changes or not, there's no way she's going to lift the quarantine."*

El looked up at the rising pillar of smoke. *"There's not a drone in the sky right now."*

"The Babble sucked them all in."

"How long you think that'll last?"

"Before Josephine gets them up and working again? Not long."
"Leaves just a little window of opportunity."
"To flap it? Have to find one of these flying bugs—"
"—that already has its brain taken out."
Zeta.

Clo nodded, tapping our little brother's shoulder twice.

His whole body stiffened at the touch. Out in the forest, a double tap on the hunt meant no matter what was going on, stay quiet and listen. He turned silently from his marvel at the Josephines battling back the flaming appendages.

Clo jerked her head twice toward the manor, just like we might have done back in the forest.

Dyre shot us a look, as if to say, "Why? I just got here."

But El repeated the silent double tap, and the meaning was clear: Be quiet and start moving. *Now.*

The three of us took advantage of the chaos in the courtyard to slip coyote-silent through the smashed manor.

We could tell Dyre had a million questions: Who is Josephine? Why am I damp with seawater? Why did that gorilla have no ears? But like a good little brother, he kept them all to himself, just following as quickly as possible our path to the front of the building.

He did, however, skid to a halt on the smoldering cobblestones when he saw the giant cicada sitting there.

"What is that big thing, and how do we kill it?" he whispered.

"We're not going to kill it. It's our ride," Clo shot back. "Don't worry, its brain's already smashed."

"Who smashed its brain?"

"A big, cute, floating face," Clo said impatiently. "Now come on."

The first Josephine's head was still there, waiting patiently at the bottom of the open carapace, and her eyes looked sideways at us.

"You don't need to be scared, all right?" the head assured us. "My sisters'll—"

She didn't know what we were about yet, and we didn't bother explaining. We were up into Zeta in an instant, El in the pilot seat, firing up the vehicle.

"Can you fly her?" Clo asked.

Zeta's humming got louder.

"If Maynor could do it, I can do it," El said.

"Yeah, and then you could just *do* him," Clo commented snidely.

"Uh, someone's already in here," Dyre said.

Clo spun, her knife ready. Sitting in the back row of seats, already buckled in and waiting silently, was April. She smiled at us. She had predicted this move: that we Yettis were going to rabbit if we saw the opportunity. Still, Clo didn't like her.

"What are you doing here, Tik-Tok?" Clo demanded. "We're stealing this bug. Get out!" She waved with her knife.

"It's okay," El assured her. "She's on our side."

"How do you know?"

"She helped us out, remember?"

Outside, the dismembered Josephine seemed to have realized that we weren't running out of fear, but actually making a getaway. "Hey! Get outta there! You can't take this vehicle!" She started yelling back toward the manor, calling to her sisters in her secret language. Fortunately, most of the supergirls were gathered on the other side of the building. Still, we had only seconds left.

Clo sized up the see-through angel. "All right, we're going to take April along?" She put her knife away angrily and reached outside, just as the carapace was starting to close. "Then I'm going to take a friend, too!"

"Hey!" the Josephine yelled as Clo grabbed her Afro and lifted her head from the cobblestones, just as Zeta's insectoid feet left the earth.

Clo pulled the Josephine head onto her lap as the doors closed and we all rose shakily into the air. We weren't sure at first if the other Josephines had heard their sister's cry for help, but as Zeta floated up past the second story of Gunry's mansion, we saw them: dozens of little supergirls dressed in white began appearing, in windows, in the courtyard, on the roof.

"Bring us down now!" the Josephine head in Clo's lap demanded. "Or my sisters'll *take* you down!"

"Not if they can't catch us!" El said, and yanked the control sticks back like she'd seen Maynor do the day before.

Zeta shot into the sky, and just in time, as scores of Josephines came launching through the air, their small fingers gripping onto nothingness just below the cicada's dangling legs. They all missed us.

And it was fortunate they hadn't had enough time to form their human catapults like we saw earlier, or it would have been all over right then and there.

Below us, thousands of frustrated girls turned into white dots and the beautiful rolling hills of Saturnalia turned into a mere patch of moss beneath the clouds as we went up and up. Satisfied with our altitude, El stopped ascending and carefully steered Zeta westward.

"We sure are high up," Dyre said, looking over the expansive seascape ahead of us and gripping his seat tightly. "I've never flown before."

"Sure you have. Everyone strap yourselves in," El growled. "Now."

Clo placed the Josephine head in the seat next to her, making sure it was propped up as well as possible before trying to place the seat belt across Josephine's face.

"Are you kidding me?!" Josephine demanded, doing her best to wriggle free.

"Suit yourself." Clo shrugged and put her own belt on.

"Just what in the hell do you girls think you're doing?" Josephine demanded.

"We're doing what we do," El answered, carefully angling the craft as best she could. "We're going hunting."

"Where?" Josephine asked incredulously.

"You know where," Clo said. "Where this whole Babble virus came from."

"Siberia," El finished the thought.

"You can't just go there!" Josephine said. "It'll violate the treaty!"

"We didn't sign any treaty," El said simply.

"Yeah," Clo echoed snidely. "We're stragglers, remember?"

"You—" Josephine fell silent, her vast mind suddenly resigned, but clearly still trying to figure out what to do next.

Dyre, his own mind also spinning, reached into the silence as El angled the flying craft.

"CloEl?" he asked uncertainly. "What are we hunting?"

We looked at each other.

"Your papa," El said.

"Your *real* papa," Clo clarified. "Antonov."

El opened the throttle.

CRACK!

With a sonic boom we shot forward, and in moments we were across the ocean, into the sky, and entering another world. The real one this time.

ABOUT THE AUTHOR

Michael Ferris Gibson is a writer and former actor, director, documentary filmmaker, producer, head of product at a tech start-up, and frozen-fish chopper at the Marine Mammal Center. He grew up in San Francisco and takes inspiration from his city and the changes it has undergone over the years. He still lives in his hometown, now with his Westie and two children.

OCT 2021

CPSIA information can be obtained
at www.ICGtesting.com
Printed in the USA
JSHW021032120821
17775JS00006B/6